CALL OF THE WILDE
THE MEMOIRS OF H.H. LOMAX BOOK 8

PRESTON LEWIS

WOLFPACK
PUBLISHING
— EST 2013 —

Call of the Wilde
Paperback Edition
Copyright © 2023 Preston Lewis

Wolfpack Publishing
9850 S. Maryland Parkway, Suite A-5 #323
Las Vegas, Nevada 89183

wolfpackpublishing.com

Paperback ISBN: 978-1-63977-610-8
eBook ISBN: 978-1-63977-609-2
LCCN: 2023932587

In Memory of
William "Bill" Dale Tiedtke
An Avid Reader Who Loved to Laugh

INTRODUCTION

Call of the Wilde is the eighth volume in *The Memoirs of H.H. Lomax* series and provides some of the backstory referenced in *Outlaw West of the Pecos*, the preceding volume in the chronicle of this Old West vagabond who had a knack for running into some of the most colorful and dangerous characters of that place and time.

In *Call of the Wilde* H.H. Lomax relates his brief employ as a bodyguard for Oscar Wilde, the eccentric Irish poet and eventual playwright and novelist, who covered the breadth of America from New York to San Francisco during an 1882 speaking tour. The Irish writer made his name in America as a proponent of aestheticism, an art movement of the period valuing painting, sculpture, music and literature solely for their beauty rather than their practicality or their social, cultural and political functions. Some interpretations of the movement valued human creativity and pleasure over logic. Consequently, aestheticism provided a philosophical paradigm for many British and American sophisticates, though it went over the head of most

Americans of the time, especially those in the West who lacked the cultural opportunities available back east in the big cities, specifically New York, Boston and Philadelphia.

Sophisticated and prosperous urbanites may have been drawn to the philosophy, but western folks—such as Lomax—who lived on the edge just to survive stood as skeptics who ridiculed the movement for its impracticality. Besides their philosophical differences on the intrinsic value of the arts, Wilde and Lomax also diverged on their levels of sophistication. Highly educated at Trinity College in Dublin and then Oxford, Wilde circulated among the literati and royalty of London, amusing fellow sophisticates with his wit, his ostentatious attire and his overall flamboyance. Traveling in those social circles, Wilde arrived in America with broader experience in intimate relationships than Lomax, who seems completely naïve of some of his encounters with Wilde, even when he wrote about them years later.

Lomax, by contrast, had limited formal education beyond what he picked up in Cane Hill, Arkansas, before and during the War Between the States, as he calls the Civil War. What he lacked in classroom experience, Lomax made up for in common sense—or horse sense as he preferred to label it—and an ingenuity that helped him survive challenging times on the frontier after encounters with some of the most lethal legends of the time.

For those new to Lomax and his memoirs, I will just say they are based on his handwritten recollections I discovered in a university archive more than three decades ago. Details on his papers are to be found in the earlier volumes of the series. Having now read about half of his memoirs, I am amazed at his recall of events from decades past. Even so, his writings are not without some factual issues, though generally his recollections match with historical facts. In this volume I find a strained timeline with some events in *The Redemption of Jesse James*, but I will leave it for the reader to resolve those, if they even matter. Either way, Lomax tells a wonderful story, true or not.

Like all of his writings, *Call of the Wilde* is more episodic rather than linear, one encounter leading to another often unexpected episode or character. How then do the likes of H.H. Lomax meet someone so far removed from his social class and standing as Oscar Wilde? By Lomax's telling, it started with him being falsely accused of robbing a bank in West Texas, then deciding to look for him a wife or wives in Utah Territory among the Mormons and next running into an older sister instead. As a result of those encounters, Lomax meets Wilde, who is enamored with him for reasons that seem beyond Lomax's understanding, and accompanies him for less than a week before escaping the law for a murder he supposedly committed in Colorado five years earlier. The killing is first referred to in the initial Lomax volume *The Demise of Billy the Kid* and fully explained in the sixth volume, *North to Alaska*.

As with previous volumes in his memoirs, *Call of the Wilde* is not politically correct, which is part of their charm or their chagrin, depending on your viewpoint. They were, after all, written at a different time about a distant period in our history. While some readers may cringe at his descriptions or his opinions, Lomax like the rest of us deserves to tell his own story in his own way without the scorn that accompanies so much of contemporary cultural debates. Take, for instance, his assessment of Mormon women as plain if not homely creatures. Both Mark Twain and Oscar Wilde themselves so reported similar conclusions after their visits to Utah Territory and Salt Lake City. Lomax, however, at least acknowledges their essential decency and the sincerity of their faith.

While Lomax is ingenious, some might say devious, in addressing some of his challenges, he is at his basic a soft-hearted fellow as evidenced by his visit to a Fort Worth dentist as described in this volume. Further, his effort to help his theatrical sister out of a financial bind is what draws Lomax to his brief and unlikely partnership with Oscar Wilde. By the end of their short acquaintance, Lomax found himself struggling to avoid a date with a hangman.

Should this be your first encounter with *The Memoirs of H.H. Lomax*, I will refer you to the introductions of previous volumes for details on him, his family and his amusing adventures out West. What I have enjoyed about editing his recollections has been his entertaining—often irreverent—perspective on the people and events of the frontier. Generally, Lomax possessed a knack for being at the wrong place at the wrong time, but somehow survived, partially on cunning and largely on luck with a smattering of wit thrown in. As I've said many times before, H.H. Lomax may not have won the West, but he sure made it fun.

Preston Lewis
San Angelo, Texas
December 21, 2022

CALL OF THE WILDE

CHAPTER ONE

Bank robbing was not a line of work I chose on my own, but it was a job forced on me twice during my adventures out West, once by the scoundrel Jesse James and the final time by the elected officials of Buffalo Gap, the seat of Taylor County, Texas. Those public leaders in 1881 cared more about securing a stop on the approaching Texas and Pacific Railway and ensuring their future as a community than they did about me receiving the justice I deserved. The sheriff, the mayor and the county judge all tried to railroad me for a crime I didn't commit before I lived up to their expectations out of desperation and revenge. But that was what I had come to expect from Texans over the years, as they had more ambitions than brains.

Down on my luck, I had ridden into Texas hoping to locate my brother James Monroe Lomax, who I had heard was a successful rancher near the community of Colorado on the banks of the river of the same name. I hoped to hire on with him until I could get back on my feet with a few dollars in my pocket. As it turned out, the law and politics of Buffalo Gap almost got me lynched and kept me from finding Jim. The unintentional result of the unfortunate Taylor County incident pointed me to Utah in search of a wife—or wives—and led me to find older sister Melissa Irene or "Lissa" as we called her. In trying to do Lissa a favor, I met the oddest character I ever encountered in my travels across the frontier. He wasn't American or Indian or Mexican or Chinaman or maybe even human, but an Irishman named Oscar Wilde, who was traveling the West lecturing folks about nothing. And people actually paid to hear him speaking nonsense, though he named it beauty or aesthetics. Beauty was an odd topic for a man as ugly as Wilde, as he wore long hair like a girl and had a plain, elongated face that would have looked better on a horse—either end for that matter. His head was usually clouded in a fog of cigarettes, which he smoked like a locomotive. Repulsive as he was, I wound up working as his bodyguard for a few days until an unsolved Colorado killing put me on the run. It was just as well because Wilde grated on a fellow, as he was odder than a three-headed duck and ten times as looney as your average politician making a stump speech.

As it turned out, though, I left Buffalo Gap with more money than I had entered with and decided it was time to settle down, maybe take on a wife or two and live like a regular fellow rather than a saddle tramp as had been my experience generally since leaving Cane Hill, Arkansas, at the end of the War Between the States. I'd heard that in Utah Territory the Mormons guaranteed a fellow as many wives as he wanted and that sounded like a good option, sitting back and letting the women do all the work. So, I considered changing my religious views from Baptist to Mormon, but that was before I saw Utah women. They were certainly a sturdy stock and most likely smarter than all Texas women put together, but they must've missed school the day the teacher passed out looks.

As I went through Buffalo Gap that fall afternoon, I wasn't thinking of my future marital state or anything else other than finding my brother and asking for a job. The town earned its name from a gap between the mountains where the buffalo crossed between the Brazos River basin to the north and the Colorado River basin to the south. By the time I rode through the region, the furry beasts had been killed off, and the Comanche and Kiowa had been settled on reservations in Indian Territory, making the country safe for civilization, if you ever considered Texans civilized.

By the hand-painted wooden sign identifying the community on its eastern limits, I learned Buffalo Gap boasted a population of twelve hundred folks, though likely only a fifth of them being of sound mind and body—Texans being Texans—and even fewer than that being sober. As I rode my gray mule down the dusty street, I noticed the imposing two-story stone jail and courthouse, not realizing I would be spending a spell there before night's end. The town also boasted a drugstore; a livery stable and carriage house; one blacksmith stand; a hotel that looked less inviting than the jail; two saloons; four mercantile, grocery, or hardware stores; a tiny newspaper office; an eatery or two; and a bank. As I had no money, I saw no sense in stopping to ask for a meal, and I didn't figure the bank would give me a loan. The men and women on the street ignored me, except for one bum, who looked worse off than me. He staggered my way from the plank walk in front of the Watering Hole Saloon.

"Could you spare a nickel, mister?" he called, raising his palm upward for my expected donation.

"Get a job, fellow."

"I can't," he replied indignantly. "I lost my legs during the war."

Throwing him a hard stare as he started walking beside my mule, I shook my head as he must've thought I was blind. "Seems to me you're making good time for a man with no legs. Thought you said you lost them during the war."

He nodded. "I did, but I found them a few years later."

"Where you from, cripple?"

The fellow smiled like he thought he had won me over. "Texas," he answered.

"Figures," I said, nudging my mount's flank with the heel of my boot, and he trotted away from this beggar, who blessed me with a wish that I spend eternity in a warm climate.

Nobody else paid me any mind as I hit the western edge of town and followed Elm Creek for a spell, letting my mule water and filling my canteen along the way. I had a few strips of jerky in my saddlebags, but I was saving them for the two days or more I figured it would take me to reach Jim's ranch. I didn't want to arrive at his place so hungry that it would scare him off from giving me a job or at least feeding me if he didn't need any hands. Even so, I felt pretty good about my chances. We were brothers, after all!

About an hour west of Buffalo Gap, I had followed

the trail away from the creek when the approaching sound of galloping hooves and an occasional gunshot caught my ear. I directed my mule off the trail and swiveled around in the saddle to check on the commotion. Three riders charged my way, one of them twisting and firing his pistol at an enemy I had yet to see beyond the veil of dust the thundering hooves of their horses kicked up.

This wasn't my fight, so I backed my mule farther away from the road, pulled my pistol from my holster and held the weapon at my side in case I needed it.

When the lead rider saw me, he waved his revolver my direction. I shook my six-shooter at him and shrugged. "None of my business," I cried.

The fellow glanced at his pursuers, slapping the reins against his dun's lathered neck as he passed me. When the second rider neared, he veered off the trail and tossed a canvas bag at me, then spurred his own sweaty mount westward. I snatched the packet from the air, hoping it might be a little grub that would end the growling in my stomach. The third horseman galloped past, firing a revolver over his shoulder at the pursuers, who I could barely t make out in the distance, well beyond pistol range.

I backed my mule farther from their path in case the coming riders fired at their quarry, then glanced at the sack as I slid my six-shooter back in its holster. Stenciled on the canvas bag were the words: BUFFALO GAP BANK. I slipped my hand inside and felt a stack of paper money, not thick but enough even in small denominations to buy me some grub. I thought about stuffing the pouch under my shirt, but decided that would make me look guilty of a crime I didn't commit. Instead, I held it on the side of my mount opposite from the six approaching riders. Four of them raced past me, but two stopped.

"What's going on?" I cried.

"Bank robbery," shouted a red-haired, narrow-eyed fellow about my size and sporting a deputy's badge on his vest.

"And murder," added the second guy, "as if you didn't know." He waved his revolver at my face, then wiped his sleeve across his sweaty cheeks.

I gulped hard. "That's news to me."

"You best raise your hands slowly, fellow, and tell us who the rest of your gang is," the deputy suggested.

"You've got this wrong," I replied, letting the bank bag slip from my hand to the ground, startling the mule, who danced over the canvas sack. I lifted my arms in the air, and the lawman leaned over and took my pistol from my holster, tucking it in his belt.

"Well, look what I found." The deputy pointed to the canvas sack beneath my mule. "How'd you come to have one of our bank bags if we have this wrong?"

"The second rider tossed it at me as he galloped by. Don't know why, but that's the honest-to-gospel truth."

The deputy gestured for his partner to fetch the canvas sack. Dismounting, the fellow drew his sleeve across his perspiration-pimpled face again, bent and retrieved the money pouch. As he straightened, he opened the mouth of the canvas and stuck his hand inside, pulling out a stack of bills that he waved at me. "Now why, fellow, would a robber throw you a bag with our money in it?"

"Naturally generous, I suppose."

The deputy rolled his eyes and spat as the other fellow climbed into his saddle with the money bag and cash. "You may think it's funny, fellow, but the folks whose money you stole won't look so kindly on your humor."

"I didn't rob your bank, and I didn't kill anybody. I passed through town, minding my own business. Once I reached here, I heard a commotion and gunshots. I eased off the trail to let the trouble pass. I saw three horsemen firing at you. One tossed me the money bag when he rode by. Then I spotted you riders following them." I leaned over and patted my mule on the neck. "Look at him. He hasn't even broken a sweat. No way I could've ridden as hard as they rode their mounts without my mule breaking a sweat. Besides, they were riding horses."

"Maybe so, maybe not," the deputy replied. "Fact is, you got a money bag with our cash in it, and you can't 'splain that away, now can you?"

"I already told you, one of them pitched it to me as he passed."

The deputy eyed me and shook his head. "That's the dumbest story I ever heard." He glanced over at his as his pal, who was thumbing through the bills.

"There's a hundred and seventeen dollars here," the bill counter announced, glaring at me. "That's cash our folks worked and sweated over to feed their families. Then you and your bandit band come to town and just take it." He shoved the money back in the bag. "I ought to plug you right now, fellow."

"And keep the money for yourself?" I asked.

"I ain't a thief like you," he shot back, drawing his

sweat- and dust-stained sleeve across his fleshy face once again.

"Easy, Snooter," the deputy replied. "We'll wait 'til the sheriff returns to decide what to do with him." The lawman turned to me. "What's your name, fellow?"

"H.H. Lomax," I answered.

"I'm Deputy Callus, and this is Snooter Johnson. You'll be our prisoner until we get this straightened out."

"At the end of a rope," Snooter suggested. "You're the type of scum that gives Texas a bad name, Lomax."

"I'm from Arkansas," I protested.

"You should've stayed there," Callus informed me.

An uneasy quiet enveloped us as we waited for the rest of the posse to return. I considered my options, whether to escape, which would make me seem guilty, or to convince the two imbeciles that I was innocent. Neither prospect seemed manageable, though I realized my captors had not taken my carbine from my saddle scabbard. Just as I thought about using it to gain my freedom, Callus realized the danger, edging his gelding beside me and yanking my long weapon from its leather case.

"You won't be needing this," he said as he slipped his pistol back in its holster and covered me with my long gun.

For the next half hour, we sat in our saddles staring at one another, awaiting the return of the posse.

"Where's a fellow get a name like 'Snooter'?" I asked Johnson.

"My mother was a Snooter."

I nodded. "I bet she was."

Johnson's beefy cheeks turned red as he tried to

determine if my response was a compliment or an insult. By the scowl on his face, he'd about decided it was a slur, but the deputy distracted his attention, pointing my carbine down the road.

"Here comes the sheriff," he announced, standing in his stirrups to get a better view of his approaching allies. "Don't appear he's bringing back any prisoners. They're either dead or escaped with our money."

"All but a hundred and seventeen dollars," Johnson reminded us.

"That won't go far divvied up among all the folks that put their money and faith in the bank," Callus said, then scowled as his black eyes glowered at me. "Some men steal from others rather than do honest work."

Shaking my head, I glared back and informed the pair, "I didn't rob or kill anybody. I only spoke to one fellow in town, a guy claiming to have lost his legs in the war, even though he was standing on two feet."

"His name was 'Legless Larry'," Callus announced.

"He never hurt nobody," Snooter informed me, "and you didn't have to kill him."

"What?" I cried. "I didn't kill anybody."

The deputy scowled. "Larry was a little touched in the head, but harmless as a fly. You shouldn't have shot him."

"I didn't!" I screamed, furious at being wrongfully accused. "Never killed him and never robbed your bank."

Snooter held up the money bag. "This says otherwise, Lomax."

As the chief lawman neared, I took a deep breath, hoping he had more sense than these two, though I had little faith in his intelligence, as he was, after all, another Texan.

Riding a speckled gray gelding, the sheriff shook his head as he reined up in front of us. "The other two got away," he announced.

"You mean the other three," I corrected.

The sheriff ignored me. "We didn't recover any money, either."

Snooter held up the bank bag. "We found a hundred and seventeen dollars on this bandit."

Bobbing his head, the sheriff eyed me as his men circled and studied me. The lawman sported a ruddy and rugged face and skeptical eyes above a nose that looked like it had been broken a time or two. He tweaked his mustache, squeezed his snout between his thumb and forefinger, and blew snot and trail dust from his nostrils. He aimed the glistening tip of his trigger finger at me. "Robbing's one thing, but killing Legless Larry is lower than a snake's belly."

"I didn't kill Legless Larry, and I didn't rob your bank."

The lawman pointed to the bank bag. "How do you explain the money Snooter's holding?"

"One robber tossed it at me as he passed."

Cocking his head, the sheriff asked a simple question. "Now, why would he do that?"

Snooter Johnson answered for me. "Naturally generous, is what Lomax told us."

The sheriff shook his head and wiped his slick fingertip on his dusty britches. "Another fellow that thinks he's smarter than the law, are you? Well, pardner, you're dealing with Saul Minter, sheriff of Taylor

County, Texas. I don't take kindly to lawbreakers that run at the mouth, rob our folks and kill our people."

"I didn't do it," I answered, though nobody believed me.

One of the other riders untied a lariat from his saddle and held it over his head. "I say let's hang him right here, right now."

Minter waved the rope away. "There'll be no lynching until there's been a trial and a conviction. After those formalities, then I'll be glad to spring the trapdoor that sends this murderer to hell." He turned to me. "What's your name, fellow?"

Before I could answer, the deputy spoke. "H.H. Lomax is what he calls himself. Says he's from Arkansas."

The sheriff nodded at me. "Is that so, fellow?"

"That's the truth, just like everything else I've told you and your posse."

"What's the name of the other two robbers?"

"There was three," I reminded him.

"After your mule gave out, we only saw two," he informed me.

"The three robbers were riding horses."

"Two of them were," Minter responded, then paused. "The smart two. The dumb one was riding a mule."

I figured I'd have to pay for a lawyer I couldn't afford to get out of this mess, as the lawmen weren't listening to me or to reason.

Things got serious when Minter twisted around in his saddle and extracted a set of wrist shackles from his saddlebags. He rattled them at my face. "Let's fit you with these bracelets and start back to town, Lomax."

The fellow with the lariat held the coiled rope above his hat. "Wouldn't it be better just to hang him right here, Sheriff? It'd sure save the fine citizens of Buffalo Gap from having to do it themselves or pay for a trial, especially after losing all their money."

Minter chuckled. "It's mighty tempting, I admit, but I took an oath to enforce the law, not break it."

The other men groaned with disappointment. Deputy Callus, though, scratched his chin. "Maybe, Saul, there's a way out of this. You and I are the only ones wearing badges. We could ride off in search of the other two bandits—"

"Three bandits," I reminded him, as the sheriff leaned over and snapped the bracelet around my wrists.

"—and while we trailed them, the other posse members could take care of Lomax."

The badgeless quartet nodded their approval of the scheme, though I had my reservations, especially after Sheriff Minter stroked his chin and spoke.

"That's not a bad idea, Callus."

The deputy grinned and thrust out his chest. "Then we could find him hanging from a tree when we returned and report him lynched by parties unknown."

"That's not legal," I shouted. "I'll know who lynched me."

Minter laughed. "I doubt you'll be in any condition to testify." He shoved his hand in his pocket. "Let me remove the shackles, and you boys can have at him once Callus and I ride out of sight."

"That's not right," I screamed.

"Neither's robbing a bank and killing Legless Larry," Minter answered as he fished around in his right pocket. He extracted his empty hand from his britches pocket, then shoved his left in the other pants pocket before removing it with the same result. He patted the pockets in his vest, grumbled under his breath and dismounted from his gelding as the fellow with the lariat formed a noose. I figured I was a goner. The only thing I had going for me was that if I died in Texas, Saint Peter'd let me pass the Pearly Gates since I'd already been to hell.

Minter untied the flaps on his saddlebags and shoved his hands inside, still searching for something but with no better results. He strode around to the other side of his gelding and continued his fruitless search. All he came up with was a curse word. "Damn!" he spat.

"What is it, Sheriff?" Callus asked.

"I can't find the key to remove the cuffs."

"That'll make him easier to hang," Snooter noted.

The sheriff clinched his lips and shook his head. "If somebody finds a hung man wearing my wrist cuffs, they'll know the law was involved. That'll implicate me and Callus."

"Way I see things, it'll buy you plenty of votes for the next election, boss," Callus observed.

Snooter offered his solution next. "I'll ride back to the house and bring us an ax so we can chop his hands off and remove the shackles, key or no key."

The fellow with the rope eased his horse to a tree and threw his hemp line over a sturdy live oak limb.

Callus grinned. "We could even scalp him and say some Comanches left the reservation for a little revenge."

As everyone—me especially—awaited the sheriff's

answer, he tied down the final flap on his saddlebags, stepped back around his gelding and mounted. "That's a fine solution, boys, but too many ways it could go wrong. Somebody might spot us or spread word about possible Comanche attacks, terrifying the womenfolk and their little ones."

The other members of the posse grumbled, and the fellow holding the rope yanked it from the live oak.

"The way I figure it," the sheriff continued, "I'll get with the mayor and the county judge and decide how we kill Lomax. We've our town's reputation to think about, especially with the Texas and Pacific building west from Fort Worth. If Buffalo Gap is going to win a stop on the railroad, we've got to be careful of our reputation and how we handle this."

I began to believe I might live to see another sunrise until Snooter Johnson spoke.

"Why don't we take him down by the creek, put his pistol barrel under his chin, pull the trigger, and tell folks he committed suicide as we closed in on him?" Snooter crossed his arms over his chest and smirked like a Democrat with a bribe in his pocket.

Minter shook his head. "Too messy, and who wants to dig his grave? Any volunteers?"

His five accomplices just looked at the ground.

"I thought so," the sheriff announced. "Let's start back to town. You first, Lomax."

When Callus shook my carbine at my gut, I nudged my mule in the flank, and we headed toward Buffalo Gap. I alone among the seven riders seemed pleased with the outcome, though with this dim-witted bunch I didn't know how long my meager luck might last. They complained about how much money they had deposited in the bank and wondered how they were going to recover from my thievery. They speculated who the other robbers were, the deputy even wondering if the most famous outlaw of the time was involved.

"You wouldn't be riding with Jesse James, would you, Lomax?"

I doubted it would help my cause to admit I had ridden against my will with Jesse on his first bank robbery, so I ignored the question. "I didn't rob your bank, so I wouldn't know who the robbers might be."

The sheriff scolded me. "*Our* jury will decide if you robbed *our* bank. If there's one fellow we don't want in these parts, it's Jesse James and his filth. We're not gonna let a bank or train robber kill our chances of getting a stop on the Texas and Pacific Railway. No, sir, that ain't happening, not while I'm sheriff."

After a spell the conversation turned from me to the railway and how its arrival would secure a prosperous future for Buffalo Gap and hush those upstart Abilene boosters fifteen miles to the northeast with ambitions of the railroad stop for themselves. As we reached the outskirts of town, posse members drifted to their homes until it was just me, Minter, and Callus.

The two lawmen directed me toward the stone courthouse and jail, ignoring questions from the crowd if they had recovered all the money and killed the other two robbers.

"We'll give you answers in good time," the sheriff announced. "Right now, I want to lock this robber up and make sure he never breaks the law again."

Several booed, though I was uncertain if they were showing their displeasure at me or the sheriff. A couple of women picked up clods and threw at me, while one fellow grabbed a horse apple and tossed it my way. I raised my cuffed hands and doffed my hat at my admirer. My neighborly gesture only drew more hoots from the fine citizens of Buffalo Gap.

As we passed a crimson-stained spot in the road, Callus pointed to it. "That's where you shot Legless Larry."

"I didn't shoot anybody," I protested, snugging my headgear back in place.

At the jail, the lawmen dismounted and helped me from the saddle. They escorted me inside the sheriff's office to an iron-barred cell in the back corner and locked me up.

"Should one of us stay the night with him?" Callus asked.

"Nope. If folks break in and lynch him, so be it."

I held up my shackled wrists. "What about unlocking me?"

Minter shrugged. "I'll search for the key tonight. If I can't find it, I'll get the blacksmith to remove it."

"What about some supper?"

"I'm not wasting grub on you until I know how—and when—we're gonna execute you."

Both men turned and left the office, locking the door behind them and leaving me to worry about my fate.

CHAPTER TWO

Come morning, I awoke with a chain around my wrists, a knot in my gut and kinks in my muscles after a hard night on a bed with wooden slats for a mattress and a single woolen blanket for cover. Daylight slipped in through a narrow, barred opening high in the stone wall. I could stand on my tiptoes on the bed boards and just see down the town's main street, as folks arose for another hot Texas day. The only activity I observed was four men loading a pine coffin into a freight wagon. Half of the fellows walked into a weathered wooden building, and the other pair climbed into the seat and started the rig down the road. I figured they were taking Legless Larry to his final resting, and the two mourners were a bigger crowd than I would draw if I was wrongly hanged. I jumped on the floor, sat on my meager bedding, and waited.

About midmorning I heard a key rattling in the office door, which swung open on squeaky hinges, allowing Sheriff Saul Minter to stride in. He wore a broad grin beneath his thick mustache as he closed the entry and slipped over to his desk. "You're in luck, Lomax. I found the key to your wrist shackles. That'll save the county money from hiring a blacksmith to free you, though Snooter still offered to bring his ax and remove the iron along with your hands."

"Snooter's a helpful cuss, isn't he? Where'd you find the key?"

"You won't believe it, Lomax, but in my Bible."

I was shocked he was smart enough to read.

"Yes, sir, I'd used it for a bookmark. You know God works in mysterious ways. If I hadn't been reading the Good Book, I wouldn't have used it to mark my place. If I hadn't marked my place, I would've pocketed the key, and I could've freed you yesterday to let the others string you up. That would've saved the county time, trouble, and money. You're one lucky prisoner."

"I don't call it luck when I'm jailed for something I didn't do."

"A hundred and seventeen dollars and a bank money bag says different, Lomax."

"It wasn't a hundred and seventeen dollars," I responded, figuring I was about to dig an even deeper hole for myself.

The sheriff eyed me. "What do you mean?"

"It was more than six hundred dollars before Snooter and your deputy divvied it up, taking closer to two hundred and fifty dollars apiece."

Minter stared at me and scratched his chin before shaking his head. "They aren't that smart or that crooked."

I shrugged. "They outsmarted you and the rest of the posse. Why do you think Callus suggested riding off and leaving me to be lynched? Or why did Snooter want to chop off my hands? Yep, they made money out of this and made you out to be a fool. It wouldn't surprise me if they even killed Legless Larry."

The sheriff cocked his jaw and tugged at the end of his mustache. "I don't believe you."

"Why would you? You haven't believed a thing I've said. Maybe Snooter and Callus were in cahoots with the robbers to begin with, just waiting for a stranger like me to ride through town to throw you off their trail, all the while stealing the honest earnings of their neighbors."

Minter scoffed, but I could tell I had planted seeds of doubt in his barren brain. He ambled over to the iron bars and had me stick my hands out. After extracting a key from his vest pocket, he unlocked the cuffs and removed the iron bracelet from my chafed wrists. As I rubbed my fingers together to restore the feeling, the sheriff returned to his desk, sat down, and reclined on his hind chair legs.

"How about taking me to the outhouse?"

"That's how Billy the Kid escaped. We don't do that in Taylor County because we don't let our murderers escape."

"I can't hold it forever."

Minter pointed to the cell's back wall. "There's a slop bucket in the corner. Use it and cover it with the towel so it doesn't perfume my whole office."

I found the container beneath a rag so filthy that I could've planted and raised a potato crop on it. After I tended to my business and re-covered the container, I turned to the sheriff. "What's for breakfast?"

"Whatever Mandy Mae brings," he answered as he

scooted toward his desk and began rifling through papers that I realized were a stack of wanted posters.

I prayed he didn't have any legal flyers from Leadville, Colorado, where I was hunted for shooting a crooked lawyer in the back, though I had no recollection of performing that valuable public service. "Who's Mandy Mae?"

"My daughter. She cooks for the inmates, gets two bits a meal from the county."

I sat on my bed. "That's a cozy arrangement, the taxpayers paying the sheriff's daughter to feed the prisoners."

"No secret there, and nobody else would do it. The county judge and the commissioners approved it. Mandy Mae's a fine cook, better than her ma. You'll eat well because we'll want to fatten you up a bit. The extra weight'll help snap your neck when we hang you."

That was a reassuring thought. "Glad you're considering my well-being, Sheriff."

Minter grimaced, then slapped the wanted posters on his desk. "I was hoping there was a reward on your head I could claim for a little more cash to get me through, now that you stole what I had in the bank."

"I didn't wind up with any cash, Sheriff. Check with Snooter or your deputy for a loan since they cleared a couple hundred dollars from the robbery. Could've been your savings, Sheriff. They're probably laughing right now about what a sucker you are as they spend your hard-earned money."

"Shut your pie hole, Lomax, and quit spreading lies. Callus and Snooter aren't smart enough to pull off something like that."

I laughed. "They said the same about you, Sheriff, while they waited for your return."

Before he answered, the squeaky door flung open and in marched a cute little lady with hair the color of corn silk. She carried a wicker basket that I assumed held my breakfast, but left the door ajar. Her emerald green eyes sparkled above a button nose and full, rich lips. I considered her as pretty as a Texas woman could be until she smiled at me. She had the crookedest teeth I had ever seen on man, animal, or rock.

"Morning, Pa," she said as she passed Minter, who arose to close the door she had left wide open. "So you're the killer," she said, approaching the cell. "You have a handsome streak about you, better looking than the others I've fed in jail."

The sheriff slammed the door to show he disapproved of Mandy Mae's flattery. "He's a killer who stole your ma's and my savings."

Her smile widened until her mouth was a repulsive half-moon, resembling a pile of white bricks from a demolished building. "That's why I keep my money under my mattress." She flitted her eyelashes at me as she neared my cell. "Aren't you gonna unlock the gate for me so I can deliver his breakfast, Pa?"

"No, young lady, he's too dangerous."

She winked at me. "Perhaps he will take me and ravish me."

Minter scowled. "Your taste in men repulses me, Mandy Mae."

"I know," she tittered. "That's why I do it."

Mandy Mae thought she was winning me over with her smile, but it was the food in the basket I craved. I hoped her cooking was as good as her father suggested.

"Besides," she cooed, "I like dangerous men, men that can bring excitement to a town as dull as Buffalo Gap."

"You know he killed Legless Larry, shot him in cold blood."

"Larry was crazy. He was so annoying, nobody liked him. Nobody went to his burial this morning besides the two that dug his grave." Mandy Mae studied me a moment more, then looked at the cell, empty of everything save the bed, the blanket, the bucket, the filthy towel and me. "Your guest needs a table and chair to eat his meal on plus a water bucket and dipper."

Exasperated at his daughter, Minter growled. "He don't deserve any special treatment, Mandy Mae, and I'm not doing anything until Deputy Callus gets here. One of us has to keep him covered, so he doesn't escape."

"I'm warning you, Pa, there better be a table, chair, and water bucket in his cell when I return for lunch or I might help him escape and ride out of this boring town with him."

Her father grimaced. "You should spend more time reading the Bible and less on those tacky dime novels."

"They're more exciting and less preachy than the Bible." Mandy Mae paused. "And your guest is more thrilling than you are, Pa." She flashed her repulsive smile at me.

"I don't mean to interfere in your family matters, but I'm famished. I haven't eaten anything substantial in two days, so I'd like whatever's in your basket, Miss Minter."

"Certainly," she replied, "but call me Mandy Mae. And your name?"

"Just call me Lomax."

She smiled again. "That sounds dangerous, like the hero in a dime novel."

I grimaced at the sight of her teeth, and she noticed, but didn't let it offend her.

"This isn't much, but it'll get you by until lunchtime when I bring you a more filling meal." She lifted the blue gingham dishcloth from the basket and handed me a mason jar through the iron bars. "It's coffee."

Twisting the lid off and holding it aside, I took a couple gulps of the warm liquid. Next she passed through the bars a bulging cloth tied at the top. Taking it, I marched over to the bed and sat down, opening the material to find three boiled eggs still in their shells, a trio of cold biscuits and six slices of fried bacon cooked perfectly. I placed the cloth on the bedding, put my coffee jar on the floor, and grabbed a biscuit, gobbling it down to add something of substance to my stomach. I peeled the eggs and alternated between bites of hen fruit and bacon.

"My, but you were hungry, Lomax. I didn't bring any butter or preserves because I didn't care to waste good food on a fellow I disliked." She batted her eyes at me. "I will next time."

I ignored her until I finished the grub, consuming everything but the eggshells and the cloth. "Mighty fine meal," I offered. "Best I've had in days."

"Believe me, Lomax, I can do better and will, just for you."

"Until we hang him," the sheriff interjected.

Mandy Mae dropped her basket, both hands flying to her mouth as she turned around and glared at her father. "No, Pa, you're not hanging Lomax, not if I have anything to do with it."

"You won't," Minter shot back. "It's a matter for the law."

"That's not right, law or not. He's innocent. Look at those eyes. A man with eyes as soft as his would never murder someone, even a tramp like Legless Larry."

The sheriff planted his balled fists on his hips and glowered at his daughter. "Girl," he scolded, "fetch your basket and scat."

Mandy Mae raised her chin toward her father, as if daring him to sock her. "I'm a woman, Pa, all of seventeen years old."

I finished the coffee, grabbed the cloth and jar lid, and stepped to the iron bars. Sticking my hand between the iron rods, I offered her the serving pieces. "You best do what your father suggests, Mandy Mae. Don't anger him over a no-account like me." My words had the desired effect as she turned and inspected me, batting her eyelashes and flashing her awful tusks.

She stared at me as she answered her father. "See, Pa. A man of such humility would never kill a man, rob from others or lie about it. You've read the Good Book so much you should see the good in others, like Lomax."

Grabbing the jar, lid and cloth from me, she bent over and placed them in the basket, which she lifted as she spun around. "I'll return with your lunch, Lomax." She marched to the door without another word. The door groaned on oil-starved hinges as she yanked it open and left it unclosed behind her.

Minter stared at the gaping entry, as if he were stunned by his daughter's impertinence, then shook his head, walking over and gently shutting it. He pinched the bridge of his nose as he returned to his desk. "Young 'uns," he said to himself as he sank into his chair.

Barely had he sat down than the door burst open, and Deputy Callus walked in. "What's a matter with Mandy Mae?" he asked. "I know she can be touchy, but I've never seen her so riled. Fairly spit at me when I told her good morning."

The sheriff sighed. "She thinks she's a woman, thinks I'm a tyrant, and thinks Lomax is innocent."

"Two out of three ain't bad for a gal her age," Callus replied, instantly realizing he should have kept his mouth shut rather than antagonize her father and his boss.

Minter either didn't catch the slight or ignored it, though Callus's eyes widened when the sheriff asked him to fetch the double-barreled shotgun from the gun rack. The deputy obeyed, backing away from the sheriff once he had completed the task. Minter broke the scattergun and confirmed it was loaded, then snapped the barrels back in place.

"Deputy," he ordered, "I want you to go fill the water bucket and get the dipper for our prisoner. When you get back, I'll have you open the cell and put it inside, along with an extra chair and the little table, so our prisoner can eat his meals in a civilized manner. It's the least we can do for a doomed man."

"Yes, sir," Callus answered, grabbing the bucket and dipper from a shelf near the cell, then marching outside, gently closing the door behind him. A couple of minutes later, he returned. "Fresh water from the hand pump rather than the horse trough," he announced.

Minter tossed him the keyring with the cell key on it, and waved the shotgun toward me. "Lomax, back over by the slop bucket. Don't make any sudden moves or I'll fill you with so much buckshot you'll whistle when the wind blows."

I did as ordered.

Callus unlocked the cell, opening the door wide enough to slide the bucket with the dipper inside. Next he scurried across the room and grabbed the little writing table and cane-bottom chair, then delivered them to the cell and shoved them inside, slapping the bars shut with a clang and slipping the key inside to secure the lock.

"Thank you, Sheriff," I said. "Now your daughter won't get mad at you once she sees you've done what she ordered."

The deputy cocked his head and stared at his boss. "Mandy Mae's never cared about the comfort of a prisoner before."

Minter shrugged. "She's taken by him, says he has soft eyes and would never murder anyone."

Callus yanked off his hat and scratched his forehead with his free hand. "Has she gone plumb loco?"

"Those trashy dime novels she reads have given her a warped idea of right and wrong. She thinks excitement is more important than decency. I don't know where her ma and I went wrong. I figure I could've raised a boy, beat him when he needed it to knock a little sense into him, but I never quite understood how to raise a girl, especially a headstrong one."

The deputy inhaled a deep breath and expelled it slowly. "What she needs is a husband to straighten her up, put her on a proper path since you've done all you can."

I cleared my throat to get their attention. "I'll marry her and right her course from now until death do us part," I offered.

Minter stood up, cocked the hammers on the shotgun and pointed it at me. "Ever mention that again, and I'll send you to kingdom come, Lomax."

I shrugged. "Just an idea, Sheriff."

"Well, keep your ideas to yourself," he responded. "I've got plenty on my mind, so don't rile me, Lomax."

"Your daughter's wedding wouldn't be one of those things, would it?"

"No," he spat. "The mayor and the county judge are coming over before lunch to discuss what we're gonna do with you."

"Reward me for recovering over six hundred dollars from the robbery," I suggested.

"Six hundred?" cried Callus. "There was only a hundred and seventeen when Snooter counted it."

"Pay him no mind, Deputy."

"A hundred and seventeen was what was left after you and Snooter helped yourselves to a share of the loot."

Callus stepped toward my cell, yanking his pistol from his holster. "That's a lie, Lomax, a damn lie."

I shrugged. "Maybe so, maybe not, but I wouldn't want to be in yours and Snooter's boots when the fine citizens of Buffalo Gap learn some posse members made out better than others in the stickup."

"Put your gun up, Deputy. Lomax aims to rile you, start some rumors that'll help him avoid the hangman. Spreading lies about the robbery and murder won't keep a noose from closing around his neck, but he's desperate. That's why he's making all this stuff up. Neither you nor Snooter are crooked enough or smart enough to pull off something like that."

Callus grinned. "Thanks, Saul."

Perhaps Minter was right, but I enjoyed planting ideas in the sheriff's head. "Your deputy said he was gonna run against you for sheriff when you come up for election. He's gonna electioneer that he caught a bandit and you didn't, Sheriff. Not only that, he recovered some money, and you didn't."

"That's a lie," screamed Callus.

"Of course, he and Snooter kept most of the bills for themselves."

"Shut up, Lomax, and calm down Callus," Minter commanded. "Lomax hopes to turn us against each other, so we get sloppy enough for him to escape."

The deputy growled with a low, menacing voice as he patted his pistol. "I hope he tries. I'll fill him with lead."

"Just trying to help, fellows," I said as I took a seat in the cane-bottom chair and rocked on its hind legs.

Minter gently released the hammers on the shot-gun, returning it to the gun rack. "Why don't you make your rounds, Callus? Cool off a spell. The mayor and county judge are due any time, and we intend to visit about how we're gonna get rid of Lomax here."

Callus nodded at the sheriff. "If you need any assistance, let me know. I'll be glad to dispatch him for you, and I won't charge the county a cent." He turned and glared at me.

"Why should you, Deputy? You've already made a couple hundred dollars from your robbery pickings." I crossed my arms over my chest as Callus's eyes widened.

"Scat," the sheriff commanded, pointing at the door.

As Callus retreated outside beyond the groaning hinges, Minter shook his head. "You have a way of galling a fellow, getting under his hide, Lomax."

"Just naturally likeable," I replied.

"Not in this town you aren't. You best behave when the mayor and county judge arrive, you understand?"

"Whatever you say, Sheriff." I got up from my chair and plopped down on the wooden slats of my bed as the lawman dragged two chairs from across the room to the front of his desk.

We both waited a quarter of an hour before the elected officials entered, doffing their derbies and greeting the sheriff, who pointed his trigger finger at me. "There's the cause of all our troubles. H.H. Lomax is his name."

One of my visitors was older and frail, a puny fellow in his sixties with thinning gray hair in disarray, wire-rimmed spectacles that made his green eyes look too big and narrow shoulders that made his coat look too large. He walked with a slight limp, using a polished wooden cane to steady himself. Under his free arm, he carried a leather-bound ledger, barely visible under the oversized coat. He looked so puny, I doubted he could knock a poot out of a bean-eating toddler.

The other fellow I took to be in his forties. He stood ramrod straight and cocked his clean-shaven face at me before striding to my cell, grabbing two iron bars and staring at me with mean brown eyes. Unlike his older, shorter accomplice, who sported no visible weapon, this official carried a dual holster with pearl-handled revolvers. He wore a red vest over a white pressed shirt with a new collar, wool pants and a pair of black boots that could blind a fellow from the shine. By his attire, he was telling people he was an important man, who was due the public's respect. I found him pompous, even more so when he spoke.

"I'm Howard Tindle, county judge," he announced.

"Never heard of you," I answered.

"I run Taylor County and with the commissioners' court set the laws, determine the tax rates, and distribute the county payroll. It's the sheriff's job to enforce the law and collect the taxes." He paused and pointed to his frail partner. "That's Thermopolis Chesterfield, town mayor and president of the Buffalo Gap Bank, the one you robbed yesterday."

"I robbed nothing, Howard," I protested.

"Call me Judge Tindle or nothing at all."

"Have it your way, Nothing At All."

Tindle glared at me as Sheriff Minter came to my defense. "Lomax has a way of riling folks. I don't know if it's intentional, or he's just so dumb he doesn't realize what he's doing."

"I'd figure the latter," said Chesterfield in a surprisingly firm voice that seemed at odds with his frail frame.

"It won't matter," pronounced Tindle, "once we try him and hang him."

"That's why I wanted to meet with you two," the mayor replied. "We've got some financial problems we need to work through."

Minter pointed to the chairs in front of his desk.

"Have a seat, gentlemen, and let's see if we can get this resolved."

The two politicians seated themselves, putting their derbies on the desk. Chesterfield dropped the ledger beside his hat, then opened the journal to the middle and pointed to a column of figures. "We had close to five thousand dollars in the bank at the time of the holdup." He tapped his finger three times on the page. "That's all the money left after the robbery."

Tindle and Minter leaned in to study the figure. Tindle grimaced. "Three hundred and seventeen dollars."

Chesterfield nodded. "That includes the hundred and seventeen the sheriff recovered off the bandit."

Minter nodded. "Where'd the other two hundred come from?"

Chesterfield offered a larcenous grin. "I always kept two hundred dollars in my desk for emergencies. This, gentlemen, is an emergency."

"The sooner we finish the trial," Tindle said, "the better. Then we can move on."

The banker cocked his head and shook it vigorously. "You don't understand. A trial costs money. We'll have to bring in a judge, pay for his food and a place to stay, pay jurors for their services. When our robber is convicted—"

"Hey," I cried, "don't I get a fair trial?"

The trio ignored me and the mayor continued, "—we'll have to build a gallows and hire a hangman to do the job. After that, there's burial expenses. We can't afford it, if—" He left his unfinished sentence hanging in the air like they planned to leave me.

"If what?" Tindle asked.

"If we want to get paid the rest of the year. There's not enough funds left to handle the expense of the legalities and still pay us the salaries we're due."

"What about everyone else that lost money?" Minter asked.

"They're out of luck," Chesterfield answered. "The best thing we can do now is look out for ourselves until we collect the next round of taxes. It's three months yet until January when we can bring in new taxes. And, we may need some more money to bribe Texas and Pacific officials. We've got a railway construction engineer and supervisor coming to town this afternoon to inspect route possibilities. We want to impress them with a few spending dollars, so they know how much we deserve the railroad instead of Abilene. I hear those Abilene crooks'll do anything to secure the railroad at our expense."

"Damn," Tindle exclaimed, twisting in his chair toward me. "You robbers have put us in a tight spot."

I got up from my bed and marched to the iron bars, grabbing them and shaking the cage until it rattled. "Sounds like you politicians'll make out better than everybody else."

Tindle snarled. "That's why we run for office!"

Chesterfield giggled. "Once we secure a train stop, we'll make out like bandits."

Incensed, I rattled the cage harder. "So, it's okay for you three to rob folks, but not the three bandits that did the same thing."

"We do it legal," Tindle replied. "Now, shut up, Lomax."

There was a question I had to ask. "Are you fellows Republicans or Democrats?"

Tindle's face turned red with anger as he stood up and shook his fist at my nose. "Don't ever accuse us of being Republicans."

"We're proud Democrats," Chesterfield said as he puffed out his puny chest with indignity.

"Politics aside," Minter interrupted, "what are we going to do with Lomax?"

"That's easy," the county judge announced. "We'll see that he's lynched! Folks are plenty angered about losing their savings, so we stoke that hatred today and tomorrow, then offer some free drinks for rowdies at the saloons, starting at dusk tomorrow and let the mob take care of our problem, all for the nominal cost of a few bottles of whiskey."

"I like the way you think, Howard," offered the mayor.

"Do you agree, Sheriff?" asked Tindle.

"Well, I want to get paid, that's for certain."

Chesterfield nodded. "As do we, Sheriff."

"As do we," Tindle repeated. "As do we."

I feared I would be hanging from a Buffalo Gap live oak by midnight the next day.

CHAPTER THREE

"You look sadder than a cowboy afoot," Mandy Mae Minter told me as she marched to my cell, leaving the squeaky office door wide open, as was her habit.

In her wake, her exasperated father arose from his desk and closed the door, likely still wondering where he had gone wrong in raising his daughter.

"Give me that smile I saw this morning, Lomax. I know I'm late, but I made a special meal for you, enough for both your lunch and supper." She lifted her wicker basket with both hands and smiled with those crooked teeth. "Don't look so glum."

"They're gonna lynch me tomorrow night, Mandy Mae. Your pa, Chesterfield and Nothing At All—"

Lowering the container to the wooden floor, she cocked her head at me. "Nothing at all?"

I nodded. "That's what the county judge told me to call him, Judge Tindle or Nothing At All."

"Don't pay him no mind, Mandy Mae," the sheriff said, as he slipped back to his seat. "He's been making things up right and left to save his ornery hide."

"There's not enough money remaining for the county to pay for a trial, so they plan to rile up the fine, law-abiding men of Buffalo Gap, get them drunk, hand them a rope and point them to the jail and me. I'll be swinging from a tree midnight tomorrow, sure as I'm sitting here."

Mandy Mae spun around, planted her balled fists on her hips and shot fire from her eyes and brimstone from her mouth. "You better stop this mischief right now, Pa. It'll hurt your re-election chances."

"You don't know politics, *girl*," he replied.

"I'm a woman, Pa, and don't you forget it." She stamped her shoe on the plank floor for emphasis and jerked her indignant nose in the air, causing her corn silk hair to bounce on her slender shoulders.

"He'll hang one way or another, whether he has a trial or not. If he should be lynched—and I'm not saying he will be—it'll save the county tax dollars and make sure I have the monthly pay necessary to provide for you and your ma."

She yanked her hands from her hips and clapped her palms. "I'll not let them lynch him, Pa. If I hear talk on the street tonight or tomorrow about men angering at him, I'll know you're involved in whatever scheme Mayor Chesterfield and Nothing At All worked up." She paused, pointing her index finger at him. "I'll never forgive you if something happens to Lomax, Pa. And if you won't stop a mob from lynching him, I will. You taught me to shoot, even gave me my own pistol, and I can handle a rifle and shotgun as well."

Slowly, the sheriff leaned forward in his chair, planted his palms on his desktop and pushed himself deliberately up from his seat, clenching his jaws, his lips and his eyes. His words came out in a low, threatening snarl. "You mind your manners, *girl*, and leave men's business to the fellows that know what they're doing."

Mandy Mae paled at the pronouncement, like she'd never before heard such a menacing rebuke from her father. She stood silent as he turned and removed from a peg on the wall the ring that held the keys to the jail.

"I'm going for a walk while you feed the prisoner." He rattled the cell keys to make a point. "I'm taking these with me so you don't get any wrong-headed ideas that can get you in trouble, *girl*."

"Yes, sir," she responded, turning to me, her eyes watering with embarrassment. Mandy Mae stepped toward the wicker basket and melted onto the floor beside it as her father marched outside, shutting the door forcefully in his wake.

By the rattle of the office key in the lock, I knew he had secured the door so no one could enter. I slipped to the iron bars, squatted down, stuck my hand through the barrier, and stroked her soft hair. As she raised her head from the floor, a pair of tears rolled down each of her rosy cheeks. She grimaced at me. Her soft beauty touched me until she opened her mouth, her teeth giving her the look of a rabid dog.

"Pa doesn't like it when I talk back," she whimpered, "but I can't believe he and the mayor and the judge would kill you."

Stroking her hair softly, I nodded. "It's true. The bank was cleaned out of its holdings, except enough to pay their salaries until they can start collecting new taxes in January." I was honest with her, as she was the only person in Buffalo Gap who cared about my fate. I didn't tell her the lies about Snooter Johnson and Deputy Callus divvying up the loot.

"If they come for you, Lomax, what will you do?" She looked at me with her wide and caring emerald eyes, wiping a tear from her face.

I leaned through the bars enough to dab the tear on her opposite cheek. "I suspect I'll grab a bed slat and hold them off as long as I can, then douse them with the fixings in the slop bucket. That should send them running."

Mandy Mae giggled, her titter falling like music into my ears. When her lips curved upward at the corners, the innocent softness in her smile made me overlook her teeth as she removed the cloth cover from the wicker container. She handed me a Mason jar with a soft brown liquid inside. "It's sweet tea. Wish I had some ice for it, but you'll like it. I put plenty of sugar in it."

I pulled my arm and the glass through the bars, then twisted off the lid and sipped at the tea. "It's tasty," I said, "and cooler than I expected."

She smiled. "I wrapped it in a wet towel to cool it as best I could." She lifted a tin plate from the basket and removed a white cloth from atop it, revealing a fried chicken leg and thigh, boiled potatoes, hominy and sliced pickles.

As she slipped the plate under the iron bars, I licked my lips. "Looks and smells good."

"Hope you like the dark meat. Pa demands the breast and pulley bone for himself, even if the county pays for it."

I grabbed the drumstick and bit in. "It's delicious," I replied as I started on my first substantial meal in days.

She slid under the door a tin spoon, a fork and a paring knife sharp enough to cut through rawhide. I enjoyed the food and her approving nods as I dined on the floor opposite her.

"Oh, I almost forgot," she said, as her hands flew to the basket. "I baked a loaf of bread and buttered you four pieces." Mandy Mae passed through the bars the slices wrapped in a napkin.

I took the gift and unwrapped it, licking my lips at the aroma of the still warm bread.

"That's why I was late getting you dinner, because I wanted to bake you fresh bread."

"Thank you, Mandy Mae, but why are you so good to me?" I asked between bites.

She sighed and lowered her head. "You looked like you needed a friend, same as how I've felt all my life. No feller's ever been interested in me, much less kissed me." Mandy Mae raised her face, her eyes watering again. She forced a smile. "I know my teeth are horrible and no man would ever take to me, me being so ugly."

"You're a fine-looking young lady, Mandy Mae."

She shrugged. "That's why I read dime novels, to make up for the excitement I've missed. I barely know you, but you are more exciting than all the fellers in Buffalo Gap put together. I hoped you might take me away."

Now I felt bad for thinking poorly of Mandy Mae just because of her teeth.

"The way things stand today, they'll take me away in a pine box after tomorrow. So don't count on me taking you anywhere."

She snickered. "Maybe I can spirit you off. Wouldn't that be exciting?"

"Don't get yourself hurt, Mandy Mae. I'm not worth it."

"You're worth more than any other man in town."

I held up the last slice of bread before taking a bite. "A young lady that can bake this good'll get a fellow one day."

Once again she smiled, and I answered her with a grin of my own as I cleaned the plate, doing all I could save lick the tin to consume every morsel. "Superb meal, Mandy Mae. Your cooking is the best thing that has happened to me on this trip to Texas."

"You're not done," she informed me, inserting her hand into the basket and removing another tin plate covered in a cloth. "Here's a slice of apple dessert I made for you." She yanked the cover away, and my eyes and mouth widened at the biggest piece of pie I'd ever seen. It had to be a quarter of the whole pie.

I took the plate from her and attacked the dessert. It was as tasty as the rest of her meal. "Absolutely delicious," I announced after swallowing the last crumb. I handed her the tin dishes, followed by the fork, spoon, and knife.

She smiled at me. "You've made me so happy."

"How?" I grimaced.

"By returning the knife," she answered. "It was a test."

"A test?"

"If you were guilty of robbing the bank, I figured you would've hid it for an escape try when you got a chance."

The thought had entered my mind, but I didn't admit it. Perhaps the sheriff was right, and God *did* work in mysterious ways. "I won't do anything that would keep you from bringing me such tasty meals. If they do hang me after I've eaten one of your fine meals, I'll die happy."

Mandy Mae smiled at the compliment, but chided me for the thought. "Don't talk like that. I'll protect you."

Doubting she could save me, I nodded anyway. "I'll hold you to that promise."

She seemed pleased, but her smile melted away when she heard a key rattling in the office door lock. Moments later, the door opened, and the sheriff walked in with his deputy.

"You've spent enough time with this scoundrel, Mandy Mae," her father said as he walked to the peg and hung the jail keyring while Callus shut the front door.

"If you say so, Pa." She pushed herself up from the floor and brushed the ruffles on her skirt, looking at me. "Tomorrow I'll bring you breakfast, dinner and supper."

The eavesdropping deputy laughed. "Lomax, won't need meals after tomorrow," he announced.

Mandy Mae caught her breath, her green eyes narrowing, her lips tightening.

"Shush your mouth," ordered the sheriff.

Never had I seen such a look of grim determination in a young woman as was frozen in her face in that moment. She bent over and grabbed the handle of her basket. When she straightened, she curtsied and nodded to me, whispering through clenched teeth, "You were telling the truth."

"Thank you," I answered, "for such a delightful

meal and such pleasant company. I hope to see you again."

"You will," she replied forcefully as she spun about and, without acknowledging her father or his deputy, strode across the room, yanked open the noisy door and marched outside.

In her wake, Minter pointed to the door, and Callus scooted over to close it.

"You better enjoy her meals, Lomax, because they'll be the last you ever eat," Callus gloated. "Men around these parts are greatly riled on account of you."

Minter nodded and approached the cell, grabbing the bars when he was opposite me. "The deputy's right. All that will save you now is telling us who the other robbers are."

"Why should I think you'd show me any mercy when you don't believe in protecting a prisoner in your charge, Sheriff?" I crossed my arms over my chest and cocked my head. "Your daughter's got more grit than you or your deputy or your mayor or your Nothing At All."

"Name your gang."

"Snooter Johnson and Deputy Callus," I answered smugly.

"What?" cried Callus.

"We'll see how cocky you are tomorrow after dark." Minter rattled my cage and spun around for his desk.

The deputy stepped toward me, but the sheriff grabbed his arm and yanked him about. "Don't waste your time on him. He'll get his comeuppance tomorrow night."

They hovered around the desk the rest of the afternoon, speaking in whispers, casting suspicious glances my way and finally leaving for the night. I wasted my time lying on the roughhewn bed and wondering if tomorrow would bring my last sunrise, a sobering thought. Twice I'd come near being hanged, first back in Washington County, Arkansas, at the close of the War Between the States and then on the Chisholm Trail after I led a herd of Texas longhorns to the new railhead in Abilene, Kansas. In both cases, the timely arrival of allies or friends saved me, but I never forgot the squeezing finality and the rope burns from a hangman's noose. Now, Mandy Mae Minter was my only ally in a godforsaken town in a godforsaken state.

I realized local animosities were building against me from the occasional commotion on the street, men yelling obscenities at me as they passed by the sheriff's office. Once about dusk and a couple times after midnight, someone pelted the building's back walls with rocks, two coming in the barred window over my bed. I made use of the slop bucket as much as I could because I wanted it plenty ripe and full for the next day's festivities. My thoughts and words weren't the only thing I planned to share with the mob if they got to me. The fellows in the front would get a dose of my perfume if they ever reached my cell.

The shouted profanities and the occasional splat of rocks against the back wall left me edgy. Besides that noise, a lovesick tomcat took to yowling outside my window and sleep came fretfully. A couple hours before dawn when I was finally dozing off, I heard the gentle rasp of a key being inserted and turned in the entry lock. I slipped off the bed onto my hands and knees and crawled to the corner, removing the dirty towel from atop the slop bucket and preparing to shower my assailant with the terrible tonic I had been saving. I waited.

The door opened so slowly it never squeaked, and a hooded figure inched inside, gently closing it without waking the dry hinges. Just as I was preparing to rise and ambush the intruder, a soft voice whispered, "Lomax, it's me, Mandy Mae."

Sighing with relief, I covered the slop bucket with the filthy rag and stood up. "I thought they were coming for me. What are you doing out so early?"

"Came to bring you something," she confided as she inched across the room.

"How'd you get the key for the jail?"

"Pa's a heavy sleeper. He keeps the office key in his pants. I slipped it from his britches after midnight, then waited until early this morning so there was less chance of being spotted." She reached the iron bars as I did.

"You could unlock the cell and let me escape."

She answered with an emphatic, "No! Everyone would think you were guilty."

"If they ever learn I had an opportunity to escape and didn't, they'd think I was stupid."

"You're neither, Lomax. Stick your hands through the bars."

I did as I was instructed. When she handed me her surprise, I felt the cold steel of a revolver in my right hand and a carton of cartridges in my left.

"It's my pistol and ammunition," she said. "You gotta promise you won't use it to escape or harm my pa, that you'll only use the weapon if a mob breaks in to lynch you." She didn't release her grip on either the pistol or the bullets until I agreed.

"I promise."

"Good," she said, "but now I want you to do one thing for me."

Pulling my arsenal into the cell, I nodded. "Sure, Mandy Mae, what is it?"

She hesitated, then spoke shyly. "Kiss me."

So surprised was I that I dawdled for a moment, not knowing how to answer.

"Just a little peck," she suggested. "Please."

"Sure, Mandy Mae. Let me put the gun down." I retreated to the bed, placed the pistol and carton on the blanket, and returned to the bars. As my eyes focused in the darkness, I saw she wore a shawl over her head. As I approached the cell door, she lowered the cover and stepped to the bars. Sliding my arms through cold rods, I wrapped them around her as best I could. She leaned toward me, and I dropped my head to hers, our lips meeting for an instant. Then it ended.

She pulled away from my embrace. "I've gotta get home and return the key to Pa's britches before he gets up. I'll be back for breakfast." Mandy Mae lifted the shawl over her head, let herself slowly and quietly out the door, locking it behind her.

Alone again, I found myself moved by her sweet innocence as I retreated to my bed and sat down on the hard wooden slats. I checked the cylinder in the revolver and confirmed it was fully loaded. I emptied the carton of bullets into my hand and split the cartridges between my right and left britches pocket. If it came to a shooting, I'd need the extra ammo handy so I could reload quickly. I stood on the bed and tossed the empty carton through the barred window overhead. Next, I hid the pistol between the bedpost at my head and the cold limestone wall. I dozed off for a spell until the door squeaked open ahead of the sheriff.

We ignored each other, both of us understanding what would transpire on this warm Texas day. Arising, I stood on my tiptoes on the bed slats and stared out the barred opening toward the sunrise, uncertain whether or not it would be my last on this earth. Not until after sunset would I learn if I would soon be dancing from the business end of a noose.

A half hour later, Mandy Mae arrived with my breakfast, leaving the door open for her father to close. Nearing my cell, she handed me a jar of coffee and a bundled napkin holding a peeled boiled egg and a chunk of ham. "It's not much, but I'll bring you a better dinner and supper."

"Thank you," I answered as I consumed my meal.

"No, thank you," she said.

"For what?"

She leaned closer to me and whispered, "For the kiss last night, it was as thrilling as I had always imagined it should be."

Bless her heart, she was so lonely, but I was pessimistic about our chances together.

"Don't worry," she whispered. "I won't let anything happen."

"What are you two whispering about?" Sheriff Minter called.

"We're planning to elope," Mandy Mae answered, me almost coughing up a bite of breakfast.

"Don't fun me, girl. Finish up with Lomax and get on home so I can close up my office early tonight."

"Sure, Pa," Mandy Mae answered, motioning at me to down my meal.

As I gulped on the last bit of coffee, she stuck her hand through the bars and offered me a dime novel.

"This'll help you pass the time. It's a thrilling story, especially on page thirty. You should read it."

I exchanged my napkin and empty Mason jar for the pulp narrative. She smiled, turned and marched behind the desk, where she planted a kiss on her father's cheek. Then she exited the office, closing the door on its squeaky hinges.

Minter looked to me, shaking his head. "Women," he said. "I'll never understand them."

"She's lonely," I answered.

The sheriff scoffed. "She's got me and her ma. What more does she need?"

"Me," I replied, drawing the sheriff's disdain as his face reddened.

"I'm looking forward to tomorrow, Lomax, when you're gone," he replied as he opened a desk drawer and took out a whiskey bottle, tossing back a healthy slug before rifling through some papers.

Sitting in my chair, I opened the Beadle's dime novel about a scout named "Texas Star" and turned to page thirty, where Mandy Mae had left a message in an elegant hand. "I'll not let them hang you," she wrote. I hoped she was right as I started reading the hundred-page pamphlet to pass the time away. The dime novel's hero always called the villains "lowdown sidewinders" or "rotten rascals" or "brazen brigands"—the imaginary Texas Star knew more words than the average flesh-and-blood Texan—before demanding his enemies "reach for the sky" prior to shooting them to pieces.

An hour later, Deputy Callus came in, glanced at

me, then snickered as he turned to his boss. "The mayor and the judge wanted me to tell you the meeting is going well with the Texas and Pacific representatives. Our folks are squiring them around, and they'll leave in the morning. The mayor thinks the railroad is as good as ours."

"Hot damn," Minter replied.

"With a train stop a near certainty," Callus continued, "the mayor thinks he can convince a Fort Worth bank to loan us a thousand or two dollars to help get everyone back on their feet. With the railroad as much as ours, the mayor says Buffalo Gap has nothing but prosperity ahead." The deputy glanced at me. "In spite of Lomax and his gang of robbers."

"If you see Tindle and Chesterfield before I do, tell them that's great news. Inform them that our other problem," Minter said, staring at me, "will be gone come morning."

Callus smiled so broadly I thought he would crack his ugly face. "I'll be glad to."

Shortly, the deputy left to make his rounds, and I resumed reading the pulp novel as the hero Texas Star rescued a captive young girl Mandy Mae's age from the redskins, killing hundreds, if not thousands, of the savages in the process and leaving Texas safe for civilization, if you could call it that, Texans being Texans.

My benefactor brought me my lunch, more sweet tea and two mason jars of a beef stew. She handed me a bulky napkin tied at the top. "It's cornbread," Mandy Mae said, "but it didn't turn out as light as usual."

When I took the bundle, it was as heavy as a brick. Untying the knot, I found a spoon and two squares of cornbread atop another carton of cartridges. I turned my back to the sheriff as I placed the packet on my small table and slipped the ammunition into my pants pocket. Then I sat down and ate.

"I'm enjoying your stew and your dime novel. You were right, Mandy Mae. Page thirty is exciting."

The lawman glanced our way. "You might want to let him borrow our Bible tonight, Mandy Mae, so he can get right with God before sunset."

"You are so thoughtful, Pa," she replied. "I'll do that."

We said little else as I finished my midday meal and returned the spoon and containers to her.

"I'll see you later," she whispered. Again Mandy Mae walked behind the desk and kissed her father on the cheek, then sauntered by the gun rack and the peg holding the keyring to my cell. She gently closed the door behind her, leaving her father to shake his head again and me to slide the additional ammunition under my bed.

The afternoon dragged by, the tedium only interrupted by a quick visit from Mayor Chesterfield and Nothing At All to confirm what Deputy Callus had told him and to report that the railroad prospects looked as good as done. I remained on my bed, pretending to read, until Mandy Mae brought me my supper of four biscuits, two sausage patties and a tin of cane syrup. After I returned her supper containers, she loaned me a Bible as her father had suggested. "I left a bookmark at a special passage," she announced. When she left, I watched her stride over to her father's chair, kissing him on the cheek. Next she swung by the wall and quietly removed the keyring from its peg holder before sauntering outside and gently closing the door behind her.

Her father shook his head as I opened the Good Book at the marked location. Mandy Mae had written on the plain marker, "I'll be back tonight to save you."

An hour later, the sheriff arose from his desk, grabbed his hat, and started out. He paused and turned to me, then said, "I'll see you tomor—" He stopped and coughed. "Have a good night and read your Bible, Lomax." He plopped his hat on and stepped outside. To my relief, he locked the door behind him.

I gave him a couple minutes to make sure he didn't return, then prepared for the lynch mob that would be coming. After retrieving the revolver from behind the bed and tucking it in my waistband, I opened the carton of bullets and left it on the little table, patted my pockets, still full of cartridges from Mandy Mae's earlier visit. I retrieved the slop bucket and placed it by the table, ready to douse my attackers if they entered my cell. Finally, I sat down in the chair facing the door, and waited.

Everything remained quiet through dusk, but once daylight faded away, things changed. Passing men shouted profanities at the jail. Some took up the chant, "Lynch him! Lynch him!" Others threw rocks at the back wall, several flying through the barred window. Down the street, the saloons emitted more boisterous noise than the previous night. The louder the commotion grew, the more dangerous the mob was becoming. I could do nothing but wait. Around midnight, I heard a commotion on the street and watched the flickering glimmer of torches through the barred front windows.

Moments later, I spotted a shadowy figure in a

sombrero through the front glass. The fellow stopped at the door, and I detected a key in the lock. I picked up my revolver, aimed it at the entry and cocked the hammer, preparing to defend my life.

As soon as the lock unlatched, the door swung open and the fellow burst in, slamming the door behind him and securing the latch again. I pointed the barrel at the fellow's heart, ready to kill him if he came any closer.

"Lomax," came Mandy Mae's familiar voice, but it took a moment for it to register because she wore a man's britches, shirt and boots.

I hesitated answering.

"It's me, Mandy Mae," she cried. "I told you I'd be back. There's a mob down the street, but I'll stop them from harming you."

Lowering my pistol, I greeted her. "I'm sure glad to see you, though I didn't recognize you in your new outfit."

"It's the only way I could get past them," she said, running across the office. She jabbed her hand in her pocket and retrieved the keyring, shoving it through the bars at me. "Take this so they can't open the jail cell."

As soon as I clenched it, she bolted to the gun rack, grabbing the shotgun, breaking it open, confirming it was loaded and snapping it shut. She then snatched two Winchester carbines from the rack, tucked one under her arm and brought me the second one, which she shoved through the bars. I accepted it as the noise and the flickering torchlight came nearer.

With her free hand, Mandy Mae doffed her sombrero, then leaned against the iron bars.

"Kiss me," she commanded.

I leaned between the cold bars and planted a long smooch on her lips.

When we broke from each other, Mandy Mae sighed and turned toward the door, the only thing that stood between me and the approaching lynch mob. "Now I can die happy," she said as she flung open the door, propped the Winchester against the wood frame, lowered the shotgun to her hip and stepped outside.

CHAPTER FOUR

The flickering light of the torches grew brighter as the unruly mob yelled insults at me and stopped in front of the plank walk where Mandy Mae Minter made her stand. Holding the scattergun at hip level, she earned the grumbling rabble's attention as they gradually hushed.

"Who the hell are you?" called a voice I recognized as Snooter Johnson's. "The sheriff told us no one would be manning the jail tonight."

Mandy Mae cocked the twin hammers on the shotgun and spoke as deeply as she could, but her words came out raspy rather than intimidating. "Call me 'Texas Star,' you lowdown sidewinders," she answered.

Some in the crowd chuckled, but not those staring at the two scattergun muzzles aimed at their guts.

"Back away and go home, you rotten rascals," she called, the hoarseness in her voice fading into her natural tone.

"Hey," cried Johnson, "it's the sheriff's daughter.

Now get out of our way, honey, and let us attend to our business."

"Yeah," echoed others in the mob.

"Your pa won't be happy about this," Snooter shouted. He stepped toward my protector.

"Scat, you brazen brigands," Mandy Mae responded.

The crowd halted, several mumbling among themselves. "What?" they asked.

"Move on, you brazen brigands," she repeated.

"Brazen brigands? What the hell does that mean?" Snooter answered for the lynching horde.

"It means you best reach for the sky before I start firing and filling you with hot lead. Leave unless you want me to plant you in graves beside Legless Larry."

The crowd inched forward, uncertain if Mandy Mae had gall to fire on them.

Slowly, she lifted the shotgun to her shoulder. "Another step and I'll fire."

As she threatened them, I raised the Winchester. If any man came near her, I planned to plug him if I could get a clear shot through the doorway. I doubted she would fire the scattergun.

"Reach for the sky or head home, you heathen hombres," Mandy Mae demanded, her voice crackling with fear—or determination.

The men looked at each other, wondering who was brave enough to take the next step until one fellow stumbled toward her as if he had been pushed or was too drunk to know what he was doing.

KA-BOOM!

Mandy Mae's shotgun exploded over their heads, sending shot whistling into the darkness.

The crowd scattered like a covey of quail, dropping their torches and escaping like the cowards they were.

KA-BOOM!

She fired the second barrel for emphasis, dropped the shotgun to the plank walk and grabbed the Winchester by the door frame, swinging its muzzle toward the slower of the disappearing lynch mob. "You should've reached for the sky, you rabid polecats," she shouted triumphantly. "Now run, you cowering coyotes, and don't come back unless you want another dose of lead and powder." As the cowardly vigilantes scattered to their homes or the nearest saloon to forget their failure, Mandy Mae marched back into the office, the flicker of the dying torches in the street behind her giving her the look of a demon. She grinned. "Wasn't that thrilling, Lomax?"

"You have a way with words and shotguns, Mandy Mae." I lowered my Winchester.

"I kept my promise. I didn't let them get you," she said as she strolled to the desk and dragged her father's chair to the doorway.

"Even the real Texas Star couldn't have done it better," I told her.

Mandy Mae smiled as she placed the Winchester across the seat and retrieved the shotgun from the plank walk and carried it to her father's desk where she lit a lamp, then re-loaded the two barrels. "I'll wait here a spell as someone will tell Pa. Then he'll storm over all hot and lathered because I did his job for him."

"The sheriff may be upset about it, but not me. I'm plenty grateful, Mandy Mae."

She smiled again as she walked to the open entry, picked up the carbine, and plopped down in the chair, waiting for her father as the torches finally burned themselves out. I sat down, Winchester across my lap, and rocked on the hind legs as I, too, awaited the lawman.

Deputy Callus arrived first, stomping on the plank walk and puffing his chest out like a bullfrog. "What the hell is wrong with you, Mandy Mae? And who the hell is Texas Star?"

"He's the bravest, most decent man in the Lone Star State. That's who he is," she shouted. "He saves maidens from the savages, protects the innocent, hunts down the guilty and makes Texas a place safe for women and children and even cowards like you, Deputy Callus."

"You've been reading too many of those worthless dime novels, Mandy Mae."

"And you haven't read enough of them. Maybe it would give you some backbone if you did." Mandy Mae spit out the words.

Gazing beyond her to me in my lamp-lit cell, Callus grabbed for his handgun when he saw I was holding a carbine.

Before he cleared leather, Mandy Mae jumped up from her seat and poked him in the gut with her shotgun. "Reach for the sky or die," she growled.

Callus released his pistol, letting it slide back in his holster. He pointed at me as he raised his hands. "Lomax has a Winchester."

"And a pistol and plenty of cartridges," Mandy Mae added.

"But he'll escape," the deputy cried.

"He's had the keys to the cell as well. If he was guilty, he would've escaped by now."

"Are you crazy, Mandy Mae?"

Before she answered, her father ran up as bewildered as a Republican in church or a Democrat anywhere. "What's going on, Mandy Mae?"

"I stopped a lynching, Pa. Aren't you proud? You always wanted a son, but a son couldn't have done any better, holding off a band of vigilantes, just like Texas Star."

"Mandy Mae, you shouldn't have interfered. You don't know what you've done, girl."

"I know exactly what I did! I did your job, preventing a hanging. That's what I did, and I'm not a girl. I'm a woman now!"

"You're a troublemaker, Mandy Mae, interfering in places you're not wanted or needed. This is man's work," scolded her father.

"Then do your job like a man, rather than a coward," Mandy Mae screamed.

Reaching his daughter blocking the doorway, the sheriff pushed the barrel down. "Let's get inside, shut the door and discuss this away from the street, *girl*. We don't want to be overheard, or it'll give folks the wrong idea about how I'm handling my duties."

Lowering his hands, Deputy Callus pointed at me, grinning and rocking with the carbine across my lap. "Uh, Saul, you might ought to know that Lomax is armed."

Minter's gaze shot toward me, and his eyes widened.

I smiled and lifted my hand, wiggling my fingers at him with a lazy wave.

"What the hell, Mandy Mae?"

Callus continued. "In addition to our Winchester,

he's got a pistol, plenty of cartridges, and the keys to his cell."

"But how?" The sheriff glared at his daughter.

She cocked her head and thrust out her defiant chin. "If you and your deputy won't protect him, I made sure he could defend himself from the lynch mob."

Perplexed, Minter threw up his arms in frustration. "Let's get inside where can we talk without being overheard." The head lawman glanced at me. "Or, without being shot?"

"Lomax promised not to shoot either of you, as long as he can protect himself," Mandy Mae informed them.

"Lomax can't be trusted," Callus grumbled.

Mandy Mae defended me. "Sure he can. He could've shot you before now and escaped, but he didn't, just as he vowed to me he wouldn't."

"Get in the office, now," the sheriff growled, "so we can sort this out."

Mandy Mae shoved her chair from the doorway, grabbed the extra Winchester propped against the wall and strode to my cell, handing me the carbine, then cradling the barrel of the shotgun in the crook of her left arm.

Minter waved for Callus to enter as he looked both ways down the street. He slipped inside and closed the door. Minter slid his hand first in his right pants pocket, then his left, both times coming out empty. "I lost my office key."

"Did you bookmark your Bible with it?" I asked.

Mandy Mae retrieved the office key from her britches pocket. "Here it is," she said. "I found it at home."

Minter clenched his lips and shook his head, grousing, "Most likely in my pocket."

She nodded. "At home nonetheless."

Exasperated at his failure to raise a proper daughter, Minter took the key, locked the door and turned to his deputy. "What are we gonna do with Lomax now?"

Continuing to rock on the back legs of my chair, I listened for the next half hour while they argued about remedies for the mess Mandy Mae had gotten them into. They came up with no solution that resolved their dilemma short of shooting me, though their odds of success were only fifty-fifty, me being well armed. The officials plotted about turning me over to the Texas Rangers or dynamiting the building so I would be blown up or crushed beneath the rubble, but those solutions created more problems than they solved, especially since they had no money until they collected new taxes in January. The conspirators even discussed poisoning me, but realized that would be near impossible with Mandy Mae fixing my meals.

"She might poison us instead," Callus offered.

After a half hour of fruitless scheming, they panicked when someone banged on the door. The sheriff blew out the lamplight on the desk and jerked his revolver from its holster. Mandy Mae stood up and pointed the shotgun at the entry as the sheriff and deputy slipped to a window on either side of the doorway.

The banging continued. "Let us in. We know you are in there. We saw you kill the lamp."

Minter pressed his cheek against the glass and quickly yanked his head back to curse.

"Is it who I think it is?" Callus asked.

The sheriff gulped and nodded. "It's the mayor and county judge." Minter let out a slow breath of frustration. "This'll cost me the next election."

"Hurry up and let us in," Nothing At All demanded.

"Mandy Mae, re-light the lamp, would you?"

"No, Pa. I'm protecting Lomax."

"Then you do it, Deputy."

Callus walked to the desk, took a match from the carton on the corner and quickly lit the coal oil lamp. As the yellow ball of light spread across the room, Minter took the office key from his pocket and unlocked the door, which instantly swung wide as Chesterfield and Tindle pushed their way inside, knocking the sheriff backward toward his desk until he caught his balance.

Quickly, the two elected officials slammed the door behind them.

"Who stopped the lynching?" the county judge demanded.

"Yeah," echoed the mayor. "Who's responsible for saving our prisoner? Someone called Texas Star is what I heard."

As neither the sheriff nor his deputy spoke, Mandy Mae lowered the barrel of her shotgun and stepped forward. "I did."

Chesterfield and Tindle looked at each other, then smiled and jumped across the room, both ignoring the scattergun and wrapping their arms around her.

For a moment, I thought the two were going to squeeze her to death for saving my life, but when they broke away, both wore the smile of a politician who had conceived of a new way to tax honest folks of their hard-earned money.

"Thank you, Mandy Mae," said Mayor Chesterfield.

"I second that emotion." Tindle concurred.

Looking from Nothing At All to the sheriff and his deputy, I saw they were as confused as I was.

Finally, Minter scratched his head. "What am I missing here, fellows? You boys wanted Lomax lynched so we would have money for our—" The sheriff left his thought unsaid as he apparently realized Deputy Callus might think poorly of them for not protecting his salary like they had their own.

Grimacing at Minter's incomplete sentence, Tindle explained. "That was the plan that we believed best, but the Texas and Pacific representatives here to consider Buffalo Gap as a railway stop, heard the commotion and watched from the hotel window all that happened."

"Yeah," Chesterfield added as he picked up the story. "They came to my house afterwards to talk about the attempted lynching. The way they explained it, they would have had trouble recommending a lawless Buffalo Gap as a stop on the new line across West Texas, but they were impressed by how we stood up to the vigilantes in the name of justice. Mandy Mae guaranteed the future of Buffalo Gap as a railroad town."

Tindle placed his hands on the shoulders of the savior of both me and Buffalo Gap and stared into her emerald eyes. "Young lady, everyone in Buffalo Gap owes you their gratitude for your selfless act. Miss Minter, you have ensured our future; Abilene be damned. Thank you for your brave stand against lawlessness." He released her and turned to her father. "Of course, Sheriff, we still have a few problems to resolve, like why did you leave the prisoner unguarded in a jail cell, knowing a violent mob was building?"

Minter lifted a defiant chin, then scowled at the judge. "Because you told me to, Tindle."

Nothing At All shook his head. "That's not what I recall."

"It's the truth and you know it, Judge."

They argued back and forth about who had the most accurate memory until I jumped into the conversation. "Perhaps you can just say that the sheriff was feeling poorly and went home to take some medicines that left him drowsy. When Mindy Mae heard the noises of the mob, she feared her pa was too sleepy to protect himself and his honest, charming, handsome and innocent prisoner—"

Tindle bobbed his head and raised his hand. "I liked everything except honest, charming, handsome and innocent." Then he motioned for me to continue.

"—so she took his key and ran to the jail to do her father's job and help his re-election chances."

As Tindle nodded, Chesterfield shook his head in agreement. "There's potential here for certain," the mayor added. "I can notify the newspaper, and we can start spreading the story about what a decent, law-abiding community Buffalo Gap is, where even girls on the verge of womanhood know right from wrong and will take a stand for what is good and decent."

I clapped my approval. "Mandy Mae might be the next hero of a Beadle dime novel."

Her father scowled.

"I can see it now," I continued, "Mandy Mae Minter, the Lawful Lady of the Plains, or Manly Mandy, the vigilante's nightmare, braver than her father, smarter than his deputy and true to the man she protects."

Minter's face reddened, and Callus pointed a threatening finger at me.

"As for me, I think it's a grand idea," Tindle said, "once we set the embellishments aside."

"Come morning I'll notify the paper," Chesterfield volunteered, "and we'll shape this into the grandest story that's happened in Texas since the Alamo."

"Remember the Alamo," Tindle said, placing his hand over his heart.

Callus cleared his throat. "And what's my story?"

"You were arresting innocent men," I suggested.

The deputy scowled, shaking two fingers at me.

"Better yet," I continued, "Callus was drunk and wallowing in the slop with hogs during the dustup."

The deputy gritted his teeth, turning to the judge and mayor. "Y'all are forgetting one major problem."

"What's that?" Tindle asked.

"Lomax. He started all of our difficulties. What are we gonna do with his sorry butt?"

"Only one thing to do," Mandy Mae offered, "and that's to free him. He's innocent because I can see all the way to his soul. There's no better citizen on two feet than Lomax."

Only Mandy Mae and I liked that idea.

Mayor Chesterfield pointed at me and shook his head. "He's armed. He could kill us in cold blood right now, just like he shot Legless Larry."

"And he's got the cell keys," Mandy Mae pointed out. "He could escape any time, if he wanted, but he doesn't. Why? Because he's innocent."

As she crossed her arms over her bosom, I leaned back in my chair and picked up the keyring from atop my bed. I rattled the keys and waved the carbine at the pair of lawmen and the two politicians. "Things are gonna change around here," I announced. "First, I want a mattress so I can get a decent night's sleep."

"We don't have the budget for that," Nothing At All protested.

"Take it out of the deputy's wages," I suggested.

Callus scowled at me. "You'll get yours one day, Lomax."

I pointed the Winchester barrel at the slop bucket. "And, you'll get yours if you're not careful, Callus."

"Gentlemen, gentlemen," cried Chesterfield. "We're missing the point, worrying about Lomax. The price of a mattress is nothing compared to what money the Texas and Pacific will bring when it arrives in town. I've got land that'll be perfect for the Buffalo Gap Depot."

Tindle scoffed. "I've got property much better suited for a depot than your tiny plot, Mayor."

"Already I can see how the railroad is gonna bring this town together," I said, "but right now I'm not concerned about where the depot will be located. What I *am* interested in is a soft mattress to make my stay more satisfactory."

"It's not coming out of my salary," the sheriff announced.

The mayor and the county judge eyed each other, as if they were trying to figure how to get the other one to pay for it.

Finally, Tindle shrugged. "We'll figure out what to do with the mattress and Lomax after the railroad representatives catch the stage this morning. They're stopping in Abilene before heading back to the main office in Fort Worth."

"Yeah," the mayor said, "once they're gone, we'll

have more options on dealing with Lomax and the predicament he's put us in. Fortunately, the twelve-hundred-dollar loan from the Fort Worth bank will get us through the end of the year. It'll be tight, but we'll make it."

"Don't forget my mattress," I reminded them.

"And don't forget Lomax has a carbine, a pistol, plenty of ammunition and the jail keys," Sheriff Minter said.

"Don't forget Lomax is innocent," Mandy Mae cried out.

I smiled at my benefactor and savior. "Well said, Miss Minter."

She turned and nodded. "Wasn't it a thrilling night? I'll remember it forever."

"As we all should," I added. "Perhaps Buffalo Gap should make an annual holiday of your birthday, just like the Fourth of July, so future generations will know how you saved Buffalo Gap and H.H. Lomax from oblivion."

"Mandy Mae hasn't saved you just yet," Nothing At All reminded me. "We've still gotta decide what to do with you."

"First, get me a mattress," I commanded. "After that, you can release me and reimburse me for my lost time in your jail."

"Shut up," the county judge ordered. "You've gotten free room and board since your arrest. And we rescued you from a lynch mob."

"*We?*" I shot back. "Mandy Mae and she alone kept my neck out of a hangman's noose."

"It came out the same," Tindle replied, pulling his watch from his vest pocket and checking the time. "It's after two this morning. We've got to be up in six hours to see the Texas and Pacific men off to Fort Worth. Buffalo Gap's future depends on a rousing sendoff. Let's retire, Mayor, and leave Lomax to the men we are paying to enforce the law. Once the railroad delegation departs, we can discuss how to dispose of Lomax."

Both politicians stepped toward the door.

"Don't forget the mattress," I reminded them, "and a new slop bucket would be nice. My other one's getting full."

Chesterfield and Tindle ignored me, barging outside and leaving the door ajar as if they had taken lessons from Mandy Mae.

Minter waved at Callus. "Make your rounds, Deputy, and close the door when you leave. I'll see you in the morning."

Callus marched outside, shutting the squeaky entrance forcefully and leaving me with the sheriff and his daughter. Minter pinched the bridge of his nose. "I've got a terrible headache. Too much excitement for one night."

"Aren't you proud of me, Pa, for standing up to the lynch mob and bringing the railroad to town?"

"The railroad ain't here yet, and Lomax still is," he replied. "That's two problems for us to solve. Are you going home with me or staying here with Lomax?" His words brimmed with frustration.

Mandy Mae looked at me with her striking green eyes.

I patted the barrel of my Winchester. "I'll be fine with my guns and the keys."

She turned to her father. "I'll see you home." Mandy Mae took her carbine and the shotgun and slid them through the cell bars to me. She stepped to her father as he blew out the lamp, slid her arm in his and escorted him out. One of them locked up, and they headed home.

After securing my arsenal and hiding the weapons under my bed, I retired and slept as good as possible on the wooden slats. I awoke midmorning to the sound of applause and then cheers. I got up and stood on my bed to glance out the barred window. Down the street I saw a throng of citizens around a stagecoach, thanking the railroad delegation for their visit and looking forward to the impending decision to make Buffalo Gap a stop on the T&P line as it went westward across Texas. Both the mayor and the county judge offered brief speeches of gratitude, then sent the stage on its way, confident that the sooner the stage left, the sooner the railroad would arrive to make Buffalo Gap prosperous forever.

Once the coach departed, Mandy Mae showed up with my breakfast, unlocking the door herself, sauntering over and kissing me through the bars. "It's just boiled eggs, cold bacon and biscuits. I was up late last night."

As I finished the meal, the two lawmen arrived, dragging a cotton-tuft mattress. I unlocked the cell door, then grabbed the shotgun to cover them as they dumped the padding on my bed.

After they exited, I locked myself back in the cell.

"No need to lock it," Minter said.

"I want to keep you fellows out," I replied as I twisted the key in the mechanism. "What about my new slop bucket?"

"In due time," the sheriff answered.

Things settled into a routine the next two days with

Mandy Mae bringing me meals, the two lawmen grumbling about my ongoing presence with the mayor and county judge occasionally dropping by to discuss my future. The second day, Mandy Mae shared with me the newspaper account of her valiant stand at the jail and how it had secured prosperity for Buffalo Gap forever.

On the morning of the third day after the failed lynching, Chesterfield and Tindle joined Minter and Callus to settle my fate.

"We've decided to release you tomorrow, Lomax," Tindle announced as the other three nodded.

"Why not release me now?" I asked.

"We're not ready, but we can't afford to keep feeding you past tomorrow, and we can't afford to try you."

"Evidently, you can't afford a new slop bucket, either."

Chesterfield ignored my observation. "Since we have no witnesses that can place you at the bank or identify you as Legless Larry's killer, a conviction might be iffy. We'll release you at ten in the morning, once Mandy Mae's fed you breakfast."

As he spoke, I noticed Callus smiling broadly and rocking on the back of his boot heels. His smirk bothered me, like he knew something I didn't. "I'll want my mule saddled and tied outside with my carbine in my rigging and my pistol and holster hanging on the saddle horn."

They all smiled and nodded, sending a chill up my spine. It was all too easy. Come suppertime when Mandy Mae and I were alone, I asked her if she had heard anything about me being released the next day.

Shrugging, she answered, "I can only dream of that day arriving."

"I feared it was only a rumor." I ate my meal and sent her home.

Come morning she brought me an early breakfast, saying her pa wanted her to run some errands for her mother, so she left me my food and departed under the close gaze of her father. An hour later the mayor, the county judge and the deputy came in, all smiles and handshakes.

"It's the day you've been waiting for," Nothing At All announced. "Your mule's hitched outside and we've placed your carbine and pistol on your mount as you requested. Now all you've got to do is let yourself out of your cell, mount up and ride out of Buffalo Gap," Tindle said. "All we ask is that you never return to our community." His fellow conspirators all nodded and grinned, increasing my suspicions.

Finally, it dawned on me they wanted me to leave the jail so they could shoot me and claim I was escaping. I figured I would be the top story in next week's paper.

"That's mighty generous of you fellows," I said as I took off my shirt, my boots, and my pants, keeping Mandy Mae's revolver nearby as I disrobed.

"Have you gone loco, Lomax?" Sheriff Minter asked. "Are you planning on leaving Buffalo Gap like Lady Godiva?"

"No," I said, eyeing the quartet and pointing at Callus, who was about my size but not nearly so handsome. "I want him to put on my clothes and go outside first."

Callus gulped hard and shook his head. "No, I won't do it."

Minter, Chesterfield and Tindle looked at each other. Finally, the county judge spoke. "You will if you want to keep your job, Deputy. It seems Lomax doesn't trust us."

I shoved my clothes through the jail bars and then grabbed my hat from the mattress and squeezed it through as well.

"Take off your duds, Callus, and put on mine, then go mount my mule."

The deputy paled, looking from Tindle to the sheriff, who nodded.

Callus swapped clothes and reluctantly marched out the door, leaving it open in his wake. I watched him approach my mule, stick his foot in the stirrup, and pull himself into the saddle.

That's when the gunshot exploded from across the street!

CHAPTER FIVE

The sheriff, mayor, and county judge bolted outside to Callus, sprawled on the ground as my frightened mule stomped at the dirt around the downed deputy. As shouting spectators circled them, the trio squatted beside Callus, grabbed his arms and eased him up from the dusty street.

Callus moaned, gasping for breath at a sudden pang and mumbling, "I can't believe Snooter shot me."

"He's out of his head," Sheriff Minter shouted as he yanked the bandana from his deputy's neck and stuffed it in his mouth. "Bite on that for the pain," he instructed, but I knew he was trying to shut the injured lawman up.

Together, the elected trio straightened him up, and eased him into the office. "Somebody fetch the doctor," Chesterfield cried.

As they walked him inside, I saw a bloody blossom on Callus's right shoulder and heard a screeching scream that sounded like a wounded cougar. Just as they were maneuvering Callus inside and shutting the door behind him, the shriek came again with my name.

"Looomaxxx," cried Mandy Mae. The entry flung open, and she burst into the room behind it, charging straight to the suffering man in my clothes. She yanked my hat from the deputy's head, then stepped back, confused at the contorted face she saw. Perplexed, she looked up and spotted me in my long johns. Her hand flew to her mouth as she disguised a giggle. "What happened?"

I pointed to Chesterfield, Minter, and Tindle as they worked Callus into the sheriff's chair. "They attempted to assassinate me."

Mandy Mae dropped her hand from her lips, cackling as she did. "You look cute in your union suit."

"At least I look alive," I said. "I figured they were up to something when they planned to release me without telling you."

She spun around and shook her fist at her father. "That true, Pa?"

"Hush up, girl," Minter answered. "I don't have time for this." He yanked the bandana from Callus's mouth. "You shut up, too, Deputy, or you'll give the beans away."

"But Snooter—" Callus began before the sheriff stuffed the kerchief back between his lips. The deputy finished his thought in an incomprehensible mumble.

"Then it is true, Pa!" screamed Mandy Mae.

"Not now, girl! We'll discuss it at home."

Before Mandy Mae could respond, the doctor barged in, carrying a medical bag and wearing a worried look. He was a short fellow, sporting a string tie, a derby and wire-rimmed glasses resting on a tiny nose. Before he looked at the patient, he turned to Tindle. "You think this'll ruin our shot at getting the railroad, Judge?"

Tindle shrugged. "We'll keep it quiet and out of the paper."

The doctor grimaced. "But you know how word gets around. Those Abilene folks are sure to find out and spread the news to strangle our railway hopes."

Chesterfield nodded. "It could be a problem if he dies, but not if you save him, so shut up and treat him first. We can discuss T&P implications later."

"Okay, Mayor, anything for the good of Buffalo Gap." The sawbones turned to the patient and gasped. "Oh, no, he's turning blue. I don't have much time."

"Maybe this will help," Minter said, pulling the bandana from Callus's mouth.

The deputy heaved and shook his head, slowly regaining his color.

"Graciousness, Sheriff, what were you trying to do?"

"Keep him from saying things that people might take the wrong way," Minter replied. "A railroad's at stake."

"And...my...life," the deputy snorted.

The doctor took scissors from his medical bag and cut my shirt off of Callus, finding the bullet hole and sticking his little finger inside as he studied the deputy's face. "His color's coming back. That's good. And the slug doesn't seem to have struck anything vital. He'll live as long as you don't stick that bandana in his mouth again and smother him." Working quickly, the physician pulled a bottle of chloroform from his bag and yanked the red bandana from Minter's grasp. He poured the liquid onto the cloth, and held it over Callus's nose and mouth. Moments later, the deputy went limp as his eyes closed. After he pulled the bandana away from Callus's face, the doctor slapped his patient on the cheek.

"Damn," said Minter, "what was that for?"

"To see if he was knocked out or if he felt pain," the doctor said without looking up. "He's out now, so I can extract the bullet." Tossing the rag aside, he grabbed a needle-nosed instrument from his bag and carefully inserted it in the hole. After wiggling it for a few seconds, he squeezed the handle and slowly extracted the metal jaws, which held a lead slug. He lifted it for everyone to inspect, then placed the device and slug on the desk. The physician yanked a bottle of liquid from his bag and poured it on the wound. Next, he pressed a bandage over the hole and held it in place with a cloth that he wrapped around Callus's shoulder. When he finished, he looked at the sheriff. "Somebody needs to take him home and put him to bed. He'll be gimpy for a spell, possibly four to six weeks to fully recover."

Minter sighed. "I don't know what I'll do for a deputy until then."

Mandy Mae stepped forward, waving her hand at her father. "You can deputize me, Pa."

Rolling his eyes, the sheriff frowned and shook his head. "Whoever heard of a girl deputy? You wouldn't know what to do?"

"From what I read in the paper," the doctor interrupted, "I'd say she did pretty well in holding off the lynch mob and securing a railroad stop for Buffalo Gap." Then the physician pointed at me holding my carbine. "Best I figure, she'd also know not to arm her prisoner and give him the keys to his cell."

Minter scoffed and pointed at his daughter. "Mandy Mae's the one that gave them to him a couple days ago."

The doctor shrugged. "Maybe so, but he hasn't shot anyone or broken from jail. How do you explain that, Sheriff?"

"He's too dumb," Minter answered. "Just look at him standing there in his underwear."

"They tried to get me to escape," I jumped in. "I figured it was a trick, so I sent the deputy out in my clothes. You treated the result."

Running his fingers through his thinning hair, the practitioner cleared his throat and responded. "Dumb, you say? He was smart enough to send a decoy out for the ambush."

Minter hesitated, then replied listlessly. "It must've been an accident."

The discussion changed when Callus moaned and shook his head. "I need help putting him to bed," the doctor said as he closed his medical bag. "Can you gents help me?"

Silence answered the request until Nothing At All answered. "That's not a job for us elected officials. Get some volunteers off the street. Besides, we've got a problem to deal with." Tindle pointed at me. "We've got to decide what to do with Lomax here before he creates more vexations for Taylor County and the fine folks of Buffalo Gap. He declined our offer to walk away a free man."

"Nothing At All here wanted me carried away in a pine box," I shouted.

The physician tilted his head and narrowed his eyes. "Nothing at all?"

I nodded. "When we first met, he told me to call him Judge Tindle or Nothing At All."

Laughing, the doctor turned from me to the sheriff and the county judge. "He's either the dumbest man alive or smarter than all of us put together. Don't do any horse trading with him, especially with our tax money, Judge, or we'll wind up broker than we are now." He picked up his bag and walked to the door. "I'll find volunteers to carry Callus home, seeing how that is beneath the dignity of the elected officials responsible for this shooting."

As soon as the doctor stepped outside, Tindle scowled at me. "You've got to go, Lomax. The sooner you leave Buffalo Gap, the sooner we can grab our future. Go ahead, let yourself out and scat." He paused, scratching his chin, then continued. "In fact, do Buffalo Gap a favor and go to Abilene. It shouldn't take you long to kill their chances of getting a rail stop." He pointed to the cell lock. "Get out of town, Lomax. We never want to see your ugly face in Buffalo Gap again."

"It's not that simple anymore because I can't trust the lot of you," I responded. "Mandy Mae's the only person in town that believes I'm innocent. Everybody else wants to shoot me. I'm not leaving here until you meet my demands and guarantee my safety when I depart. I'd trust a Comanche before I would you, Nothing At All."

Mayor Chesterfield stepped to my cell. "Just so you know, I had nothing to do with the assassination attempt. I'll work with you on a safe departure. What are your demands?"

"To start with, bring me a padded rocking chair this afternoon. I think better when I'm in a rocker. Then I want you to double what you pay Mandy Mae for my meals."

"That's robbery," cried Tindle.

Chesterfield lifted his hand at Nothing At All. "Hush, Judge. Let me handle this."

Before I could answer, the doctor barged in with three volunteers, including Snooter Johnson, who was still carrying the carbine that I suspected had shot Callus. Our conversation halted while the trio eased the moaning deputy up from the chair. Between the groans, I overheard Snooter whispering, "I thought you were Lomax. I didn't mean to shoot you."

The men got Callus to his feet as the doctor lifted the deputy's left arm over a volunteer's shoulder, then attempted the same with the right arm near the wound, but Callus screamed in agony. The physician pointed to Snooter to grab the deputy's holster on that side, while the third man clutched the gun belt from behind. Carefully, they moved the wounded lawman outside.

Once they exited, Mandy Mae closed the door, and I resumed negotiating. "If y'all aren't emptying my slop bucket, I want three more and heavy towels to cover them."

"No one wants to dump your—," Tindle started until Chesterfield interrupted.

"Shut up, Tindle. All you do is pick at our scab of a problem." I spotted frustration building in the mayor as his face reddened and his cheeks puffed out. He turned to me. "That's fine, Lomax, but it has nothing to do with you escaping, err, I mean being released from jail."

"Maybe not, but meeting those requests will demonstrate your good faith and allow me to think more clearly about how I want to be freed."

"This is ridiculous," Nothing At All shouted, "us negotiating with a scallywag who has brought a wagonload of trouble to Buffalo Gap."

Chesterfield stomped his shoe on the floor and pointed to the door. "All you do is gall him, Judge. I'm trying to work this out in the calm, rational manner of a mayor who intends to watch this community blossom with the railroad's arrival."

Minter stepped between the two elected officials. "I agree with Judge Tindle. This should be county business."

The mayor's cheeks reddened even more as he pointed a finger at each of their noses. "You forget, gentlemen, that I am not only the mayor, but also the president of Buffalo Gap Bank. It was me that got a loan from the Cattleman's Bank of Fort Worth to help us through this. If you gentlemen persist in antagonizing our jailhouse guest, I will tell the newspaper how you plotted to ensure that the money remaining after the robbery paid your salaries at the expense of all my other depositors."

The sheriff and the county judge paled. "Go ahead, Mayor," Tindle replied.

Forcing a smile, Chesterfield turned to me. "What else do you need, Mister Lomax?"

"Time," I said. "I want time to figure out how to leave this cell, this town, and this county without getting shot."

The mayor nodded. "I understand. We'll get you a rocking chair this afternoon and start doubling Mandy

Mae's meal reimbursement tomorrow. I'll also make certain that three new buckets are sent over for your slop."

"And heavy blankets to cover them," I added.

"That, too," he replied.

"Plus clothes, since my others now have the deputy's blood on them. Also, put up my mule and retrieve my carbine, pistol and holster."

Chesterfield bobbed his head. "Fair enough." He turned to Minter. "Sheriff, fetch his weapons and stable his mule."

"And, Mister Mayor, I want to negotiate with you, not the sheriff or Nothing At All."

Chesterfield agreed. "I understand. My intent is to get you out of town safely so it doesn't harm our fair community's reputation. We all want Buffalo Gap back to normal as soon as possible." The banker turned to the sheriff and the county judge. "And that's what Minter and Tindle want, whether they admit it or not." He pointed to the door. "It's time for us to leave, Tindle, and no more tricks, Sheriff."

Once they exited, Mandy Mae rushed over, stuck her hands through the bars and grabbed my proffered hand. "You'll eat well, Lomax, because I'll buy you the best groceries I can find in Buffalo Gap." She squeezed my fingers tightly, then leaned her face between the iron rods for me to kiss her.

As I obliged Mandy Mae, the sheriff turned away and stepped outside so he wouldn't view his only child kissing the worst thing that ever happened to Buffalo Gap. He returned moments later with my carbine and sidearm, placing them on the gun rack.

Pulling my lips and my hands from hers, I told

Mandy Mae what I wanted. "Buy me plenty of tinned food. You can either feed it to me, share it with your ma and pa, or throw it away, but whatever you do, save all the tin cans. They'll come in handy when I leave town."

Overhearing my instructions, the sheriff turned, looking as perplexed as a preacher with a noose around his neck. "You're the dumbest thing ever to arrive here," he mumbled.

Mandy Mae twisted about and plopped her balled fists on her hips. "Pa, that's a terrible thing to say about Lomax."

Not willing to stand and argue with his daughter about my intellectual capabilities, Minter tugged his hat snug on his head and started out again. "I've got rounds to make and tend Lomax's mule, seeing how Callus has been shot."

"That's on you and the judge," I called after him as he slammed the door. Waiting a moment, I placed the Winchester on my bed, grabbed the keyring and let myself out of the cell. Mandy Mae stepped to me and threw her arms around me, hugging me without bars between us.

She kissed me, then grabbed my wrists and looked at me with her inviting emerald eyes. "You're the most thrilling man I've ever known."

"Me standing here in my underwear isn't exactly thrilling for me."

"That doesn't matter. When you leave Buffalo Gap, I want to go with you."

"That's too dangerous," I replied.

"Like I said, the most thrilling man I've ever met."

Despite her resistance, I pulled myself from her grasp and strode over to the gun rack where I removed another shotgun, a rifle, and a pistol, plus my carbine and holstered pistol the sheriff just returned. I toted them into my cell and slid everything under my bed, save for my holster, which I buckled around my waist. I checked the load in the pistol and marched back out, inspecting the drawers on the gun rack and in the sheriff's desk for ammunition. I found seven cartons of various calibers. Mandy Mae helped me carry the boxes to my cell, where I shoved them under my bed. As soon as that was done, I gave Mandy Mae another hug and kiss, then shooed her out of the cell and locked myself back in, hiding the keyring under my mattress.

"How do you plan to get away?" my green-eyed ally asked me.

"Give me a couple days to sort things out, Mandy Mae, but save the empty food cans."

"Okay," she answered, "but remember to take me with you."

"I can't do that without risking your life."

"I'd rather die than live without you, Lomax," she said in a voice so sweet it would've embarrassed a hundred-pound sack of sugar. "Promise me you'll take me with you."

Knowing I had no other option without losing the only friend I had in town, I nodded. "I promise, but you've got to promise you'll do exactly what I tell you to and not ask any questions or share what I said with anyone."

She nodded. "I promise. You're my only friend in Buffalo Gap, the only one that doesn't mock my ugly teeth."

"Then you best head home and start working on my next meal. Remember to save all the empty tins."

"Why do you need the cans?"

I waved my index finger at her. "Tsk, tsk, Mandy Mae. You promised not to ask any questions. Also, while I'm thinking about it, buy a ball of twine for us."

She smiled, but didn't inquire. "I'll see you in a spell with a little lunch, since I don't have time to prepare much now."

"Just bring me an early supper, Mandy Mae, a big meal."

"I'll do that," she answered, scampering out the door as happy as if she had marriage on her mind.

While I appreciated her support, I couldn't saddle her with a vagabond like me. I would certainly need her to escape the mess I found myself in, but after that I feared she would be a chain dragging me down. Inside, I felt bad about not returning her affection, but I couldn't tie any knot with her that would hinder my options in escaping from Buffalo Gap. I grappled with that pang of conscience as well as a fail-proof plan to leave Taylor County for good.

True to his word, Mayor Chesterfield that afternoon sent over new clothes, a comfortable rocking chair, three sparkling buckets for slop and a heavy blanket to drape over the pails and reduce the stench. Though Sheriff Minter scowled at the deliveries, he said nothing until he realized the weapons and ammunition in the gun rack were missing. He yanked open his desk drawers and discovered all his cartridges had been removed as well.

Slamming the desk shut, he arose, hitched his pants, and marched to my cell as I rocked contentedly in my padded rocker in my fresh clothes. He growled. "What happened to my arsenal?"

"It's mine now."

"What?"

"Everything's under my bed, except my revolver." I pointed to the holster buckled to my waist.

"This beats all I ever saw. My prisoner with my guns and cartridges, as well as the key to the cell."

"Who's the dumb one now, Sheriff?"

"Worst of it all, my daughter's taken a liking to you, Lomax." He scratched his chin and shook his head. "I don't see it. You ain't that smart, and you ain't that handsome."

"It's my natural charm." I paused a moment, then issued a command. "Sheriff, I have an errand for you to run."

"What? Have you gone plumb loco, Lomax?" He grinned. "That's what I'll call you, 'Loco Lomax.' It fits."

"I've been called a lot of things over the years, Sheriff, but loco is a new one. Now I want some more reading material, so run on home and tell Mandy Mae to include two or three of her dime novels with my supper, something to keep me occupied. Fact is, one of those dime novels might give me an idea for a daring escape, as your daughter would say."

"And what if I don't do it?"

"I suppose it's up to you, Sheriff, you being the law in Taylor County, but it sure would be embarrassing if I let myself out of jail and told folks how I had hoodwinked you out of all your guns and ammunition. That wouldn't look good come election time."

He tapped his fingers on the butt of his revolver. "I ought to shoot you right now."

"Do that and you might lose the railroad. On top of

that, you would break your daughter's heart, killing the first man who ever kissed her."

He cleared his throat like he was about to spit until he remembered he was indoors.

"Which is it, Sheriff? Shoot me or fetch me reading material."

Minter hesitated.

"I'll also need light in my cell so I can read after dark. You don't know how boring it is when you can't go to sleep and can't do anything else because of the darkness."

The sheriff clenched his jaw and gritted his teeth. "You're just a friendless saddle tramp, Loco Lomax."

Standing up from my rocking chair, I marched to the iron bars and grabbed them. "I make friends enough to get by. In Buffalo Gap I made friends with the one who wears the pants in the Minter family, Mandy Mae. Now are you gonna fetch the dime novels, or am I gonna have to complain to your daughter? She don't think too highly of you at the moment, but if you do what I say, I'll put in a good word for you with her."

Minter grabbed the butt of his revolver, but I pulled my gun from its holster before he freed his.

"Remember the Texas and Pacific," I reminded him.

Slowly, he released his pistol, then turned around, grabbed his hat from a peg by the door and burst out onto the plank walk, leaving entryway wide open. Deciding an open door might draw unneeded spectators, I took the jail key from under my mattress, unlocked the cell and walked across the office to shut the doorway. As soon as I was done, I locked myself behind the bars and awaited my supper.

Minter arrived first, inquiring who had shut the door.

"I did."

"Then why didn't you escape?"

"I'm innocent, Sheriff. I believe in justice triumphing over injustice."

The lawman closed the squeaky door, dropped his hat on the peg and took his seat behind his desk, where he remained until Mandy Mae arrived with my supper. Without a word to her or me, the sheriff grabbed his hat and trod outside, leaving us alone.

Mandy Mae carried two baskets, so I knew I was in for a fine meal. From one basket she removed a half dozen dime novels, a box of candles, a candle holder, and a carton of matches. I unlocked the cell door so she could bring in my light and reading materials. She moved to the small table and extracted a cloth that she used to cover the surface. Next, she put down eating utensils for us both.

"I decided to eat with you tonight."

"I'm honored, ma'am."

She giggled at my formality as she unpacked my supper, a Mason jar of sweet tea, and batter-fried steak, cream gravy, mashed potatoes, green beans, deviled eggs, pickles, warm biscuits, and butter on fancy china dishes. After she placed the elegant silverware by our plates, I stepped behind her and pulled out the chair for her to sit down. She chuckled again as I went to my side of the table and slipped into my rocker and slid it across from her.

"Everything smells delicious, Mandy Mae. You outdid yourself on supper!"

Her sincere smile would have been beautiful, except

for her teeth. "Thank you, Lomax. Now that they've doubled my food allowance—thanks to you—I can offer more and better dishes, but wait until dessert."

"I'm anxious to find out."

She giggled. "I can't keep a secret. It's peach cobbler. I used three tins of sweetened peaches and Ma's dough recipe. It was all I could do to keep from eating it."

"You saved the cans, didn't you?"

"Just like you said, and I won't ask why you need them."

Her meal was as good as it smelled, delicious to the last morsel, and the fruit cobbler was as sweet and tasty as any I had ever spooned between my lips. I figured Mandy Mae would make some old boy a wonderful wife, just not me.

After we finished our supper, Mandy Mae hesitated before cleaning up the dishes. "Do you know how you're going to escape?"

I grimaced. "Not for sure, though I am certain of one thing—I'll need your help. I may even have to take you as a hostage."

Her face brightened and her eyes widened as she lifted her hands beneath her chin and softly clapped them together. "Goody, goody!"

"I see no other way of keeping them from shooting me. Of course, if they all aim as poorly as Snooter Johnson, I stand a good chance of surviving."

"This is all so thrilling," she tittered. "It's just like one of my dime novels, me the maiden in distress."

"Beyond needing you, Mandy Mae, I don't know what else I'll need other than all the empty tin cans you can save, plus a ball of twine. Buy me some twine.

When you have time, find a ten-penny nail and a hammer, and knock a hole in each can around the lip."

"Why?" she started before shaking her head and lifting her index finger to her lips. "I know, don't ask any questions."

"And I won't have to deceive you," I answered.

"As long as you take me with you, I don't care, Lomax." She arose and strode around the table, leaning over and planting a kiss on my lips as her father entered and stomped his boots.

"What's going on here?" the sheriff demanded, slamming the door.

Mandy Mae broke from me and backed away.

"Something got stuck in my teeth," I replied. "Your daughter, being the gentle, caring soul that she is, was only trying to help me get it out."

"Loco Lomax, I ought to shoot you."

"And kill Buffalo Gap's chances of getting the railroad after your daughter saved the town's reputation mere days ago? That's not smart, Sheriff."

He threw up his arms, grabbed his hat, and flung it at his desk. "What I don't want is some citizen coming into my office and seeing you two cavorting like you have the run of the place."

Mandy Mae gathered up the dishes and shoved things back in the baskets, tears moistening her eyes. I stepped to help, but she waved me away, then turned to her father. "This is the only man that's ever thought enough of me to kiss me, and you want to kill him, Pa. It just ain't right."

"What's right's what's in the Good Book, which you should read more and those trashy dime novels less! I swear, girl, I don't know what I am going to do with you or how I'm gonna support your ma and you if I'm not re-elected." He plopped into his chair, dropped his elbows on the desk and buried his face in his open palms. "Keeping the law's easier than keeping a daughter," he decried.

When she finished gathering her goods and filling her baskets, she placed them on the bed and came to me, grabbing me and planting a long kiss on my lips. As she broke away, she cried out for her father to hear. "I'll look forward to seeing you again tomorrow, unlike some men in this room." With that, she grabbed her wicker containers and strode out. When she exited, she left the door wide open for her pa to close. As he did, I locked myself back in my cell and retired to my mattress, figuring to read one of the dime novels for ideas how to get out of my predicament.

Minter lingered at his desk well after dark, fearful I suspected of encountering his daughter and not knowing how to deal with her. I lit a candle to read. When he finally left, I'd never seen a fellow's shoulders and spirit sag so low. He likely tripped over them walking home.

The next three days Mandy Mae exulted in our relationship; the sheriff sulked; and I pondered a fail-proof plan to get me out of Buffalo Gap, alive and prosperous. On the fourth day, I informed Sheriff Saul Minter that I needed a pencil and pad to write out my demands and that I wanted to meet with him, Mayor Chesterfield and County Judge Tindle the next day.

"If this don't beat all," Minter said under his breath as he got me the writing materials, "a criminal telling the law what to do."

"Get used to it, Sheriff, until I leave town."

CHAPTER SIX

"I'm not leaving Buffalo Gap until we switch places," I informed the sheriff, the mayor, and the county judge, as Mandy Mae looked on. I sat in my jail cell, swaying back and forth in my rocking chair while the three men leaned against the edge of the sheriff's desk, shaking their heads. Nothing At All reddened with anger while Minter jutted his surly chin toward me. Only Mayor Chesterfield agreed he was ready to end this drama.

"What do you mean, us change places?" Tindle growled.

"Yeah," grumbled Minter.

The mayor nodded. "Go ahead, don't mind them."

"What I mean," I answered, standing up from my rocker and stepping to the iron bars, "is I'm not leaving until I'm on the outside of this jail cell and the sheriff and the county judge are inside. On top of you two, I want Deputy Callus and Snooter Johnson locked in here with you."

"What about the mayor?" Tindle demanded.

"He'll be at the bank. I'll lock the four I named in

jail and deliver the keyring to the mayor at his desk. He can free you when I'm out of sight."

Chesterfield smiled broadly, straightened from his perch and hooked his thumbs in his suspenders. "I'm fine with that."

"I bet you are," snarled Tindle.

"That's the starting point, gentlemen. If you can't agree to that, I'll stay here until you can afford to pay for a trial."

"If that's what it takes to get Loco Lomax away from Mandy Mae, I'm for it."

Shaking my head, I raised my trigger finger at the sheriff. "It's not that simple, Sheriff."

"Huh?" he asked, moving from the desk toward me.

"I'll be taking Mandy Mae as a hostage and a shield in case you send Snooter Johnson or someone else out to shoot me."

"That's outrageous," Minter spat the words out like bullets and turned from me to his smiling daughter. "I don't want her hurt."

"And I don't want Lomax shot," she answered.

"I don't like it," her father said.

"It's okay by me," Mandy Mae replied. "I trust him more than I do y'all."

"Sheriff, you best get used to it because you have no choice. Besides, I may marry her."

Mandy Mae glowed with my pronouncement, but her father's face clouded like an approaching storm, and he clenched his fists and jaw.

"Is that acceptable to everyone?"

"Yes," replied Mandy Mae, clasping her hands over her bosom, tilting her head and smiling at me.

"It's fine with us," Tindle responded.

Minter turned his murky gaze from me to the county judge. "She's not your daughter, and you don't speak for me, Judge."

"You have no choice, Sheriff," said Chesterfield, "if we want to get this resolved and Lomax out of town."

The sheriff let out a long, slow sigh, as he nodded. "Let's get it over with."

I returned to my rocker and sat down, enjoying the growing tension among my three antagonists. "Nobody'll get hurt if you go along with my plan."

"No matter how stupid," Tindle said.

"Or embarrassing, my daughter marrying a common thief," Minter added.

Chesterfield waved away their reservations with a sweep of his arm. "Let's end this. How does tomorrow work for you?"

"What's tomorrow, Mayor?"

"Saturday."

"Nope. Too many people in town on Saturday. The fewer folks around, the less chance of someone trying to be a hero."

"Then when?" the mayor asked.

"Let's aim for Monday."

"Monday's not what I would like to aim at?" the sheriff grumbled.

"Pa!" cried Mandy Mae. "Don't say that about my future husband and your future son-in-law."

"Thank you, Mandy Mae," I said, then turned to the mayor. "Monday should work, but I've got a list of things I want. If you can't provide everything, the deal's off and the Texas and Pacific could wind up in Abilene, not Buffalo Gap." I took my list from the table and stared at the three officials. "Ready for me to go over them one by one?"

They all nodded, two of them reluctantly.

"First, I want my mule, saddled, fed and ready to go. Next, I need two fast horses, also saddled and fed and ready to run."

"Where are we gonna buy two horses?" Tindle wanted to know.

Shrugging, I answered. "That's your problem. Borrow someone's or let me use yours."

"Then I want a wagon with a team for Mandy Mae to manage," I said and pointed to Minter. "Now, Sheriff, I want you to load her things in the wagon before we go."

Minter stood before me, silent and simmering.

"I demand that the sheriff, the judge, Callus, and Snooter bring the wagon and mounts to the jail and hitch them outside the door here. Once you arrive, leave your gun belts in the back of the rig and come in. I'll be armed and waiting. You'll walk in here and load the office arsenal in the wagon. Are you fellows still with me?"

They nodded.

"Once you're locked in the cell, I'll deliver the keyring to the bank and leave it in the hands of the honorable mayor. Only when Mandy Mae and I are out of sight, can he free you, but don't give chase or Mandy Mae might get hurt. Do you all understand what you're to do?"

Again they assented.

"Any questions?"

"Yeah," Tindle smirked. "How tall are you?"

"What difference does it make?"

"It'll save us having to measure you for a coffin."

I laughed. "It looks like I'll cost Taylor County money no matter what happens. Knowing you, Nothing At All, I suspect you'll bury me in a blanket and pocket the difference like any politician."

"Hell, Lomax, why even buy a blanket when I can bury you naked and pocket the whole sum?" he shot back.

"Now, now," said Chesterfield, "let's not insult each other. I don't want any animosities tearing up this arrangement. We've got to think about our salaries and Buffalo Gap's future. Agreed?"

The sheriff and the judge bobbed their heads.

"Then, gentlemen, I suggest you get busy, as you have a lot of arrangements to make before Monday and my departure from Buffalo Gap."

"You've caused us a bushel of problems," Tindle said.

"Deputy Callus and Snooter Johnson are the varmints at fault. They wrongfully arrested me and started this whole mess. I didn't want to be here, just like you didn't care to host me."

Chesterfield nodded. "We understand, but that's all water under the railroad bridge. We'll work it out." He turned to his allies. "Let's pow-wow outside to determine how to handle things to get rid of Mister Lomax."

"Mister?" Tindle spat the word out like it was poison.

"Son-in-law?" Sheriff mumbled as he marched past his daughter and opened the door for Chesterfield and Tindle.

"Have a good day," I said as they exited.

As soon as they closed the door, Mandy Mae scurried over, her blond hair bouncing with each step.

"Did you really mean what you said about marrying me, Lomax, or was I just dreaming?" She came to the cell, pressed her cheeks between two bars and puckered up. "Tell me. I must know."

I stood from my chair and stepped to her, softly kissing her lips. "Mandy Mae, you'll accompany me so I don't get shot, but I'm not sure a marriage would work. I'm almost twice as old as you. You'll find a younger man that can take care of you better than I can, now or later."

She bared her choppers. "Not with these teeth."

"Let's get out of Buffalo Gap, then we can discuss marriage. Just don't let your father know that our marriage is unlikely."

"You're still the most thrilling man I've ever met or even read about, more so than even Texas Star. I can't wait for Monday. Wouldn't it be exciting if they shot at us?"

Frowning, I shook my head. "I've been shot at, and I hope never to be shot at again. A fellow could get killed that way."

Mandy Mae backed up from the cell, wrapped her arms around herself as if she were dancing, and twirled across the office floor. "Imagine," she said. "Come Monday, I can leave Buffalo Gap forever. I can't wait."

"You know what I'm ready for, Mandy Mae?"

"No, what?" she said, stopping her dance.

"Supper."

"I get the hint. Time for me to go fix you some grub."

"That's the idea. I'm powerfully hungry from

scheming my liberation without being shot and or getting hitched."

She grimaced. "Don't tease me. Remember, I could still poison your food."

I nodded. "Your pa would like that, but my future is in your hands."

"And mine in yours."

With that, she scampered out the door and returned a couple hours later with some chili, soda crackers, and a pastry she called "butter rolls," which was pie dough flattened out and covered with sugar and chocolate powder before being rolled up on itself like a jelly roll and baked. It was all good.

The next two days, I worked out the final plans for my liberation, as that sounded so much better than my escape because I had done nothing wrong to begin with. To pass the time, I read Mandy Mae's dime novels as my potential father-in-law ignored me. I immersed myself in the rousing tales of Texas Star, the greatest Texan ever, subduing outlaws, saving young lasses and fighting Indians everywhere. Had he had been with Custer instead of me five years earlier, the Seventh Cavalry might have survived the Little Bighorn.

I informed Minter that I wanted to meet with the mayor and county judge Sunday afternoon following church, and they showed up with the sheriff as Mandy Mae was clearing my table of another fried chicken meal.

When my invitees arrived, I took charge, checking the details of my plan. "Gentlemen, where do we stand for my liberation tomorrow?"

"We've identified some horses we can borrow,"

Minter announced. "If you don't return them, we can arrest you for stealing horses."

"One ahead of you, Sheriff. That's why I want Mandy Mae to accompany me. She can return the horses."

The sheriff's eyes lit up, and a smile bloomed on his face. "You mean you're not eloping with her? You won't be my son-in-law after all?"

"I'm sure you're disappointed, Sheriff, but there's that possibility."

Mandy Mae groaned and frowned. "Pa's not, but I sure am."

Winking at her, I offered my reassurance. "Of course, I could always change my mind, love being so unpredictable." I turned to Tindle. "What about the wagon? Any developments?"

"We've got one lined up, but if it isn't returned, you'll be charged with theft, Lomax. We still have to follow the law."

"Why, Nothing At All, I've known from the very first time I laid eyes on you that you were only interested in carrying out the law." Looking back at the sheriff, I continued my questions. "What about Snooter Johnson and Deputy Callus? Do they understand they'll be caged here for a spell on Monday?"

Minter nodded. "I'm going to talk to them as soon as this meeting is over. They'll do what I tell them or they'll be in jail for disobeying."

I turned to Chesterfield. "Tomorrow afternoon, Mayor, I want you to send all your employees home thirty minutes before closing time. I don't care for anyone seeing me give you the keyring. Can you do that?"

"Yes, sir, Mister Lomax."

"I like how that sounds, Mayor." I smiled at Minter and Tindle. "You boys might imitate the mayor there. Calling me Mister Lomax will keep you on my good side."

Tindle and Minter stood silent and hesitant.

"Did you fellows hear me?"

The sheriff looked at his boots and whispered, "Yes, Mister Lomax."

Tindle remained mute.

Tapping my boot impatiently on the floor and crossing my arms over my chest, I waited.

Finally, the judge sighed, nodded, and spoke softly. "Yes, sir, Mister Lomax."

"Let me thank you all for coming this beautiful Sunday. I'll look forward to seeing you three tomorrow afternoon for my liberation," I said.

The county judge growled, but Chesterfield grabbed his arm and patted it. "It'll be okay when we get the railroad. It's for our future, Buffalo Gap's future."

Were I staying in Buffalo Gap, I decided I would vote for Chesterfield in any election he ran in. "Well spoken, Mayor. Have you ever thought of running for county judge?"

Tindle looked at me like I'd put gunpowder in his mother's snuff.

"Maybe you should aim higher, Mayor, like governor, which draws a better class of candidates than a measly county judge's office." Even though I knew I was grating on Tindle, I enjoyed watching the roiling lava in his gaze.

"Why thank you, Mister Lomax. I'm honored that

you think so highly of my political skills. Not everyone does," he said, releasing Tindle's arm and staring at the county judge.

"If there's nothing else, gentlemen, I suggest you go your way on this fine Sunday afternoon while I pack up for my impending departure, though I would like Mandy Mae to stay for a few moments so we can visit alone. After all, I don't want my hostage getting hurt."

She stepped forward. "I'll be okay," she reassured her father, who ushered Minter and Chesterfield out the door.

"Now Mandy Mae," I said, "you know the tin cans I've been having you save?"

She nodded. "I've already punched holes in them. There must be twenty or more cans."

"Now I need you to reel off about thirty feet of twine. About midway down that length, I want you to tie those tin cans to the twine. Do that with two lengths of twine, ten or so cans on each one, then pack them in your bags so your pa doesn't see them. We'll need them tomorrow after we leave of town."

"I won't ask what the cans are for."

"That's good, but you might let it slip casually that I intend to head northwest toward Mitchell County. My brother has a ranch there, but just tell them I've got an unnamed friend that will hide me out along the Colorado River. Can you remember that?"

"This is so thrilling," she remarked as she gathered her wicker basket to head home. "Anything else you need me to do?"

"You might say a prayer that neither one of us gets hurt."

"Texas Star never prays," she answered.

"Yeah, but he doesn't worry about folks getting injured, like I do. Now run along. I'll see you at supper before our big day."

Smiling, Mandy Mae came over to give me a peck on the cheek before she left. As she departed, her father entered, slammed the door, yanked his hat off his head and hung it on the wall peg. He glared at me as he spoke. "This is the most foolishness I've ever seen," he said to himself as much as me.

"Why should I trust you, Sheriff, after you colluded with Snooter to assassinate me?" I picked up a dime novel, sat back in my rocker and started reading for any ideas that might help me get out of a pickle or put my enemies in one. The day passed slowly, the tension building as I wondered if the elected officials of Buffalo Gap were still plotting to get rid of me somehow. Mandy Mae delivered my supper, but her father never left us alone, so we couldn't discuss any developments as we had in the past.

Come Monday morning, Mandy Mae gave me a simple breakfast of biscuits and cane syrup as her father studied us. I asked her to bring me a ball of twine and a pocketknife when she returned around noon. At lunch time she supplied me a jar of stew, the twine, and the knife. As I gobbled down the food, I checked on the final details. "Is everything ready for our liberation?"

She nodded as her father eyed her. "Best I can tell."

I whispered, "Any suspicious activities by the judge or your father?"

"Not that I've noticed. They want to get you out of town before you embarrass them further, though Pa's mad you're taking me as a hostage and threatening to marry me. I'd enjoy that just to anger him. He always wanted a son instead of a daughter."

A half hour after Mandy Mae left, the sheriff departed, leaving me alone in the office. I got on my hands and knees and pulled all the weapons and ammunition from under the bed. I removed the cartridges from each weapon, dropping them on my mattress. When the guns were empty and harmless, I scooped up as many bullets as I could in my hands and stepped over to the slop buckets, which had never been emptied in my time in custody, and nudged the blanket cover aside, dropping the bullets in the murky soup. It took me two trips to baptize the rest of the bullets I had extracted from the weapons. Then I sat aside two cartons of cartridges for my revolver and my carbine. The remaining boxes I took over and emptied into the slop buckets. After I disposed of the ammunition and covered the pails, I placed the long guns crosswise at the end of the mattress, then rolled them up inside the bedding. With my knee atop the padding, I cut off two lengths of twine and slipped them under and around the mattress, tying it into a bundle atop the bed slats. I stacked Mandy Mae's dime novels on the cushion.

I wished I had included in my demands a hot bath, a haircut, and a shave, because I knew I needed them after my extended stay in the crowbar hotel. But there would be time—if not the money—for that once I liberated myself from my wrongful incarceration. Then I sat back in my rocker and re-read one of the Texas Star dime novels.

About midafternoon Minter returned with Deputy Callus, whose face looked pale and his body seemed thinner than I remembered. The bullet that was meant for me had taken its toll on the deputy.

Callus scowled at me as he walked to the sheriff's desk and eased himself down in the chair. "You caused all my misery. I'll be glad when you leave, even gladder when you die."

"You've only yourself to blame, Callus. If you and Snooter hadn't taken me into custody, you'd never gotten shot." I paused and studied him, then continued. "Of course, you'd never gotten to skim money from the bank bag. How much did you two take, two hundred and fifty dollars apiece, wasn't it?"

The deputy cursed, then jumped up from the chair, took a step toward me, grimaced and sat back down in his seat, the pain of the sudden movement warping his face. He called me every vile name he could think of as the sheriff tossed his hat on the desk.

"Shut up, you two. I don't choose to listen to your palaver. I just want to get this over and hope news doesn't get out about the arrangements we made to get rid of Loco Lomax. If word gets around, it'll cost me votes."

"Whatever you say, Sheriff," I replied, then turned to Callus. "Is it true you're gonna run against Sheriff Minter, Deputy?"

"Ignore him, Callus," Minter ordered.

The deputy seemed relieved at the command, as he appeared to be much too weak to follow up on his threats.

After a spell, I heard the rattle and jangle of a wagon outside. Shortly, Nothing At All entered, the glower on Tindle's face showing he was not in a forgiving mood. "The wagon's outside with Mandy Mae's belongings in the back," he announced.

Five minutes later, Snooter Johnson arrived. He came in shaking his head and grumbling about his ruined afternoon. "The saddle horses and the mule are tied to the hitching post." He moved by the desk with the others.

"So glad y'all could make it," I said, getting up from my rocking chair. "Once my hostage arrives and confirms y'all have met my demands, I'll be leaving your fine community."

"Don't you harm Mandy Mae," the sheriff grumbled.

"I'd never hurt the only person in Buffalo Gap that treated me decently, but you better not have assassins waiting for me anywhere, or she could get hurt." I pointed at the sheriff's holster. "Now, gentlemen, you forgot to remove your gun belts and leave them in the wagon. Now remove them and drop them on the floor by the door."

"I'm not wearing one because I can't buckle it with my bum arm," Callus said.

"I left mine at home as well," Tindle announced as he pulled back his frock coat to prove he was unarmed, though I didn't trust him.

Minter and Johnson slowly unfastened their holsters and carried them to the door. With them unarmed, I lifted the revolver from my holster and picked up the keyring from my table to let myself out of my cage. I inserted one of the two keys in the lock and twisted it until the metallic click freed the door and it swung open. Waving my pistol at Minter and Snooter as I stepped from behind the bars, I motioned for them to enter the cage. "I want the two of you to take the rolled mattress outside and place it in the back of the wagon. No funny business or I shoot Nothing At All."

The pair eased past me, grabbed the mattress at each end and slowly carried it out of the office to the dusty street.

"Tindle," I said, "you come inside and take the dime novels out to the wagon. Callus, you can enter the cell and enjoy the rocking chair, as I won't be needing it now."

The deputy men did as I ordered. Shortly Minter, Johnson, and Tindle returned from the wagon. Once they shut the door, I motioned for them to join Callus inside. "Up against the back wall," I ordered. After they obliged, I kept my gun on them as I stepped to the iron door, clanged it shut and locked it with the key. I rattled the two keys in front of them once I backed away. "I'll leave the keyring with the mayor. Once Mandy Mae and I have cleared town, he can free you, but don't follow us or the girl might get hurt."

The jailed men nodded, then the sheriff spoke. "We saw you bundled our shotgun and carbines in the mattress, but it wasn't heavy enough for the ammunition. Where'd you put our cartridges?"

"I hid them in the jail when you weren't around. You'll have to find your bullets."

With that, I slipped my pistol back in its holster and stepped to the window, checking the street outside. Everything seemed normal, with but a few men and women scattered about, handling their Monday afternoon duties. I grinned when I saw Mandy Mae striding down the dusty street, a smile as big as a crescent moon on her face.

When she entered the jail, she wrapped her arms around me, much to the disdain of her father. "This is so thrilling," she said, then gave me a kiss on the cheek. "I watched the mayor send his people home a couple minutes ago, so you shouldn't encounter anyone there but him."

Pointing to the two holsters on the floor, I told Mandy Mae, "Put those in the back of the wagon, will you, while I say goodbye to all my friends." I hung the keyring over the butt of my pistol, patted my pants pocket where I had slipped the ball of twine and knife. Next, I turned to the captives. "Gentlemen, I would say I enjoyed your hospitality, but I didn't. If you get the railroad, I hope the first locomotive through town runs over you all." I tipped my hat at them, then eased to the door, sticking my head outside and looking both ways for trouble. Everything seemed normal as Mandy Mae dropped the gun belts into the wagon.

"Mandy Mae, tie my mule behind your wagon, then climb aboard and head for the bank. I'll follow you there."

"This is so thrilling," she said. Once she completed my instructions, she got in the wagon, released the brake and rattled the reins.

As she did, I slipped across the plank walk to the hitching post and slid between the two horses, untying their reins and turning them toward the bank. I grabbed the chin straps on their halters and fell in behind the wagon, staying low between the two animals in case some assassin planned to take a shot at me. All around me, everything seemed normal, but I remained tense, each step angering me at how much time and worry my stay in Buffalo Gap had caused me.

That's when I determined I was due some compensation. That's when I decided I would rob the Buffalo Gap Bank.

CHAPTER SEVEN

We made it safely to the bank, where I tied both horses to the back of the wagon beside my mule. At that point, I lifted the keyring from over the butt of my pistol and unhooked it, removing both jail keys. Retreating to Mandy Mae, I gave her the two keys. "Keep these where you can find them later," I instructed her.

Cocking her head, she offered a puzzled look. "I thought you said you'd give the keys to the mayor to release the others after we escaped."

Raising the iron band in my hand, I responded. "I promised I'd leave the keyring, not the keys."

Mandy Mae snickered. "You've got a devilish streak in you, Lomax. Yes, you do."

"As I see it, I'm just trying to escape Buffalo Gap alive. Wait here until I return." Looking around the street and seeing no threats, I hitched up my gun belt and strode into the bank where the mayor stood behind the teller cage. Beyond him, I saw the safe still cracked open. The only thing between me and the money was the waist-high gate that walled off the banker section from the customer area.

Chesterfield smiled. "I hope everything's been satisfactory so far."

"No complaints yet, but I'd like to visit with you before I leave and thank you for your belief in me. Mind if I close the door?"

The banker grinned. "Go ahead. In fact, take my key and lock it so no one can disturb us."

I took the key and retreated to the entry, locking it and pulling the blinds in the windows to ensure our privacy.

The mayor continued, "You working with us to slip out of town solves a lot of embarrassing issues all around."

"Mind if I join you behind the counter?"

"Of course not." He unlatched the gate, and I walked past him. As he turned, I slipped my gun from my holster and held it at my side.

His smile shone like the afternoon sun as he extended his hand for the bank key.

Instead, I handed him the metal loop.

"What's this?"

"The keyring to the jail cell, like I promised."

He scratched his head. "Now, what is it you want to visit about?"

"I'd like to make a withdrawal," I announced.

He laughed, then stammered when I lifted my revolver. "But, but, but..." He dropped the keyring, which rattled around at our feet.

"Sorry, Mayor. I take no pleasure in this, but Buffalo Gap and Taylor County owe me for my time behind bars. Clear out the safe and give me the cash you stash in your desk drawer."

"But, but, but..."

I cocked the hammer on my weapon. The metallic click convinced him I was serious.

He grabbed a bank bag and stepped to the safe, hesitating before he opened it.

"Don't shut it or you won't live to open it again."

Chesterfield slipped the door partially ajar.

"All the way," I said. "Don't hide any money from me."

The mayor shoved the safe door back on its hinges, and then filled the bag with all the cash. He offered me the sack, but I refused it.

"Don't forget your personal cache."

He eased to the desk. "That'll be over six hundred dollars total."

"Y'all shouldn't have arrested me."

Chesterfield sighed, sat down at his rolltop desk and opened the bottom drawer on the right side of his chair. He reluctantly picked up a cigar box and lifted the lid where I could see a stack of bills. As he fingered the paper money, I instructed him to shut the box and shove it in the bank bag. He obeyed, dropping the sack on his desk.

"Put your hands behind the chair, Mayor."

He pulled a handkerchief from his pants pocket and wiped the sweat from his brow, then obeyed.

I stepped to him, slipped my gun in its holster, and pulled the ball of twine from my pocket. I quickly tied his hands together with several loops of the twine and secured them to the slats on the chair back. Then I squatted down and secured each of his ankles to a chair leg.

"Sorry, Mayor," I said as I yanked the handkerchief from his hand to stuff in his mouth.

"No," he begged. "Please don't do that. It'll smother me, if you do. I promise I won't yell for half an hour, just don't gag me or I'll die."

Nodding, I dropped the kerchief on the floor. "Sorry I had to do this because I don't feel right about it, but I don't feel right about what Buffalo Gap did to me. I'll let myself out and return your key and the jail keys this evening." I grabbed the money bag, exited the teller cage and unlocked the front door, locking it back when I got outside. Looking around the town, I calmly walked to the wagon where I handed Mandy Mae the bank key.

"Add this to the others."

She slipped it in her pocket, as I quietly placed the bag of loot in the wagon bed with the rolled mattress. "Is everything okay?" she asked.

"Let's leave town. No hurry about it, but after we put a few miles between us and Buffalo Gap, I'll explain things."

After I unhitched my mule from the wagon and climbed in the saddle, Mandy Mae rattled the reins and the buckboard lurched forward, the two tethered horses trailing. I followed her, tugging my hat low over my forehead to avoid anyone recognizing me. We passed the jail, then swung west along the road where I had first been arrested. About five miles out of town, I called for Mandy Mae to stop while we visited. I reined up beside her.

"Let me be straight with you, Mandy Mae. I robbed the bank."

Her face clouded at first, then she broke out laughing. "Serves them right."

At that point, I explained my plan and what she should do to avoid being implicated in the robbery. "Then you can either join me or return home and pretend we never met."

Mandy Mae smiled and started to speak.

"Don't say a thing," I told her. "You know what to do if you want to go with me. If not, no hard feelings. For now, hand me the cans you brought."

I dismounted and led my mule to the back of the wagon, where I untied the two saddled horses. When Mandy Mae handed me the two cords strung with tin cans, I tied one to a stirrup on each horse, then slapped both animals on the rump. The geldings bolted down the road, the jangling cans terrifying them into a panicked run.

"When the posse comes looking for me, they'll follow the trail of those two mounts. By the time they catch up, I'll be long gone in the other direction."

"You're devilish! Yes, you are, Lomax. It's thrilling."

I retrieved the bank bag and tied it to the saddle horn on my mule. After I mounted and guided him to the front of the wagon, I stood in my stirrups, leaned over, and kissed Mandy Mae on the cheek. "Thanks for your kindness, though I suppose I betrayed your devotion by robbing the bank."

"It was as thrilling as reading a Texas Star tale. I wouldn't trade it for anything."

Then I reminded her I would backtrack wide around

Buffalo Gap. She was to linger for half an hour before heading home, returning the keys and pointing the lawmen toward the fleeing horses. If she wanted to join me, I told her how to play her hand when she arrived in town. I assured her I would stay for her until sundown near the road five miles northeast of Buffalo Gap.

"Wait for me because I'll be there," she said.

I pointed to the holsters and long weapons wrapped in the mattress. "If they think to retrieve the guns, tell them they can fish their ammunition out of the slop buckets."

Mandy Mae laughed, then leaned over in her seat and kissed me on the cheek. "Like I said, you're devilish."

Tipping my hat, I turned my mount south off of the road and put him into a lope so I could backtrack and loop around town. Fortunately, I saw no one else, nor did I encounter any barbed wire fences to slow my journey. Using the hills and trees to screen myself, I circled wide of Buffalo Gap, not close enough to see it or to be seen, finally angling back to the road east of town. I found a spot near a creek crossing where I dismounted to water my mule and watch the approach from both directions. As I waited, I untied the money pouch from the saddle horn and counted the bundled cash and the additional bills in the cigar box. The total came to six hundred and thirty dollars. Dropping the bank bag, I placed all the money in the box, which I stuffed in my saddlebags. Figuring it unwise to leave the bank sack where someone might find it, I picked it up, filled it with rocks and tossed it in the creek, where it sank out of sight. Then I waited, hiding from a pair of west-bound riders and staring toward the sunset for Mandy

Mae. Though she said she would join me, I wasn't sure she meant it or if her pa might lock her up in jail to prevent it. If she didn't show up, my escape would be much simplified.

About a quarter of an hour before dark, I spotted a wagon approaching and mounted my mule to watch the road. As the rattling wagon neared, I realized the driver was wearing pants, shirt and hat, not skirt, blouse and bonnet, as I had last seen on Mandy Mae. I eased my mule back among the brush to let the fellow pass.

Then the driver cried, "Lomax, it's me, Mandy Mae. Can you hear me?"

I waited until the wagon came closer before answering.

"It's Mandy Mae," she cried again, removing the wide-brimmed hat and waving it over her head, her blond hair falling free and bouncing with her movement.

She seemed jittery, so I didn't know if she was being followed or just concerned that I had betrayed her and ridden on alone. I shook my reins, and my mule stepped ahead and cleared the brush. Removing my own hat, I windmilled it her direction. "Over here," I shouted, then slapped my mule's flank with my war bonnet before yanking it back on my head. The mule trotted forward.

"Oh, Lomax," she squealed. "I feared I'd never find you before dark, and you would leave me forever."

"You've been reading too many dime novels, Mandy Mae." I reined up in front of her. "How did it go?"

"Perfect," she cackled. "When I rode into town, things were quieter than I expected. I stopped at the jail and ran in, crying my head off, saying you had not only betrayed me, but had robbed the bank leaving town. I told them the last I saw of your ornery hide, you were riding hell bent for Mitchell County, taking both horses so you could swap mounts rather than running them to death."

"Hold on a moment." I directed my mule behind the wagon, where I dismounted and tied him to the tail-gate. Then I strode to the front, climbed into the seat, took the reins and started toward Fort Worth. "Go on," I said, as Mandy Mae slid her arm beneath mine and leaned her head against my shoulder.

"They were furious when I gave them the three keys. Pa unlocked the cell and asked about the third key. I told him it was to the bank where you had tied the mayor up and taken the cash. Judge Tindle grabbed the key and raced to check on Chesterfield. They wanted to know if I had their weapons. I told them they were in the back of the wagon, the long guns still wrapped in the mattress. Pa and Snooter ran out and retrieved their arms, returning shortly. They asked about the ammunition and almost puked when I said the cartridges were in the slop buckets."

"What did they do?"

Mandy Mae giggled. "Pa ordered Callus to fish them out to save time since he wouldn't be riding with the posse. The deputy protested, but Pa told him to do it or get fired. Pa and Snooter ran out to get horses and gather a posse. All the time I was sobbing and wailing about how you had betrayed me. Within thirty minutes, Pa led two dozen men out of town, galloping as fast as they could to catch you."

"Once they left," she continued, "I drove the wagon

to the edge of town, stopped at an outhouse and changed into men's clothing that I had in my belongings and rode out to join you. I figured anybody coming our direction would look for someone in a skirt and bonnet, not pants and hat."

"Smart thinking. You must've picked that up from your dime novels. Are you certain nobody followed you?"

"Absolutely. Everything worked like you planned it. My only worry was not finding you and having to return to Buffalo Gap. Where now?"

"We'll head to Fort Worth, then decide where to go from there."

She squeezed my arm tighter as I guided the team through the creek crossing and headed northeast toward Abilene in the enveloping darkness. "That's so thrilling. I've never been to a town as big as Fort Worth."

I glanced over my shoulder and made out the mattress unfurled in the wagon bed. "We won't stop tonight so we can put as much distance between us and Buffalo gap as possible. We'll alternate driving and sleeping. Whenever you get sleepy, climb in back to doze, and I'll wake you when I want to switch."

In a couple hours we passed through Abilene, the vacant street dimly lit by the jaundiced light slipping out of a handful of homes that dotted the modest community. On the far side of town, we turned east toward Fort Worth, the rising crescent moon illuminating the road. A half hour later, Mandy Mae crawled in the back and went to sleep. I drove until I was exhausted, swapping places with her three hours before dawn.

I awoke to a brilliant Texas sunrise as Mandy Mae hummed a song I couldn't place. When she realized I was awake, she greeted me and told me she had brought some biscuits and a tin of cane syrup for us.

"You'll make some old boy a good wife, Mandy Mae."

She smiled. "I hope it's you."

"No guarantees," I said.

Shortly, we came to a creek crossing on the road and pulled up beneath a spread of pecan trees to eat our breakfast. As the team seemed fagged, I decided to let them rest and graze after I watered them and my mule.

"What's your plan, Lomax?"

"Let's ride until we find the railroad. Then we'll take the train to Fort Worth."

Mandy Mae clapped her hands. "Oh, goody! I've never ridden on a train. This is all so thrilling."

A day later we reached Ranger, then the terminus of the Texas and Pacific Railway that the fine folks of Buffalo Gap so coveted. We spent the night in the wagon by the new Ranger depot and the next day purchased passage to Fort Worth for us and my mule. Mandy Mae changed from her men's clothes into a skirt and blouse in the women's lounge. After that, we unloaded Mandy Mae's trunk and carpetbag and my saddle and saddlebags, which I left her to guard on the railroad platform. A block away I found a livery stable and paid the owner ten dollars to return the wagon, team and mattress to Buffalo Gap in three days. Then I retreated to the station, checked our luggage except for my carbine and saddlebags with the money-filled cigar box.

Within the hour, the train arrived from Fort Worth. It took thirty minutes to unload the cars of passenger and freight, then turn the locomotive around. Mandy Mae fidgeted with excitement. "This is so thrilling," she said. "I never thought I'd be able to ride a train. I've heard they can go thirty-five to forty miles an hour. Is that true?"

"I can't say," I answered. "I've never tried to race one."

Mandy Mae laughed, then giggled when she heard the cry, "All aboard!" She scampered across the platform, where the conductor waited at the steps to help her into the passenger car. He smiled as he took her hand, but his beaming face clouded when she grinned back and exposed her teeth. The T&P employee looked away as she climbed aboard, but Mandy Mae was too excited to care.

A married couple beat me to the conductor and the gray-haired wife turned to her husband. "Did you see that poor child's teeth?"

He nodded. "Horrible. She'll have a hard time attracting a husband."

They boarded, then I did, embarrassed for Mandy Mae and the challenges she would face for the rest of her life. Mandy Mae found a padded seat and scooted by the window, patting the place beside her like an excited schoolgirl.

I slid onto the cushion next to her, handing her my carbine to prop between her place and the wall panel. I rested my saddlebags on my lap.

"Isn't this exciting?" she chattered. "I can't believe I'm seated in a passenger car about to go to Fort Worth. I thought the only chance I'd ever have to ride a train

was when it came through Buffalo Gap and only then if
Pa let me." She paused, then resumed. "Though, I must
admit, I'm a little scared. I've never gone as fast as I'm
about to."

"You'll manage just fine, Mandy Mae." I patted the
top of her hand. She kept talking, but I missed most of
what she said as I studied the rude passengers, slyly
pointing at her and grimacing at her teeth. Several
times I wanted to stand up and teach the busybodies
some manners, but that was a rash thing to do after
robbing a bank.

After the fifteen minutes it took folks to board and
seat themselves, the locomotive tooted its whistle and
the train lurched ahead, Mandy Mae grabbing my hand
and squeezing it tightly. I was glad when we gathered
speed and left Ranger so the passengers would have the
countryside to look at rather than Mandy Mae's teeth.

So exhilarated was she, that she smiled the entire
way to Fort Worth, never realizing the other riders were
mocking her for her tusks. With the stops along the
way for water, coal, freight and riders, we covered the
hundred miles between Ranger and Fort Worth in just
over four hours, though it seemed longer to me with so
many people deriding Mandy Mae. At times, I thought
some passengers in our car stepped into the next one to
invite other folks over to see the freak.

When we pulled into the Fort Worth Depot, Mandy
Mae arose and hugged me. "I can't believe we went a
hundred miles in less than five hours. That's amazing."

"And thrilling?" I asked.

She smiled. "And thrilling."

I suggested she sit down until the car emptied, as I
didn't want other people mocking her as we exited.

Once the car cleared of those mean folks, and the conductor clambered back in to see that it was empty, I stood up, draped the saddlebags over my shoulder and grabbed my carbine. Mandy Mae arose like the beautiful young woman she was, at least until she opened her mouth. As we marched down the aisle, the conductor looked away when she thanked him for the exhilarating ride. I wanted to punch him in the nose, but just strode past him, glad to be exiting his train.

Once on the platform, I sent Mandy Mae inside to await her luggage while I marched to the stock car where they were unloading my mule. I grabbed my saddle and blanket from the freight cart and toted them to the end of the wooden landing as they led my mule down the ramp. I followed my mule to street level, propping my carbine against a bench and dropping the rest of my load on the seat. Grabbing my rigging, I quickly saddled my gray mule and slid my long gun in its scabbard. I draped my saddlebags over my shoulder and led the mule around to the front of the depot where I secured him to a hitch and headed in the depot to find Mandy Mae, who waited patiently at the baggage claim, oblivious to the pointing and mockery aimed at her by the three dozen nearby travelers. Perhaps she had been so accustomed to it throughout her life that she could ignore the stares. I couldn't. She deserved better.

When the baggage carts arrive, I held her back, screening her from other passengers until they had cleared out. She had a modest trunk and a carpetbag to collect, and they were the only items remaining on the three carts when we stepped up to retrieve them. I carried the trunk out of the station as she followed with her valise. Outside I found a hack driver who agreed to take Mandy Mae and her luggage to a clean and decent hotel for a dollar. As he loaded the luggage, I helped Mandy Mae into her seat. As they drove away, I mounted my mule and followed, passing the Cattleman's Bank that had loaned money to the Buffalo Gap Bank, cash that I now claimed as my own, rightfully or wrongfully. On Fourth Street the hack driver stopped in front of the Mansion House Hotel.

After helping Mandy Mae down, the driver approached me with an outstretched palm. I pointed to the luggage. "Not until you drop those in the hotel."

He grumbled, but delivered the pieces in two trips as I dismounted and hitched up my mule. I'd pulled a dollar from my cigar box by the time he returned. I paid him, and he went on his way as I stepped inside to find Mandy Mae.

She was waiting and joined me as I marched to the registration desk. The clerk, a small fellow with a squeaky voice, big ears and wire-rimmed spectacles, eyed us suspiciously, probably because I had a ragged beard and shaggy clothes. "This is a high-class hotel, fellow, no riff-raff allowed, especially with women of questionable morals."

I leaned over the counter, grabbed the runt by his shirt, and jerked him off his feet. "She's my cousin," I growled, "and I expect an apology."

He hesitated.

"Now," I demanded.

"I'm sorry, ma'am, no offense meant."

I released him, and he slid back to his feet.

"As for me, I've spent two weeks chasing thieves. I

haven't had time to clean up, but I intend to. I want two rooms across the hall from each other."

"Can you even afford it? Cost is two dollars and four bits a night per room."

I slammed my saddlebags on the counter and pulled out my cigar box, opening it up wide enough for him to see I had a considerable stack of bills. Extracting five dollars, I shoved them across the counter. "I want a place to bathe and get a haircut and a shave and a place to buy some new clothes."

"There's hot running water in your rooms," he announced.

Mandy Mae gasped. "Really?"

Lifting his indignant nose in the air, the clerk responded. "This is a first-class hotel." He turned back to me. "There's a barber around the corner and a couple clothiers nearby. Just sign the register, and I'll get your keys."

Our rooms were on the second floor, across the hall from each other, as we requested. I saw Mandy Mae to hers and made sure she locked herself in. I dropped off my saddlebags in my room, extracting fifty dollars from my cigar box, which I slid under my pillow.

After leaving the hotel, I first stabled my mule. Next, I got a haircut and a shave, then bought me some new duds, returning to my quarters where I took a hot bath. When I was done, I dressed in my new shirt, trousers, vest, coat and socks and headed back to the registration desk. I had a question for the runty clerk.

"I need one of those—what do you call it?—tooth doctors."

"You mean a dentist?"

"Yeah, that's it."

"There's Dr. Henson over on Calhoun Street at the corner of Second Street behind City Hall. Henson's probably the best dentist in town, maybe the state."

"It's for my cousin."

He shook his head. "With teeth like hers, what you need is a blacksmith!"

CHAPTER EIGHT

"Where are we going?" Mandy Mae asked as we left the hotel the next morning.

"It's a surprise," I replied.

"I like surprises." She giggled and squeezed my arm.

"Not me, unless I know what they are."

"Then it's not a surprise."

"Exactly!"

With me bathed, shaved, shampooed, and attired in new clothes and her wearing a yellow blouse with a high collar and a dark blue skirt, I decided we looked as fine as any couple in Fort Worth until Mandy Mae smiled, but I hoped to change that.

I guided her down Rusk Street to Second, where I spotted the clapboard city hall, and then to Calhoun Street, where I saw a whitewashed wooden molar hanging from a pole over the plank walk in the front of a narrow, two-story limestone building. The structure being more substantial than most of the buildings we had passed, I figured the dentist was quite good or terribly expensive.

When she realized where I was going, she yanked my arm, and we stopped. "You're taking me to the dentist?"

"That I am."

She looked at me with tears moistening her emerald eyes. "I can't afford a dentist. They cost too much."

"You'll never know unless we ask, will you?"

She winced. "I'm scared."

"It shouldn't hurt that much."

"Not about the pain, but that he can't do anything for me. I see how people look at me, turn away, and ignore me when I smile. I've always dreamed of getting my teeth fixed, but if the dentist tells me nothing can be done, I'll be devastated."

"You're brave, Mandy Mae. It won't be as risky as holding off my lynch mob. Besides, you've got Texas Star's grit in your craw."

Mandy Mae pursed her lips and nodded. As we stepped to the entry, I read the name and title of "Bartholomew D. Henson, Dentist" emblazoned in gold gilt lettering on the glass. Beneath his name in smaller letters was the statement "Teeth and Smiles Fixed." Through the window I saw a slender, middle-aged woman with gray hair tied in a bun sitting at the desk across from four empty chairs for patients. As I opened the door for Mandy Mae, a bell tinkled overhead, announcing our arrival.

The woman smiled. "Good day. Do you have an appointment?"

"No, ma'am."

"Then it'll be next month at the earliest before Dr. Henson can schedule you."

Removing my hat, I rolled the brim in my hands and pleaded for a session. "Ma'am, we arrived in Fort Worth yesterday afternoon, coming from West Texas to visit what we heard was the best dentist in the Southwest."

She smiled. "My husband is the best in Texas, no doubt. That's why his schedule is packed. You'll just have to wait your turn."

I pulled Mandy Mae beside me. "Smile for the lady, will you, Mandy Mae?"

As soon as Mandy Mae opened her mouth, the woman's hands flew to her own lips. "Lordy, lordy, lordy," she cried behind her fingers as she turned her gaze to the wall. "Let me check with Bartholomew." She jumped from her chair and knocked on an adjacent door, then entered as a patient cried, "Ouch, that hurt."

We heard her tell the dentist there was a young lady he needed to see immediately.

Instantly, the practitioner strode out of the door, still holding a fancy pair of pliers with a bloody molar in its jaws. His wife trailed behind him.

Mandy Mae bared her teeth for him, but unlike others, the dentist offered a gentle smile and reassuring words. "Have a seat, my dear, and I'll work you in as soon as I can." He spun around and went back to his patient.

The woman pointed to the wooden chairs. "Take a seat. I'm Mrs. Henson, but you can call me Claudia."

"Thank you, ma'am," I answered as I seated Mandy Mae.

"You poor dear," Claudia said, turning to the door

as the bell rang and an older woman in a black mourning dress entered. "Be seated, Mrs. Fillmore, and Bartholomew will see you shortly."

About ten minutes later, the fellow who had lost a molar emerged, and the dentist invited Mrs. Fillmore inside. I feared we might be there all day, but the female patient came out within a quarter of an hour, and the dentist waved us into his examination room. As we entered, he removed and wiped his spectacles, then put them back on a narrow nose between blue eyes beneath a thinning mop of black hair flecked with gray. After I introduced myself and Mandy Mae, he spoke with a soft, soothing voice.

"Please take the examining chair, young lady, and let me have a look at your mouth. I see a few issues, but nothing that can't be fixed."

Mandy Mae looked at me with smiling lips as a tear rolled down her cheek. She settled into the dentist's chair.

"You can be seated over there, sir," the dentist said, pointing to a cushioned chair in the corner. After sitting on a stool by her side, Henson eased the dental recliner back, grabbed a probe and a tool with a small round mirror on the end, then asked Mandy Mae to open her mouth. He spent five minutes examining and probing her teeth and gums before lifting her chair upright. Putting his tools on a metal tray by his side, he took her hand and patted it gently.

Henson informed us that the major problem was seven of her baby teeth had never fallen out, which meant they had strong roots as would her permanent teeth, which was good. Since the baby teeth remained firm, the others had come in at crooked angles behind and between her original teeth. He then confirmed that her teeth and her smile could be fixed, but it would take time and money.

Mandy Mae frowned. "I don't have any——"

I bounced up from my chair and shook my head for her to hush. "How much time and how much money?"

"It's hard to be precise," Henson responded, "but I'd say twelve to eighteen months and four to six hundred dollars to pull the baby teeth and straighten the permanent ones."

As her lips quivered, I knew Mandy Mae verged on releasing a flood of disappointed tears.

"Just a minute, dentist."

"Doctor is the proper appellation," he informed me.

"Okay, doctor, here's the problem. Mandy is seventeen years old with no family to count on beyond me, her no-good cousin. She has no place to go. I could pay you three hundred or so dollars in advance, but she'd need room and board because she can't go back and forth between Taylor County and here for regular treatments. We can't afford that after paying money up front, nor can we pay to board her in town."

Henson stood up from his stool and stroked his chin. "I understand your predicament. Give me time to think it over and discuss with my wife so we can consider some different options." The dentist nodded at Mandy Mae. "She's a lovely young lady, except for her teeth. I'd hate for her to wind up as one of the saloon girls around here, just to get dental work. Come back tomorrow before lunchtime, and we'll have an answer for you."

Mandy Mae smiled as he offered his hand to help

her from the examining chair. "I'm grateful to you, Doctor Henson."

I thanked the doctor and told him we would return the next day, as he opened the door for us to exit. Two patients were waiting, but we thanked the dentist's wife before departing. As soon as we stepped outside, Mandy Mae threw her arms around me and gave me a kiss on the lips.

"For years I've dreamed about getting them fixed, but I never thought it possible. Thank you, Lomax. You are more dashing than a dime novel hero."

"More so than Texas Star?" I asked.

"Even more than Texas Star!"

We strolled around town, arm in arm, and checked out Fort Worth. Mandy Mae stopped in a couple of women's clothiers and held up dresses to her front, twirling around and thinking how pretty she would be once her teeth were straightened. As for me, I counted twenty-three saloons and three bawdy houses. My only worry with her getting her teeth fixed was her safety while in Fort Worth, if the details could get worked out. I didn't like the idea of her staying by herself in such a town and having to work for her room and board while she received treatments.

"If you stay here for dental work, I fear for your safety, Mandy Mae."

She stopped and shook her head at me. "Won't you be here with me?"

"No, ma'am. You forget, I'm now an actual wanted bank robber. Your pa and his allies won't be as forgiving this time if I'm caught. I should leave Texas as soon as I can, and I can't take you with me, though I'm stumped about leaving you here."

"I've got my revolver in my carpetbag, and I know how to fend for myself."

"Indeed you do, but mean men frequent these parts."

"Remember, I faced down a lynch mob? I'm not scared."

"But I am."

She grabbed my arm and tugged me down the street. "I'm so happy, I don't care."

"But it might not work out, Mandy Mae."

"Lomax, everything's worked out since I met you. This will, too."

She was correct. The next day, we arrived at the dentist's office a little before noon. The Hensons closed the place and took us to an eatery down the street for lunch. While we consumed bowls of beef stew and squares of cornbread, Henson said he and his wife had discussed Mandy Mae's predicament and their own. It seemed his reputation had grown such that people from across Texas were coming to visit him with challenging dental problems. He hated to turn away patients, and didn't have the money to hire staff because he tried to maintain affordable fees for average folks.

"Claudia and I've been thinking we might use Mandy Mae in the practice. We live upstairs and have an extra room we'd thought of renting out to the right person, but this would be even better. She could work in the office, but would also be expected to help Claudia keep house and cook. Can you cook?"

Before Mandy Mae answered, I responded. "She sure can. Mandy Mae fixed me fine meals when I was jailed." The moment I said it, I realized that might not have been the wisest thing I ever blurted out.

"Jail?" Henson asked, lowering his head and looking at me over the top of his spectacles.

Mandy Mae stepped in. "He was falsely arrested before Taylor County officials admitted their mistake and let him go."

The dentist eyed me. "Perhaps we should contact Taylor County to ensure everything's on the up and up before we reach any agreement."

For a moment, the table went dead silent until Mandy Mae burst out bawling. "I knew this wouldn't work out, and I'd go through life with terrible teeth," she sobbed. "Come on, cousin. If they don't trust us, we'll find a dentist that will. Maybe it's better we leave now. I hear there may be some good dentists in Dallas. It's not too far away, and there's Waco to consider. If there'd been a dentist in Taylor County, I'd never have let you bring me to this wicked city, anyway." Mandy Mae bounced up from her chair and grabbed my arm. "Let's go, cousin!"

Though I wasn't through eating, I stood up to walk away until the dentist grabbed my other arm.

"No, no," Henson insisted. "I didn't mean to insult you, but the men that come to Fort Worth aren't always the most honorable fellows on two legs."

Mandy Mae daubed at her tear-filled eyes. "Taylor County treated us poorly, and I sicken at the sound of its name."

"Please," Claudia interjected, "sit down and finish your stew. We can work this out."

I watched Mandy Mae. When she released my arm and slid down to her seat, I did, too, and resumed dining. She calmed down, and when the couple glanced away from the table, she winked at me. Henson checked his pocket watch, then said he and his wife must return to the office in the next ten minutes. He outlined his proposal for fixing Mandy Mae's teeth with me paying three hundred and twenty-five dollars up front for the dental work. In exchange, Mandy Mae would room and board with them, helping around the office and doing household chores as needed or assigned. After her teeth were fixed, Henson would reassess the dental charge based on actual costs, less the contributions of her labor. If her contributions exceeded my payment and her labor by ten dollars or more, he would give her the difference. Further, if she worked out as an office assistant, Henson might hire her at regular wages.

"If you need some time to think about it," the dentist said, arising and helping his wife from her chair, "let me know by the end of the day tomorrow."

Before Mandy Mae spoke, I shook my head. "The arrangement is fine. I'll pay you tomorrow afternoon and bring her belongings to your office so she can lodge with you."

"Do you want a written contract?" the dentist asked.

"No. You trusted Mandy Mae and me, so we'll return the favor."

The husband and wife smiled. "We'll see you tomorrow," Claudia said as they walked away, the dentist stopping at the counter to pay for our lunch, then leaving the restaurant to get back to work.

Once they left, I grinned at Mandy Mae. "Where'd you learn to cry like that?"

"Little girls discover early on that's one method of getting their way with their fathers. And I read of a woman doing that in a Texas Star dime novel."

"You realize this means I'll be leaving you here."

She nodded. "You'll always be my first kiss and my first love." She paused, giving me a gentle, reassuring smile. "Once I get my teeth fixed, I'll be able to find me another beau."

"So, you were just using me?"

"Maybe. Weren't you using me?" she countered, patting the top of my hand.

Part of me was disappointed that she had gotten over me so quickly, but the rest of me rejoiced that leaving her behind would be so much easier now. After exiting the eatery, we strolled about town for a spell, then returned to our lodging where I paid the clerk for both or our rooms that evening and my room only the next night.

The following afternoon, I pulled money from my cigar box and hired a hack to come by the hotel, pick up Mandy Mae's baggage and deliver us to the dentist's office. After dropping her off at the front to alert Claudia to unlock the back, we drove around to the rear entrance. After unloading her trunk and carpetbag, the driver stuck out his hand for pay as Mandy Mae opened the door. I ordered him to wait and take me back to the hotel, where I would settle up. Mandy Mae grabbed her valise, and I picked up the trunk by the handles and wrestled it upstairs. Claudia waited at the top to point me to a room, where I found Mandy Mae staring out a window over Fort Worth.

"Where do you want your trunk?"

"Put it on the bed beside my carpet bag," she instructed.

I did as she said, then examined the room with its single bed with a feather mattress and pillow, plus a rocking chair, a washstand and a reading table with a lamp and Bible atop it.

I pointed to the Bible. "You need to read more of the Good Book, rather than those trashy dime novels."

Mandy Mae turned from the window and aimed her finger at me. "You're sounding just like Pa." She hesitated as her lip quivered. "You're a good man, Lomax. I'm gonna miss you."

"Not for long," I said. "Once your teeth get fixed, you'll be fighting off suitors."

"When they're fixed, I'm going back to Buffalo Gap to show everyone."

At that point, Mrs. Henson walked in. "Is everything satisfactory?"

I let Mandy Mae reply.

"It's wonderful," she answered with a lilt that touched my soul.

"Claudia," I said, "I have something for you." I dug into my pocket and pulled out a roll of bills, quickly counting out three hundred and twenty-five dollars and offering her the payment. "Here's the money we agreed on. Take good care of Mandy Mae."

She accepted the bills, then hugged me. "We'll watch after your cousin." She turned and trod down the stairs as Mandy Mae and I snickered.

For a moment, I stood looking at her, not knowing what to say. "I suppose this is goodbye, Mandy Mae."

She sighed and we fell into each other's arms, sharing a hug and kiss as friends.

"I'll always remember what you did for me," she whispered, "even if it was with stolen money."

I laughed. "When you return to Buffalo Gap, you can show them what their money bought."

"Do you want me to accompany you downstairs?"

"No, Mandy Mae. I think it's best you stay here."

She nodded. "I do, too, or I might cry."

Breaking from her arms, I grabbed her wrists, then stood looking at her. After I gazed into her emerald eyes a final time, I released her hands and bolted down the stairs, thinking I heard her crying softly. My eyes watered as I jumped in the hack and started back for the hotel.

Once in my room, I bathed, shaved and washed my old clothes in the water when I was done. I draped my pants, shirt, socks and long johns over the chair, the bedstead and the side of the tub for them to dry overnight. Next, I laid down for a good night's sleep, but was overwhelmed with melancholy as I thought about the special women I'd lost like LouAnne in Arkansas, who I'd abandoned for her own safety; like Ruth on my initial foray into Texas, when I had vowed to marry her once I returned from a trail drive to Abilene, Kansas, but she had died in my absence; and now like Mandy Mae Minter. She was younger than me, but older men had married even younger women many times before me. I tossed and turned throughout the night, waking up tired and fretful. I toyed with staying another night in hopes of a more restful sleep, then decided I should leave Fort Worth before my Buffalo Gap friends came looking for me.

As I considered my predicament, I decided it was time for me to find a wife that could warm my bed and take care of my needs. After I arose and checked my lightly damp laundry, I evaluated my options for finding a woman. Over the years, I'd heard about Brigham Young's band of Mormons and how husbands could have as many wives as they wanted or needed. I figured if I had enough spouses, I would just sit back and enjoy life while they did all the work. So, I decided I'd return to Utah Territory, look for me a woman and settle down. I'd been there during the rush to complete the transcontinental railroad so I knew what to expect from the terrain and weather, but not from the women, as there weren't many decent ones following the construction crews. I'd even been in Ogden, Utah, the week after the grand celebration of the driving of the Golden Spike. There I'd actually seen Brigham Young himself turn the first spade full of dirt to begin the laying of the Utah Central Railroad line that would connect Ogden with Salt Lake City. Though I remember seeing the Mormon patriarch, I didn't recall gazing upon any of his more than fifty rumored wives. If I had seen some of them, even just one of them, I might never have departed Texas for Utah Territory.

I dressed and rolled up my clothes, then stuffed them in my saddlebags. Emptying my cigar box, I counted out slightly less than three hundred dollars. I put a third of the bills in my pants pocket and divided the remainder into stacks I wedged in both boots. Placing my hat atop my head and looking in the mirror at my reflection, I decided I was plenty handsome enough to find me a wife or two or three or four, though I doubted I could manage Young's fifty-plus.

Suitably pleased at how I looked in my hat and new duds, I grabbed my saddlebags and carbine, stopping at the desk to drop off my key with the clerk and inform him I was heading south to Waco. I intended to ride to Dallas to catch a train to Utah, but wanted to throw off any Taylor County pursuers that might trace me to the Mansion House Hotel. Leaving the lodge, I walked the two blocks to the Texas Wagon Yard, where I had stabled my mule. I paid the proprietor, who fetched my mount and even saddled him for me. I secured my saddlebags over his rump, slid my carbine in its scabbard, and mounted, heading east for Dallas, though I was tempted to ride by the dentist's office and catch a last glimpse of Mandy Mae, but I decided I should put her in the past and look for a Utah woman or two to marry. I never knew for certain what happened to Mandy Mae, though well after the turn of the century, I read a newspaper article about the passing of a Texas state senator from Fort Worth leaving behind a widow named Mandy Mae. If it was her, I laughed that her first love had been a bank robber and her last love a robber of the public till.

Arriving well after dark in Dallas, I found a cheap hotel, spent the night, and asked for directions for the nearest livery stable. At the livery I sold my mule and saddle, but kept my carbine and saddlebags as they held my modest belongings. From there I walked to the train depot and checked with the agent for the best route to Utah Territory.

"Cheapest or shortest route?"

"Cheapest," I answered, "but don't route me through Colorado. I can't handle the mountain cliffs and ledges. They leave me edgy." Actually, I wanted to avoid the murder warrant hanging over my head after a

Leadville killing I was blamed for, though I had no memory of committing.

The agent wound up sending me northeast to Kansas City, then northwest from there to Omaha, where I could link up with the Union Pacific and ride it into Ogden. I paid my fare and killed the ninety-minute wait for the train by walking down the street to an eatery, where I had a hearty breakfast of four fried eggs, eight slices of bacon, a stack of pancakes with cane syrup, and four buttered biscuits with apricot preserves. My breakfast weighed heavily on my stomach, but I didn't know the next chance I would get to eat. As I covered my breakfast costs at the counter, I purchased a couple of newspapers to pass the time away on my long train ride. With the end of the year approaching, I knew I would need to acquire a coat somewhere to ward off the cold weather I would face up north.

When the eastbound locomotive convoy arrived, I answered the "All aboard" cry and found an empty bench seat where I could sit and store my saddlebags and carbine. I had to admit this train trip would not be as much fun as the one with Mandy Mae, but told myself I had to let go of her memory. The passenger car was half full, so nobody sat on my bench, leaving me plenty of room to stretch out, though the wooden bench was hard on my tailbone.

Once the train lurched forward and picked up speed on my wife-hunting expedition, I started reading through the newspapers, and found a story datelined "Mitchell County," my intended destination before I was arrested for the bank robbery. According to the story, a pair of Texas Rangers found three dead men at a camp on the Colorado River. Among their possessions were four bank bags filled with money stolen from Buffalo Gap. The lawmen discovered the three lying around a blanket where they had spread a deck of cards and apparently been gambling when they got in a dispute that ended in the gunfire that killed them all. The Rangers buried the bandit trio where they fell and returned the money to Buffalo Gap. I would have been vindicated of the original crime had I not subsequently robbed the same bank. In the long run, I suppose I came out the loser, but at least Mandy Mae got corrected teeth out of my misdeeds.

Because of the roundabout route, layovers and switching trains, it took me a week to reach Ogden, arriving a few days before Christmas and heading first to a store to purchase a coat to fight off the late afternoon chill blowing in from the surrounding mountains, which were splotched with snow. The town had grown since I had last seen it and had taken on airs of respectability. I started looking for a woman that would make me a good wife, but wasn't impressed with their plain attire and somber expressions, nor did any of them give me a second glance.

Figuring I could find a hotel easier than a woman during my first hour in Ogden, I walked toward the business district, my carbine in my hand and my saddlebags draped over the shoulder of my new coat. I passed a theater that promoted a performance of Charles Dickens's *A Christmas Carol* and thought little about it until I turned the corner and saw three gaudy red, yellow, blue and green painted wagons of a traveling acting company parked near the alleyway. I would've walked past the trio of wagons had I not noticed the name painted in huge letters on each: LOMAX and COKER THEATRICAL TROUPE. In smaller letters beneath the name was the line: FEATURING LISSA LOMAX, THE ARKANSAS SONGBIRD.

I caught my breath. Lissa was the second of my three sisters! I hadn't seen her since I left our Cane Hill, Arkansas, home more than fifteen years earlier.

CHAPTER NINE

I spun around on the plank walk and trotted to the theater's locked double doors where I banged on the green-and-gold entryway, drawing no response, though I detected a slight movement of a curtain in the box office. I jumped across the steps to the ticket booth and rapped on the glass long enough for the emerald velour curtains to part an inch, allowing an eyeball to stare at me.

"Tickets go on sale at seven. Come back later," came a voice muted by the thick drapery and an unwillingness to help a needy fellow.

"I'm here to see Lissa Lomax."

"Buy a ticket, why don't you?" replied the eye. "That's why we sell them."

"But I'm her brother," I cried.

"Fellows are always trying to meet her, but you're the first one to claim to be her kin. Anyway, she's married. You're disgusting." With that, the green drape snapped shut, leaving me frustrated and mad. I considered bashing in the door, but figured the local constabulary would frown upon my impatience. Too, with the reach of the telegraph, you never knew when word of your misdeeds—like robbing a Texas bank—might have beaten you to town. Progress wasn't always for the better in my mind as I descended the stone steps to the plank walk to consider how to meet my sister.

By my estimation, it was about four o'clock, and I had but an hour of sunlight. After dusk it would turn cold. I figured I could rent a place to stay, then return and buy a ticket to watch the production, but there was no guarantee I would get to meet her afterward as protective as the management seemed to be of her. At the corner, I turned down the intersecting street, stopped and stared at the horseless theatrical rigs with their gaudy, painted sides promoting the traveling troupe. Evidently, the acting crew was doing well enough to stable their teams at a local wagon yard. I don't recall my name ever painted on anything, though it had appeared on a few wanted posters in Colorado for murder and perhaps in Texas for bank robbery. I walked past the first wagon and slipped between it and the second, noting that the door in the back was padlocked. As I inspected the other two carriages, I discovered comparable security. Apparently, Lissa and her company had many valuables inside. As I strolled beyond the wagons, I looked down a service alley that ended at a limestone brick wall. In the back of the theater, I spotted two doors, the first being of regular size and the second large enough to drive a wagon through. I turned down the alley and stepped to the closest entryway, pounding as hard as I could on the thick wood. I hammered the door for a couple minutes with my right hand, stopped, switched my carbine to that hand and continued with my left until someone inside pounded back.

"Be gone, scoundrel," cried a man. "We can't rehearse with your infernal noise. We have a performance tonight, forsooth!"

I beat the lumber as hard as I could with my left hand, then slammed the butt of my carbine against it. "This is important, forsooth," I shouted back. I heard a rattle of chains and saw the door crack open. I yanked my gun around and leveled it at the fellow inside.

The old codger's arms shot up in the air. "We're being robbed," he cried, drawing screams from inside. For an old man, he stood straight and defiant.

"Scoot away from the door," I commanded, waving the gun at him a last time, then stepping inside. "Now lock it up."

The elderly man obliged me, complaining "We don't have any money." Behind him I saw a dozen adults and children in costume, their arms all raised.

"I don't want your money. Put your hands down. I'm not a robber," I cried, realizing the folks in Texas probably disagreed. "I'm looking for Lissa Lomax."

"So is every other libidinous male in Utah Territory, but I'm her husband."

Bewildered about what the old fellow meant about the livid men of Utah, I waved my carbine. "Drop your hands, everyone."

"It'd help if you quit pointing your Winchester at us."

"No, no!" I shouted. "I'm not robbing or hurting anyone. All I want is to see Lissa Lomax. She's my sister."

"Oh my heavens," gasped an older-looking woman,

whose hands flew to her face. She stepped forward, hesitated, then threw out her arms and raced toward me. "Henry Harrison Lomax, is that you?"

Recognizing the lilt of her voice, I nodded as she grabbed me and hugged me tightly.

"I can't believe it," she said, breaking from my grasp and shouting to the other actors. "This is my kid brother! Put your worries aside."

"Forsooth," I said.

"Forsooth," she echoed as the old fellow walked up beside her. "Henry, I'd like you to meet my husband, Aaron W. Coker, though for tonight he's Ebenezer Scrooge."

Coker extended his hand and shook mine cautiously. "You gave us a scare, Henry."

"And," said Lissa, stamping her foot on the floor, "you interrupted our rehearsal for tonight's performance. I'd love to visit, but we have a show to prepare for."

"I can return."

"Absolutely not, Henry. It's been years since I've seen anybody from home. You find a seat offstage and watch. We'll have plenty of time to visit after the play's over tonight." She looked at me once more, taking me in from head to foot, then hugged me and bolted back to her spot.

"Back in your places, everyone," Aaron cried. "We'll pick it up where I say 'Bah! Humbug!'"

I eased away from the door, passing the painted backdrop of a London street in winter and finding a stool near the pulls for the stage curtain. After dropping my saddlebags on the floor, propping my carbine against the wall and removing my coat, I watched the rehearsal. I never fathomed how much preparation and practice went into putting on a performance. From the theater seats it looked so easy and effortless, but I soon learned it was anything but, as the actors said their lines, paying attention to their gestures and expressions while moving to the proper spots on the stage. With a small theatrical group like this, performers had to play several parts, making quick costume changes between their scenes.

Whenever Lissa stepped offstage, I thought she would visit with me, but she scurried about helping with costume swaps and prepping others for their next appearance. They practiced until right before the theater doors opened and patrons scurried to their seats. At that point, they gobbled quick bites of sausages and soda crackers, which they washed down with gulps of water. Then they completed their makeup and adjusted their stage garb for the performance, all while the noise beyond the draped barrier increased as more spectators filled the hall. Even though I was nothing more than an observer, the excitement grew, and I could feel the butterflies in my belly. I wondered how the actors and actresses, especially the children, handled it. At ten minutes after eight o'clock, the curtain rose to roiling applause, and Charles Dickens's classic tale unfolded before my eyes. I found it amazing sitting where I was, seeing the action on the stage and behind the scenes with the hands moving sets, lifting backdrops, doing the sound effects of the rattling chains and helping the performers change costumes quickly, efficiently. The excitement continued throughout the performance. When the curtain came down, the audience responded with great cheers and applause, especially when the stage hands raised the curtain for the last calls. What amazed me was Lissa got the loudest roar of approval, though she only had a minor part in the play, and the Arkansas songbird never sang a note.

When the curtain fell for the final time and the noise of the crowd abated as families exited the theater, Lissa rushed over and gave me a bear hug. "Henry, I'm so glad to see you, to see any family. I've written to most everyone but you and Constance because I never knew where you were."

I nodded as she released me. "Perhaps I've been a tumbleweed of a brother, blowing from place to place, never settling down."

"That doesn't surprise me. You were always like Pa, born with a restless stripe down your back." She laughed. "Though I am shocked you've survived this long."

"Talk about surprised. How do you think I felt when I spotted your name on the wagons outside? Tell me how that came about."

She looked from me to the family that had gathered around her. "That can wait. I need to introduce you to everyone. You've met Scrooge, my husband Aaron Coker. He's not as old as he looks in makeup."

Aaron and I shook hands again as Lissa gathered her brood.

"Come here, children." She motioned for her offspring to join her. "This is your Uncle Henry. He's my little brother." She introduced me to John Adams, twelve, and Van Buren, eleven, both named for the brothers we lost in the War Between the States, then her three daughters, Constance, seven, and Harriet, four, both given names of our sisters, and LouAnne, five.

I choked up at the mention of LouAnne, the young lady I abandoned after the war, fearing threats to me might spill over and harm her. "I...I...uh—"

Lissa noticed the catch in my voice. "We loved her, too, Henry. Wish it would've worked out, so you didn't have to leave her," my sister said, patting my shoulder.

After I cleared my throat, I shook the hands of the two boys and bent over to do the same with the three girls, who were as cute as baby kittens. "Delighted to meet you all and glad to be your uncle. I can tell you some funny stories about your momma when she was your age." They all giggled, then little Harriet scooted toward me and wrapped her arms around my leg. I lifted her up and held her at my shoulder, where she rested her head.

Lissa next introduced me to the rest of her troupe. Starting with Abigail Coker Stillman, Aaron's sister, and her husband, Silas Stillman, themselves both performers, along with daughters Avon, fourteen, and Corina, ten, plus son Banner, twelve.

"That makes up the Lomax and Coker Theatrical Troupe," Lissa said. "Of course, we hire locals for stage hands and additional actors when we need them."

I tried to put down Harriet as I shook hands with the Stillmans, but she grabbed my collar and held on like a tick.

"She likes you," Lissa said. "Harriet doesn't always take to newcomers, so you're special, in her eyes at least."

"But not in yours," I teased my sister.

"How many jobs have you kept for more than a year, Henry? Not many, I suspect."

She pegged me there. "I've moved around a bit, much like a traveling theater troupe."

"But we all had a job, Henry."

"Maybe so, but I've met a lot more interesting characters in my travels."

"Like who?" asked John Adams, her oldest boy.

"Wild Bill Hickok, Buffalo Bill, Billy the Kid, General Custer—"

Lissa chided me. "No point in filling the children's heads with foolishness, Henry. It's late, and we must put the children to bed so they're rested for the show tomorrow." She pointed to Harriet, who was nodding off on my shoulder.

I handed the little one to her mother. She resisted, but this time more gently than before. "I reckon I should leave and find me a room for the night."

"You're welcome to stay with us," Aaron said, as he took his daughter from Lissa. "The theater lets us bed down backstage. It's not as comfortable as a hotel, but it's often cleaner and cuts down on expenses for us all."

Glancing at the others, I nodded. "As long as there are no objections from anyone."

"Not at all, Henry," said Silas Stillman. "If you're family with Lissa, you're family with all of us. Stick around; we might make an actor out of you."

As Abigail shooed her kids away, Lissa directed hers behind the backdrop, but Aaron grabbed her arm. "I'll see to the children. Why don't you and your brother sit in the theater and visit? You've got a lot to catch up on."

"Thanks, dear. That would be lovely." My sister took my hand and led me across the stage and through the curtain to the forestage where the gas footlights were dimming as two workers cleaned up after the performance. We descended the steps on the wing of the forestage and claimed a pair of seats in the front row.

I explained my vagabond existence, and I had indeed met all the men I told the kids, though I'm uncertain she believed me.

"What about Constance? Did you ever run into her?" Lissa asked. "She just up and disappeared before the war."

Nodding, I hesitated to tell her the truth. I had seen Constance in Deadwood, running a brothel, but I ignored the profession about our older sister. "As a matter of fact, I did in Deadwood in seventy-six or seventy-seven, I believe it was. Constance had a wandering streak like me and Pa. When I saw her, she was doing quite well in business."

Lissa cocked her head at me. "What kind of business?"

"Sort of a boarding house. Of course, it was all primitive at that time, Deadwood being a boomtown and all, but she was shrewd, knowing how to charge a pretty penny for a clean bed for the miners, freighters and the other riff-raff a mining town draws."

I feared she would ask what kind of rooming house, but she spoke of mining towns instead. "There was a time when we worked some of the mining camps in Colorado, but they were too rough and mean. We could manage before we had John, but boomtowns were no place to raise a child, boy or girl. That's what we like about Utah. The Mormon influence provides a good, stable setting for raising a family. Too, the Mormons appreciate theater and value clean drama and comedy."

"That's what drew me to Utah," I said. "I figured I might become a Mormon and marry me a dozen wives."

Lissa reached over and slapped my thigh. "Henry Harrison Lomax, the very idea that you should think about such things."

"Maybe," I said, "but it'd take a dozen wives to equal LouAnne Burke. I should've taken her with me when I left and started over somewhere else, but I couldn't see that far ahead. I've often wondered how my life would've been different had I done that."

"From what I've heard in letters from home, she married a merchant in Fayetteville and is prospering. Do you ever write home?"

Shrugging, I shook my head. "I never knew what to say."

"Telling them you were alive would be a good start. I guess you know Pa died."

"I'd heard. Pa's probably wandering about heaven looking for the gold he never found in California."

Lissa laughed. "He always believed if he had reached California sooner, he'd have come back from the coast a rich man."

Memories of home flooded back as my sister recalled the good times and the dark days of the war, when you couldn't sort friends from foes.

"That's what I enjoy about theater," Lissa said. "You can live in another world, escape from your daily problems, even if only for a few hours."

"The wagons outside list you as the Arkansas songbird."

Lissa smiled. "I'm better known for my singing in Utah than for my acting. So I give several concerts to bring in money in the gaps between different plays. It's easier than running a boarding house or wandering around the country like you, Henry, looking for something you'll never find."

"Believe me, Lissa, I've found it several times, but I've always lost it."

"Just like Pa," Lissa answered, then eyed me with a harder gaze than she had until that moment. "I'd like to ask you something, if you don't mind?"

"You're my sister, ask away."

"We performed in the Tabor Opera House shortly after it opened in Leadville, Colorado. My name caught the eye of a few men, who wanted to know if I knew of a Henry Lomax. I said I had a brother by that name, but I'd encountered others with the same brand in my travels. Not thinking much of it, the next morning I found a wanted poster someone had slipped under my hotel room door."

I feigned innocence, but realized maybe I didn't have the makings of a real actor after all.

"There was a reward for a Henry Lomax that was accused of murder," she continued, her gaze boring into me like a mine augur. "Was that you?"

Lifting my shoulders and letting out a slow breath, I shrugged. "I can't say with certainty."

Lissa cocked her head and stared even harder. "What do you mean?"

"I was in Leadville at the time and was swindled out of some rich mining property by the dead lawyer, but I don't recall much about that night until I woke up in his office with him sprawled across the floor and a shotgun at my side." I shrugged. "That's the truth, Lissa, as I remember nothing."

She stared at me for an uncomfortably long time before nodding. "I'll take your word for it, Henry. What about those tales you shared with the children about meeting Custer and Buffalo Bill and Hickok?"

I nodded slowly. "Those are all true and clear in my mind, but not the lawyer in Leadville. Everything about that night's still a blur."

"Anything else that's unclear in your mind I should know about? I'm trying to raise my children right, and don't want you influencing them otherwise."

Nodding, I slowly arose from my seat. "I'll be on my way, Lissa. Tell your family I enjoyed meeting them."

Lissa grabbed my wrist. "I'm not asking you to leave, Henry. You're family now and forever."

I settled back in my chair. "You should know I haven't led a perfect life, Lissa. I've run with bad company, sometimes by choice, sometimes not. Though I've tried to do what was right, things didn't always work out. Sometimes that was my fault, sometimes not."

My sister smiled and patted my hand. "I'm not judging you, Henry, just looking out for my children. Some people think raising a family in a traveling theater troupe is not good for kids, but they are learning values that will serve them well for life. That's why we run the theater circuit in Utah where the folks are decent. The Mormons are good folk, not perfect, but good folk nonetheless."

"My life's been far from pure since I left home, so what do you want me to do, Lissa? Stay or go?"

She squeezed my hand. "Like I've said, Henry, you're

family, so stay as long as you like, though we may put you to work. Everybody in our troupe has to carry a share of the load. Besides that, don't tell outlandish stories about your past and some of the bad fellows—"

"Bad gals, too," I interrupted.

"—that you've run with." She paused, releasing my hand and scratching her chin, then cocking her head at me. "What's your most outlandish adventure, Henry?"

Pursing my lips, I considered the possibilities like being stalked by Billy the Kid the night he died, going against my will with Jesse James on his first bank robbery, having Calamity Jane save me in a gunfight with Wild Bill Hickok, robbing the bank in Buffalo Gap or accompanying Custer to the hill where he met his demise. "I suppose it was being at the Little Bighorn when General Custer perished."

Lissa snickered. "I can't believe you were in the cavalry."

"I wasn't. It's a long story, but Custer was out to kill me. If he'd listened to me, he might have survived, but I saw him die."

Shaking and lowering her head, she ran her hand from her forehead to her chin. "Now, Henry, everybody knows no white men survived Custer's command that day."

"That's what the army said, but I know better."

"Henry, that's such an outlandish tale. I can't help but think you've eaten some locoweed since you left home."

"I've had lots of adventures, Lissa, but most folks doubt my stories when I relate them, so I won't tell them to your young 'uns."

"No, Henry, share with them what you like. They sound so outlandish even the little ones won't believe you, but keep the stories clean, nothing about drinking, gambling or carousing. Can you do that?"

As I nodded, Lissa arose, taking my hand for me to stand.

"It's getting late, and I've still got to take off my costume and makeup." She pointed to two theater employees at the back of the auditorium. "Besides, they're waiting on us to turn off the gaslights." She nodded at the pair and they dimmed the lights as we stepped on stage and behind the curtain.

My eyes adjusted to the backstage dimness, but I could see a row of children asleep on blankets on the floor as Aaron and the Stillmans tiptoed around them, preparing their own bedding. I retreated to my carbine, saddlebags, and coat. After I fetched them, Lissa brought me a pair of blankets and pointed to a corner opposite where the others slept.

"Make your bed there," she told me. "It'll give you a little privacy, though it won't be as comfortable as a feather mattress. You'll grow accustomed to it."

"It'll beat sleeping in a wooden railcar seat."

Lissa hugged me for a final time. "It's so good to run into you, Henry. I'm glad you're well." She kissed me on the cheek. "Sleep tight."

I made my bed and slept soundly. When I awoke the next morning, Lissa and Abigail were already giving school lessons to their eight children. When I got up yawning and stretching, little Harriet spotted me and came running across the stage, wrapping her arms around my leg.

"Good morning, little one," I responded, picking her up.

"Miss Harriet," her mother called, "return to your place and finish your drawing."

I carried her back to her spot and sat her down by her paper and pencil.

That was my first lesson in the routine of a theatrical troupe with children. They arose midmorning to do lessons after a plain breakfast of bread and sausage. Then they went out to lunch or fetched food to the theater for the noon meal. Afternoon was for rehearsal time for the current play, the upcoming production or Lissa's next musical concert. When I saw Lissa without her *Christmas Carol* makeup, I understood why the eyeball between the box office curtains did not let me in. She was strikingly beautiful. I understood why she was a desirable object among the Mormon men accustomed to plainer women.

That afternoon during the rehearsal of a London street scene from the Dickens play, Lissa informed me I would perform that night. During the scene, I was to walk in front of the street backdrop like a normal London pedestrian. I did as directed and learned I would play three parts. I would enter stage right with a wrapped gift in my hand and cross behind the real actors as they said their lines. After I exited the stage, I was to quickly put on a winter coat, swap hats, pick up a Christmas tree and place it on my shoulder, then retrace my path. Next, I swapped my coat and hat for a shawl and a cane, bending over and hobbling back a final time as the scene ended.

I realized I had found my true profession, as everyone complimented me on my acting skills. That evening, though, after they had put on my makeup and costume, I understood it was a little different strolling across the stage without an audience and doing the same thing with the gaslights ablaze and a theater full of critics. The closer it got to show time, the more the butterflies fluttered in my stomach, to the point I feared I might throw up.

Fortunately, my debut came early in the play. As I strolled by the audience on my first trip, I recognized it was hard to act natural when you were acting, at least for me it was. I made it across the stage carrying the gift without a problem, switched costumes and toted the tree to the other side awkwardly, but successfully. As the old man, I crossed halfway across the platform when I tripped over the end of my shawl, and tumbled to the floor, my cane clattering ahead of me.

Embarrassed, I picked myself up, kicked at the stage, crying, "Darn rock." As the audience snickered, I gathered my cane and hobbled the rest of the way out of sight. I feared my career as an actor was over, but after the final curtain fell, everyone came up and patted me on the back, complimenting me for my clever impromptu comment.

At that moment, I realized I might have found my calling in life: H.H. Lomax, actor.

CHAPTER TEN

The Lomax and Coker Theatrical Troupe closed *A Christmas Carol* after a matinee and evening performance Christmas Day. I continued my three pedestrian parts for the rest of the run, never again tripping, nor drawing another laugh. After the last show on Christmas night, we decorated the small tree I carried in the play and let the children open their modest gifts and empty their stockings filled with apples, nuts and peppermint sticks. Their toys were simple, little rag dolls for the girls and spinning tops for the boys. Simple though they were, their gifts surpassed anything I remember Lissa and me receiving for Christmas during our childhood back in Cane Hill, Arkansas, particularly during the war.

On New Year's Day, the troupe opened a concert that featured Lissa's talented voice. Everyone took part except me, as my musical talents wouldn't have filled a gnat's ear. The show began with the duet of Silas and Abigail Stillman singing popular songs, followed by the children's choir, where all of them sang before culminating with my sister, warbling a variety of songs, including several religious hymns. The show ran for a week with a capacity audience of eight hundred at the beginning, tapering off to half that by the final presentation.

When the concerts concluded, the performers took a two-week break to prepare for their next play, a melodrama titled *Ten Nights in a Bar-room*. That struck me as an odd subject for a show that would attract a sober and somber Mormon crowd, but Lissa informed me the melodrama provided a moral lesson on sobriety that rested well on the Mormon conscience that had always believed in temperance in all things and abstinence in liquor. My role in the play was as a saloon patron, whose only line was "barkeep" as I lifted an empty bronze beer bottle that the bartender, a character named Simon Slade played by Aaron Coker, replaced with another one which he uncorked for me. I either sat at a table or at the bar, drinking my fake beverage. It was a part I was destined for, as I had been in more saloons than churches since I left home. My acting success, though, was dashed because my "beer" bottle held water instead of the genuine article. So, I had to sit through each performance night after night after night, hearing the same lines time and time again from the others.

In the play, the bartender Slade entices a sober young father Joe Morgan, played by Silas Stillman, to drink, turning him into the town drunk that his young daughter Mary must always fetch from the saloon. One night Slade and Morgan are fighting when Mary arrives just as Slade throws a liquor bottle at Morgan, missing and plastering the girl instead with a fatal wound. On her deathbed, she extracts a promise from her father to give up alcohol and live a righteous life from that point onward. Meanwhile, Slade gets into a fierce argument with his son. When things turn violent, the son pounds the tavern owner over the head with a beer bottle, ironically, causing the bartender's own demise. I debated whether the melodrama was testament to the evils of alcohol or to the dangers of bottles. In the end, righteousness—or liquor bottles—prevailed over drinking's sinfulness, at least on the theater stage.

During this time what I learned about acting was that except for the time beneath the lights when you were performing for an audience, it was a tedious, boring profession, much akin to sitting through a mind-numbing sermon on a beautiful day. But I stayed through February, pitching in to help and playing my roles as best I could. Lissa perceived I was getting restless, but convinced me to stay until after the troupe moved to the Mormon capital.

"We start our new season in Salt Lake City the second week in April," she said. "The venue is always our biggest moneymaker. We'll open with *Ten Nights in a Bar-room*, before moving to one of Shakespeare's plays. Fact is, Aaron is taking the train south tomorrow to sign the contract for the Salt Lake City Theater. You won't find a more striking theater in all the West, save maybe in San Francisco. It cost a hundred thousand dollars to build. You'll continue your role in *Ten Nights*, and we'll find a spot for you in the bard's play."

"I admit the free room and board is fine, though a stage-floor bed doesn't rate with a feather mattress, but I'm getting a different kind of bored, if you understand me."

She nodded, "Bored as in tired, jaded, uninterested, and wearied."

"Exactly."

"You never had much patience as a boy."

"Still don't."

"I'm not surprised, Henry, but stay, if you please, until we get settled in Salt Lake City, where we make the bulk of the money that carries us through the year."

I nodded. "Sure, if that's what you want."

She smiled. "If it'll ease your boredom, tell us about your adventures out West, though I'll likely explain to the children you are relating tall tales."

"A drink of whiskey in the beer bottles on stage might help," I answered.

Lissa stomped her foot and clapped her hands. "Absolutely not! We can't afford to offend the Mormon Church or we risk losing our livelihood."

Grinning, I nodded. "I was just joshing."

My sister eyed me. "I'm sure you were." She paused, pointing at me. "If you relate any of your accounts to the youngsters, do it at lunch time rather than at supper, so they aren't too keyed up to remember their lines or what they are supposed to be doing."

I agreed and during lunch the next day, I asked if the young ones had ever heard of the Indian fighter George Armstrong Custer. The boys all nodded, but the girls shrugged and didn't seem to care, so I focused on the little fellows, whose eyes widened as I told the story of the Sioux attacking me, Custer, and his troopers of the Seventh Cavalry atop a lonely hill near the Little Bighorn.

"One by one, the soldiers around me fell by arrow, by bullet or by fear until it was just me and the maniac

Custer. Indians to the left of me, Indians to the right of me, Indians all around me."

"Alfred, Lord Tennyson," Aaron interjected.

I turned and looked at my brother-in-law, my browed furrowed in confusion. "No, George Armstrong Custer."

"*The Charge of the Light Brigade*," Aaron responded.

"It was the Seventh Cavalry, not some brigade," I replied.

"Cannon to the right of them, cannon to the left of them, cannon in front of them," he answered.

"The Sioux didn't have any cannons," I insisted. "I know because I was there."

Aaron waved his hand at me. "Never mind. Go on with your fable."

Though uncertain what in tarnation had gnawed at Aaron's brain, I continued. "Then it was just the two of us, but the general collapsed into my legs, knocking me down. I sprawled across the bloody battlefield, my mind muddled, my senses dulled. I spotted an Indian hulking over me."

Everyone was listening now with rapt attention, even the girls, so I paused to add suspense to my tale. They all leaned toward me, desperate for more.

"What happened?" asked little Harriet.

"The warrior raised his hatchet to scalp me."

Everyone's eyes and mouths widened.

"He grabbed me by a necklace I was wearing and lifted me to smash my brains out."

The girls gasped, and the boys grimaced.

"You know who the Sioux brave was?"

"Sitting Bull," Banner Stillman guessed.

"No, even meaner than Sitting Bull. It was Crazy Horse himself."

Even the adults gasped this time, though I think it was more in mockery than in fear.

"When he saw the necklace, he realized it was one he had given me for saving his life weeks earlier. Believe it or not—"

"I don't believe it," Silas said.

"—he carried me to his horse and delivered me to other soldiers a few miles away, repaying me for saving his life."

"How did you rescue him?" Van asked.

"I found him bitten by a rattlesnake and sucked the poison out."

"Yuck," said the girls.

"Why?" asked John.

"Because I like Indians better than rattlesnakes or even General Custer, who was impressed with himself more than any other man I've ever met."

"Children," said Lissa, "that is what we call a tall tale. You know what a tall tale is? It's a story with an element of truth and a large dose of exaggeration."

Van looked at his mother. "Are you saying Uncle Henry is a liar?"

I grinned at my sister, wondering how she would answer.

"No," she answered. "I'm telling you, he's a wonderful storyteller, one who knows how to stretch the truth a tad to spin a good yarn."

I cocked my head, looking at the kids. "Who do you believe, boys and girls?"

"You, Uncle Henry," they shouted.

Triumphantly, I cast my gaze back at my sister, who shook her head.

"Sometimes things aren't worth explaining," she responded.

Offering her a victorious smirk, I turned back to the young ones, figuring I should add a moral to the story to instill the proper values I knew their parents wanted in their offspring.

"Do you children know the moral of this tale?"

"Never ride with Custer," Van offered.

Young Van was a smart boy, I thought as I tried to disguise my snicker. "That's good advice, but the greater lesson is you should always help people in need because it will come back to bless you in unexpected ways."

"Very profound, Henry," Lissa said. "You can keep telling your outlandish stories as long as they contain a lesson about life."

Every day after that at lunch time, I would share my adventures, some true, some not, most a combination of fact and fiction, but each ending with an adage about living right so that their lives might not be wasted as most of mine had been.

After a three-day absence in Salt Lake City, Aaron Coker returned to Ogden with signed papers for a month's run at the best theater in Utah Territory and perhaps in all the West. The Lomax and Coker Theatrical Troupe would get three days of setup with *Ten Nights* to start on Saturday, the eighth of April. While he was in town, Aaron purchased advertisements in the *Deseret News* and the *Salt Lake Tribune*, announcing the play's two-week run, followed by a midweek break, a week of musical concerts, featuring the Arkansas Songbird, and ending with a week of Shakespeare. Additionally, Aaron paid extra for the *News* to print colorful broadsides to post around town and promote the cast and their performances. Aaron returned excited that he had gotten a discounted rental from the theater and a bargain on print ads. Even so, the cost was three hundred and fifty dollars, which meant things would be tight for the ensemble until after the first week of shows, when the money would roll in as the dramatic company always drew well in Salt Lake City.

The enthusiasm in their final Ogden performances grew and the optimism of a great new theatrical season ballooned. After the closing show in Ogden, everyone pitched in that night to take down the sets and load the three wagons with their costumes, props and baggage. We slept a final night on the stage floor, packed our remaining belongings, and loaded them up. Everyone was excited to head south to Utah's biggest city and milled about impatiently around the wagons, awaiting Aaron and Silas to return with the teams they had stabled at the wagon yard.

Then the telegram arrived.

"Telegram for Aaron Coker with the Lomax and Coker Theatrical Troupe," the courier cried as he approached our rigs.

Lissa looked at me. "What's this?" She raised her arm and turned to the messenger. "I'm his wife. I'm Mrs. Coker."

The courier strode to her, handed her a clipboard and pencil to sign for the communication. After she wrote her name and returned the clipboard, he handed her a yellow envelope, which she tore open to skim the message. Her hand flew to her mouth. "Oh, no!"

Abigail came to her side. "What is it?"

"The theater is postponing our opening for a week," Lissa answered, her eyes moistening.

"They can't do that!" Abigail stomped her foot on the walk and planted her hands on her hips. "We've got signed papers."

Lissa shook the yellow sheet. "It says 'Performance postponed one week; contract paragraph nine.' That's the only explanation."

"What'll we do?" Abigail asked, her anger dissolving into worry.

"Wait for the men to return," she answered, handing the message to me.

The telegram made little sense, but I hadn't read the contract, or any other theatrical ones for that matter. I returned the yellow sheet to Lissa, who paced back and forth on the walk, as we waited for their husbands to return with the teams. In a half hour, we spotted them leading the animals down the street toward us. As soon as she sighted Aaron, Lissa darted to her husband, waving the telegram over her head. When she reached him, she dashed into the road to deliver the message.

Aaron stopped, took the missive, and read it. He jammed the yellow sheet in his pocket and handed Lissa the lines to the lead team. As he dashed away in the opposite direction, Lissa and Silas continued with the horses to the theater. Abigail and I herded the children until the pair arrived with the teams.

"He's gone to the telegraph office to wire for clarification. Said he'd read the contract when he returned.

We're to hitch up the teams and be ready to start for Salt Lake as planned."

I took the harness lines from my sister for the first team as Silas approached with the other four horses. He and I spent thirty minutes hooking the horses to the wagons, then waiting for Aaron to return. We all rested in the shade of the theater, Lissa pacing about.

Aaron came back an hour later, face downcast, shoulders slumped. Lissa ran to question what he had learned. He said a few words to her. Both trod toward us, wearing bewildered grimaces.

"What's the problem?" Abigail asked.

Aaron ignored her, walking to the back of the lead wagon, which he unlocked and climbed inside.

"We don't know yet," Lissa explained. "He's checking the contract. He telegraphed the theater, but received no response after forty-five minutes, so he returned for us to drive the wagons to the telegraph office and wait there for an answer."

As she finished, Aaron emerged from the wagon door and eased down the step as he read the contract in his hand.

"Figured it out yet?" Silas asked.

Aaron held up his palm, motioning for everyone to be quiet. Our eyes focused on him. When he finally looked up, he clenched his lips. "The contract says our rental can be postponed for as much as a week if our dates conflict with a national touring troupe or lecturer. The provision had never been in any of our previous contracts. When I hesitated to sign, they offered me a reduced rate if I accepted the clause." He sighed. "So, I inked the papers, not really considering possible consequences."

"You did what you thought best," Silas said, walking over and patting Aaron's shoulder.

"Thanks, Silas, but I've thrown away close to three hundred and fifty dollars on advertising and broadsides that are now wrong."

"Send a telegram to the printers and tell them to hold off," Abigail suggested.

"If it's not too late," Aaron responded, releasing a long, slow breath. "I'll put the contract back in my satchel, then let's head to the telegraph office. I'm hoping we get an answer before we leave town." He hesitated. "I guess there's no rush if they deny us the theater for a week." His shoulders slumped, and he twisted his head from side to side as he stepped back to the wagon to file the theater agreement.

The theatrical wagons had two bench seats in the driver's box, so everyone loaded up in their accustomed places. Each of the men driving a team and the two women handling the third.

"How about the women ride with their husbands and I'll drive the extra wagon?" I suggested.

Little Harriet cried out from her seat in the front wagon, "I want to sit with Uncle Henry."

The children clamored to join me. As it worked out, I took Harriet and the three boys in my wagon while the remaining girls rode with their parents. We all climbed in and headed for the telegraph office. After we reached the building, we waited while Aaron went inside. An hour later, he returned, holding a telegram and wearing a dejected look.

"What does it say?" my sister asked as everyone gathered around him.

Lifting the yellow paper, he sighed. "Oscar Wilde Lecture April tenth."

"Who the hell is Oscar Wilde?" I exclaimed.

"Henry, watch your language," Lissa chided me.

Turning to the kids, I confessed, "Uncle Henry said a no-no. Don't use that word, young 'uns."

"It's a long story, Henry," Aaron responded.

Lissa picked up the explanation. "You ever heard of Gilbert and Sullivan?"

Stroking my chin as I considered the question, I finally nodded. "Weren't they a pair of horse thieves that were hung down Texas way in McLennan County?"

The adults laughed.

Shaking her head, Lissa turned to me. "Have you ever heard of *H.M.S. Pinafore* or *The Pirates of Penzance*?"

"Are they any kin to the Light Brigade?" I asked.

Now all the adults were shaking their heads, and the kids were snickering.

"Not really," Lissa answered. "They are musical plays written by dramatist W.S. Gilbert and composer Arthur Sullivan."

"Are they kin to this fellow Oscar Rowdy?"

"No," my sister laughed. "It's Oscar Wilde, not Rowdy."

Shrugging, I responded. "Y'all are the first theatrical types I've been around, so I don't know all these fellows."

"Okay," Lissa replied, "just listen, no questions. Okay, Henry?"

I nodded.

"Last year Gilbert and Sullivan wrote another comic

opera called *Patience*, a satire on the aesthetic movement and its proponents like Oscar Wilde."

I raised my hand like a schoolboy.

"Yes, Henry?"

"Can I ask a question?"

"Go ahead."

"What's the athletic movement?"

The other adults snickered as she lifted her chin and rolled her eyes. "It's aesthetic, not athletic. It's probably over your head, but aestheticism is a philosophy, a view of life that values drama, literature, music and art over everything else."

Lissa was right. It made little sense to me. I shrugged. "What about Oscar Untamed?"

"It's Wilde," she cried, stamping her foot to show her impatience. "He's parodied in *Patience* as a fool named Bunthorne."

"So?"

"When the play came to New York last year, Wilde visited the States to prove himself the fool. He started a lecture tour across the nation when the opera premiered. *Patience* is playing to this day in New York's Savoy Theater, which features electric lighting, believe it or not."

"And they are kicking you out of the theater because of a fool?" I could only shrug.

"Actually, it's only a postponement," Aaron interrupted, "but it'll cost us plenty and likely cut our profits significantly. It seems he's drawing full houses wherever he speaks, though he only stays for one or two nights before moving on."

"That's what's so unfair," Lissa said. "We could've set up and cancelled our Monday performance for him to speak. They don't need a week to prepare for a lecture." My sister bowed her head and sobbed. Aaron put his arm over her shoulder as her children gathered around her.

"It'll be okay, Momma," said LouAnne. "Don't cry, Momma."

At that moment, I abandoned looking for me a passel of Utah brides and instead vowed to find justice for the Lomax and Coker Theatrical Troupe. I didn't like to see my sister cry.

When Lissa calmed down, we all climbed in the wagons and headed south for Salt Lake City, about forty miles distant. We took our time, making it easy on our teams and spending the night about halfway to our destination. From a distance, we saw the Great Salt Lake and the surrounding Wasatch Mountains that enveloped our route down the basin. While riding with the boys and Harriet, I told them more of my adventures, sometimes true, most times not, and they sat enthralled as I spun the tales. Whenever we stopped for meals or camped by the road at night, I visited with Aaron, asking questions about the theatrical business and how it worked. I wanted to learn how plays, concerts and lectures were booked and what arrangements were made for visiting celebrities or fools.

"You thinking of getting into the theatrical business?" Aaron asked.

"If idiots can sell out theaters by doing nothing but talking, perhaps I can get rich spinning yarns from the stage. After all, I am an accomplished actor based on my roles in *A Christmas Carol* and *Ten Nights in a Barroom*."

Lissa choked, and Abigail giggled at my review of my own performances.

"Perhaps you should try *Hamlet*," Silas suggested.

For the life of me, I couldn't figure out what breakfast had to do with my acting, but I tried to gauge my response, so it wasn't condescending to Mister Stillman. "I ate an omelet once in a fancy Denver eatery, but I can't say I ever had a hamlet."

"You'd find it hard to chew own," Silas responded, a note of snootiness in his reply that had been absent in mine. I figured he was acting.

Aaron tolerated my questions and answered them, but I could read in his pinched brow he doubted my fitness as a theatrical manager, actor, or lecturer, at least a successful one. But folks had always questioned my abilities, and yet I had outlived most of those who cast doubts on my capabilities. Granted I never made a fortune, though I lost a few, and I'd never had a dime novel written about me like Buffalo Bill or Wild Bill Hickok or Texas Star. I wondered if Oscar Wilde would ever be the subject of a novel, if he was such a fool and assuming he would survive his lecture tour out west. Then the thought hit me I could shoot him or take him hostage for a month, so the Lomax and Coker performances could go as scheduled.

A lot of possibilities raced through my mind the next day as we entered the Mormon capital and headed for the Salt Lake City Theater, so Aaron Coker could take up his dispute face-to-face with the theater management. The first thing that struck me about the city was its cleanliness. I'd never seen streets so wide and spotless. It wasn't just that there were no saloons visible to my eye at least, but it seemed like even the horses knew better than to leave droppings on the roads—at least the horses other than ours.

Aaron led the three-wagon caravan through town to the theater on the corner of First East and First South streets. I had to admit it was a fine looking facility, one any actor would be thrilled to perform in, provided the theater hadn't postponed his contract. When we stopped outside the building, I secured my team, jumped from the wagon seat, and reached Aaron as he was climbing out of his wagon.

"Would you like me to accompany you to discuss the matter?" I said, patting my revolver at my side. "I can fetch my carbine from the wagon as well."

"No, thanks, Henry. The Mormons don't take kindly to threats. I think they even prohibit guns on the street. Further, threats would only harm our cause."

I nodded. "Do me a favor, Aaron. Find out the name of the traveling manager who is booking this fool in your place. His name might come in handy."

CHAPTER ELEVEN

The whole troupe fidgeted on the street in front of the theater as Aaron pleaded with the managers to honor the troupe's performance contract. As we waited, several folks afoot, on horseback and in wagons pointed at us and our parked theatrical rigs. Many waved and one woman even stopped her buggy opposite us, inquiring if Lissa Lomax was among us. The kids wagged their fingers at my sister, who turned toward her admirer and gave an impromptu bow.

"Would you sing for us?" the black-clad buggy driver asked as she set her brake.

With so many worries on her mind, I knew Lissa preferred not to sing. "Maybe another time. It's been a trying day," she responded.

But her fan was not to be denied. She twisted in her seat and folded the top of her buggy down, then stood on the floorboard. "Look everyone," she shouted. "That's Lissa Lomax, the Arkansas Songbird."

Lissa's face flushed, even more so when several

pedestrians gathered around her and traffic stopped on the road.

Spontaneously, the crowd applauded and chanted, "Sing, sing, sing."

After several seconds, Lissa finally nodded. She looked for a spot to perform, then stepped toward her female fan. Reaching the buggy, she shook the hand of her admirer. Putting her foot in the step, Lissa lifted herself into the rig beside her devotee. She hugged the woman and motioned for her to sit.

Lissa turned to the crowd. "Thank you for your kindness, ladies and gentlemen," she said. "I would invite you to watch us perform in the theater, but there has been a mix-up in the scheduling, and I can't say when we will take the stage."

Her admirers groaned.

"We were to start this coming weekend, but it seems the theater has booked the lecturer Oscar Wilde at the same time as us, so our productions will be postponed. If you like, I will sing one song, if you promise to see us when our run begins. We'll start with *Ten Nights in a Bar-room* for a week, then my concerts and finish with Shakespeare."

The crowd cheered, nearly all nodding their support as they clapped.

Lissa smiled for the first time in two days. "Thank you," she said. "With your permission, I will sing my favorite, a beautiful hymn written by John Newton."

Several people applauded her choice, though I had no idea the song she chose. When the crowd quieted, Lissa started *Amazing Grace*. As she sang, a stillness fell over the spectators as if they were in church, and Lissa's melodious words wafted over the street like the sound of an angel from heaven. I knew she had a fine voice, as she had since she was a child, but I had never heard a song so beautifully rendered. As she sang the chorus, she raised her arms to the heavens, and I saw the woman at her side dab her eyes with a lace handkerchief. When she finished, Lissa lowered her head and shut her eyes. Her admirers stood silent for a moment, then applauded politely before raising an enormous cheer. Lissa lifted her head, smiled and bowed to acknowledge their approval.

I stepped from the walkway to the buggy to help her down. "That was beautiful," I said.

"Thank you, Henry. Perhaps it'll help attendance and profits here. If not, it'll be a tough year financially for us."

Lissa received another polite round of applause as traffic resumed. When Lissa returned to her family, they gathered around and congratulated her for a spontaneous performance well done. After that we waited for Aaron to rejoin us. Thirty minutes later, he emerged, his face drawn, his lips tight. He shook his head and everyone understood he had failed to correct the situation. Aaron motioned for all to return to our places in the wagons, and we followed him to the edge of town. There he stopped at a grassy meadow with scattered shade trees beside the River Jordan, as the Mormons had named the watercourse.

We parked the rigs in a triangle to give us an enclosure and a little privacy from those passing on the nearby road. Everybody nervously awaited Aaron's explanation, but nobody dared raised the issue because of the defeat in his eyes. We unhitched the teams, watered them and staked the horses where they could graze on the emerging spring grass.

After we set up camp, Aaron grabbed five stools from the back of a wagon and asked everyone to gather as he placed the seats in a circle. He motioned for the adults to join him and for the children to find a place on the ground. When everyone was seated, he plopped down on his stool, sighed and spoke.

"I failed us," he began, "in signing a contract with paragraph nine. I knew it had the cancellation provision for a nationwide tour, but I didn't think it would affect our schedule, not this early in the year."

"Don't be so hard on yourself," Silas said, his wife and Lissa nodding.

"The theater operators apologized for the inconvenience, but were threatened by a San Francisco impresario to keep the week open for Wilde or he would make sure no future national tours stopped in Salt Lake City."

"How's that possible, Aaron?" Lissa asked.

Aaron then explained that the promoter, who manages several theaters on the west coast paid Oscar Wilde five thousand dollars to deliver twenty speeches in California over three weeks. After Bunthorne collected the money, he decided to only give ten talks in California, as the audiences there bored him. Consequently, Locke demanded to schedule Wilde's next ten lectures. Wilde agreed, provided the tour started him back east as he had wearied of the West and its vast distances. Aaron explained that Salt Lake City was the first lecture on a tour that would take him across Utah and Colorado and into Kansas before Locke would consider their verbal agreement settled.

"It's unfair," Lissa cried.

Aaron loosed a deep breath. "You know how promoters are, honey, always getting their money first. That's why I do it for us, so they don't siphon our earnings away."

"And you've done a fine job, Aaron," Silas said, everyone nodding their agreement.

"What's the San Francisco fellow's name?" I asked.

"Charles E. Locke," Aaron answered, "but don't you do anything that could harm our troupe's future."

Smiling, I responded. "I wouldn't think of it."

"Best I can tell, Locke is working as the advance man for Wilde, at least through Kansas, setting up venues and buying advertisements to promote the lectures."

"What do you know about Wilde's traveling party?" I asked.

Lissa clapped her hands. "What kind of mischief are you up to, Henry?"

"I'm naturally curious, Lissa, sort of like a cat."

"Are you gonna shoot him," asked twelve-year-old Banner Stillman, "like you did all the other outlaws in the West?"

"What kind of tall tales have you been telling my son?" Abigail demanded.

"Nothing that ain't true, more or less." I paused, eyeing the adults. "I can pack up and leave if you don't trust me."

"You're family," Lissa replied.

"Sort of the black sheep of the family, right?"

Everyone, even the kids, nodded at my statement of fact.

"Either tell me what you learned, Aaron, or I'll leave before dusk."

"Promise me no violence," he demanded.

"Not unless I have to defend myself."

Finally, Aaron relented and told me what details he had gathered. Oscar Wilde traveled with a road manager and a Negro servant. J.S. Vale, the traveling manager, had accompanied Wilde since he arrived in New York in January. As part of his contract, Vale handled the business needs of the tour and supervised a servant to attend to Wilde's personal needs. All Wilde's expenses were covered by the promoter. In addition to his share of the box office, Wilde received first-class accommodations on the rails and in the towns where he spoke.

"It's a comfortable setup that has earned him thousands," Aaron concluded.

"And cost us hundreds," Lissa interjected.

"Others as well," her husband answered. "The Home Dramatic Club had the theater reserved before we arrived, but their performances of *Saratoga* and *Our Boarding House* will now be offered in another location after he leaves. At least we got priority over the local dramatic club for the theater, once Wilde is done, of course."

"Where'll his majesty be staying in town?" I asked.

My sister shook her head. "I can't help but think you're up to no good, Henry."

"The show must go on," I replied. "Isn't that an old stage saying?"

She nodded as Aaron spoke. "Nobody said specifically, but I suspect it'll be the Walker House on Main

Street. There's no better accommodations in Salt Lake City."

"You're saying it's better than our lodging," I said with a sweep of my arm, drawing laughs from everyone, though Lissa eyed me suspiciously like I was plotting something. I was, though I remained uncertain exactly what. At least I had a few days to think about it.

We spent the next three days camped beside the river, me killing time in thought while the others practiced their lines for upcoming shows or repaired costumes. Lissa had the men remove the treadle sewing machine from the costume wagon, then started work on a new gown for her concert. Abigail and the girls fixed meals, making simple dishes of soup and biscuits.

Six Mormons visited us that Saturday, inviting us to the Tabernacle for Sunday services and asking us to ponder converting to Mormonism. When I had arrived in the territory, I might have considered the conversion while I was still thinking about multiple wives, but a few looks at Utah women convinced me it was better to stay Baptist with one wife instead of Mormon with a dozen spouses. Whenever the Mormons stopped to greet or convert us, I always asked what they thought about Oscar Wilde. Generally, the men shrugged their indifference, though the women seemed curious, especially when it was announced that he would speak that Monday night on "The Decorative Arts." The women thought a dollar fifty for a reserved seat or seventy-five cents for a gallery seat was a small price to pay for the culture that he would bring to Salt Lake City and Utah Territory.

Not all—especially the husbands—agreed the cost was worth it, but many locals remained curious to see this young writer, even though none could name anything he had written. They had heard he penned poetry, but nobody had read a line of his verse. His promoters had spread around town copies of the photograph he used as a calling card, and one of our visitors had been lucky enough to secure a copy, which she passed around to us. When the image reached me, I held it and studied the fellow. Oscar Wilde sure wasn't drawing crowds based on his looks. His photo could've made a blind man wretch. Compared to him, Utah women were the belles of the ball, any ball, anywhere.

"Is he single?" I asked the bearer of the image.

"Oh, yes," the matron replied. "Twenty-six and not a wife yet."

"I can see why," I responded as I handed the piece to her. "Are you gonna pay to see him?"

Taking the photo and slipping it in her purse, she shrugged. "My husband thinks he's a waste of money. Seventy-five cents for drivel were his words, but rumor has it that John Taylor—he's the Mormon president—plans to attend. Can't say I'll pay for such expensive tickets, but I am curious about him. His train arrives after church tomorrow in the early afternoon. Many of my friends and I hope to see him then."

I thought about asking if those friends were her husband's other wives, but held my tongue.

"Some of us will wait at the depot to see him for free and others will gather at the Walker House to glimpse him."

"Why?" I asked.

She shrugged. "He's celebrated in all the newspapers."

"Why?" I repeated.

"For being famous, I suppose."

The woman reminded us we were welcome at Sunday's services in the Tabernacle, bade us farewell and parted. As she left, I decided more than a handful of women would be on hand to greet his royal highness the next day at the hotel. I would be there, too, with a business proposition for Mister Wilde.

When Lissa resumed her sewing after our guest departed, I sauntered over and told her I felt like going into town the next day to see Mister Oscar Wilde in person.

"Not me," she said as she sewed away, never looking up.

"But I'd like to go as a gentleman, not a frontier ruffian. Are there any costumes in your collection that'd make me look like a proper Englishman, say?"

Lissa jerked her foot from the treadle and looked at me as the whirr of the sewing machine faded into silence. "You're up to no good, aren't you, Henry?"

"I'm only looking after my big sister's well-being. What do you think I am, a bank robber or something?"

"Nothing would surprise me with you, Henry."

"Well, are you gonna outfit me with suitable duds or do I have to go into town and steal—err buy—a suit of clothes?"

"Okay," she said, pushing herself from the sewing machine and leading me to their costume wagon.

I opened the door for her and she climbed the two steps into the coach. I could see two walls lined with togas, military uniforms, gowns, knee-britches, and suits. Lissa headed to the back corner of the rig and spent a couple minutes pulling a shirt, trousers and jacket from the racks. She tossed the costumes to me. "You'll have to provide your own underwear, Henry."

I caught the clothes, took the shirt and held it up, figuring it and the jacket would fit, though I wasn't certain about the pants as they looked a little big. "What about some suspenders, a vest and a derby? I should appear cultured, so you might add a gold watch chain."

"Don't have a watch," she replied.

"Neither do I, but a chain will do," I responded. "Also, I want a carpetbag."

"Pray tell, what for, Henry?"

"In case I have to leave town fast after I meet Oscar Wilde."

Shaking her head, she retreated into the enclosure, coming back with everything I sought.

"What about a cane? That would be a nice touch, something a gentleman would carry and something I could beat the hell out of him with if he didn't reimburse you for your trouble."

"Henry," Lissa cried, stomping her foot on the wagon's plank floor, "don't use such language where the children can overhear it. Further, don't go beating folks up on our account. We'll make do. It's in the Lomax family nature."

I bowed to my sister. "I am your obedient servant."

"You're dragging the pants on the ground," Lissa chided.

Straightening up, I nodded. "You'll forgive me tomorrow, Lissa."

"Not if we have to get you out of jail because we can't afford your bail, Henry."

"That's okay. I won't need bond money, as I tend to

break out of jail on my own."

Lissa brought to the rear of the wagon a watch chain, carpetbag and cane, which she waved my direction. "Don't make me use this on you, Henry."

"If you do, big sister, I'm not bailing you out of jail, I guarantee you that."

"One more thing, Henry," she said as she retreated in the wagon and returned with a pair of shiny black patent leather shoes. "You'll need these rather than your boots. These may be a little big but, that's better than them being too small." She stacked the latest addition to my costume in my arms.

I toted the items to my bedding beneath another rig and laid them on the blankets where I slept. My odd journey caught everyone's attention, but nobody inquired, as I figured they feared being dragged into my diabolical scheme, whatever it was.

That evening after supper, when the skies darkened, I pulled my razor and bar of soap from my saddlebags and went to the river to bathe, shave and wash my hair in the cold waters. Come Sunday I would need to look the part. I slept well that night and sat in on the regular devotional the Cokers and the Stillmans held each Sabbath. Over the year's I'd prayed when I got in trouble, but seldom to prevent difficulties. On this morning, I asked for patience so I wouldn't harm Oscar Wilde, even if he needed a sound thrashing with my cane. In fact, such a whipping might improve his looks.

After the final amen, I excused myself and went to my bedding. "Look the other way," I told everyone, "as I'll be changing clothes." As actors, they had seen enough costume changes that my brief moments of indecency were routine in their world. I swapped attire, putting on my spare underwear and socks from my saddlebags, then donning my shirt, pants, vest and coat. Finally, I slipped into the patent leather shoes. Never had I worn such shiny footwear in my life. They were a little big, so I stuffed my dirty socks in the toe of the shoes and that made them a better fit, easier to walk in. After that, I packed my hat, my regular outfit and my remaining cash in my carpetbag along with my holster and revolver, as well as a box of ammunition I brought from Buffalo Gap. Everything fit except my boots. To top things off, I grabbed the derby, placed it over my head at a roguish tilt, and took the cane.

"Now you can look," I announced as I walked among the troupe, twirling my cane until it slipped from my grasp and bounced on the ground.

"Very stylish," Aaron snickered.

"Cultured," Abigail added.

"Refined," Silas noted.

Lissa hesitated before speaking. "Henry, what the hell are you up to?"

"MOM!" shouted her offspring in unison.

Their mother sighed. "I'm sorry, children, but I'm worried what kind of fix he'll get himself in, maybe us, too."

"But, Mom," her oldest son John said in my defense, "he's always gotten out of whatever mess he's created, whether with Custer or Billy the Kid or—"

"Or Jesse James," added Van.

"Even Wild Bill Hickok or Calamity Jane," Banner contributed.

Little Harriet eased my way, picking up the walking stick and handing it to me. Then she sidled up beside me and hugged my leg. "I like your stories, Uncle Henry."

"Thank you, Harriet, and I love you, too." I looked around at everyone else. "I won't do anything to embarrass you, I promise." It was a vow I hoped I could keep. I touched the brim of my hat with the crook of my cane, picked up my valise, and offered my farewell. "I've business to attend. Not sure when I'll be back, but I will return the costume and carpetbag. Watch after my things." With that, I headed for town. I covered twelve blocks, reaching the square where the Tabernacle stood and the Mormon Cathedral towered over everything else. Never had I seen such structures devoted to the worship of God, and it left me thinking of my many shortcomings and failures. I wondered if I was about to fail again with Oscar Wilde and his associates before I righted the wrong they had done to my theatrical family.

I turned on Main Street, looking for the Walker House, and found it between Second and Third South streets. Compared to the cathedral, it was a hovel, but otherwise as nice as any hotel I had ever visited. Opening the brass door, I walked inside on a granite floor that reflected the gaslight from the fixtures around the lobby. Plush chairs and sofas, several filled with couples or families in their Sunday best, dotted the foyer. Marching up to the mahogany registration desk, I acknowledged a clerk wearing a white shirt, black vest, and black bowtie.

"May I help you?"

I reached for the gold chain in my vest and pulled it out like I was checking the time, though I had no watch. After inserting the empty chain back into my vest pocket, I responded. "Right on time, I am. I'm here to check on Mister Wilde's room and arrangements."

"Mister Locke left no such instructions, and I can assure you the suite is in perfect order, only awaiting our distinguished guest."

Shaking my head, I smiled at the young man, who straightened his bowtie beneath my gaze. "I am not surprised as Mister Charles E. Locke is a busy man with multiple responsibilities as you would expect of a San Francisco theater impresario. That's why he hires me to follow up on the details. All I need is a key to the suite so I can do my job."

"I'm afraid I can't give you a key without authorization."

"Let me speak to the manager," I demanded, dropping my carpetbag on the floor and slamming my fist against the counter.

"He's not back from church."

"If Mister Wilde finds anything amiss in his room, he might cancel his talk tomorrow and leave tonight. Do you want that on your conscience, that you deprived the fine folks of Salt Lake City the chance to hear his lecture on the decorative arts?"

Bewildered and indecisive, the wide-eyed clerk shook his head.

I pounded my fist on the shiny wood again and screamed. "I demand satisfaction—"

"But, sir, I can't give you a key, and you're causing a disturbance," he said in a low voice as he gazed at guests staring at him.

Leaning across the counter, I whispered, "Give me a key or I'll demand that satisfaction be accorded me for all the rats in my room."

"But, sir, there aren't rats. Besides, you don't have a room."

I swept my hand toward the hotel guest. "They don't know that."

The clerk's eyes widened further. "But, sir, that would damage the fine reputation of Walker House."

"If Oscar Wilde cancels his lecture, that will harm your reputation as well. Believe me, I'll spread word that a certain Walker House clerk was responsible for his cancellation. What do you think the hotel's reputation will be if that word gets around?"

With a quivering lip, the young man twisted his head from side to side, uncertain what to do.

"Perhaps your stubbornness is why the father of our country never slept here."

He blinked his perplexed eyes. "George Washington never slept here?"

"And neither will Oscar Wilde if this isn't resolved immediately," I said, bending to pick up my carpetbag. "If you don't give me a key, I'm walking out and looking for another place for this great man to stay."

The clerk hesitated.

I turned to leave, everyone staring at me.

"Just a moment," he said meekly before retreating to a wall of pigeonholes where he pulled a key from a mail slot.

"It's suite number one on the top floor," he said.

"Thank you," I called loud enough for everyone to hear, "for your fine consideration and forgive my momentary lapse of manners. I am completely satisfied with the resolution of this issue." I turned and walked up the stairs, leaving behind a relieved clerk.

I ascended the stairs, plenty pleased that I had

talked my way into Oscar Wilde's suite. After the final flight of stairs, I turned down a red carpeted hall, seeing a room with a brass number one on the door. I inserted the key and unlocked the door, pushing it open and entering a hotel chamber unlike any I had entered before. I stood in a small sitting room with a three padded chairs, a small writing desk and a door opening into a parlor with two sofas between end tables and four padded chairs. Beyond them was a dining table suitable for six. To one side were two more doors, one leading into a large bedroom and the second into a water closet. On the opposite side were two more doors, each opening into smaller sleeping quarters. Apparently, lecturing paid better than acting.

I retreated to the entry and locked up, backtracking to the parlor, where I dropped my valise on the sofa and sat down beside it to wait. About forty-five minutes later, I heard a hurried key in the lock and saw the door swing open.

In marched a man who strode furiously toward me. "Who are you?" he demanded.

"H.H. Lomax."

"Get out," he ordered.

"Certainly," I replied, turning to grab my carpetbag, quickly unlatching it, yanking my pistol free and aiming it at the fellow's head. I didn't recognize him, but he wasn't Oscar Wilde because he wasn't nearly as ugly as the picture I'd seen. "Now who are you?"

"I'm Charlie Locke."

"You're not who I'm looking for, but you'll do," I said.

CHAPTER TWELVE

Scowling as his shifty eyes studied me, Charles E. Locke of San Francisco raised his arms. "I don't carry a gun or cash on me, so I'm no threat and no candidate for a robbery."

"You're the robber, not me," I replied, motioning for him to step to the corner while I moved to the ante-room and shut the door.

"I never robbed anybody in my life. I've given folks quality entertainment for a fair price."

"You as good as robbed my kin, booking Oscar Wilde in the theater they reserved weeks ago."

Locke cocked his head and lowered his arms, crossing them over his chest. "That's between your folks and the owners. They negated the contract, not me."

"But you and Oscar Wilde are the cause. It's cost the Lomax and Coker Theatrical Troupe close to a thousand dollars as a result," I said, exaggerating the loss to give me some horse-trading flexibility. "But I'm willing to negotiate."

"I'm not!" His eyes narrowed as he shook his head. "Oscar Wilde has already cost me thousands, not living up to our agreement. Thousands of dollars I paid him for twenty lectures in California. He delivered ten. He's cost me more cash than he did your ensemble. Once I get the return on my investment, I'm done with that vapid weasel."

I gathered Locke despised the esteemed Mister Wilde, so I lowered my gun.

"One more thing," Locke continued, "I can fix it so the Lomax and Coker troupe never plays another venue west of the Mississippi. So you best be careful with your threats, as I have more clout than you realize."

Though I wanted my kin reimbursed, I worried about damaging their future ability to play theaters in Utah and elsewhere they might travel. I turned about and put the revolver back in its holster and snapped the carpetbag shut. "What do you suggest, then?" I asked as I collapsed on the sofa.

Locke strode across the room and extended his arm. "I didn't catch your name."

Standing up, I shook his hand, and slipped back on the divan. "I'm H.H. Lomax, Henry Harrison Lomax, to be formal, but most people call me Lomax."

"Where you from, Lomax?"

"Everywhere mostly, though from Cane Hill, Arkansas, originally."

"You any kin to Lissa Lomax, the Arkansas Songbird?"

"I'm her younger brother."

"Wonderful voice, your sister has, and an excellent reputation with her acting company," Locke said, then settled into a chair opposite me. "Now, Lomax, as to your question, I'm fine with anything you can skin off of Oscar. After expenses, he gets half of all the earnings from the lectures. On top of that, he charges anywhere from fifty to five hundred dollars for showing up at a gathering or meeting with people outside the theater, and that money is all his. Fact is, I think he's scheduled —for a fee—to meet with the president of the Mormons tomorrow before his evening lecture. John Taylor is his name, I believe."

"You don't care for Wilde?"

"Can't stand him! The best I can tell, all he's done is written a few mediocre poems and ingratiated himself with English royalty, who are amused by his incomprehensible theories of art and beauty, so much so that Gilbert and Sullivan wrote a comic operetta parodying him as the fool he is."

"*Patience*, isn't it?"

Locke stared at me. "You surprise me with your knowledge of the theater, Lomax. You don't look that cultured."

Figuring to impress him even more with my intelligence, I said, "I believe he is represented in the play as Bunthorne."

"That's right, Lomax, but I call him butt-thorn because he's a pain in the ass." Locke shook his head, "But I have to admit he draws a crowd, though I can't understand why. I've heard him lecture a half dozen times, and I never carry away from his talks anything I didn't already have when I entered the theater. The more you can squeeze from him, the better, as far as I am concerned, just as long as it doesn't cut into my share."

"I'm obliged," I responded, "and I'd be further

obliged if you informed the hotel desk that I belong to your advance party since I bluffed my way in."

"I'll let them know. Now there are some things you should understand before he arrives." Locke pulled his watch from his vest, popped the cover and checked the time, then returned the timepiece to his pocket. "His train arrives in ninety minutes, but it'll be an hour later before he reaches his suite. He insists that his valet, a Negro named William Traquair, precede him to prepare the room for his holy presence. Besides Willie, his road manager J.S. Vale will accompany his holiness."

Locke told me about Wilde's peculiarities, which were more than I could remember, and his expectations, including that a fine meal be awaiting him in his suite. After he dined, he received screened visitors desiring to meet him, provided Traquair approved. Further, Wilde always made time to answer questions from newspapermen seeking an audience.

"Now, Lomax, how do you intend to convince his foolishness to repay you a thousand dollars?"

"Sweet talk him, play on his conscience."

"He has no scruples other than for himself."

"Then I'll pull my gun and rob him."

"That'll never work, not dressed like you are, way too cosmopolitan. That's not your normal outfit, is it?"

"It's a costume from my sister's stage costumes."

"Let me suggest you leave and change into your regular clothes. Wilde's enamored with roughhewn, robust western characters, not men in suits and derbies. He's always talking about finding his 'True American,' a man entirely the product of the American condition and landscape."

Patting the valise, I responded, "My regular clothes are in the carpetbag."

"Change once I leave and be sure to put on your holster so he can easily see your revolver. It certainly got my attention."

I chuckled as Locke arose. "I'll meet him at the depot after I let the desk know you are with me, so the hotel shouldn't bother you anymore. Also, I'll advise Willie you'll be here and are to stay until Wilde arrives."

"What about Vale and Wilde? You telling them?"

"Gracious, no! I want to watch their faces when you settle scores with Oscar."

Standing up, I shook Locke's hand and thanked him for the information. I escorted him through the ante-room and out the door, then locked the suite. Returning to the parlor, I swapped the costume for my regular attire, which hung more comfortably on my body than the stage clothes. I pulled out my crushed felt hat and worked the wrinkles out as best I could, then reached for my boots before I remembering I lacked the space to pack them. For a moment, I considered running out to buy a pair, but realized it was Sunday and the stores were closed in Salt Lake City. I decided not to head back to camp to fetch them because I didn't want to risk any problems with the hotel staff when I returned or not being in the room when Wilde arrived. So, I could either wait in socked feet or put on the black patent leather shoes again. I opted for the shiny footwear, doubting anyone would notice.

I stepped to the window overlooking Main Street. Church must have just let out as the avenue teemed with families in their Sunday best, strolling along the walk or riding in buggies. After the church crowd thinned, I heard a distant train whistle and suspected Mister Oscar Wilde himself was shortly arriving in Salt Lake City. I wondered who would be the most surprised, him when I pulled a gun or me when I first glimpsed his homely countenance.

A half hour later, as I watched the street, I saw a wagon loaded with luggage pull up in front of the Walker House, the driver and a black man jumping from the rig. I assumed the Negro was the valet Willie Traquair, as he disappeared into the hotel and returned with four staff to unload the baggage. As I studied them, they piled two enormous trunks, six portmanteaus, a hatbox, three carpetbags, and a dressing case on the walk. I observed the valet pay the driver, who jumped back in the wagon box and departed. As Traquair directed the porters on handling the luggage, I took a seat on the sofa and waited.

Shortly, I heard a noise in the hallway and a key rattling in the lock. When the entry swung open, the valet entered, offering me a broad smile with the whitest teeth I had ever seen. "You must be Lomax," he said. "I'm William M. Traquair."

I stood up and stepped to him, grabbing his hand and shaking it warmly as he inspected me from top to bottom.

"Pleasure to meet you," I told him.

His gaze stopped at my feet. "Nice shoes, Lomax. Master Wilde will appreciate them, him being a devotee of art and beauty. I prefer the practical, a good old pair of work boots or brogans." Traquair directed the hotel staff where to deposit the luggage, all of it going to the large bedroom, save for a single carpetbag in each of the other two sleeping rooms. As the porters finished their work, Traquair pulled out a change purse and tipped his helpers a quarter each. "Remember to bring up his meal within thirty minutes. It must be here before Master Wilde arrives. Otherwise, he will pout."

As soon as the door shut, the valet turned back to me. "Mister Locke indicated your intentions." He hesitated.

"And?"

"I endorse them. He is a hard one to work for, insisting I say 'Massa Wilde' rather than 'Master Wilde,' as massa rolls more melodiously off the tongue. I'm educated with some university work to my credit."

"Why's an educated man like you working as a servant?"

"It was a chance to get paid while seeing the country."

"What about you?"

"I've seen more of the country than I have of the classroom."

Traquair smiled. "It doesn't matter where you get your education, Lomax, as long as you keep learning. I'd like to visit, but I must prepare the suite for Master Wilde."

"One more question. Should I call you William or Willie or Master or Massa?"

He grinned again. "My friends call me Willie. You can, too." With that, he spun about and hurried into Wilde's bedroom, quickly turning the two trunks on end at the foot of the bed. Next, he unlatched and opened the twin wings of the cases, each with sliding drawers filled with clothes. From the large drawer at the bottom, he extracted the hide of a tiger and another of what I took to be a gray wolf. He strode past me to the sofa and spread the gray pelt on one end and the tiger coat on the other. Traquair returned moments later with a gold silk handkerchief, which he placed on the armrest. The valet glanced at me, smiled, and offered an explanation. "It's where he rests his delicate head."

As Willie scurried about, I moved behind the dining table to the window and watched the street where a crowd, mostly women, stood facing the hotel and waiting for Wilde's arrival. The servant worked quickly, moving a small writing table from the wall by the entrance to the end of the sofa, where he placed a stack of writing paper, a pen, and inkwell. "That's in case Massa is inspired to write," Willie informed me. Beside the writing materials, he set a gold cigarette case and a sister container of matches. He moved an ashtray to the small table as someone knocked.

The valet bounded across the room and admitted two white-jacketed hotel staff, who pushed twin carts covered with dishes to the dining table, where they spread the food out for the esteemed visitor. I licked my lips as the attendants uncovered baked trout, braised quail breasts, grilled steaks, omelets, green beans, baked potatoes, salad, a basket of rolls, and a tray of sweets. They also left a bottle of champagne. "Will there be anything else?" one asked Traquair, who inspected the layout.

"That will be all, provided he arrives on time. He turns prissy when the food is cold."

As the two attendants exited, I heard cheering on the street and looked out the window to see a buggy expel its occupants. I recognized Locke and figured the second to be Vale, the road manager. The third fellow, the tallest of the trio, was surely Wilde by his eccentric dress topped by a broad-brimmed hat that would've looked better on an ugly woman or a dead mule.

"Massa wears a long green overcoat with a gray fur collar," Willie said.

The guy in the wide hat wore a green overcoat.

Traquair scurried about, attending to the final details. He twisted the top of a bottle of perfume and flung drops across the suite. Soon the place reeked with the sick flower smell of a funeral parlor.

"Question for you, Willie. How do you think I should approach Massa about repaying my drama troupe's lost money? Should I reason with him or meet him with my gun drawn?"

Traquair twisted the lid back on the perfume, returned the container to the bedroom, where he stood in front of a mirror and checked that his coat and tie were straight. Emerging, he grinned. "I like the idea of you standing there, gun drawn. He's big into dramatics, and I'd love to see the look on his face when he knows he's about to die. I'll announce that he has a visitor, but he'll be angry because he doesn't accept guests until after he completes his meal. Once he's eaten, I admit newspapermen or visitors with proper calling cards, so he can put on his parlor show for them."

"Gun drawn it is, Willie."

"I'll close the parlor door and greet him in the ante-room. I intend to lead him in here, so I can watch his expression." Traquair disappeared as he shut the door behind him. I moved beside the sofa and thought about sitting down, but decided against it as I preferred not to disturb Willie's careful setup of the tiger and wolf hides.

The next few minutes dragged by slowly until I heard Traquair welcome his boss. I pulled my revolver from the holster and waited.

"Welcome to Salt Lake City, Massa Wilde. I have prepared your room to your liking, and your dinner is ready," he said as he opened my door. "And, a guest awaits you, Massa Wilde."

The lecturer grumbled as he entered. "You know how much I despise visitors before I dine," he chided.

Traquair moved to the side, and Wilde stepped past him, halting the moment he saw the gun aimed at his chest. I studied him as he looked me over.

Wilde stood tall, six-feet and two inches tall by my estimation, looking even taller because of the crown of his floppy hat. His tawny hair hung down to his shoulders, framing an elongated face that would clabber fresh milk. Wilde's deep-set blue-gray eyes looked down at me over an angular nose that pointed to lady-like lips parted just enough for me to see a pair yellow-stained, protruding choppers that were the worst teeth I'd seen since Mandy Mae Minter in Buffalo Gap. His flamboyant attire muted his homeliness as he wore a red bow tie big enough to top a funeral wreath, a brown shirt, light green corduroy knee britches, brown stockings, and black patent leather shoes that made me ashamed of my footwear. Butt-thorn stood in front of me, his right hand flying to his lips.

"You owe my sister a thousand dollars," I announced. Behind him I saw Vale reach inside his coat —for a gun, I feared—but Locke grabbed his wrist and yanked it away.

"Oh, gracious me," Wilde said. "I can't believe this is happening."

"Your lecture bumped my sister's theatrical troupe out of the theater they had reserved for weeks," I explained.

"It's really him," Wilde cried, dropping his hand and stepping fearlessly toward me.

Uncertain of his motive, I cocked the pistol's hammer, but that didn't slow him. He stepped to me, shoved my gun aside with his left hand and reached with his right to lift my chin. He moved my jaw first to one side, then to the other, next retreating a step and clapping his hands softly like a little girl. Bewildered, I released the hammer of my revolver and stuck the weapon back in the holster.

"The money," I said. "Pay up."

Wilde lifted his right index finger to his pursed lips for me to remain silent before inspecting me from my hat to my feet. "It's providential," he announced. "I have found him in Salt Lake City, no less."

"Who, Massa Wilde?"

"The True American! I have been seeking him ever since I landed in North America, a man shaped by the continent, a roughhewn frontiersman who's carved civilization out of a wilderness without the thought of art, and yet is a man who appreciates beauty as reflected by his patent leather shoes, which he prefers for their artistry rather than their practicality on the trail." He grabbed my empty gun hand and shook it. By the softness of his fingers and palm, I determined he had never worked hard in his life. It seemed the only thing that was hardened was his mind, which was callused with nonsense.

"What's your name, sir?"

"H.H. Lomax," I answered. "Now, about that thousand dollars."

He touched his finger to my lips. "Such a strong, powerful, alliterative name, H-H. It reminds me of H-R-H, his royal highness. You, sir, are but one letter—the letter R—away from royalty."

And he was about one drip away from insanity, I thought. I looked behind him at Traquair, who raised his arms palms up to show he was as bewildered as me.

"Where are you from, H.H.?"

"Arkansas, originally."

"Ah, Arkansas," Wilde mused, removing his hat and flinging it on the tiger end of the sofa, "the Athens of the Western Hemisphere, the intellectual, and cultural center of the North American Continent."

Behind him, Vale and Locke snickered, lifting their fists to their mouths to stifle their chuckles.

"Now about the money?"

Wilde waved his finger at me, "Tsk, tsk, tsk. Your patience and your silence are what I desire." He grabbed my shoulders and stood at arm's length, studying me like he would the menu in a fancy restaurant. "This is indeed a providential day, me finding the True American. I have heard that Mark Twain claimed to be the True American, but he is a humorist. You, H.H. Lomax, are a realist, the genuine True American."

"Is it worth a thousand dollars?" I asked.

He shook my shoulders. "With your every word, you prove you are the True American, always looking to the West, an American metaphor for riches and wealth, the desire of all but the destination of few. And you, H.H., are on that journey to prosperity, a man with beauty in his soul, art in his dreams and patent leather shoes on his feet. You are a patron of beauty, H.H., and everyone else is a mere philistine."

I had no idea who Phyllis Steen was, but by that point I was befuddled whether Wilde was serious or merely mocking me for his own entertainment, like a kitten playing with a wounded mouse before the kill. Maybe I should have shot the lecturer and been done with the negotiations, sacrificing Lissa's reimbursement for my own sanity. As I'd gotten away with robbing a bank—up to then at least—perhaps I could manage the same for murder if I plugged him and put the country out of the misery of having to listen to the rest of his lecture tour. A single bullet didn't cost as much as a ticket to one of his talks, so I would save a lot of decent citizens, though not me, the True American, considerable money that could go to better uses, such as roulette wheels or political bribes.

Wilde finally lifted his arms from my shoulder and removed his coat, tossing it atop his hat on the sofa. With a sweep of his arm, he gestured toward the dining table. "Would you care to dine with me, H.H.? My preference is to dine alone so that everyone at the table recognizes my brilliance, but I can see by your footwear that you are a man of discernment, a man who appreciates art, even in a dreary country."

"Only if we talk about money," I replied.

"Of course, H.H.," he answered as he led me to the buffet. Once we moved away from the sofa, Traquair filled our wake, plucking Wilde's coat and hat and taking them into his bedroom to brush and hang.

At the end of the table, Wilde pulled out a chair and seated me before striding to the writing stand, picking up the cigarette case, extracting a rolled one, and lighting it from a match from the sister case. He exhaled deeply and blew out a ribbon of smoke between his effeminate lips as he marched to join me. It was the first of hundreds of cigarettes he smoked during our brief acquaintance.

Taking his place at the opposite end of the table from me as Traquair rushed from the bedroom and quickly placed the ashtray by his plate, Wilde grabbed a folded napkin, shook out its folds, and stuck it in his shirt collar to protect his big red bow of a tie. As he did, Vale and Locke stepped to a pair of parlor chairs and sat on the cushioned upholstery.

"Don't mind them," Wilde told me as he spewed smoke. "They handle my arrangements. Unfortunately, they lack our appreciation of true art and beauty. Look at their footwear if you don't believe me."

Locke actually raised both legs so I could see his dull, scuffed shoes above the sofa. Vale merely scowled.

Never having had a catered meal in a hotel room before, I remained uncertain about the appropriate manners, so I followed Wilde's lead, shaking my napkin and tucking it in my collar. At that moment, I made my first mistake, reaching for the basket of rolls.

"Tsk, tsk, tsk," Wilde said, waving his index finger at me as I yanked my arm back to my side. "William," he called, "I and my guest are ready to be served."

Traquair picked up a bone china plate. "What would Massa Wilde like?"

He pursed his lips and tapped his chin with his index finger, mulling over his choices. "Serve me the baked trout, the salad greens, an omelet, and a roll."

The valet dutifully dropped modest servings atop his plate and placed it before him, leaving me to wonder if Traquair was going to cut and chew his food for him as well.

"Now please assist my guest, William."

"Yes, sir, Massa Wilde," Traquair said, turning to me and rolling his eyes.

"What would you prefer, Mister Lomax?"

"One of everything," I replied, drawing a guffaw from Wilde.

"Delightful, H.H. I adore your American sense of humor. It is good for the soul."

Realizing Wilde thought I was joking, I reduced my request. "I've had an omelet before, but you don't happen to have a hamlet, do you? I've heard good things about it in theater circles."

Wilde roared. "That's a witty one, too. I should introduce you to the queen. She has a literary sense of humor as well."

Perplexed by his reactions, I changed my dinner order to things I knew. "I'll take the steak, braised quail, a baked potato, green beans, and a roll."

The valet served me with bigger portions than he gave my long-haired host. After sliding my plate in front of me, Willie stepped aside, and Wilde picked up his fork and toyed delicately with his food, which he chomped with an open mouth and his protruding teeth. Watching him eat reminded me of a sausage grinder.

"Now about what you owe my sister," I said, trying to focus him on my problem.

"When I was young," Wilde answered, "I thought that money was the most important thing in life. Now that I'm old, I know it is indeed just that."

I was relieved he realized my concern, but to be conversational, I asked, "How old are you now?"

"Twenty-six in years," he replied as he churned his bite of trout, "but a hundred in wisdom and brilliance."

"Your appearance in the Salt Lake Theater bumped my sister's theatrical group from the stage for more than a week, though they had a signed contract. We estimate it has cost the Lomax and Coker Theatrical Troupe a thousand dollars or more."

Road manager Vale bounced up from his seat. "Mister Wilde, a provision in the theater's contract allowed management to postpone that arrangement in the case of a national touring company or lecturer. You, Mister Wilde, are of national significance."

Wilde harrumphed. "World significance," he corrected.

Locke grabbed Vale's arm and tugged him to sit down, which he did.

"Now," I continued, "in consideration of your worldly importance, I am prepared to reduce our claim by half and will settle for a payment of five hundred dollars."

Vale coughed, but Locke swatted his arm and motioned for him to stay silent.

Wilde pondered my proposal.

"There's four adults and eight children, ages four to fourteen, in the troupe, spreading art, beauty, and morality to the fine folks of Utah Territory."

"Morality," responded Wilde, "is simply the attitude we adopt toward people whom we dislike."

"You would value my folks for elevating art and beauty on stage."

"Five hundred dollars, is it?"

When I nodded, Wilde snapped his finger at his managers. "Arrange it," he commanded, turning to me, "on one condition. H.H. is to accompany me the rest of my tour."

Me, Vale, and Locke shared bewildered looks. Traquair snickered.

"And it's not to come out of my share," Wilde announced.

"Nor mine," Locke insisted.

Everyone stared at Vale. "Mine neither."

Wilde yanked his napkin from his collar and flung it across the table toward me. "The lecture tour is over," he announced as he stood up from his chair. "Cancel tomorrow night and get me back to New York immediately, so I can return to England, even if I have to swim."

"Now, now, Oscar," cried Vale. "Don't be rash. Give us time to consider our options."

"I can be petulant when I am denied my way," Wilde reminded them.

"We know," Locke said. "Give us a few minutes to discuss, Mister Wilde. Perhaps you can change into more comfortable clothes. I told the desk to keep callers away for ninety minutes, so you would be rested before seeing visitors."

The petulant poet strode around the table, stopping beside me and patting my shoulder. "We'll work this out, H.H., or my tour ends today." He marched into his bedroom with Traquair following and shutting the door.

Once Wilde disappeared, Vale and Locke jumped up from their seats and dashed to the table, grabbing and filling plates with food, then sat down, one on either side of me.

"We've got a problem," Vale said, "unless we figure how to charge this to expenses."

"I'll consider accompanying him," I announced, "but only if I get the money in advance so my kinfolk aren't left stranded and broke."

They gobbled down their food, discussing options with mouths full of delicacies, nothing productive coming out of it other than my opinion that it was less disgusting watching them eat than Wilde.

"Perhaps I could shoot him," I offered. "That would solve a lot of our problems."

Locke gulped down a big bite, almost choking when he swallowed. "That's it."

"Shoot him?" Vale cried. "Don't you think that's extreme?"

"No," Locke responded, then looked at me. "You can handle a gun. At least you know how to point it at folks, right, Lomax?"

"I can pull a trigger and hit a target, if that's what you mean."

Locke nodded, glancing to Vale. "We've had threats against Mister Wilde since we left California. Perhaps we could hire Lomax as his bodyguard. We could charge that to expenses. Though it would cost us a little, it would cost him as well."

Both turned to me. "What do you think, Lomax? Are you agreeable?"

"As long as I have the money in cash before we leave town."

"Today's Sunday. It'll be tomorrow, but we'll get you the money."

"Cash," I reminded them.

"It'll be cash," Locke said.

"And time for me to deliver the money myself to the family."

Locke cocked his head. "On two conditions, Lomax."

"You keep wearing the patent leather shoes, as he seems smitten with them."

I nodded. "And?"

"You get from your theatrical folks a long-haired wig as close to the color of Oscar's locks as you can and bring it with you."

"Sure," I replied, thinking the request silly and not realizing it would put my life in danger.

CHAPTER THIRTEEN

When Oscar Wilde emerged from his room, he was sucking a cigarette and calmly blowing puffs of smoke at the ceiling. He stood in the parlor with his balled fists on his hips. "Well," he said, "am I still lecturing or am I swimming back to England?"

Vale spoke first. "You'll be pleased with our arrangement, Oscar. We plan to hire Lomax as your bodyguard to accompany you for the rest of the tour."

Wilde jumped and clapped his hands like a little girl. "Goody, goody," he cried, yanking the cigarette from his mouth, barreling toward me, throwing his arms around me in a tight hug and kissing me on the cheek. I twisted from him and saw Traquair giggling at my predicament.

I could've sworn I felt his wet tongue against my flesh, but without a doubt I smelled his rancid breath. It was enough to make a maggot puke. I wrestled free of his grip and wondered what I had gotten myself into while trying to help my sister.

"I'll be paid in advance," I reminded them.

"Soon as the banks open in the morning," Locke said.

"Until I get my money, I'm staying with my sister's troupe."

"Oh," said Wilde, "and I'll want H.H. to accompany me on the town tour by the head apostle of Mormonism, John Taylor. Isn't that his name?"

"I'll arrange it," Vale said. "And yes, John Taylor is his name."

"Splendid," Wilde announced. "Let's celebrate with champagne." He walked over to the table, picked up the green bottle and cried, "William!" He slammed the flask against the table.

When the valet came to his side, he pointed at the drink. "Is this the best you can acquire?"

"Yes, Massa Wilde. This is Utah Territory, Mormon country, where the church frowns on liquid spirits. Their champagne choices were narrow. This was the best the hotel could offer."

"Oh, the travails I go through to spread the gospel of aestheticism to the unwashed and unsophisticated of this new world."

"Massa Wilde, you have fifteen minutes before callers arrive. Don't tax your nerves as a newspaperman will be among them. You must charm them to boost tomorrow's attendance."

Wilde jammed his cigarette back in his mouth and retreated to the bedroom. "I'll change into something they will talk about." He disappeared through the haze of smoke he exhaled on the way to swap outfits.

Vale and Locke grinned at Traquair. "We'll leave you to tend to Massa," said Vale.

"I'm sick of hearing his interviews," Locke noted. Both men grabbed their hats and departed through the anteroom, leaving me and Traquair alone.

"Welcome to the freak show," the valet said, disappearing into Wilde's bedroom to prepare him for his adoring public.

When Wilde emerged, he carried a small, thin book and wore a petite red turban with a black tassel, frilly white shirt, red smoking jacket, black trousers, red stockings, and black patent leather shoes. He reclined upon the sofa, his head on the gold kerchief on the armrest, his body on the tiger and wolf hides. The lecturer opened the volume and began reading.

"Are you settled, Massa Wilde?"

"Yes, William."

Traquair turned to me. "Massa Wilde sees callers for an hour. I might suggest you stay by the window, arms across your chest to let people know you will broach no foolishness and that you stand ready—" he winked, "—to give your life in defense of this young literary genius, who has blessed all thirty-eight of these United States of America with his presence the last four months."

Wilde smiled at his valet's words, as if they were holy and truthful.

As I took my position, I heard soft chatter from the hall. William headed for the anteroom, closing the parlor door behind him.

"Is your traveling party always you and three others?" I asked.

"Sometimes more, like now with you as my fourth," he answered.

"That's a lot of folks."

"Nothing compared to the Prince of Wales."

"Whales? I didn't know fish had kings and princes."

"Whales are mammals, not fish, and it's Wales, spelled W-A-L-E-S. The Prince of Wales is Britain's king in waiting, Bertie to his friends. He travels with a personal valet; two equerries or stablemen, each with his own valet; a sergeant footman and two other footmen; two loaders when he goes shooting; a brusher; a telegrapher or telephonist; various gentlemen-in-waiting; a chef; and even an Arabian youth who makes his special blend of Turkish coffee." He chuckled, "And, of course, various female consorts for his bedtime entertainment. You do believe in bedtime entertainment, do you not, H.H.?"

I nodded. "When the occasion and price are right. It beats going to the circus."

"The prince gets it free, as do men of renown, such as myself."

"I've always had to pay to attend the circus."

Wilde winked at me, then resumed his reading, mouthing the words and smiling to himself at his cleverness.

The noise picked up in the anteroom until I heard Traquair call for quiet, saying the visitors should speak softly so as not to disturb the genius in the next room, as he was resting after a long and tiring trip from Sacramento to Salt Lake City. Moments later, a tapping on the door was followed by the formal voice of the valet.

"Massa Wilde," he announced, "I am pleased to present Mister and Mrs. Victor Kline of Salt Lake City."

"Enter," Wilde responded, exhaling a puff of smoke from his dwindling cigarette.

The servant led the couple into the parlor, the frowning husband holding his hat by the brim and the grinning wife carrying a bouquet of sunflowers. As they stepped to his sofa, Wilde closed the book and removed the butt from his lips, holding it over the side of the sofa as Traquair picked up the ashtray from the dining table and presented it to the reclining poet to extinguish his smoke. Wilde crushed his cigarette in the receptacle, clasped the book in both hands and pressed it against his chest as the valet placed the container on the writing table.

"Oh, Mister Wilde," gushed the woman. "I am so honored to meet you. Please accept this humble bouquet as a gesture of our admiration for your devotion to beauty."

Never arising from the sofa, Wilde motioned for her to present the flowers to Traquair, who carried them around the divan and placed them on the dining table amid the dirty dishes.

"Honored, I am indeed by your token of kindness, though I beg your indulgence as my journey here was so tiring that I lack the strength to arise and greet you formally. I should save my energy for my lecture."

The woman nodded vigorously. "We understand," she replied, then elbowed her husband in the ribs. "Don't we, Victor?"

"Yes, dear," he replied. "Whatever you say, dear."

"You are so kind, both of you," Wilde said, in a voice so low it was almost a whisper. "Might I ask a favor?"

"Yes, indeed," responded the wife.

"Would you step this way and offer me your hand? Please, tell me your name."

"Beulah," she shot back.

"Such an enchanting appellation, Beulah. It is most poetic in cadence as it tumbles from the tongue," he continued. "Beulah, would you extend me your hand?"

She eased toward him, her fingers outstretched. He lifted his right hand from the book and took hers, drawing it to his face, where he leaned forward and kissed her wrist. As Beulah tittered with joy, I wondered if he licked her like he had my cheek.

"Oh, thank you, Mister Wilde. I shall remember this moment forever," she gushed.

"Me, too," grumbled her husband.

Traquair stepped to the couple. "Massa Wilde has many other callers to greet, so let me escort you from his presence."

Beulah clasped her hands to her bosom. "Thank you for honoring us with an invitation into your parlor. Perhaps we could host you at our home during your visit. We are quite prosperous, as Victor is the most successful merchant in town and likely in all of Utah."

"That would be such an honor," Wilde replied. "My valet will advise you of my visitation fee on the way out."

Traquair escorted the couple to the parlor door, Victor passing through first as Beulah turned about, kissed the fingers of the hand he had smooched and flung him an imaginary kiss.

As soon as the door shut, Wilde twisted on the sofa, his poetry book falling to the floor, as he reached for the writing table. "I need another cigarette," he said, grabbing the gold case. "Care for one, H.H.?"

"Don't smoke."

He lit a cigarette between his lips, which immediately seeped a veil of smoke. "I prefer Turkish tobacco like the Prince of Wales," he announced as he posed on the couch, "but I can't find any out west so 'Old Judge' is the best I can do. Why don't you smoke?"

"Can't afford it."

Wilde scoffed. "A cigarette is the perfect pleasure. It's exquisite, but leaves one unsatisfied and desiring another. What more can one want?"

"Food or liquor! Besides, I'd rather save my money for circuses."

He smiled. "Perhaps we can create a circus of our own, H.H., you and me."

His comment perplexed me, as I had no interest in feeding elephants or taming lions, though I was curious about one thing. "When you greeted the couple, were you sincere, or was that an act?"

"My whole life is a performance, H.H. To begin with, I am an Irishman pretending to be an Englishman. Thanks to Gilbert and Sullivan's *Patience*, I am a poet imitating a fool. I give people the truth of what they imagine, not the truth of what is."

Wilde settled into the sofa, leaning his shoulder on the arm rest, half reclining as he retrieved from the floor his book of poems. Traquair William tapped on the door again and brought in three Mormon women in plain but immaculate dresses. After them I lost count, but by the time he quit accepting visitors an hour later, I suspect he had greeted close to fifty people, mostly females. In addition to that, he had signed four autograph books and a dozen of the photo cards with his portrait taken by the famous New York photographer Napoleon Sarony.

Traquair returned after escorting the last two

callers out the door and reported that a newspaperman from the *Salt Lake Herald* would call on him in thirty minutes for an interview. The servant moved to clean the dinner table.

"Narcissuses of imbecility, that's what newspapermen are," Wilde grumbled as he arose from the sofa. "They lack a sense of splendor, instead focusing on the money I make rather than the philosophy of art and beauty I impart."

"Then why grant them your precious time?" I asked.

"My fame and my wallet are more important than my opinion."

"So it's another performance?"

Wilde nodded and ordered Traquair to empty his ashtray. When the valet entered the water closet with the full ashtray, the poet looked at me. "What do you think of my slave? Everyone needs a slave, even in a free country."

"I thought that was what marriage was for," I responded, drawing a chuckle as the valet returned and placed the receptacle on the writing table.

Wilde lit the cigarette, blew out the match and flipped it in the clean ashtray. With every breath, the self-proclaimed genius polluted the air until the room reeked of burnt tobacco. He paced the room finishing that smoke, then another, until a knock sounded on the front door. "That must be him," Wilde said, crushing the cigarette in the holder and reclining on the sofa as he retrieved his book of poems and turned to the middle of the slim volume.

I retreated to my place by the window as Traquair

welcomed the newsman and escorted him into the parlor, introducing him as a distinguished representative of the *Salt Lake Herald*.

Wilde lifted his palm for silence as his eyes focused on his poetry. After ten seconds, he gently closed the book. "Great literature should not be interrupted," he said, "especially mine." Instead of remaining on the sofa, Wilde rose to his feet and strode across the room, shaking the fellow's hand and escorting him to a chair by the sofa. As the reporter settled into his seat, Wilde stood opposite him, preening so the visitor could note his dress and his looks for the newspaper account to follow. He eyed the apostle of the press, who penciled notes on a tablet. I wondered who was predator and who was prey in this encounter.

When he thought his visitor had captured the essence of his attire and his presence, Wilde began his performance. "I am honored to accept your call," he began. "Some of the brightest, most satisfying hours I have spent in this country since my arrival have been with the distinguished gentlemen of the press like yourself. Gentlemen with ink on their hands understand art and literature better than even the university faculty that I have met, so I welcome you and stand ready to answer your inquiries."

The reporter pointed his pencil at the window and me. "Who's he?"

"That is my *Praetorian* Guard. His name is H.H. Lomax, in my mind the True American, a man molded by the roughhewn west, though sensitive to the value of beauty such as his footwear, patent leather as I wear, the perfect cut of man to protect me from the threats

I've received since leaving California. Some people fear art and beauty and might harm me like they would snip a beautiful lily from the bush."

"How to you spell *Praetorian*?" the fellow asked.

Turning to me, Wilde rolled his eyes and spelled the word for him.

After the spelling lesson, the visitor inquired about Wilde's fascination with art and beauty.

"The essence of all art," Wilde replied, "is the combination of perfect freedom with perfect beauty. That is why I am associated with sunflowers and lilies." He pointed to the dining table where the sunflower bouquet remained from the afternoon's first visitors. "Sunflowers and lilies are England's two flowers most perfect in concept and design. The implements of our everyday life should equal the sunflower and lily in application so we can enjoy beauty in even the most mundane aspects of our day-to-day existence. We are better to have no art than bad art, as we can live without art but we cannot live with bad art. True art and beauty can elevate the life of man and woman, even in our industrial times. Life without industry is barbarism, and industry without art is barren."

I don't know if the newspaperman was as befuddled as I was, but he at least was able to ask another question. "Is that the essence of aestheticism?"

Wilde strode back and forth in front of the correspondent, stroking his chin as if he were contemplating before answering. "The aesthetic movement values literature, theater, music, and arts for more than their social use or their political function. Not only should art be produced for its own sake, but everyone should also appreciate it for that sake above all others, regardless of other uses."

The reporter scratched his head before turning aesthetic art against its proponent. "Then, sir," he asked, "is Gilbert and Sullivan's *Patience* art or bad art?"

Wilde glared at the newspaper man. "I saw the comic opera *Patience* while it played in London. I failed to see its point, sir, but thought it was a lovely opera with some charming music. As a satire on the philosophy of the beautiful, sir, I think it is the greatest twaddle."

The reporter grinned. "So, art is truly in the eye of the beholder?"

Wilde fumed that this ignorant, ink-stained newsman had outwitted him. I wanted to ask Wilde if he could spell beholder, but Traquair entered the room. "Massa Wilde, I must remind you of the evening appointment you should prepare for to keep your commitments."

"Goodness, yes," he said, running his fingers through his long hair, then turning to the newspaperman. "My servant will see you out." Wilde spun about and charged into the bedroom, closing the door behind him, leaving the journalist to scratch his own head.

Traquair approached the reporter, thanking him for his time and apologizing for the abrupt ending to the interview. "Master Wilde has a packed schedule. I hope you understand." The valet escorted the visitor out.

When he returned to the parlor, Traquair smiled. "He nailed Massa's hide to the wall."

I nodded.

"My favorite interview came from a writer who dubbed him 'Lord La-de-dah.' It fits."

"Nothing made sense to me. He doesn't have a dinner appointment, does he?"

"No, sir. He instructs me to interrupt all journalist interviews after twenty minutes, or if he gets in trouble. Seems the *Salt Lake Herald* tied him in knots today. I haven't seen him this mad in weeks, so I'm glad you'll be here this evening for company, Lomax."

"Hate to disappoint you, Willie, but I'm not staying with him until I'm paid." I waved my hand at the murky atmosphere. "Besides, I need some fresh air. You can tell the money men in the morning that I'm camped with the Lomax and Coker Theatrical Troupe near the iron bridge over the River Jordan. They'll see the theater wagons. If they don't have the money—all of it—the deal's off and Massa Wilde can fend for himself."

"It's gotta work, Lomax. It'd be nice to have someone sane around me for a spell."

I shook his hand and gave him a hug, though I didn't kiss him on the cheek, as was Wilde's custom. Traquair helped me gather my carpetbag, my cane, and my derby, then escorted me to the hallway. I descended the stairs and marched through the lobby area where the clerk at the desk greeted me.

"Good evening, Mister Lomax. I hope everything has been satisfactory for you and Mister Wilde."

"Indeed it has."

"Can we do anything for you or Mister Wilde?"

I waved the offer away, then reconsidered. "Might I get a ride to the river? I must visit a theatrical troupe camped there."

The attendant smiled. "On Sundays, we keep a carriage for the convenience of our guests interested in church services. Let me check its availability." He disappeared behind a registration desk door, returning moments later. "It'll be about five minutes, but if you'll wait out front, the driver will be around to pick you up, Mister Lomax."

"Much obliged," I said.

"Anything for Mister Wilde and his party."

Oscar Wilde was enjoying courtesies far beyond what he deserved, I thought, but I didn't refuse the ride to the river. After a pleasant stay in the fresh evening air, I saw the carriage turn the corner and stop in front of me. "Mister Lomax," the driver called.

I waved, picked up the carpetbag and cane and carried them to the rig. The young man offered to help me load them, but I put them behind the seat and climbed beside him. He was a pleasant, youthful Mormon with sandy brown hair and freckles. I instructed him to take me to the bridge over the River Jordan, and he rattled the reins, beginning the journey toward my kin. As we rode, I told him I'd never seen a cleaner town. He smiled and bragged about the city, taking especial pride as we turned the corner on North Temple and passed the cathedral and the tabernacle. He was confident in his faith, and I asked him if he had any wives. The driver chuckled, informing me that was what most visitors always wanted to know. Though he had not married yet, he hoped to one day. After that, God would determine the number. While I had given up on getting me a passel of Mormon wives, I realized that my conviction was not as strong as his, and I should not mock a religion I didn't understand.

We had a delightful conversation, so different from my visit with Oscar Wilde that we seemed to reach the river in no time. I jumped from the seat and grabbed my belongings. The driver asked me if he should wait to return me to the hotel, but I told him I would find my way back, likely in the morning. "God bless you," he said, then turned the rig toward the Walker House.

As soon as he departed, everyone else gathered around me.

"You must've failed," Lissa noted, "because you're not in jail, and the law isn't chasing you."

"That we know of," Aaron added.

Lissa next asked, "Did you get our money?"

"Maybe," I responded, "but it'll cost you."

"What now?" Aaron inquired.

I pointed to the patent leather shoes. "You'll need to give me these brogans."

"Those are much better than brogans," Silas said.

"They are part of the deal," I replied to everyone's disbelief. "Also, I need a woman's wig, shoulder-length, tawny brown but not black. Is that possible?"

"Maybe," Lissa said, "but are you keeping the suit, derby, and cane?"

"Nope, they'll go back to you. I'll want the carpet-bag, though."

"You got three hundred and fifty dollars for a pair of prop shoes and a woman's wig?" Lissa queried. "Oscar Wilde and his manager must be crazy."

"The deal's not done yet," I informed them. "His men promised to deliver the money here tomorrow morning. Five hundred dollars is what we agreed on. I'm figuring four hundred for the troupe and a hundred for me."

"Five hundred dollars for prop shoes and a wig?"

"Not exactly," I explained.

"If they pay up, I return with them and work as Oscar Wilde's bodyguard until his tour takes him to Kansas. That's why I'm taking a hundred bucks for my pay."

Lissa and Abigail rushed over to hug me. I liked their affection much more than Oscar's. Aaron and Silas slapped me on the back.

"You're some horse trader, Henry," Aaron said.

"Did you negotiate with Wilde himself?" Abigail asked when they broke their grip.

"I met him, and he's stranger than a three-legged duck with hiccups."

"We're proud of you, Henry," Lissa announced.

"Let's not celebrate until we get the money. If they don't bring the cash, I'll be in jail before sundown tomorrow night."

We marched to the wagons where I unpacked the carpetbag and returned the clothes to my sister, who invited me into the costume wagon to look for a suitable wig. As she hung the suit, she crinkled her nose. "This outfit smells like an ash heap."

"Oscar Wilde smokes like a locomotive and is as strange a fellow as I ever encountered. Even kissed me on the cheek, Lissa. I don't understand the fuss over this odd cuss."

"Popularity is a hard commodity to weigh," Lissa answered. "It's one tenth talent, two tenths luck and seven tenths mystery as to what strikes the public fancy." She took the cane and derby from me. After putting them in their place, she walked to a chest and opened the biggest drawer, extracting a handful of long-haired wigs for me to inspect.

In the dwindling daylight it was hard to tell the true

color in the wagon, so I stepped to the back and held up three, though none matched exactly the color of Wilde's long tresses. Lissa brought me a half dozen more to check. I finally settled on one as near a match as I could make in the dusk. After handing her the others, I tugged the wig over my head and gauged the length which reached to my shoulders. "This one should work."

"It's yours, though you'll have to return it if they don't show up with the money," Lissa informed me, "it and the patent leather shoes."

"I figure you'll get your money, one way or another."

"Then you can keep the wig and shoes."

I jumped from the wagon and strode to my blankets under the adjacent rig. I pulled off the patent leathers and slid my socked feet into my boots, which were much more comfortable. I packed the wig and shoes in my new carpetbag. Come morning, I'd need to take it plus my saddlebags, coat, hat, and weapons when the money men picked me up. I wondered if I would ever rejoin the Lomax and Coker Theatrical Troupe.

Everyone realized my future was indefinite with them as we sat around eating boiled potatoes for supper. I regaled the group with observations about Oscar Wilde and his idiosyncrasies, ignoring the part about the hug and kiss.

After we finished, little Harriet sidled up to me on my stool and took my hand. "Will you be leaving us tomorrow, Uncle Henry?" she asked.

I nodded. "Most likely, sweetie."

"Will you be coming back?"

Shrugging, I told her the truth. "It's unlikely."

Tears welled up in her eyes and trickled down her cheeks. "I'll miss you."

"And I'll miss you," I replied, picking her up, placing her on my knee, and hugging her.

"I love you," she whispered.

"And I love you, little one."

She lifted her face and kissed me on the cheek, leaving me choked up. She rubbed her eyes, slid from my knee and ran to her mother. Lissa comforted her. Everyone's affection startled me as they seemed saddened that I would likely leave in the morning. After the kids went to bed, the adults joined Lissa and me as we reminisced about the good and bad times growing up in Cane Hill, Arkansas, especially during the war.

We adults retired late and awoke up early. I fretted for almost three hours before Vale and Locke arrived. Locke insisted on meeting Lissa, the Arkansas Songbird. I introduced them while Vale counted out five hundred dollars. I took the money to Aaron, doling out his four hundred and pocketing the balance. I strode to my things, pulling my hat over my head, grabbing my carpetbag with my pistol inside, saddlebags, carbine, and coat, then telling each member of the troupe goodbye. With little Harriet in her arms, Lissa rushed up, all excited that Locke might be interested in her doing some California concerts.

Harriet reached out for me to take her, but my hands were full. I leaned over and kissed her cheek and she grabbed my neck, holding me tight. "Bye, bye, Uncle Henry," she said softly.

I waved a final time with my carbine hand, dropped my things in the buggy, and climbed in the back seat. Vale circled the wagon and headed to town.

My eyes misty, I didn't look back at my kin. I wondered if I would ever see any of them again. My consolation was the pride I had in recovering the money they had lost because of the contract postponement, but I feared I was leaving a decent theatrical company for the biggest freak show on earth.

CHAPTER FOURTEEN

As soon as I settled in my seat, Charles Locke turned and queried. "Did you bring the wig?"

I pointed to the carpetbag in the wagon bed. "It's in there, the patent leather shoes, too."

"Good," Locke answered. "You'll need them." He nodded to Vale. "Let's get back to the Walker House."

Vale shook the lines, and the buggy lurched forward, heading at a rapid clip.

It was Monday morning, and I saw no reason to hurry. "What's the rush?"

"We're running behind."

"Oscar's lecture is not until tonight. You afraid he'll burn the place down with all his smoking?"

"The president of the Mormon church is picking him up in fifteen minutes to tour Salt Lake City. You'll accompany him as his bodyguard. That's what we're paying you for, to protect him," Locke said.

"Protect him from what?"

"From himself," Vale scowled. "The Mormons believe in temperance in all things from liquor to tobacco. We can make sure he doesn't carry a bottle of champagne with him, but he's likely to pull out a cigarette and light it up."

"It'll do wonders for the box office tonight if Taylor is spotted driving Wilde around town," Locke explained. "But if anyone sees him smoking on the tour, it will embarrass the leader of the church and cut into his appeal to the local audience."

"Why don't you just tell Lord La-de-dah himself?"

"He can't control his urges," Vale said.

"What should I do if he pulls out a cigarette? Shoot him?" I patted the revolver at my waist.

"Not until I make my money back," Locke answered. "After that, do what you want with him."

Soon we passed the cathedral and tabernacle, turning down Main Street toward the Walker House. As we drew nearer, it appeared as though Taylor had arrived early, because a throng of folks circled a team of white horses harnessed to a large surrey with four bench seats beneath a canvas top. I counted three women on each of the last two benches and another one alone in the second row.

As we pulled up to the building, Oscar Wilde emerged from the hotel beside a distinguished white-haired gentleman with a receding hairline. Though his cheeks and chin were closely shaved, he had a short white beard that hung from his jawline down to his necktie. He dressed as a president with a starched shirt, a pressed coat, and trousers with a sharp crease. The gloss of his footwear reflected the early morning sunlight, but without surpassing the glimmer of Wilde's black patent leather shoes. Wilde wore his fur-collared, green overcoat that failed to hide the yellow bow of a tie that tumbled from his neck like a boulder rolling down a mountain. He wore brown corduroy trousers beneath a pale green shirt. As he descended the steps with Taylor, his dark brown hair bounced under a floppy tan hat the size of a locomotive drive wheel.

"We're just in time," Vale said, yanking the reins and drawing the buggy to a quick stop.

Locke bailed out. "Come along, Lomax."

"What about my things?"

"We'll get them to your room." Since I was going as a guard, I grabbed the carbine.

"Leave the long gun," Vale ordered. "Your sidearm'll be plenty."

Locke reached the walk and motioned for me to hurry. I jogged to him, and he elbowed his way through the crowd to the surrey, as Taylor and Wilde reached the wagon. The Mormon president introduced the poet to his wives. On the rear bench sat Josephine, Margaret, and Harriet, who was nowhere as cute as my little niece of the same name. In front of them were Sophia, Mary Ann, and Jane. Seated in the second row was Elizabeth. Except for Josephine, who look to be in her twenties, the rest appeared to be in their late forties or older. Whatever their ages, they perched straight-back prim and proper in their subdued gowns and bonnets.

Wilde flashed his stained teeth at each woman, then looked at Taylor and the team. "Lovely harem," he said.

Taylor spun about. "What, Mister Wilde?"

"Lovely pair, them horses," Wilde responded, winking when he saw me.

The elderly gentleman sighed. "My hearing's

getting worse and worse, one of the problems of growing old." He apologized. "I thought you said something else."

"Never would I be so crass as to demean such a lovely band of wives," Wilde responded as Locke eased behind him.

Before Wilde could climb into the wagon, the theater impresario slipped his hand in Wilde's pocket and delicately extracted the green bottle of champagne, deftly hiding it under his own coat.

Wilde turned to confront the thief. "Oh, it's you, Locke. I feared someone else was lifting my cheer. You've eliminated the need for me to wear my coat." He slipped it off and gave it to the impresario. "Another of my manservants," Wilde told Taylor, "as I don't have a single wife, much less seven."

Locke's face flushed with embarrassment as Wilde turned to his host.

"Reverend Taylor—should I call you reverend?"

Elizabeth answered the poet. "As leader of the Mormon church, our husband is the Prophet, but he is addressed as 'President.' Within the faith, our men are called 'brother' and our women 'sister.' In addressing our husband, President Taylor is proper."

"Thank you, Elizabeth," said the Mormon leader, who turned back to Wilde. "You were saying, sir?"

"Most enlightening, Elizabeth," Wilde replied as he turned to me. "I would like to introduce you to H.H. Lomax. He serves as my *Praetorian* Guard because my views on art and beauty offend some folks, though I am bewildered why. Who can be against art and beauty, except the philistines, and I know there are none of them among the Mormons, are there?"

I decided I would like to meet this Phyllis Steen someday, if she was such a thorn in his behind. I nodded at the church president and he extended his hand. We shook.

"You, young man, should sit behind us with Elizabeth so Mister Wilde and I can ride in the front seat, allowing him an unobstructed view of our beautiful city."

"I am pleased to accompany any of your lovely brides," I replied, casting a friendly smile to my seatmate. Her thin lips answered with a quiver of an upturn at the corner.

"Let's begin," Taylor instructed, motioning for the visiting poet to take his seat up front, while he marched around and climbed aboard. I perched beside Elizabeth. Begrudgingly, she scooted from the middle of the padded seat to the far edge behind her spouse while I kept to my end of the bench.

"Is everyone settled?" Taylor called.

"Yes, brother," the wives answered in unison.

The women's response tickled me, calling their husband brother.

Taylor rattled the reins and began our excursion, showing us the city hall, federal and county courthouses, and Walker House's competitors, the Townsend House and the Wasatch Hotel. He bragged about the beautiful Wasatch Mountains and boasted even more when he pointed out Deseret University and the Salt Lake Museum.

He drove by the Salt Lake Theater, where Wilde would lecture that evening, and touted its many amenities, claiming it was the best opera house between New York and San Francisco. "It offers the cleanest entertainment you will find in the country," he said with abundant pride.

"At least until tonight, when I speak," Wilde retorted, reaching inside his suit coat and extracting a gold box.

Taylor shook his head, at first worried, then understanding. "Your English humor sometimes catches me unaware. I was born in England. Did you know that? The Good Lord welcomed me to this earth in Milnthorpe, Westmorland, England."

"I'm still waiting for Him to welcome me," Wilde replied, pulling a cigarette from his case and snapping it shut.

Instantly, I leaned forward and snagged the tobacco from his hand, drawing his scowl and an approving nod from my seatmate.

Taylor looked over his shoulder at me. "Young man, is everything okay?"

"Yes, Brother Taylor, err President Taylor, sir. Master Wilde has been helping me break my smoking habit." I sat back down in my seat. "When I least expect it, he'll offer me a cigarette to tempt me, like Satan tried Christ. He's a caring man, Master Wilde, endeavoring to help me move past this filthy habit. I once asked him if he minded if I smoked. He responded I could burn for all he cared, as long as it wasn't in hell. He's a caring man, this Oscar Wilde, the man that so many think is a fool, yet he is anything but. Weren't the apostles considered fools in their time? Oscar Wilde is an apostle for our time."

I held the cigarette up to my nose, smelled the putrid tobacco and next tossed the vile smoke onto the road, littering the otherwise pristine street. Beside me,

Elizabeth clapped softly, joined by her fellow wives, letting me know it was better to litter than to smoke in Salt Lake City.

"Praise be to God for you both."

"Indeed," Wilde said as he shoved the cigarette case back into his suit coat, turning around to glare at me, even though I had saved him from creating an incident among potential Mormon ticket buyers. The prophet next guided us to Gardo House, his own residence, where we had a fine dinner, confounding me as I had no idea who prepared it unless he had more wives hidden somewhere. Before the meal, Wilde asked if he could explore the garden-like grounds alone to meditate and enhance his appreciation of this Mormon promised land. Taylor agreed, touched by Wilde's devout inclinations, but I knew all he wanted to do was disappear somewhere for a quick smoke before the meal. After dining, he repeated his request to tour the grounds alone, though it was merely to burn another cigarette.

During our meal and the ensuing ride back to the Walker House, Taylor told his story of being converted to Mormonism from a Church of England background and being with the religion's founder, Joseph Smith, when he was murdered by religious bigots in Illinois. Taylor had been the assistant editor under Smith for *Times and Seasons*, the official organ of the Latter Day Saints church, when the attack occurred. The pocket watch, which he still carried, had stopped a bullet and saved his life during the assault.

"Like you, Mister Wilde, I, too, am a writer."

"Another newspaperman," Wilde responded. "I can't escape the men of the press anywhere I go."

"I'm no longer a journalist. Instead, I write poetry and verse, the lyrics to a handful of hymns that are still sung in our churches."

"As well they should be as the works of a prominent Mormon leader," Wilde responded.

"We have been blessed with two outstanding leaders," Taylor said, modestly lowering his head. "The first was Joseph Smith, and the second was Brigham Young."

"Tell me of your poetry, President Taylor."

"It is nothing compared to yours."

"No one's writing compares to mine," Wilde proclaimed.

"Except God's," Taylor noted.

"Except God's," Wilde repeated with little enthusiasm. "The poetry of most Americans I consider mere prose. Rhymesters are many, but a genuine bard comes but once a century." Wilde lifted his chin awaiting acknowledgement from the reverend that he was that poet. Taylor, though, disappointed him with his response.

"I have written verse about California and Deseret, though I'm proudest of my ode, *The Upper California, Oh, That's the Land for Me*. Some have called me the 'Poet Laureate of Zion.' I would be honored to share my compositions with you, if you would be so kind as to read them and share your thoughts as a man of great literary skills."

As we loaded the wagon, Taylor joined us with a stack of papers tied together by a string. "Copies of my poetry, I hope you enjoy." He handed them to the Irishman.

"I know I will," Wilde said, turning in his seat and

giving the bundle to me. "Guard these with your life, H.H."

We started back for the hotel, but Taylor had saved the best for last, taking us around Temple Square, which was surrounded by a high-plank fence with four gates for the faithful. The tabernacle was an oblong building, roughly two hundred and fifty feet by a hundred and fifty feet, with a copper-sheathed roof, supported by forty-four exterior stone columns.

"Our tabernacle is the largest hall in America, seating thousands, and our organ, built in England, has seven hundred pipes," Taylor bragged. "You should hear the choir sing in the tabernacle. It's as if the angels came from the heavens to offer a concert."

Wilde shook his head and commented on the structure. "Reminds me of a soup kettle."

Taylor failed to catch or simply ignored the comment, pointing to the adjacent edifice.

Soaring above the tabernacle were the towers of the temple, some two hundred and twenty-five feet high. Though work continued on the building, Taylor said it was a hundred and eighty-seven feet long and a hundred feet wide with walls eight feet thick.

"Like a fortress," Wilde observed.

"A mighty God is our fortress," Taylor replied, explaining the significance of the symbols carved in the stone facades. "Each side has an all-viewing eye, representing how God sees all things. The clasped hands above each exterior door represent brotherly love and the covenants that are made within the Temple. You'll also see carvings of the sun, the moon and the stars around the building, symbolizing in the Mormon faith the celestial, terrestrial, and telestial kingdoms of glory in the afterlife."

Taylor spoke with sincerity and conviction. I'd been around a few circuit riders in my years and had attended many Baptist river revivals in Arkansas, but I had never encountered a man this high in any denomination's hierarchy and never one that voiced such pride in his faith, his beliefs, and his flock. I understood Mormon beliefs were far deeper than multiple wives.

"You may not be able to see them from here," Taylor continued, "but carved in each door and embedded in each doorknob is a beehive, the perfect symbol for Mormonism as it represents the industriousness of our people, their thrift with the gifts God provides them, and their perseverance through the hard times and persecution that drove us to this, our promised land."

The Mormon president spoke with an inflection and resonance that gave his words power far beyond their meaning. He cared for his God and his people, unlike Lord La-de-dah, who cared only for his god and himself. Of course, he was his own god, so it was one and the same for Oscar Wilde.

After turning the final corner around Temple Square, Taylor headed the rig down Main Street to the Walker House. Wilde remained silent, likely untouched by the top Mormon's sincerity and probably craving a cigarette. When our host reined up in front of the hotel, Wilde jumped from the surrey. "Thank you for the lovely lunch and tour," he said, then turned and bounded up the steps for his suite, an abrupt conclusion to a generous visit.

"My poems," Taylor called, "don't forget them."

Wilde ignored him.

"I have them, President Taylor, and I will see that he reads them, though you must understand he is a busy man," I responded, knowing the only thing he was busy with other than glorifying himself was smoking.

The stately Mormon leader smiled. "Thank you, young man. You are blessed that a man as brilliant as Oscar Wilde would devote his attention to helping you break the vile hold of tobacco in your life."

"Indeed I am blessed," I said, turning to smile at Elizabeth, who offered a slight grin, likely for my departure. "I hope we will be honored tonight with your presence at the theater. It will be an experience you will not soon forget."

"We wouldn't miss it. All of us will be there, young man."

I slid out of my seat. "I'm not that young anymore."

"At my age," he responded, "all men are young."

Standing beside the wagon, I held up his papers. "I'll make sure he gets this."

"Splendid," Taylor answered. "We shall see you this evening, and please watch out for anyone that might do him harm."

"I will do that, confident of success now that I have your blessing, President Taylor. I tipped my hat at him and turned for the hotel as he drove away.

As I walked through the lobby to the stairs, I overheard a pair of elderly women commenting on Wilde's rudeness and pomposity. They had a good fix on his character. I climbed the steps slowly, dreading the upcoming night in a smoke-filled suite with him. I at least had a key so I could let myself in, though I would've gladly traded it for one that would lock Lord La-de-dah out.

When I reached the top floor, I found Traquair standing in the hallway. He smiled. "Didn't know if you'd return or not, Lomax. You don't seem as infatuated with him as he does with you, but thank you for keeping him occupied for the last four hours. I enjoyed the quiet."

"And the fresh air," I added.

"It's stale now."

He noted the stack of papers in my hand. "What's that?"

"Poetry."

"You've known him but a single day, and you've already written that many poems? You must really be impressed by him."

"Not as much as he's taken with himself. These aren't mine. They belong to President John Taylor."

"I thought our president was Chester Arthur."

"President of the Mormons, John Taylor."

Traquair grinned. "Just pulling your leg."

Lifting the papers, I replied. "I promised the president that I would have your boss read his poetry."

"Good luck with that. He reads his own poetry, no one else's. He's taking a smoke right now and has asked me to draw a bath for him shortly. Next, he'll dress and dine, then depart for the theater to confirm the stage is situated to his liking. After that, he will fret until time to talk. At that point, he'll bore them all to sleep."

He opened the door, and I passed through the anteroom into the parlor, which was veiled in cigarette smoke. Wilde stood by the window, looking down upon Salt Lake City. When he heard me approach, he turned and scowled.

"I could've killed you for grabbing my cigarette."

"Vale and Locke ordered me to shoot you if you started smoking. They didn't want you embarrassing the President of the Mormons with your vile tobacco habits."

"My cravings dictate when I smoke, not the prudish beliefs of a religious zealot."

Traquair marched between us to the water closet.

Lifting the stack of Taylor's writing toward Wilde, "Where do you want me to put this?"

"In the trash."

"That's petty."

"I suspect it's the best review his poetry will ever get, to be deposited in an ashcan at the direction of Oscar Wilde."

Lowering the papers to my side, I shook my head. "That's not right. At least let me return them to his place."

"Never did I promise that pompous old fool I'd read his poems." Wilde drew savagely on the nub of his cigarette and expelled smoke like venom.

I gritted my teeth, asking myself what I had gotten myself into, agreeing to protect this arrogant ass for God knows how long.

Wilde gauged my anger as I heard water running in the adjacent room. He crushed his butt in the ashtray that Traquair had cleaned, then stepped toward me.

"No reason to be upset, H.H.," Wilde said, putting his arm around my shoulder.

He smelled like an arsonist.

"Once my valet draws my bath, perhaps you should join me. We can discuss matters more, see if we might reach an understanding about the esteemed churchman with a half dozen wives. I'm surprised he has time to write a poem, much less insightful poetry, like mine."

He turned and walked toward his bath, while I stood there holding the unread papers. After the running water stopped, Traquair emerged, a wide grin on his black face. "You've upset his holiness, as have I," he informed me.

"How?"

"Not only does Massa Wilde have me draw his water, he always asks me to bathe him as well. I find the thought repulsive. I refused. What did you do?"

I shook the stack of poems. "I refused to trash the Mormon president's poetry. Lord La-de-dah ordered me to throw this in the ashcan, saying it would be the best review of his poems ever received, to be discarded by Oscar Wilde. I'm not trashing the honest work of a decent man, but I don't know what to do with it. Any suggestions?"

Traquair pointed to a bedroom on the opposite side of the parlor. "Put it in there. Vale's taking another room so you could protect Wilde. In fact, I think he was glad to get out of this jail. You'll find your carpetbag, coat, carbine, and saddlebags already in there."

Nodding, I thanked the valet and started across the parlor, as Wilde called for me.

"H.H., please join me so we can discuss your concerns."

I dropped the papers on the feather mattress, hesitated for a moment, and then unbuckled my gun belt and placed it on the bed so I wouldn't shoot my charge. Taking a deep breath, I emerged from my bedroom and walked toward the water closet. Before I entered, Traquair grabbed my arm.

"Be careful," he warned. "Massa Wilde can be a bit peculiar when he bathes."

Not sure what to expect, I grimaced. After he released my grip, I knocked on the door.

"Enter my roughhewn rapscallion."

Twisting the doorknob, I opened and stepped inside. Against the back wall I saw Wilde in a claw foot porcelain bathtub with soap bubbles up to his neck.

"Care to join me? I've found a hot bath can not only wash away the grime from our torsos, but also the worries from our minds." He lifted a bar of soap above the bubbles and waved me over.

Shaking my head, I declined his invitation.

As his arm retreated into the suds, I heard a thud when he dropped the cake of soap.

"Ooops," he said, "I seem to have lost my soap. H.H., might you retrieve it? I can't seem to find it."

Crossing my arms over my chest, I shook my head again.

"My, aren't we difficult this afternoon, H.H.?" Wilde leaned forward in the tub, patting the bottom for the soap until he recovered it. "Ah, here it is." He lifted his arm above the bubbles to prove he had found his cake of cleanser. "Would you wash my back for me?"

"I'm hired to guard you, not to bathe you."

Wilde frowned. "H.H., you disappoint me. This is not how I expected the True American to respond to my simple request."

"I'm not one of your men-in-wading or whoever accompanies the Prince of Whales."

"It's men-in-waiting, and it's Wales, H.H., not whales. I'm astounded you are so distraught over my refusal to read Taylor's poetry."

"Seems it would be a decent gesture simply to look at a few and write a note."

Wilde smiled. "I prefer the indecent gesture. That aside, I am a genius, unwilling to diminish my brilliance by reading the inferior works of a religious man. You should understand that religion is like a blind man looking in a black room for a black cat that isn't there, and finding it."

"What's wrong with offering the old man a little encouragement with his writing? Besides, my momma always taught me the basic principle of religion was following the Golden Rule. You know, do unto others as you would want them to do to you."

"There is no Golden Rule, H.H., only the fact that gold rules. Whoever has the gold makes the rules."

"Or, makes fools of themselves," I replied.

Wilde slapped the sides of the tub with his palms. "Be gone, H.H. You are oblivious to the lessons I am offering you. I have a lecture to consider, and you have disappointed me greatly."

I spun around and stepped to the door.

"Discard Taylor's poetry before we head to the theater, H.H. I care not to discuss the matter further."

Exiting the water closet, I gritted my teeth.

"Did he ask you to pick up the soap or wash his back?" Traquair asked.

"He did."

"Strange, that man certainly is," the valet said. "He requests the same of me every bath if I linger after drawing his water."

As I marched across the room, I saw Wilde's writing paper and instruments, then retreated to the bedroom, where I picked up the stack of Taylor's poems.

Returning to the small table, I leaned over, dipped the pen in the inkwell. I wrote a note on a sheaf of paper with Oscar Wilde's name printed at the top: PRESIDENT TAYLOR, I WAS TOUCHED BY YOUR POETRY. O.W. I blotted the wet ink, then slipped the paper under the twine that bound the poems. "I'm taking this to the hotel desk to forward to President Taylor," I told Traquair.

"You are coming back, aren't you, Lomax?"

"Unfortunately."

"Good," he replied. "We leave for the theater in two hours. You won't care to miss that."

CHAPTER FIFTEEN

I left the papers at the hotel desk, instructing the clerk to deliver the material to the Mormon president after Wilde departed town for his next stop. Then I stepped outside and walked around Salt Lake City for an hour before returning to the lodging. I enjoyed the sincerity of the Mormon people and their industriousness as I continued to be amazed by the cleanliness of their streets, the pride they showed in their community and the fact that they did their business without carrying sidearms. The folks seemed more focused on helping others than themselves, unlike the man I would be guarding for several weeks.

When I returned to the Walker House, I climbed the stairs slowly, reluctant to return to Wilde's quarters, as I had enjoyed the fresh air and dreaded returning to a room shrouded in smoke, even if it was the fanciest accommodations I ever stayed in. The accommodations certainly beat the Buffalo Gap jail, save for the companionship, as I had decided I'd rather room with an ignorant imbecile than a self-proclaimed genius.

I slipped my key in the door, let myself inside, and locked up. As I stepped into the parlor, Traquair threw me an uneasy glance. "I feared you'd abandoned me."

Waving my arms against the haze from Wilde's incinerated tobacco, I shook my head. "I needed fresh air."

"It's always worse before a talk. He's nervous and smokes like a steel mill, since his managers don't care for him to be seen smoking in public. Lord La-de-dah departs about an hour early to check the stage arrangements and then spends the rest of the time trying to calm his nerves. For a man who's so confident of himself in conversations, he's plenty skittish before going on stage and with good reason. Massa's a poor orator, and he knows it." Traquair eyed me. "Do you own any better clothes than what you're wearing?"

"I've a suit, shirt, and tie I bought in Fort Worth a while back."

"Wear them to hide your holster under your coat. It'll avoid trouble with local ordinances we don't know about." He grinned. "Wear your patent leather shoes. They're so manly."

"Like drawing baths for another fellow," I laughed.

"Remember, I didn't wash his back."

"Me neither," I countered.

"That's not what he says."

We both snickered as I stepped into my room and closed the door. I dressed in my clean shirt, suit, and my shiny footwear, then strapped my pistol around my waist and pulled on my coat. Without a matching hat, I went bareheaded to the theater. Though my attire rippled with wrinkles, that would have to do. I returned to the parlor as Wilde emerged from his quarters, his outfit looking like a rainbow had collided with a freight train. He wore a black velvet coat trimmed in purple over a beige shirt which sported a Venetian green bow tie large enough to hide a pack mule. His knee britches matched his green tie. His purple stockings stretched from his black patent leather shoes over his calves to his kneecaps. In his left hand that featured a signet ring the size of a sombrero, he carried a gold-headed cane. Over his right forearm, he had draped a purple cape.

Traquair stepped back from the lecturer, cocked his head, stroked his chin and commented, "Massa Wilde, you have outdone yourself with a splendor that will keep Salt Lake City talking for months, if not years."

Wilde spun around so we could see his outfit from all angles.

I wrestled with a snicker, trying to smother it behind my lips.

The poet gazed at me, awaiting a review. I'd seen freak shows that looked more respectable. Finally, I nodded. "It reminds me of John Taylor's poems. Better unviewed and un-reviewed, as you would say."

"Alas, H.H., I shall win your affection yet. Perhaps one day I shall convince you to wear clothes that will strike folks with a smile for its daring. Your rumpled outfit today will only draw frowns for its wrinkles. You should either be a work of art, or wear a work of art. I can accomplish both."

I shook my head. "You should mate your attire with the plain dress of Mormon folk. After that, you'd never have to play the fool."

"Alas, H.H., sometimes one must play the role of fool to fool the fool who thinks he can fool you." Wilde spun around, tossing his cape and cane on the fur-covered sofa, then extracted his gold cigarette case from his coat pocket. He took a match from beside the ashtray that Traquair had cleaned a thousand times and fired up his smoke. It was like the fog was rolling in as he strolled about the room, working off his nerves as visibility steadily decreased.

He consumed six cigarettes before it was time to go. Picking up his cane and cape, he marched through the door Traquair had opened into the hall. "My adoring fans await Oscar Fingal O'Flahertie Wills Wilde," the poet announced to the empty hallway.

"That's his full name?" I asked the valet.

"Yes, sir."

"No wonder he's touched in the mind. Having to tote around a handle that long is bound to be tiring on a man's mind and body." After Traquair locked the door, he and I followed the great man—at least in his evaluation—down the stairs, through the lobby and out the Walker House doors where the hotel carriage awaited. As we loaded, passersby pointed and snickered at Lord La-de-dah, but the attention only made him prouder, holding his head higher and clenching his lips defiantly, confident that none of them could sell a reserved seat for a dollar fifty in the biggest theater in Utah Territory.

Traquair sat up front with the driver, while Wilde and I parked on the bench behind them. "What about Vale and Locke?" I asked.

"They'll meet us at the theater," Traquair said over his shoulder. "They go early to monitor the box office and sales." Once Wilde was comfortable, the driver rattled the reins, and the carriage delivered us to the theater's back entrance, where a dozen admirers waited, four of them with the photo cards distributed earlier to promote his visit. A handful of other gawkers carried sunflowers and lilies for the apostle of appearances.

As his bodyguard, I figured I should protect him from this surly crowd, so I jumped from the carriage as soon as the rig stopped and stepped between the throng and the celebrity. Waving my arms, I cried, "Stand back! Stand back! Allow the great man to emerge."

Of the backdoor bunch, all were women but one, and they ranged from the early twenties to late fifties, I guessed, though I never understood what they saw in him. To me, he was the baron of the bizarre.

Wilde handed Traquair his cane as he took a pencil and photo from an admirer and scribbled his name. I prayed he signed only Oscar Wilde because if he wrote his full moniker, we'd be there for a week. He graciously accepted the flowers, kissing the back of each donor's hand. "Please stay for my lecture," he said. "I have titled it 'The House Beautiful' but perhaps I should have named it the women beautiful, as you are all delightful on the eyes."

The females sighed as Wilde took his cane from Traquair, walked up the steps to the back door and rapped on the entry with the head of his walking stick. Moments later, the door swung open to reveal Locke. Traquair and I followed Lord La-de-dah inside. As soon as Locke closed the entry, Wilde tossed the flowers to the floor. So much for the perfect beauty of the sunflower and the lily, or for the generosity of his fans.

The poet strutted around the stage to the footlights

and next inspected the lectern and the single chair behind it.

"Would you like the front curtain open and at the appointed time you step to the lectern to speak?" Locke asked. "Or, would you prefer to be seated behind the closed curtain when it is raised?"

"I intend to strut on stage, give them a chance to admire my attire and get some of their rowdiness out before I start, so leave the curtain up."

"These are Mormons mostly," Locke reminded him. "You'll never find a more mannerly audience."

"Fine."

"Your speech is on the podium," the impresario said. "Your dressing room awaits you with a light repast for your enjoyment."

"Is there champagne?"

Locke shook his head. "We did not request any. Even if we had, I doubt the Mormons would have allowed it."

Wilde clenched his lips, then responded. "I'll be glad to get out of Utah Territory, where a man can celebrate as he desires."

"Perhaps you can make the sacrifice as it appears we'll have a full house this evening with a great box office. Even President Taylor plans to attend." Locke pointed to a section of seats in front of the stage. "That's where he and his wives will alight and where Brigham Young once sat, when he was their prophet."

"Will anyone introduce me?"

"You need no introduction, Master Wilde. You are known far and wide for your intellect and your attire."

The poet liked that response. "I shall return to

England even more famous than when I left." He chortled. "And richer!"

"Indeed," said Locke, who escorted Wilde to his dressing room, leaving me and Traquair to kill time before the lecture began.

We found and sat on stools, Traquair informing me we would leave the next morning on the train bound for Denver and arrive the following afternoon ahead of an evening speech in the capital city. I wasn't happy about visiting Colorado, not with a murder charge hanging over me in Leadville, but figured I'd be okay as long as we avoided the place where the unfortunate deed had occurred.

"Any plans to visit Leadville?" I inquired.

"No, just a lecture in Denver, then a day off, followed by a speech in Colorado Springs, and a second talk in Denver again." Traquair eyed me. "You got any problems with Leadville?"

I coughed, shaking my head. "It's the altitude. The air's so thin it's hard to breathe up there. I've even heard cats and rats can't survive because the air's too thin."

Traquair snorted. "If that's so, Massa Wilde would perish there."

We visited until twenty minutes before the program began. From our seats behind the back curtains, we heard spectators entering the auditorium. Traquair arose, motioned me to follow, and led me to Wilde's dressing room. "What he hasn't eaten from the spread the theater puts out is our supper."

"That's assuming Lord La-de-dah hasn't smoked it all."

Traquair laughed. "Nice pun, Lomax. You're quite

clever, in an uneducated way, full of common sense, which exceeds book learning."

"I prefer horse sense to common sense," I informed the valet.

"Why would that be?"

"I've never known a horse to bet on a person," I replied.

He laughed again. "I'll share that one with Massa Wilde, and one day he'll claim the clever line as his own, I'm sure." Traquair knocked on the dressing room door.

"Enter," responded Wilde.

The valet led me inside, and we found Wilde standing in front of a full-length mirror. I would've thought he was admiring himself after observing him in his suite, but he seemed shocked at what he saw.

"What is it, Massa Wilde?"

Without lifting his gaze from the reflective glass, Wilde answered. "I fear I've discovered my first wrinkle, which is so much worse than a gray hair, that you can pluck. A wrinkle stays. At twenty-six, a wrinkle is a great tragedy, the initial sign of my ultimate demise."

I ambled to Wilde's side and leaned toward the mirror, close enough to smell his rotten breath. "I don't see a wrinkle, a furrow or even a crease."

Indignant, Wilde pointed to the corner of his right eye. "There, see it now?"

I nodded. "Oh, yeah. It's like you're growing old before my very eyes."

"The man who stands most remote from his age is the one who mirrors it best," Wilde responded.

Uncertain I understood what he was getting at, I suggested an approach to address his single wrinkle and his impending senility. "Perhaps you should never look at any more mirrors."

"What," he cried, "and deprive myself of the joy others see when they gaze upon my perfect countenance?"

I'd seen train wrecks with better form and less smoke than the great Oscar Wilde. "Maybe you should imagine the mirror as a portrait of what you will be, not what you are. Only the reflection ages, not you."

"Yes, yes, yes, H.H." Oscar turned to me and clapped his hands. "That's brilliant, a portrait that ages rather than its subject, who remains forever youthful." He threw his arms around me, hugging me tightly and kissing me on the cheek again. "You are indeed the True American, H.H. My trip to America has been worth it for this idea alone. This is more than a poem, but rather a novel, a literary masterpiece. I can picture it now."

I wormed my way from his arms, but he grabbed me by the shoulders, pulled me forward and kissed me full on the lips. Dumbfounded and speechless at his show of appreciation, I broke from him and backed away, getting beyond the reach of both his arms and his lips.

Realizing my discomfort, Traquair stepped between us. "In all these months with you, Massa Wilde, I've never seen such enthusiasm."

"Nor have I encountered such brilliance in the New World than that displayed by H.H., a veritable genius in his own way and indeed my True American."

I had no idea what I had said that was so brilliant, but I would have gladly retracted it if I could have erased his kiss from my mouth and my memory. I drew my coat sleeve across my face, trying to eliminate the stain from my lips.

"An idea of this literary magnitude comes along only once in a century, maybe even once in a millennium." Wilde stepped past Traquair like he wanted to hug me again, but I backtracked to the food table, turned around and stuffed a sourdough roll in my mouth and started chewing. "H.H., we should celebrate when we get back to the suite, though I am assuming you don't mind me developing your idea into a novel."

Not having any clue what my brilliant thought was, I nodded vigorously as I chomped and swallowed the roll. "Use it, do whatever you want with it as long as you never kiss me again on the cheeks or the lips or anywhere, ever again for as long as I live and even after I die."

Wilde smiled, then mused. "Genius can be so temperamental, as I well know." He sighed. "William, you are blessed to be in this room not with one genius, but two, me and H.H."

"What an honor," he replied, "but I must remind you in a few moments *you* will be lecturing, not Lomax. Don't forget your loyal, paying guests."

"They can wait."

"They did buy tickets, and they deserve your full devotion."

Wilde sighed again. "Perhaps you're right." He preened in front of the mirror, evidently leaving his wrinkle and his worries in the reflective glass.

Traquair joined me by the food and picked up two slices of apple. I'd lost my appetite but kept a sourdough biscuit in each hand to stuff in my mouth in case Wilde approached me again with affection on his mind.

"I've never seen him so enthused before," Traquair whispered. "Perhaps it will help his delivery on stage."

As the scheduled time approached for his appearance, Wilde lit a cigarette and marched around the room puffing little clouds of smoke as the crowd grew restless, waiting for him to show. After drawing the final drag from the rolled tobacco, he crushed the cigarette in his dinner plate, stepped to his chair, lifted his cape and swung it over his back, hooking it in front of his bow tie. Next, he yanked his flowing tresses from under the cape, took his floppy hat and gently tilted it atop his magnificent brain. He admired himself in the mirror, smiling at the reflection.

"That's our cue to leave," Traquair informed me. "Once he grins at himself, he's ready to perform, if you can call it that." As the valet led me out of the dressing room, Wilde grabbed his gold-headed cane and followed. We traipsed around the back curtain to the wing of a stage now lit by gas footlights and overhead spotlights which converged on the chair and lectern. Traquair stepped aside so his charge could pass, took our two stools and moved them where we could watch without being seen by the crowd.

Wilde turned to us, took a deep breath and bowed. When he straightened, he lifted his head and strutted on stage like a peacock at mating time. As he came into view, the audience hushed momentarily before responding with gentle applause and a smattering of laughter. I suspect the chuckling would have been louder had more husbands and fewer wives attended.

Without looking at the crowd, Wilde strode to the high-backed, cushioned chair and laid his cane across the armrests. He removed his cape and draped it over the back. Finally, he lifted his hat, placing it in the throne and flipped his head so his hair rose, then settled on his shoulder. He turned and strutted to the podium where he stared at the audience for a full minute, allowing them to inspect his finery and settle down for what was certain to be the most important lecture in the history of Utah Territory, at least in his own mind.

"Good evening, aesthetes," Wilde began, "and who does not enjoy art and beauty as they transcend the human experience and unite us as people when we can agree on so little else? Tonight I shall address you on 'The House Beautiful' and some easy approaches that will make your home as handsome as the streets of Salt Lake City, which I toured yesterday, thanks to that great Mormon and poet John Taylor and his lovely wives. My aim is to teach you how to transform your meager homes into aesthetic heavens on earth in an otherwise ugly world of the philistines."

Once again, I realized I should meet this Phyllis Steen, as she sounded so much more interesting than the lecturer.

Wilde spoke in a singular tone, never lifting his voice or varying the tenor of his words. He lectured in a pattern that would begin with four, five or six words interrupted by a slight pause before reading the next phrase followed by another hitch. Even if he was a genius, he was no orator, as I had heard school kids read better from the first *McGuffey Reader* than he managed before a paying audience. I patted the revolver at my side, wondering if it would be preferable to shoot myself and end my personal misery or turn my gun on Wilde and conclude the despair of the ticket-buying public. That mental debate was all that kept me awake during the lecture.

As his opinion was definitely worth something since people had paid for it, Wilde presented his thoughts on what created a beautiful home, things like hand-carved rather than machine-made ornamentation; blown glass rather than cut glass; wax candles for their soft glow rather than gas lamps and their harsher light. If gas was preferred, the illumination should come from gas jets on the wall rather than a central gas chandelier in the middle of the room, and no matter the location, shades or screens should cover each flame. Wallpaper was to be avoided in favor of elegant wainscoted wood. Carpet should likewise be banished and replaced by red tiles, offering "a warmer, more beautiful floor" in his words. Cast-iron stoves should give way to Dutch porcelain stoves. I'm sure the men's snores would've drowned out his lecture had it not been for their wives—probably seated on either side of them—elbowing their spouses in the ribs to keep them awake. I know I was teetering between sleep and suicide as he droned on and on.

He even ventured into women's fashion, saying American women, which I took to mean Mormon females, should replace their thin and drab dresses with more substantial fabrics with more vibrant colors to enhance their natural beauty. I wondered how President Taylor's wives received that suggestion. The torture continued for ninety minutes, the audience silent, either respectful or unconscious.

Several times I thought he had reached his conclusion, but every time I thought such, Wilde disappointed me and muddled on. After giving so many tips on making a home more aesthetic, at least in his view, he spoke of the need for an artistic temperament—whatever that was—in the minds of all people, American's and Britons, Mormon and heathen, young and old, so that children especially would mature with an appreciation of beauty for its own sake and art for its broadening of beauty.

"The only way of nurturing this artistic temperament in children is by accustoming them from childhood to the abiding presence in their own homes with elegance, with joyous color and with noble and rational design. I seek to make art more than a luxury for the rich but—as it should be—the most splendid of all the chords through which the spirit of any nation manifests its power and makes its culture and refinement a part of the daily atmosphere in which people live, whether in London or in Salt Lake City."

With that, Wilde spun about and marched to the throne of a chair as the spectators—at least those that were still conscious—offered polite applause. He picked up his cape and hooked it around his neck, plopped his hat at a rakish tilt on his head and grabbed his cane. Wilde turned and stepped to the footlights, kissing the head of his walking stick and waving it toward his admirers, as if sharing a kiss with them. I wished the spectators had been with me in his dressing room earlier to take my kiss from him as well.

Wilde took a bow before his standing throng, both of them. With his free hand as he straightened, he removed his floppy hat with a sweeping gesture of admiration—most likely for himself—to the audience. He kissed the cane once again and waved it their way. "Now I bid you *adieu*."

With that announcement and the loud baritone roar that followed, I knew the men in the crowd had finally heard something they could appreciate. The auditorium would be more beautiful and majestic once he removed his ugly face. As he walked to the wings, several women rushed down the aisles toward the stage, throwing lilies and sunflowers at his feet. Where they got the flowers at that time of the year, I didn't know, but they had exerted a lot of effort to throw the garlands at the feet of the aesthete. As Wilde disappeared in the wings and a stage hand drew the curtain, another wave of baritone cheers rippled through the room as the gentlemen celebrated the disappearance of the man who had cost them a dollar-fifty apiece for all their wives. Now I was never a religious theologian, particularly a temperate one, but had I been the Mormon president that evening I would've given the rams of my flock permission to drink all the whiskey it took to wash away the memory of that expensive night.

At that moment, as the departing sounds of the tittering wives and their grumbling husbands still flowed through the auditorium, I realized why I had been hired as a bodyguard. Oscar Fingal O'Flahertie Wills Wilde would need more protection *after* the lecture than before. Granted, I had robbed a bank in Buffalo Gap, Texas, but the folks there had at least gotten something in return—Mandy May Minter's dental work. The way I saw it, these fine Mormon folk had got received nothing of value, though I disagreed with Charles Locke's assessment that he had never left a Wilde lecture with anything more than what he went in with. I was departing with an incredible headache.

As Wilde strode by, Traquair complimented him.

"Wonderful talk, Massa Wilde. Your most forceful lecture yet."

Lord La-de-dah smiled, something he never did during the lecture, revealing his protruding and cigarette-stained teeth, then scurried to his dressing room, likely to satisfy his craving for tobacco.

"Are you serious, Willie? *That* was his best speech?"

"He was on fire tonight, more vigorous than I have ever seen him."

I whistled. "Now I know why he needs a bodyguard. I'll have to be on my toes when we leave. On top of that, I've got a splitting headache."

"Protecting him shouldn't be too hard. The men want to shoot him, but their women won't allow it. From what I've observed, he could have his pick of women, believe it or not, but he shuns them all."

"So he's a rock, you're saying?"

"More like a noodle, I'd guess."

Vale and Locke walked up as Traquair and I visited.

"Good crowd and great box office," Locke said.

"And the best speech he's given yet, more fire in his delivery than normal," Vale noted.

"Lomax inspired him," Traquair noted.

Both Locke and Vale looked at me and grinned, like they understood something I didn't.

Locke said, "Once we get our earnings, we'll head back to the hotel and see the three of you in the morning for the trip to Denver." He turned to me. "Lomax, you'll need your wig tomorrow, so keep it handy on the train." With that, the duo marched away.

"What's it with that wig?" I asked Traquair.

He shrugged. "That's a new one on me."

From there, we stepped to Wilde's dressing room

and waited outside the door. When he opened it, he emerged, as well as the smoke of what must have been another dozen cigarettes.

"Ready for the gauntlet, H.H.?"

I nodded as we marched to the back of the theater and outside into the darkness, where forty or more women in plain garb awaited. They threw flowers and kisses, though I think a couple of men near the street pitched pebbles at him.

"Thank you, ladies of Salt Lake City, for enhancing my life, but I am exhausted and must return to the hotel for rest. Genius is tiring."

I watched for men with weapons more dangerous than pebbles but saw none, so I climbed into the hotel carriage after Wilde and Traquair. We made the run to the Walker House, arriving in the rear to avoid the crowd out front. We scurried in the back, up the stairs and to our room, without creating any commotion. Only after Traquair had locked the door did I let down my guard for a potential assassin seeking to revenge or a refund for a tedious evening.

The three of us were exhausted, me with a splitting headache to boot. We retreated to our respective rooms. Collapsing on my bed and kicking off my patent leather shoes without bothering to remove my clothes, I fell into a deep sleep for a spell until I heard someone approaching my bed. An assassin had followed us, intent on getting even with that aesthete scoundrel, but had entered the wrong bedroom. His mistake gave me the advantage. I gently slid my revolver from its holster, aiming at the approaching shadow and intending to kill the intruder.

CHAPTER SIXTEEN

As the stealthy prowler inched toward me, I made out his crouching form and heard a wisp of a breath as he neared, ever careful not to disturb me. I let my gun hand ease my revolver over my chest, ready to lift the weapon in his face and give this trespasser the greatest and last surprise of his soon-to-be-shortened life. The specter raised his hands as he came closer. I suspected he intended to strangle Oscar Wilde, but the moment he wrapped his fingers around my neck and I would introduce him to Judge Colt, putting a .45 slug between his eyes. This murdering hooligan neared me, his thighs bumping my mattress.

I held my breath.

He stretched his arms for me, drawing closer, leaning down, and reaching for my neck.

Taking a shallow breath, I inhaled the ashcan odor of the ruffian. I lifted my gun, cocked the hammer and shoved the barrel for his mouth.

He gasped.

I cocked the hammer, preparing to pull the trigger as my intended slayer kissed the pistol's muzzle.

The fellow straightened, lifting his arms over his head like he was the victim. "H.H.," he cried, "I thought you were asleep."

In that instant, I realized I was about to kill the man they hired me to protect, the young genius Oscar Wilde. "What the hell are you doing in here? I almost killed you." Lowering the gun and releasing the hammer, I placed the revolver on the mattress beside me.

"I thought you might desire companionship or a conversation with someone who could warm your bed."

"Not tonight," I answered. "I've got a headache." I thought for a moment. "Not tonight or any night ever."

"I couldn't sleep," he responded. "Thought perhaps we might converse." He lowered his hands and pulled something from his side, then flared a match to light a cigarette he had extracted from the pocket of his robe.

In the flame of his match, I saw he had forgotten to tie his robe, and he observed that I remained fully dressed. He blew the match out with a puff of smoke. "You didn't undress? Shall I help you get out of those clothes and make yourself more comfortable?"

"How many times do I have to tell you I've got a headache? Take that stinking cigarette out of my room so I can rest enough to protect tomorrow. I'd hate for someone to shoot you like I almost did. It'd ruin my reputation."

"And make my name immortal," he replied.

"Now scat. And don't ever enter my bedroom again without knocking."

Wilde turned and marched sullenly out the door,

shutting it harder than necessary to show his displeasure. So was I mad, as I had been sleeping soundly until he interrupted my slumber. I grabbed my pistol, inserted it my holster and stood up, undressing down to my long johns. Collapsing on the bed after that, I craved sleep but managed only fretful rest after my perplexing encounter with Lord La-de-dah.

Come sunrise I got up and dressed in my normal pants, shirt, gun belt, and boots, then packed my suit in the carpetbag and gathered my carbine, saddlebags, and coat, toting them to the parlor and tossing them on the sofa now naked of the tiger and wolf skins. Traquair was busy packing things for the wizard of words, so Wilde would not have to waste any of his brilliance on the mundane tasks of everyday life like the rest of us ignorant toads.

Traquair grinned. "I suspect Massa Wilde visited you last night."

"Yeah, but what was that all about?"

"Let's just say he gets lonely late in the evening."

"Well, last night, he almost got a bullet in the mouth."

"He would've survived. After all, he's immortal to hear him tell it, but most folks find him odd. When you're around him a lot, you realize he's imperious."

I agreed, whatever that meant. "You need any help, Willie?"

Traquair shook his head. "I've got my getaway-day routine, so I'm fine, but you can keep him occupied and out of my way when he arises."

An hour later, Wilde emerged from his room, dressed in regular trousers and shoes, but a shirt with flared cuffs and a frilly front. He saw me on his sofa and smiled, then came over and moved my belongings to a nearby chair before sitting beside me. The poet placed his hand on my thigh and squeezed. "I hope you got a restful sleep after I left."

Removing his fingers from my leg, I placed them on his own. "Don't sneak up on me in the night. It's dangerous."

"Indeed is, H.H., as I came near kissing your gun barrel. You've got much to learn about life, and love."

"I've learned enough to know not to prowl in people's bedrooms."

"Not me," Wilde snickered.

"Perhaps you should've been a Mormon."

"Too dull for me. I should've been a monarch with all the intrigue that accompanies social, political and military power." He next talked about Queen Victoria and her wayward son, the Prince of Wales, with his many mistresses, including Lilly Langtry, who he called the most beautiful creature on earth, though I took him to mean excluding himself, of course. Wilde spoke of Langtry and battleships and trysts and the cost of governing and the price of philandering. He reminded me of an old lady gossiping at a Sunday social. Seldom did I get his jokes or the point of his stories other than how important he was, rubbing shoulders with royalty and their consorts, but I kept him occupied as Traquair packed his belongings, then fetched porters to carry his luggage to the wagon that would deliver it to the depot for the afternoon train.

When the hotel staff arrived, Traquair pointed to the trunks and bags for them to handle.

"You forgot one," Wilde said, nodding toward his bedroom doorway.

"No, Massa Wilde, both Mister Vale and Mister Locke asked me to keep that one in the compartment with us."

"I have no desire to change clothes on the train."

Traquair shrugged. "I do what I am told by those that pay me."

Wilde pointed to the chair where he had moved my belongings. "What about these things of H.H.?"

Shaking my head, I announced. "I'll keep up with my own baggage."

The valet turned to the hotel porters and nodded for them to proceed.

A half hour later, we headed downstairs and out the back door to avoid the curious out front who could never get enough of the freak show that was Lord La-de-dah. I carried my belongings and Traquair toted Wilde's carpetbag. We loaded up in the carriage and rode to the depot where we met Vale and Locke, then had lunch at an adjacent eatery. We boarded the afternoon train and started for Denver on an overnight trip that would end the next morning. As a famous and monied passenger, Wilde received a large compartment partitioned in two sections with two overhead beds and cushioned seats that converted into additional sleepers. With four beds and five of us, I was the odd man out, so I knew I would sleep on the floor, which was fine with me as long as it was beyond Wilde's reach.

As I pitched my belongings beneath a bench seat, Traquair gave Wilde's carpetbag to Locke, who handed it to me. "You'll need this," he said, "as well as your wig and patent leather shoes."

Tossing the luggage on the seat, I unlatched the

catch and saw gaudy clothes that could only belong to Wilde. "These are his," I said, pointing to the poet.

"Your powers of observation astound me," Locke replied, "but you'll want to change into them."

"What?"

"Master Wilde is such a sensation that people come out to meet the train at each stop. They expect an appearance."

"Let him appear, then."

Locke shook his head. "Nope, he's got a headache."

I glanced at Wilde and grimaced.

"Headaches are so contagious," he answered.

"You were paid five hundred dollars to work as his bodyguard. This is part of the job, Lomax."

"I don't like it."

"That doesn't matter because you'll do what you're told, or I'll make sure your sister never plays in another theater west of the Mississippi or east of hell."

Locke was bluffing, I figured, but I couldn't risk her future and that of her family. I nodded. "Fine by me."

The steam whistle blew and moments later the train lurched away from Salt Lake City with me destined to play the role of the incomparable Oscar Fingal O'Flahertie Wills Wilde at every stop between the Mormon city and Denver. As the locomotive required water or coal every forty-five minutes or so, I would perform a number of times.

"You should be prepared to say a few words, impress the locals—"

"Or yokels," Wilde interjected.

"—with your observations on beauty and art."

Sighing, I turned to Traquair, who lifted his arms and shrugged.

"I had no idea, Massa Imposter."

Everyone else laughed.

"Should I help you change, H.H.?" Wilde asked.

Shaking my head, I took the carpetbag and strode into the adjacent compartment and slammed the door. After I unpacked the bag, I realized I should have accepted the valet's offer, as I wasn't sure how to wear all the clothes or even the order you put them on. As Wilde was taller than me and wider in the hips, I doubted the attire would fit, but I did my best.

I removed my clothes, rolled up the leggings on my long johns and extracted the purple stockings from the bag. While I had taken hose off a young lady on occasion, I'd never put them on anybody, much less myself. I yanked them up to my knees and poked the top under my long johns. Next I pulled the lavender shirt over my head and pushed my arms through the wide sleeves. Between the broad collar, the frills and pleats in front, I felt like a bumble bee trapped among flower petals. Extracting the green knee britches from the carpetbag, I grimaced, wondering how they worked. Sure, you put your legs in one at a time, but it didn't seem natural for a man to dress in something more appropriate for a dancehall gal. I shoved one leg in and yanked the garb up to my knee, then the other. After that, I pulled the waistband to my midsection and tucked my frilly shirt into my girly britches. The pants were loose at the waist, but tight at the knees where my bunched up long johns made my thighs look like ten miles of rough road.

Though I wanted to escape the coming embarrassment, I gritted my teeth, opened the door between units and entered. Locke, Vale, and Traquair laughed.

Wilde applauded softly. "So, manly," he noted.

Nothing he could've said would've sounded stupider than "manly." My doubts grew about the manliness of the British. "I feel like a fool," I admitted.

"I play one all the time and look at me because I'm making a small fortune living the part."

"You were born to play the fool, Oscar. Not me."

Locke studied me and nodded. "You'll pass once you put on the wig and the patent leather shoes."

From head to toe, I would be fully humiliated. Traquair removed my carpetbag from beneath the bench and held it up. "Shall I assist, Massa Imposter?"

"Why not?"

Placing the luggage on the seat, he unlatched it and pulled out the wig, handing it gleefully to me.

I snagged it over my head and adjusted it until it felt right. As soon as I completed barbering myself, I accepted the shoes from Traquair and slid my feet inside. They were a little big, but I could manage no farther than I would have to walk on the train to make my appearance.

Wilde clapped his hands together. "Goody, goody! I have never looked so stylish."

"Nor me so foolish."

Locke and Vale studied me. "You'll do, but don't say anything stupid," Vale instructed.

"In this outfit, who would ever realize it?"

Traquair closed my carpetbag and slid it beneath the seat.

Wilde tittered. "I could just hug myself." He flung his arms around me.

"Just don't kiss yourself again," I responded as he squeezed, then released me.

"Should I assist you with your elucidation or your elocution?"

I shook my head at Lord La-de-dah. "Being seen in this outfit is execution enough."

Again Wilde laughed. "You have such a way with words that I am certain my public will adore you as me."

"I'd rather they appreciate me as me, the 'True American,' and you as you."

"You hold my reputation in your capable hands, H.H. How you handle this awesome responsibility may go down in posterity as the greatest moment of your life."

Lord La-de-dah was more excited about my debut than I was, though I was not without an acting experience, having played three pedestrians in *A Christmas Carol*—by Charles Dickens, no less—and a drunk in *Ten Nights in a Bar-room*. That certainly prepared me to play the fool.

I retreated to the adjacent cubicle to await my performance in my first lead role. Traquair followed me, grinning from ear to ear.

"Has anyone ever performed Wilde before?" I asked.

"Indeed they have. An actor played him some in California from San Francisco to Sacramento. I think he gave them the idea. Massa Wilde thought it was delightful."

"How do they know Wilde—or me—is coming?"

"The telegraph. Vale and Locke pay telegraphers to wire the news ahead. It'll surprise you how many folks show up with an hour's notice."

The train slowed, and I knew my debut as a solo performer neared. "Where's my first performance?"

"Ogden," Traquair answered, giving me confidence.

"I've played Ogden before. Maybe folks'll return for my encore."

Traquair laughed. "They only want to see Wilde man without paying for the privilege."

The train slowed as we entered the outskirts of town. I gritted my teeth and marched into Wilde's compartment, where Locke stood up. "I'll introduce you to the crowd. You'll speak from the back of car."

"Are you certain the great man wouldn't care to deliver his remarks himself? Surely, he knows more about himself than I do."

"No, sir," Locke responded. "We can't take that chance."

His comment confused me, just as I figured my talk would make no sense to the curious folks of Ogden. The train slowed, the whistle blew, and the locomotive huffed as our car finally came to a stop.

"It's show time," Locke said, picking up Wilde's floppy hat and plopping it atop my head. He grabbed my hand, led me to the end of the car and out the door to the landing, where more than a hundred spectators closed in on me.

"Ladies and gentlemen," cried Locke, "let me introduce to Ogden, the world's great aesthete, the incomparable Oscar Wilde, all the way from London, England, and the court of Queen Victoria herself."

I stepped to the back railing, kissing my palm and flinging it toward the crowd, most applauding. I shook my head like a horse.

"Speech, speech," cried a bald man in overalls, and the throng took up the chant.

"What forsooth wouldeth you liketh me to talketh abouteth?" I asked.

"What you're known for," answered a woman. "Art and beauty."

"Art is liketh beauty," I started, "and beauty is liketh art."

Various members of the crowd scratched their skulls because, like Wilde, I was talking way over their heads.

"But what is beauty?" shouted a woman spectator.

"Beauty is liketh the opposite of ugly, and ugly is liketh the opposite of beauty."

One fellow held up one of the souvenir photos Locke had distributed. "How come you don't look like this image of yourself?"

"Becauseth," I said, "beauty changeth always."

"How cometh?" shouted a young man, mocking my speech.

"Becauseth I sayeth so. I ameth an ass-thete." I ran my fingers through the strands of my wig and shook my head.

"Then you are Bunthorne, the fool of *Patience*?" shouted another skeptical man.

I proudly raised my chin and nodded. "I ameth but I prefereth to calleth myself Butt-thorn as I ameth a paineth in the ass-thete."

The crowd gasped at my comment.

Deciding I could never top that line, I tipped my floppy sombrero at the crowd. "I biddeth you adieueth."

Some applauded, more jeered. I stepped back into the passenger car where Vale, Locke, and Traquair stood laughing.

Wilde showed far less enthusiasm for my performance. "Butt-thorn? A paineth in the ass-thete? You sounded like a drunk, illiterate reading a passage from the Bible. Dispense with the King James English, H.H. I prefer a subtle mockery, not blatant ridicule." He lit a cigarette and puffed vigorously on the smoldering tobacco.

Locke slapped me on the shoulder. "Great performance, Lomax, but I agree with Master Wilde, eliminate the Bible English, but not the humor. It makes as much sense as he does." He turned to Lord La-de-dah. "No offense, Oscar."

The lecturer sucked harder on his cigarette and plopped down on the cushioned seat, spreading his long legs across it so no one else could sit beside him. The rest of us migrated to the adjacent cubicle and sat down as the locomotive blew its whistle and the conductor cried, "All aboard!"

Shortly after that, the train lurched forward, and we resumed our journey. Once beyond the outskirts of town, the conductor visited to hand Locke a yellow envelope, which he ripped open and read, then tucked in his britches pocket. I thought nothing of it at the moment, but after every stop between Ogden and Denver, Locke always received a telegram, even in places without a depot and telegraph office. We stopped an hour later at a water tank and shed where the locomotive took on water and coal. As there were no spectators at this stop other than a dozen mules in a corral and ten times that number of crows sitting on the fence, Locke suggested I practice my delivery for the next town, where we would have an audience.

I retreated to the back platform and railed about art

and beauty, speaking plain old American English. It was all nonsense, so I felt I had given an accurate representation of Wilde's philosophy. As I spoke to the birds and the mules, I watched a railroad man with a modest wooden case run to a telegraph line paralleling the train tracks. He hung the box from a pole, unlatched the case, which opened like a writing desk and revealed a telegraph key. He removed a pair of wires and attached them to wire connectors within reach on the pole. Then he started tapping the instrument, slinging Morse code to who-knew-where and subsequently receiving messages he penciled on a yellow pad.

The engineer gave a quick toot on the train whistle and the telegrapher unhooked the wire strands, closed and locked the case, before dashing to a car ahead of ours. Having completed my performance before the animals, I stepped back into the passenger compartment as our journey resumed. Minutes later, the conductor came by and delivered Locke another message, which he read and stuck in his pants pocket.

"We've got one more water stop before we hit the next town, Lomax," Locke announced. "It would do you good to keep practicing so you can give a sterling performance, something that the folks will always remember about Oscar Wilde."

"Even if it's not Oscar?" I asked.

"Especially if it's not him!" He laughed.

Wilde pouted, still taking up the whole seat in his compartment and puffing on his latest smoke. Barely a moment had passed since Ogden that Wilde hadn't squeezed a cigarette between his lips, billowing out more smoke than a prairie fire. He completely ignored me, the True American, as I mocked him again at the next water stop. Once the train continued its journey, the conductor delivered another telegram, which Locke stuck in his pocket, whispering something to Vale, who nodded. Moments later, Locke suggested he and Vale step outside for some fresh air.

"I'll join you," I offered.

"No, Lomax, you stay here. Can't risk your wig getting blown off while the train's moving. Then you couldn't be Oscar's apprentice."

"Some understudy," Oscar mumbled.

Locke exited our compartment, bumping the door with his hip and jarring from his pocket the latest telegram, which dropped to the floor. Traquair picked it up and started to call Locke, but the promoter had already stepped outside and shut the enclosure. The valet looked at the telegraph, his brow furrowing. He signaled for me to join him outside the compartment.

"Pardon us for a moment, Massa Wilde," Traquair said as I accompanied him to the narrow passageway. He shut the compartment door.

"You should read."

I took the yellow paper and scanned the message: PROTECT OW//stop//SNIPES STILL LIKELY TO DENVER. Three times I reviewed the telegram, uncertain what the last part meant.

Traquair took the sheet from me and slipped it in his pants pocket.

Shrugging, I said, "All I can figure is folks in Colorado think he's such a greenhorn they play on taking him snipe hunting, you know, searching for a creature that doesn't exist."

"Perhaps, but what if 'snipes' is code for sniper, someone planning to shoot Master Wilde?"

"Why would someone want to shoot him?"

"Because he's different."

"No question about that, Willie."

"Since Sacramento, Locke and Vale have talked about threats to Lord La-de-dah, but I thought they were making it up to increase the box office." Traquair scratched his chin and cocked his head. "I don't know that I trust them, especially Locke. They're promoters and will do anything to get press. It could be these are genuine threats, or maybe a scheme to obtain more column inches in the newspapers. Imagine the head-lines if some assassin takes a potshot at him.

"I doubt it would be a jealous husband." I laughed.

"Or imagine the headlines 'Oscar Wilde Apprentice Shot, Takes Bullet for Aesthete.' Wow!" Traquair said.

"I wouldn't care for those headlines or a bullet meant for Lord La-de-dah."

"Think what that would do for ticket sales, maybe even let Locke earn his money sooner so he could return to California quicker, rather than traipsing halfway across the country for Master Wilde to fulfill his agreement."

"So, Locke is using me as a sacrificial lamb, is he?"

"It's possible, Lomax, as I wouldn't put anything past a promoter. You've heard there's no honor among thieves, but what I've learned is theatrical promoters are all thieves."

Our conversation ended as Vale and Locke opened the door and entered the hallway.

"Have you two been eavesdropping?" Vale demanded.

"We had to use the toilet, and Lomax wasn't sure he could manage in his new outfit."

The two promoters laughed as they opened the compartment door and let us enter first. We marched through a cloud of smoke into the second sitting area, which was little fresher. There we waited for the next stop, Vale and Locke grinning like they knew something Traquair and I didn't. When the train slowed, I gulped, wondering if this would be my last performance and if Locke and Vale had planned my demise all along. Maybe the five hundred dollars they paid me would be returned tenfold in news stories if I were get assassinated portraying the poet.

As the train crawled toward the depot and platform, Locke told me the town's name, but I didn't catch it. I focused on survival. I stood up, adjusted my wig and tugged the floppy hat down over my forehead. When our car stopped by the depot platform, Locke and Vale arose and led me out of our compartment.

Turning to Traquair, I asked, "Are you coming?"

He shook his head. "Not sure I want to be within range of you, Lomax. It's been good to know you."

I scowled, mad that my only friend on the trip had abandoned me for his own safety.

The valet jumped up and laughed, swatting me on the back. "Of course, I'm coming. I wouldn't miss this for the world."

"I'm okay, just as long as any assassin misses."

"Lomax, what's keeping you?" Vale cried.

"We cometh," I answered.

"None of that phony English this time," Locke ordered.

Traquair and I marched past the pouting and smoking literary genius and into the hallway, then out onto the landing. On the station platform another crowd awaited. Locke introduced me as the boy genius, and I stepped to the railing to talk about art and beauty while I was thinking about survival.

With my nerves tingling, I shook my tresses and surveyed the crowd, looking for a potential assassin.

"There he is," cried a young man, pointing at me.

"Isn't he marvelous?" called an elderly woman, stepping on the railroad ties and walking straight to me, her hands clasped beneath her chin. I wondered if she packed a pistol somewhere on her.

"You are a beautiful gathering," I announced, hoping to flatter any potential assassin.

Barely had I uttered those words than I heard the first explosive bang followed by a second and more. It sounded like my killers had brought a Gatling gun. I spun around to dash into the safety of the passenger car, but Locke and Vale beat me there, holding the door shut so neither I nor Traquair could find cover.

Deciding to die like a man, I pulled my coat open and turned to face the sniper, exposing my chest to him. I face by destiny, wondering only if this shooting would boost Wilde's ticket sales.

CHAPTER SEVENTEEN

With my nerves tingling, I stepped out to the platform, shook my tresses and surveyed the crowd, looking for a potential assassin.

"There he is," cried a young man, pointing at me.

"Isn't he marvelous?" called an elderly woman, stepping on the railroad ties and walking straight to me, her hands clasped beneath her chin. I wondered if she was packing a pistol somewhere on her.

"You are a beautiful gathering," I announced, hoping to flatter any potential assassin.

Barely had I uttered those words than I heard the first bang followed by the second. I spun around to dash into the safety of the passenger car, but Locke and Vale beat me, holding the door shut so neither I nor Traquair could find cover.

Deciding to die like a man, I pulled my coat open and turned to face the sniper, exposing my chest to him. I face by destiny, wondering only if this shooting would boost Wilde's ticket sales.

Bang-bang-pop-bang-bang-bang-pop   sounds

exploded above all other noises, and I stood fearless against the bullets and not a one hit me. The shots kept coming, but I remained steadfast and invincible, determined to survive, least Wilde grow richer from better box offices.

My audience applauded and cheered as the explosives faded away. A man cried out, "Every grand occasion deserves fireworks."

Realizing it was a string of firecrackers rather than a barrage of bullets, I breathed easier, proud I had faced death like a hero, even if I had wet Wilde's pants.

"Art and beauty have come to Utah," I announced, "because I am here to vanquish the ugly and promote the artistic. Beauty may only be skin deep, but ugly extends all the way to the bone. Art, however, goes deeper because it reaches the heart and touches the brain and shapes your enjoyment of life. Seek beauty in everything you have and create art in everything you do, whether it is collecting your mail or dumping your chamber pot. Only then can your nation be truly civilized. Otherwise America will evolve from artless barbarism to senseless anarchy without the pleasing existence we call civilization."

Behind me, Locke and Vale returned to the platform, clapping their hands and encouraging my audience to do the same.

"Isn't he brilliant?" shouted Locke.

"And brave!" snickered Traquair.

Removing my hat, I took a bow and grabbed my head as my wig almost slipped off. I replaced headwear and retreated inside, followed by the promoters.

"You're improving with each talk," Vale said, slapping me on the back.

"So good, in fact, we may substitute you for Oscar in some of his meetings with the newspapermen," Locke added.

"I want nothing to do with assassins who use bullets or ink," I responded, my odd remarks catching them off guard.

Both men looked at each other with widened eyes and a questioning look that told me the threats were real, not a promotional stunt.

They quickly covered their surprise as Wilde spoke.

"Don't I have a say in the matter? After all, *I* am the celebrity."

"True," Locke said, "but Lomax makes about as much sense as you do, and he's not as temperamental. Once I earn my money back from our agreement, Oscar, you can do whatever the hell you want."

The train whistle announced our pending departure, and soon we moved on. I spoke at one water stop and two small communities before dusk arrived, followed by the darkness that enveloped the majestic land. I was glad to get out of Wilde's damp pants when we bedded down for the night in our accommodations, everyone else in a bunk and me on the floor, but at least I was beyond the grasp of Lord La-de-dah. We expected to be in Denver around noon the next day in plenty of time for our group to check into the Windsor Hotel and catch our breath before the evening lecture in Denver's new Tabor Grand Opera House, named for its benefactor Horace Tabor. I had once worked for Tabor in his Leadville store before he struck it rich and before I became a wanted murderer in the town.

I spent a restless night, partially because I was bedding down on the floorboards with no mattress to soften the jarring ride over the iron rails, but mostly because of my possible assassination for impersonating Oscar Wilde and because I had that Colorado murder warrant hanging over my head ever since I escaped Leadville five years earlier with the law looking to hang me. I'd gotten drunk one night, lamenting being swindled by a crooked, long-necked, bug-eyed lawyer named Adam Scheisse out of a mining claim that would've made me as rich as Horace Tabor. When I sobered up the next morning, I found myself on the floor of Scheisse's office and him dead at my feet along with a shotgun.

As I understood it, Wilde would speak in Denver, Colorado Springs, and then Denver again before we continued our journey east into Kansas. I doubted folks outside of Leadville remembered the murder, and I suspect nobody would've cared about the lawyer's demise if they had ever met him, but it left an uneasy knot in my stomach, knowing I'd be back in Colorado in case some do-gooder had a long memory and was intent upon collecting the reward or fulfilling the letter rather than the spirit of the law.

When we awoke the next morning, the train sat motionless on the tracks. We dressed, me in Wilde's now dry clothes, and Locke went to check on the delay. He reported the conductor had indicated an overnight train wreck had delayed traffic up and down the line. We would be late getting into Denver. How late, no one could tell. As we were special railroad guests, the conductor scrounged up some food for our breakfast, an apple apiece and a tin of soda crackers. Meager though it was, our meal was more than the other passengers received.

To kill time, we got off the train for a spell, passing the delay by throwing rocks and looking at the distant snow-capped mountains. After what seemed like forever, the train blew its whistle to announce it would depart shortly. We travelers scrambled aboard and the railroad man with the telegraph key scurried away from the telegraph pole for his car.

Finally, our iron serpent started crawling along the rails, and the conductor brought Locke another telegram. The promoter read it, then wrote a message to be sent from the next telegraph office. By the conductor's best estimate, we would arrive in Denver around seven o'clock, barely an hour before Wilde's scheduled talk.

"We can't afford to cancel or postpone the lecture," Locke said. "We'll make it no matter what." He turned to Wilde. "You won't have time to change into your normal attire."

The poet pointed to me, still wearing his foppish costume. "He's dressed right for it. You've been saying he can do what I do, so let him give the speech."

"That's fraud, Oscar."

"No bigger scam than what we've perpetrated on this train, him acting like me."

"In the eyes of the law there's a huge difference, charging admission to see a celebrity and substituting someone else in his place."

Wilde yanked his cigarette from his mouth and blew smoke at Locke. "You're telling me a theatrical promoter would never sink that low?"

The San Francisco impresario smirked. "We're paragons of virtue, unlike our lecturers. This may be a sham, but it's not a scam without money changing hands."

"I can draw a crowd, Charlie. Let's see who'll pay to hear you talk."

For an instant, I considered giving them my revolver and carbine so they could resolve their differences in a manly way, rather than insulting each other like school girls. "Can I remove these girly clothes before you kill each other? And just so we understand, I won't impersonate his holiness in a coffin. He can handle that appearance himself."

"Nobody's gonna die, Lomax," Locke informed me, "and no, you can't change your outfit. We'll be cutting it close to get Oscar to the theater for his lecture. He always draws a crowd on arrival, so I intend to send you off the train first to decoy folks. I've ordered an extra carriage to deliver you to the Windsor Hotel while we run to the opera house for the talk. We can't afford to be late and lose any box office earnings."

I glanced at Wilde, who wore as close to normal clothing as you would ever see on him—straight tan trousers, a frill-less aqua shirt, a modest red bowtie and regular shoes. The only flamboyant piece was the dark blue velvet coat. "The crowd'll be disappointed in his bland attire."

"We won't have time to wait for his baggage to change," Locke informed me.

"He can have what I'm wearing," I offered.

"Not today, Lomax," Locke responded.

"Can't guard him if I'm not with him."

"It's a risk I'm prepared to take," he answered. "We have had no threats in Denver like we've had along the route." As soon as he spoke, he squinted, and I realized for certain they had used me as a substitute victim. After all, the show must go on even if an innocent man —me in this case—died as a result.

We settled back in our seats as we crawled toward Denver, the tension tight among us as we fretted away the afternoon. The train arrived at the Denver depot a little after seven o'clock and two hundred people waited on the platform to meet the great aesthete. Glancing out the window, I watched the spectators craning their necks to glimpse Wilde.

"Show time, Lomax," Locke announced as we drew to a stop.

I stood up, strapped my holster around my waist and picked up my carbine, coat, saddlebags, and valise.

"You won't need your baggage. Traquair can handle them for you."

Shaking my head, I made my displeasure known. "He's got enough to keep up with."

Locke and Vale shrugged. "There'll be a carriage in front of the station. The driver will display a sign for Mister Wilde. Tell him to leave the depot as quickly as he can, but take his time getting to the hotel so Traquair can get there and see the baggage is unloaded, as they know to give Willie the keys."

I nodded, stepped by Locke, past Wilde and into the hallway, pausing at the door to catch my breath before emerging onto the landing where I had given my previous interpretations of Lord La-de-dah. I stepped from the passenger car to the platform, stumbling as I landed but managing my balance, even with the load I carried.

"There he is," someone shouted, and the throng converged on me.

One breathless lady stopped opposite me. "Are you him?"

"Who else would dress like this?" I responded as I pushed my way through my admirers.

She smiled and clasped her hands above her bosom.

A more suspicious fellow in the crowd eyed me. "I didn't expect you to come armed and carrying saddlebags."

"You never know when a crowd'll turn on you," I replied. "The Prince of Wales told me before this lecture tour to be prepared to defend myself—"

Another man scratched his head and shouted, "Fish have princes?"

"—especially in the wilds of the American West," I finished as I worked my way through the crowd toward the station. Everyone trailed me into the depot and out the front door.

"You're still lecturing tonight, Mister Wilde, are you not?" asked a woman.

"Indeed I am, once I eat dinner and freshen up at the hotel, though I may be late to the opera house."

"You already missed dinner," noted a spectator. "That's our midday meal. We call the evening meal supper in these parts."

"Fine, I'll suffer through supper, so I shall have strength to talk to the fine folks of Denver this evening about art and beauty. You know beauty is the opposite of ugly, and ugly is anything but beauty."

Several women swooned at my brilliant observation, and another female wearing heavier makeup and a blouse that revealed the vee of her bosom winked at me. "Let me know if you'd like some companionship tonight, Oscar." She batted her eyes again. Uncertain what Oscar would've done, I ignored her, relieved to spot a carriage man holding a sheet of paper with Wilde's name penciled on it.

I scurried to the driver, tossed my belongings in the back and climbed into the rear seat as my chauffeur took his place.

"Get away from here as fast as you can," I instructed, "but once we lose the crowd, take all the time you need to reach to the hotel."

The driver whistled, and the horse moved forward. Soon we left the throng behind. "We're so excited to have a man of your fame and intellect in Denver, Mister Wilde. And I must say, your attire is fetching."

"And I am honored to reach Denver and share my genius with you, but I prefer to gossip. That's why I wear such outlandish clothing to inspire hearsay, though none is as juicy as stories of the monarchy." As he killed time showing me the town, I regaled him with tales Wilde had told me of the crown prince and his peculiarities. The driver was enthralled and disappointed when we arrived at our destination barely ahead of William Traquair with the baggage.

As soon as my escort halted the carriage at the hotel entry, he jumped out and helped me down, picking up my valise and saddlebags while I took my coat and folded it around my carbine. "It's been a pleasure to serve you, Mister Wilde."

"I hope I haven't disappointed you, lad."

"Absolutely not! I loved your stories of the queen and the crown prince. I can't wait to share with my friends."

"Remember one thing: they are no better than you."

"Thank you, sir. I'm honored to have met you."

"I see my valet coming. I'll wait on him, if you wouldn't mind carrying those items to the desk and leaving them with the clerk."

He nodded. "My pleasure, Mister Wilde."

I thanked him as he scurried away. Several passersby stopped and pointed at my stockings, knee britches, and frilly shirt, giggling at my attire. Shortly, the baggage wagon arrived with Traquair. He grinned. "Glad you made it to the hotel, Oscar junior. You left the crowd buzzing, less about your clothes than your weapons. Lord La-de-dah was tougher than they imagined."

"Did my twin get away unrecognized?"

"Indeed, he did, though his audience will be disappointed that he's not in stockings, knee britches, and blouse. Word at the depot was that the benefactor of the opera house, Horace Tabor, planned to attend the lecture. He's lieutenant governor now and he wants to meet our boy this evening after the lecture."

As we walked into the hotel lobby, a wave of relief rushed over me as I had worked for Tabor in Leadville before he was rich and before I was accused of murder. Had I been working as Wilde's protector at the theater, the lieutenant governor could have identified me and had me arrested for the murky crime. This was the type of coincidence that worried me in Colorado. If the wrong person recognized me, I could wind up in prison or on the gallows—unless I could convince Wilde to dress in my clothes and go in my place. He might enjoy the drama of the event, if not the outcome.

At the desk, I retrieved my saddlebags and valise. The clerk greeted me. "Welcome to Denver, Mister Wilde."

Before I could answer, Traquair leaned into the counter. "This is not Mister Wilde, but an impersonator we send ahead of the great one in case someone seeks to harm his holiness, Mister Wilde." Traquair pointed to me. "This man is a dangerous operative from one of the nation's pre-eminent detective agencies, an agency I am not at liberty to disclose because they fear the attire he is forced to wear might damage their reputation, but let's just say he sleeps with an open eye."

I nodded and growled as I stared at the attendant. Next, I shut my right eye to reinforce Traquair's elaboration of my role.

"Our driver will be so disappointed," the clerk responded, "as he was thrilled to drive you to the Windsor and deliver your bags."

With my eye still shut, I lifted my extended index finger to my mouth and tapped my lips. "He is never to know, or people could get hurt or killed," I warned.

As the clerk's eyes widened, I opened mine and glared at him that this confidence was not to be broken upon risk of injury or death.

"I understand," he stammered.

"We knew you would," said Traquair. "Now, what floor are we on?"

"Third."

Traquair turned to me. "Okay, killer, why don't you head on up and check that the hallways are safe?"

I nodded and tromped away, trying in silly clothes to look as threatening as an approaching tornado while I surveyed the lobby and the staircase for dangers. Traquair, I had to admit, was a talented actor as well. I paced the third-floor hallway for fifteen minutes as the servant checked in and made the final arrangements for the baggage to be delivered.

When Traquair joined me, he matched the numbers on the doors against the keys he carried and pointed me to the end of the hall. "It's a different setup than in Salt Lake City. Rather than a suite, we have three separate rooms. His majesty will have the end room to himself. You and I'll be sharing a room, as will Vale and Locke. We'll be here two nights before heading to Colorado Springs."

"Suits me, as long as I'm not sleeping on the floor," I replied.

"About that," he said, then hesitated. "You'll be sharing a bed with me."

"It beats sharing one with Lord La-de-dah or sleeping on the floor. You surprised?"

"You *are* from Arkansas, and me being black and all."

"Northwest Arkansas," I replied. "Anyway, we're too dumb to know any better. At least, that's what most people think."

Traquair laughed and slapped me on the back. "You're more open minded than our traveling genius. He's told me even in a free country, the monied and intellectual folks still need servants at worst or slaves at best. That's another reason I call him 'Massa.' It tells him I understand my place is beneath him, no matter how low he is or ever will be. Now that he's met Walt Whitman, do you know the person he most desires to meet before he returns to England?"

As I didn't even know who Walt Whitman was, I had no idea who to guess. I shrugged.

"Jefferson Davis!"

I knew who Jefferson Davis was, and I held him—along with two Yankee marksmen—responsible for the deaths of my two brothers during the late War Between the States. "Perhaps he's partial to lost causes."

"Like aesthetics," the valet answered as he unlocked Wilde's suite at the end of the hall. The doors to the other two rooms straddled Lord La-de-dah's quarters. Traquair gave me the key to Wilde's room. "You may need it as his bodyguard." He inspected the adjacent rooms, studying them, then handing me the key to the one he liked best. "This will be ours."

I carried my belongings into our room and dropped them on the poster bed. A commotion at the end of the hallway told me the baggage had arrived. I stood in our doorway as Traquair directed the porters where to place the different bags.

As the six staff member were leaving, the valet confirmed Wilde's dinner would arrive in his room no later than nine-thirty and should include baked fish, mutton chops, two cheese omelets, relishes, bread, butter, tea, and wine. After the hotel staff disappeared, I stepped into Wilde's suite as Traquair arranged the temporary quarters to Wilde's specifications, beginning with the display of the tiger and wolf furs over the sofa. "You need any help?"

"I've got my method and you'd only slow me down, though I appreciate the offer. Why don't you go in our room, remove those ridiculous clothes and that stupid wig and dress like an American once again?"

"You don't have to ask me twice." I retreated to our quarters and changed, then removed my bags from the bed and reclined on the pillows, dozing off for an hour until hall noises disturbed me. I awoke in my darkened chamber as the door opened. I prayed it wasn't Wilde checking on me as my revolver was across the room.

"Lomax," Traquair called, "Mister Locke's here to see you."

"Was Wilde assassinated?" I asked.

"Not yet, but he'll have some special visitors about ten o'clock."

I followed Traquair into Wilde's room, just as two attendants delivered his meal, placing the food on a modest table in front of the sofa.

Locke strode over. "I need you in here protecting Oscar the rest of the night. We have a distinguished guest arriving at ten."

"Won't his highness be too tired to entertain after such a long and exhausting day?"

"Not tonight," Locke announced, lifting his chin. "The richest man in Colorado wants to drop by. Horace Tabor is his name, and he's the lieutenant governor."

I grimaced. "Can't do it."

"And why not?"

"I'd rather not say, as it wouldn't be good for him to see me. Might bring back some bad memories."

"For him or for you, Lomax?"

Ignoring the question, I responded, "I can't and won't do it. Fact is, I'll quit before I show my face to Horace Tabor."

"You're hiding something in your past, but that don't matter to me. You ain't given me five hundred dollars' worth of your time, so you still owe me another week or ten days until we play Kansas."

We glared at each other as Vale entered leading Wilde, who seemed more animated that I had ever seen him, like he was about to pick Tabor's pocket or steal his bank account. I wondered if he'd be as excited to meet Jefferson Davis.

"You should've been there, H.H. Never had I been in a theater with so much money, at least new gauche money. The wealthiest man in Colorado will join us shortly once I finish my dinner."

"Supper," I corrected him.

He laughed. "You and your southern colloquialisms." He marched past me, sitting down on the sofa and taking a bite of the baked fish before complaining it was cold. As he buttered a piece of bread, Traquair entered with a small fellow with wire-rimmed glasses on his tiny nose and introduced him as a reporter for the *Denver Tribune*. The newspaperman drew up a chair and indicated he would be quick, as he had learned the lieutenant governor and his friends would arrive shortly.

Wilde took a bite of bread and a sip of tea, waving toward Traquair. "Get rid of this tea and serve my wine."

The valet stepped to the table and removed the cork from the bottle, handing the plug to Wilde to sniff. "Grave Bordeaux," Traquair announced.

Wilde smelled the cork and nodded. "Not the best, but it will do." He turned to the reporter. "Please continue."

The newsman asked about Wilde's visit to Salt Lake City and he spoke more highly of Mormon President John Taylor and his wives to the journalist than he had to me in private. I watched Locke fidgeting over what Wilde might say. It didn't take long for Locke's fears to be realized. "Salt Lake City interested me because it was the first city that ever gave a chance to ugly women. The people, as a body of humanity, have the most ignoble forms I ever saw, and the females are commonplace in every sense of the word."

Locke eased over behind the reporter, shaking his head for Wilde to stop the insults. Wilde defiantly lifted his chin and continued. While he praised Taylor's house as pleasing in art and furniture, he turned his aesthetic eye on the town and the Mormon Tabernacle. "As for the city, it is clean but drab. The tabernacle has the shape of a kettle and the decorations are suitable for a jail. It was truly the most dreadful building I ever encountered."

At that point, Locke was flailing his arms and shaking his head violently, but Wilde kept ranting about the Mormon capital. With Locke preoccupied, I slipped out the door, gently closing it, and scurrying into my room and locking it. I knew I could never let Tabor see me, but I feared this late I might encounter him on the stairs. Crossing the room in the dark, I checked a window to see if I could flee, but there was no ledge or fire escape. Another possibility raced through my mind: just shoot Tabor and be done with it. But that would probably create a bigger problem for me. I realized sometimes a man had to stand up and take his medicine, but this wasn't one of them. If escaping was out as a possibility, hiding under the bed was my only remaining option. As best I could in the darkness, I gathered my belongings and shoved them under the bed so the low-hanging spread hid them from the door. I fumbled for my gun belt, finally grasping it and strapping it around my waist. Once armed, I stepped to the other side of the bed and slid under it to await my fate.

Ten minutes later, I heard Locke escorting the correspondent out, telling him there was five dollars in it for him if he didn't publish Wilde's derogatory comments on the tabernacle and Mormon women in the next day's paper. Once the newspaperman descended the stairs, Locke stomped back toward Wilde's room. "Where is he?" he cried.

I knew it wasn't the lieutenant governor he was looking for. He twisted the knob, then banged on my door.

"Lomax, get out here." He stormed away and returned shortly. I heard a key in the door, then the click of the lock being unlatched. A rectangle of light from the hallway lit the entry.

Traquair called, "Anybody in here?" He turned on the gas lamps, and the room brightened. "He's not in here," the valet said. "Even his belongings are gone."

Locke cursed. "Maybe I can still catch him." He bolted down the hall and bounding down the stairs.

When he was beyond hearing range, Traquair whispered. "Lomax, you in here?"

"No," I answered softly.

"Then where are you not?"

"I'm not under the bed."

"Stay there," he said, "until the visitors leave. Locke is furious."

"I'll be here."

Traquair turned out the gaslights, and closed and locked the door.

I spent an hour and a half under the bedding, hearing the commotion in the next room as they evidently left their door open. I heard Tabor's familiar voice and that of the woman he introduced as his wife.

By her soft voice, I could tell she was a younger woman than I had known. From the noise, Wilde came across wittier to rich people than he did poor folks like me and my acquaintances. After the lieutenant governor and his delegation departed, Traquair returned to our room and turned on the gas lamps.

"You can come out now," he announced.

I slipped out from under the bed and found him, Locke, and Vale standing by the closed door. Locke stood with his arms folded across his chest. "Hiding on the floor like a coward."

"You didn't say that when I slept on the train floor."

Locke scowled. "That was before I knew you were a murdering back shooter. I picked up enough information from the Tabor about a onetime employee named Lomax, who killed a lawyer with a shotgun blast to the back."

He had me. "It was a long time ago."

"Here's the deal, Lomax. I don't care about your past. I only care about my financial future. So, you either accompany us until I say otherwise or I'll turn you in to the Denver authorities tonight. What'll it be?"

"You drive a hard bargain."

"I thought you'd see things my way."

"You didn't give me much choice."

Traquair shook his head. "You don't seem to be the kind that would shoot a man in the back. Seems you're more the type of fellow to drop his gun and kill someone by accident."

"I've done that," I answered. "Just ask Johnny Ringo."

"He's dead," Locke interrupted.

"My point exactly."

Locke waved his fist at me. "That don't matter, either. All that matters now is you finish this tour with Wilde. Understood?"

I nodded. "Agreed."

"Good, because there's been a change of schedule. Oscar's wanted to visit a gold mine, so Tabor's arranged for us to inspect his Matchless diggings. Be packed and ready to leave the hotel by eight in the morning."

"Where are we going?" I inquired.

"Leadville," Locke responded.

I gulped.

CHAPTER EIGHTEEN

The thought of returning to Leadville terrified me, as so many bad things had happened to me there before. The law accused me of a murder I didn't remember. A crooked lawyer swindled me out of a mining claim that could've made me as rich or richer than Horace Tabor. Worst of all, I had escorted Susan B. Anthony to her Leadville lecture on women's suffrage. Miss Anthony taught me how sour a female could be when she wasn't blessed with the looks of even the ugliest Utah woman. I tried to forget that encounter, but couldn't. I hoped the authorities in Leadville *had* forgotten my so-called crime because it was hard enough to breathe the thin air in the town's high altitude without a noose around your neck.

If I didn't go, Charles Locke would turn me in to the sheriff in Denver. If I went, Leadville lawmen might arrest me. Either way, I risked spending my last days on earth in Colorado. At least it was farther from hell in Leadville than from the flatlands. I retired that night, pondering how to change my fate. When Traquair came to bed after tucking Wilde in, he snickered.

"I never pegged you as a killer, Lomax."

"You sure you wouldn't prefer to bed down with Lord La-de-dah?"

"Good heavens, no. I'd rather share a mattress with a dozen murderers and a sack full or rattlesnakes than with that man." Traquair crawled onto the mattress, staying on his side and me doing the same. "How you gonna manage, Lomax?"

"I'm not sure, but don't call me Lomax again. For Leadville, I'm changing my name to Henry Harris, and I'll need a disguise." Once Traquair fell asleep, I fretted an hour before settling on a ruse and dozing off. I rested well until Traquair shook my shoulder to rouse me.

"It's get up, get dressed and get going time," he announced. "Leadville and your sordid past await you." The valet chuckled.

"You tell the others to call me Henry Harris. I'll kill anyone that calls me Lomax in Leadville."

Traquair's eyes widened. "So you are a murderer." He winked. "I know better."

"Yeah, but Wilde, Locke, and Vale don't. Make sure it stays that way."

He nodded and scurried from the room to pack up Wilde's belongings as Lord La-de-dah was too helpless to do anything himself. I was surprised the genius didn't force Traquair to puff his cigarettes for him.

Arising, I dressed in my disguise, fixing my hair, then packing my carpetbag and saddlebags before tossing them on the unmade bed. I draped my coat and carbine atop them, then pranced out into the hall and into Wilde's room, where the poet and his managers stood around the small table by the sofa eating biscuits, boiled eggs and bacon slices.

As the trio turned to me, their jaws dropped. Locke finally spoke, "What the hell, Lo—"

"It's Henry Harris from now on," I said.

"That's what I told them, Henry," Traquair announced as he scurried about the room, gathering things.

"What the hell, Henry Harris? You can't go to Leadville like that," Locke cried.

I shook my head and felt the tresses of my wig falling against my shoulders. "Why not? I've worn the wig, stockings, knee britches, frilly shirt, and patent leather shoes the past two days and didn't hear any complaints."

"We can't have two Oscars," Vale complained. "And besides that, tuck your shirttail in."

I grabbed the hem and lifted the shirt high enough for the trio to see I was wearing my holster and revolver beneath it. "Another killing or two or three won't much matter to me now," I bluffed. "This is how I'm traveling. You can figure whatever story you want, unless you'd like me to visit with the newspapers and tell them how you've been substituting me for Oscar."

"No, no," answered Locke. "That might cut ticket sales."

"That's okay," added Vale.

Wilde grabbed his gold case from the table, pulled out a cigarette, found a match, and started smoking.

Vale and Locke debated how to explain me and my outfit, undecided whether I should be hailed as "Apprentice Oscar" or "Oscar Junior." I didn't care what they called me, as long as it was not Lomax until after we left Leadville for certain, and likely Colorado as well.

Traquair snickered as he handled his chores. "Massa Oscar Junior," he called, "are you toting your bags today or do you want to add them to Oscar Senior's for the baggage car?"

"I'll carry my coat and carbine. The rest can go with senior's stuff."

"Very well, Massa Oscar Junior." Traquair left the room and returned with my gear, which he stacked by the door with the growing pile of Wilde's belongings.

"When you leave the hotel, Henry Harris," Locke commanded, "wear your coat and hat to cover your outfit. We'll figure out how to explain you in Leadville on the train ride up."

"And carry your carbine," Vale said. "That'll distract folks from your stockings and knee britches."

I growled. "A killer always carries his long gun." I thought I detected a tremble in Vale's lip. A worried grimace seeped across Locke's face as he pondered if I was a true murderer with him next on my list. Whether or not they feared me, I never confirmed, but they never turned their back on me then or later on the train trip to Leadville. As for me, I didn't know what I would do, but I vowed to get even with those two promoters before we parted ways.

Traquair fetched the porters, and they carried the gear outside for the trip to the station as Vale and Locke debated how to exit the building with twin Oscars. Finally, they decided I should go downstairs and out front to decoy whatever pedestrians—or assassins in my mind—might wait for a glimpse or a shot at his holiness. While I distracted the locals, Lord La-de-dah would slip out the back door for the carriage to pick him up on the side street.

When the valet returned with word that everything was loaded except us, I slipped on my coat and picked up my carbine. Traquair and I marched downstairs, me with my nose in the air. A handful of hotel guests in the lobby followed me across the marble floors and outside, where others watched the carnival with me as the top freak.

One fellow in a slouch hat looked at me, then announced, "You don't look as tall today as you did last night at the opera house."

"Lecturing takes a lot out of me," I answered.

"Listening to you took a dollar fifty out of my wallet and a wasted hour and a half of my time," he shot back.

"A decade from now, you will reflect on this as a truly glorious moment, the only time in your entire life when you were in the presence of a veritable genius."

The fellow had no answer for my comment, but Traquair did as he assisted me in the rig. "Massa Wilde would be proud of your unbridled condescension. Before long, people won't be able to tell the difference between you and the real Lord La-de-dah."

I settled in the carriage seat and waved at my admirers.

As Traquair climbed in, he offered me a purple silk handkerchief. "Wave this at them. It's a nice touch from one as courtly as you, Massa Wilde Junior."

Following the valet's suggestion, I shook the rag at my admirers. "I'm not only courtly, I'm dangerous," I whispered.

The same carriage driver who had delivered me

from the train station to the hotel turned around and smiled. "Are you ready, Mr. Wilde?"

Waving my purple hanky at him, I nodded. "Yes, son, please proceed, but turn down the side street as we have three more passengers to retrieve."

The driver did as instructed, but I had to distract him when we arrived so Traquair could direct the genuine Wilde around the carriage to sit behind the driver while Vale and Locke climbed into the front seat beside him. Shortly we made it to the station, me glad to be wearing my coat because of the chilly Denver air. It would be even colder in Leadville.

We boarded the train without incident and found our place in the palace car with a roomy compartment provided by Horace Tabor on the narrow-gauge railroad that covered the hundred miles between Denver and Leadville. The trip dragged by, taking just over six hours as the locomotive chugged from Denver at five-thousand-plus feet of altitude to more than a ten-thousand-foot elevation at our destination. It was much like our previous train rides, plenty of stops for water and fuel—in this case wood—with Locke sending or receiving telegrams at most breaks.

Arriving mid-afternoon in Leadville, the locomotive pulled up to a station depot, where a smattering of the curious awaited the arrival of the two Oscars. The conductor said the mayor and the city board waited on the platform to welcome the famous Oscar Wilde. He looked at me, then Oscar, then back at me and scratched his head. "Which is he?"

Everyone pointed at Oscar.

"Then who's this imposter?" the conductor inquired, looking at me.

"That," said Locke, "is Apprentice Oscar, an understudy who is watching the genius's every move so he can play Bunthorne in the San Francisco debut of Gilbert and Sullivan's *Patience*. He's got big shoes to fill."

"Patent leather shoes." I noted.

The conductor ignored me and nodded to Locke. "I sent the telegram you requested, so the sheriff should be waiting as well."

I glared at Locke, whose grimace told me he had betrayed me. Pointing my index finger at him, I snapped my thumb like I was shooting a pistol.

Locke gulped. "I wired the sheriff we might need protection from the miners. They're a surly group of rough men."

"You're more likely to require protection from me," I answered, patting my revolver beneath my shirt. "If he comes for me, I'm shooting you first. If you're not around, I'll plug Oscar."

The promoter paled. "Don't do that."

"Then call off the law dog. Did you tell him my real name?"

Locke hesitated before finally answering. "I can't remember."

"Is there still a reward?"

He grimaced again, then nodded. "Five hundred dollars, enough to reimburse us for what we paid to hire you."

"Is money all you promoters think about?"

"Pretty much." Locke nodded. "Him, too." He pointed to Wilde.

"You best steer the sheriff clear of me."

"I can't stop the law."

"You better," I answered, "if you and your freak show want to leave Leadville alive. I've escaped before, and will again."

Wilde grunted. "Would you two move out of my way so I can make my appearance and meet the local dignitaries?" With that, he discarded his coat, dropping it on the floor for Traquair to pick up. He stood a moment, finishing the last drag on his cigarette, which he released and crushed beneath his shiny shoe. After that, he strode out of the compartment and followed the conductor outside. As he stepped from the train onto the platform, he waved his own handkerchief and blew kisses, drawing a mixture of cheers and jeers from the few hard-rock miners and women that had braved the chill to see the celebrity fraud.

"Speech, speech," someone cried.

He shook off the request. "Attend my lecture this evening. I will speak of the decorative arts at the Tabor Opera House. Reserved seats are a dollar and a quarter, gallery seats are only seventy-five cents."

Wilde stopped, glancing around for the accustomed carriage and appearing lost without Traquair to point the way.

Meanwhile, I emerged from the train with Locke, who pointed me toward the sheriff. We walked that direction, me holding the carbine in my front, so the lawman understood I was armed.

"Sheriff," said Locke, "I sent you the telegram about the killer Lomax, but I was mistaken after hearing a rumor he was coming to Leadville to harm great Oscar Wilde."

"I'd like to get my hands on that murdering skunk,"

the sheriff said. "He's already killed one man in Leadville."

Locke nodded. "He's a despicable man, that Lomax." He turned to me. "That's why I hired Henry Harris here to protect the brilliant lecturer. Open your coat, Henry."

I hesitated.

"Do it," he commanded.

So I unbuttoned it and spread it so the sheriff could see I was dressed as outrageously as Lord La-de-dah.

The lawman sniggered. "He's as big a dandy as Oscar himself. He don't look like much protection."

"We dress him this way to confuse fellows that might harm Oscar."

I closed my coat and buttoned it against the cold.

The lawman nodded. "I'm here to preserve the peace. No harm'll come to Wilde in Leadville, not while I'm sheriff of Lake County."

"We're obliged, sheriff. After his lecture tonight, Governor Tabor has arranged for Oscar to tour a gold mine, the Matchless."

"It's a silver mine," the lawman corrected.

"So be it, but I'm worried about his safety among all these rugged miners. Henry will go with him, but I'm still uneasy."

"I'll stay with Wilde whenever you need me."

"We're obliged again."

The lawman pointed at me. "Henry here doesn't look manly enough to protect Oscar Wilde, not in his sissy britches and his ruffled blouse."

"We'll be fine, Sheriff, once we get to the hotel, but if you'll be at the theater about seven-thirty, we'd be grateful."

He nodded. "I'll be there." He turned and strode away.

Locke glared at me. "You satisfied now, Lomax?"

"You mean Henry Harris."

"Yeah, that's what I meant."

After meeting the town officials, Wilde walked around the depot while Locke and I trailed the meager group of the curious. Traquair pointed us to the carriage and announced he would follow us once the baggage was unloaded. Wilde, Vale, Locke and I climbed in the awaiting carriage, but realized none of us knew the name of our accommodations. Tabor, though, had made the arrangements, and the driver delivered us to the Clarendon Hotel on Main Street.

As we drove to our lodging, I marveled at how the town had changed in five years. It was still a rough mining enclave with pretensions when I left, but now it was one of the richest cities in the States, if not the world, with a nice train depot, fine brick-and-stone buildings, a municipal water works, a telephone system, a school, and a firehouse, which would be handy if Wilde caught on fire from smoking so much. Then there was the pride of Leadville, the Tabor Opera House, perhaps the finest theater to be found in any mining town on the globe. The roughhewn town that I had known had been polished from the wealth extracted from the hard earth beneath our carriage. While saloons still thrived, their number had dwindled by two thirds, with churches taking up the slack. The driver sang the praises of Horace Tabor for his many contributions to the community. When I had first met Tabor, he had run a store and constantly argued with his wife, who opposed him spending their money on grubstaking so many miners. Two of those miners struck the mother lode, and Tabor shared their wealth from a claim next to the one the lawyer defrauded from me. I wondered how my life might have been different had I held onto that claim and not trusted an attorney when I signed the papers that effectively sold away my title for a pittance. I pondered that, and if the sheriff would arrest me before I left town the following day.

We arrived at the hotel where Vale and Locke announced we were Oscar Wilde and associates. Immediately, we were escorted up the stairs to the third floor and three large rooms, all compliments of the lieutenant governor. The best thing about our floor was the enclosed bridge that connected the hotel to the Tabor Opera House across the street. We could all go to the theater without stepping outside in the frigid air once the sun set.

Wilde fretted in his suite, as Traquair had not arrived in advance to arrange his belongings or unfold his tiger and wolf furs on the sofa. Wilde smoked cigarettes to smooth his edginess until thirty minutes later, when Traquair arrived with a retinue of porters carrying the luggage. He ordered the evening meal for the group and then scurried to unpack for Lord La-de-dah, who calmed some when Traquair tossed the animal hides over the divan. Wilde collapsed on the sofa. "I have a headache and feel dizzy and nauseous," he announced. "I doubt I can speak tonight."

"You must," Locke said. "We can't afford to offend Governor Tabor."

"Lieutenant governor," I corrected.

Vale volunteered to help. "I'll inquire downstairs if we can find a doctor." He departed and returned shortly, saying help was on the way. Thirty minutes later, a physician showed up. He quickly checked Wilde, then turned to Locke. "It's a case of light air caused by the altitude and brought on when folks climb this high too fast."

"Will he be able to lecture tonight?"

"Perhaps," the doctor replied, "I'll write an order for laudanum if someone can take it to the druggist."

Locke pointed at Traquair. "The valet can handle it."

The doctor scribbled on a piece of paper and provided Traquair directions to the drug store. After twenty minutes, the valet returned with a brown sack and a green medicine bottle. "Two tablespoons, the druggist said," Traquair explained.

"I don't have a tablespoon," Wilde said, snatching the vial from the valet's hand, uncorking the top and taking three healthy swigs. Then he retreated to his bed, resting there while the remainder of us milled about in the hallway, wondering if Wilde would deliver his remarks and tour the silver mine. Traquair ordered food brought at six o'clock.

When the delicacies arrived, the valet let the staff into Wilde's room and found him lying on his tiger skin, smoking a cigarette. Traquair retreated to the entry and invited me, Locke and Vale to enter. "He seems better," the valet announced.

As we walked in, he was reading a book, not his slim collection of poetry but a thicker volume. On the spine I made out the title as *The Autobiography of Benvenuto Cellini*, whoever he was. Once the hotel staff finished setting up the food, they departed, and Locke asked the question we all wanted answered: "Can you lecture tonight?"

He held up his hand—"Let me finish this paragraph,"—then continued reading for a moment. Closing the book, he sat up. "No longer does my head throb. I shall deliver my expected remarks, though I will take Cellini's autobiography to read to the audience in case I worsen."

"Maybe you should eat something to strengthen yourself," Locke suggested.

"Not now as I had rather faint than throw up on stage." Wilde resumed reading.

"Then we'll help ourselves," Locke responded.

The table had the usual selections as well as oysters on the half shell and a card saying the meal was compliments of Horace Tabor. I avoided the seafood in favor of an omelet—though I was still curious to taste a hamlet—plus a pork chop and two slices of bread. Then Vale, Locke and I retired to our rooms, leaving Traquair to watch after Wilde. I returned at a quarter to eight o'clock to find everyone else there. Wilde had changed into his flamboyant outfit with the bloated bow tie and stood at the table, downing oysters from the half shell. I felt certain he would vomit on the stage with that in his stomach. Nodding he was ready, Wilde picked up the autobiography, clutched it to his chest and marched out the door.

Traquair showed us down the hallway to the enclosed passage over the street to the theater, where the nervous stage manager waited to guide us along the passages and stairways that led backstage. By the noise, we could tell the auditorium, which seated almost nine hundred spectators, was full, and the crowd was mostly raucous men. While the theater manager insisted Wilde begin his presentation punctually, so the anxious crowd wouldn't tear up the facility, Wilde said he was light-headed and needed a moment to gather his thoughts and his breath. He took a seat behind the curtains and closed his eyes like he was praying, though I knew he believed in no god except himself.

As the fretting theater man paced back and forth and the spectators grew louder, Wilde remained serenely oblivious to the growing impatience. Finally, a half hour late, he stood up, Cellini in hand and marched on stage to the relief of everyone. From the wings, I observed a roughhewn audience, mostly miners in work clothes without a single one carrying sunflowers or lilies. When Wilde began speaking of the decorative arts in his shallow monotone, the miners fidgeted like the theater operator before the talk, then grumbled they had wasted their money.

Wilde chided them for squandering the town's prosperity by making the community practical rather than beautiful like sixteenth century Pisa with its palaces of marble and its pillared architecture, where gorgeous women walked and gallant knights rode in armor that not only reflected the sunlight but also the magnificence of Pisa and its inhabitants. He then picked up the book and announced he would illustrate the refinement of Pisa by reading from the works of Benvenuto Cellini, the famed Italian sculptor and silversmith.

"Why isn't he here to speak for himself?" shouted an audience member.

"He's dead," Wilde answered indignantly.

"Who shot him?" cried an overall-clad miner.

Wilde ignored the comment, merely describing the late Cellini as the patron saint of the decorative arts and a man the citizens of Leadville should emulate to elevate their community even higher than its ten-thousand-foot elevation so it could rival Pisa. To say the audience was enthralled would be a great lie as they stomped their feet and jeered. Wilde responded, "There is no better way of loving nature than through art."

"We've got plenty of nature," cried another miner. "What we need is more women." Dozens hailed the comment with shouts and whistles.

They cheered even more when Wilde finished his lecture, took his final bow and marched behind the curtains with Cellini clutched to his chest.

The theater operator congratulated Wilde. "They loved it," he said.

"How, sir, can you say that?" Wilde responded.

"Because they didn't shoot you!"

"Nor Cellini, either," Wilde answered.

The theater boss directed Wilde behind the stage where the mayor, two mine officials and the sheriff awaited, ready to show the lecturer the town and give him the promised tour of the Matchless. Wilde insisted on returning to his room to get his coat. So everyone tromped up the back stairs to the bridgeway. Like Wilde, the rest of us retrieved our coats and bid Traquair farewell so he could prepare for the morning departure to Colorado Springs. Vale, Locke and I awaited Wilde, who took his time fetching his coat. When he stepped back in the hallway, I saw he had changed from his costume into long britches and a regular shirt. I felt stupid still wearing my wig, fluffy shirt, stockings, and knee britches.

Then the entire party marched down the hotel staircase and out into Leadville's frigid April air, where the two mine officials headed to the Matchless to await our arrival. Snowflakes fell gently from the sky and a light dusting of white hid much of the ugliness and grime of the mining town. The mayor guided our tour, but I kept my eye on the sheriff, who seemed more interested in watching me than in guarding Wilde, who might have been in great danger from any miner who thought his lecture was robbery rather than entertainment or education.

We marched along State Street with Mayor David H. Dougan, explaining the town's prosperity and its unlimited future. Wilde focused more on the saloons, with names like the Little Church, the Board of Trade, the Red Light, the Bon Ton, and the Bloody Bucket. We walked past the "French section," as it was called, where the most exotic prostitutes in the States worked and profited from mining in their own artistic ways. Wilde glanced at nary a woman of questionable repute visible in the doorways, though three gals whistled at me with suggestive offers. Wilde, instead, requested to visit a saloon.

Dougan steered the aesthete toward Pap's, which he described as Leadville's premier drinking establishment, run by the beloved Charles "Pap" Wyman. As we approached the watering hole, a tinkling piano pinged above the other celebratory noises inside. As soon as we entered, the racket dimmed for a moment.

"There's Oscar Wilde," shouted an inebriated patron, pointing at the poet.

"And Oscar Junior," cried another fellow, aiming his trigger finger at me.

"I didn't know Oscar had kids," interjected a man with a beer mug raised over his head.

Then a critic noted. "Junior's too ugly not to be his son."

I thought about punching him in the nose for insulting me, but Wilde grabbed my arm and steered me toward the keyboard player, pointing to a sign over the musician's instrument and reading it to me.

"Please don't shoot the piano player. He's doing the best he can," Wilde recited, then looked at me with a wide grin. "These folks understand that bad art merits the penalty of death and in this remote town I now can appreciate the aesthetic implications of the revolver."

"Like Cellini?" I asked.

Wilde nodded. "So you listened to my lecture?"

Before I could respond, the mayor grabbed our arms and escorted us to the bar to meet Pap, who seemed amused at the great poet's visit. Wilde praised him for the sign over the piano as the truest criticism of art that he had ever seen.

The saloon owner offered us a free drink, but I declined as the last time I'd partaken of liquor in Leadville, I'd wound up on the floor of a law office with a dead attorney at my feet. Wilde accepted the whiskey and downed it and a second jigger full.

"Show him your coin purse," Dougan suggested, and Pap pulled out a tanned leather bag with a rawhide tie at the top.

Proudly, Pap handed it to Wilde. By the droop of Wilde's hand when he took it, the bag was heavy with coins. "It's a scrotum," Pap announced.

"Poor fellow." I said.

Pap nodded. "It's a long story."

"I like the feel of it," Wilde replied, "art and natural beauty—" He shook the coin purse and continued, "—enclosing silver and gold coins. Artistry at its best and most personal." He handed the curiosity back to Pap, who nonchalantly slipped it into his britches.

I was thankful I had abandoned Leadville without having met or offended Pap. The coin purse brought an end to the conversation because what do you say after that? We visitors stood silent, but curious to ask Pap how he had secured the personal pouch, but feared we might insult him, so we remained silent.

Dougan announced it was getting late, and that he must deliver us to the Matchless, where the mine superintendent was waiting to provide Tabor's promised silver mine tour.

"It's a two-mile walk," Pap said.

"Governor Tabor is providing three carriages for us," Dougan announced. "Though they're not covered, the snow isn't that bad and us locals are accustomed to it."

Dougan pointed to the saloon door, and we threaded our way through the drinkers, carousers, and gamblers. I wasn't interested in seeing the bottom of a mine that with better luck, might have been my own. Locke and Vale had reservations as well.

"Charles and I have had a long day," Vale noted. "We'll pass on the tour, if you can spare a carriage to take us to the hotel."

"Or we'll walk," Locke announced.

"I'll go back as well," I said.

"You're staying with Oscar," Locke insisted. "You're his bodyguard, remember?"

I pointed to the lawman. "The sheriff'll be protecting his highness."

The sheriff nodded. "Indeed I will, but another set of eyes couldn't hurt anything."

With no alternatives, I shrugged. "Matchless it is!"

"Mayor," the sheriff said, "make sure Henry and I ride in the same buggy to and from the mine." He eyed me with an evil grin.

CHAPTER NINETEEN

After we loaded up two carriages, we headed for the Matchless, me and the sheriff seated behind the driver in the second carriage, while the mayor and Lord La-de-dah rode in the first. The third buggy took Vale and Locke back to the Clarendon Hotel.

While I was in no mood for conversation, the lawman wanted to gab as we rode up Fryer Hill.

"I figured we should get to know each other a little better, Henry, since we're both responsible for protecting Mister Wilde. Where are you from?"

"Here and there!"

"You ever been to Leadville before today?"

"I've been everywhere, except there and here."

"You ever worked for Mister Horace Tabor in his store?"

"I've had a lot of jobs here and there."

He changed subjects. "Why'd you decide to become an apprentice to Oscar Wilde?"

"Work is hard to come by these days, at least for me."

"Did you let your hair grow, or is that a wig?"

"A true apprentice would never substitute a fake for the real thing."

"You're a clever one, Henry."

"That's why Oscar took me as his apprentice."

"It is Henry, isn't it? Henry Harris is your name, right?"

"That's what my folks named me."

"You should know," the sheriff said as we arrived at the mine works.

The mayor escorted Wilde, and the lawman saw me into the shaft house where mine superintendent Charles Pishon awaited to boast about the mine's productivity, explaining that Tabor owned interests in multiple mines in the Leadville region, but the Matchless belonged to Tabor alone.

"Just last month we extracted eighty-two thousand dollars' worth of silver from the Matchless," Pishon bragged. "By the end of the year, we expect it to yield some two million dollars in ore. Governor Tabor is a rich man growing richer."

Wilde sighed. "Imagine all the beautiful art a master silversmith such as Benvenuto Cellini could have created with so much silver."

"Cellini's not from these parts, is he?" Pishon asked. "I can't say I've ever heard of him."

"Nor him you! Some folks mine ore," Wilde responded. "Others create art."

"And," interjected the sheriff, "some folks tell stories." He stared at me as he spoke, paused for a moment, then continued. "Or, alibis."

Realizing for certain the lawman knew of my past

and intended to arrest me, I doubted I would be lucky enough to escape Leadville this time.

Pishon next explained that a dozen miners awaited the aesthete and his apprentice at the bottom of the shaft. They planned a special celebration, a genuine Matchless welcome in the richest hole in North America. While it was frigid on the mountaintop, the superintendent indicated it would be hot and damp in the mine, and that should discard our winter coats for a rubberized slicker and hat. We doffed our outerwear as Pishon's three helpers provided us with mining attire. I felt foolish standing there in my frilly shirt, knee britches, stockings, and patent leather shoes. The two assistants snickered at my costume as one of them gave me my slick parka.

After Wilde finished putting on the covering, he tucked his hair in his headwear and noted, "This reminds me of the togas worn by Roman senators."

"I didn't know you were that old," Pishon joked.

"Art and beauty endure across the ages," the poet replied, critiquing the color of the mining gear. "Something other than a drab green would lift your workers' spirits."

The attendants snickered until the superintendent glared at them. "We aren't given a choice of colors," he responded.

"Perhaps you should line them with a rich satin, say a vibrant purple or a soft lavender, maybe with some embroidery of storks and ferns around the edges. That would bring life to the work clothes."

"We buy what they make, practicality over beauty, durability over art. I've never heard of an embroidered lining in a slicker," Pishon said.

"Such a pity," Wilde answered as the sheriff and I donned our gear.

"We'll be descending in shaft number three," the mine boss informed us. "At a hundred and fifty feet deep, it's not our deepest, but it's our driest shaft." He pointed to a battered iron bucket about waist high with an iron arch above it attached to a cable and pulley system.

"That's our ore bucket. It delivers and returns our men from the shaft and brings out our ore. It's four-feet in diameter, wide enough to drop a mule into the mine once his legs are properly bound. We'll go down two at a time, but I must caution you. Do not under any circumstance lean out of the bucket or extend your hand or arm beyond the bucket rim. We've had men lose an ear, a hand, an elbow, an arm and, in one unfortunate case, a head."

Wilde paled and shifted his weight from foot to foot as he awaited the descent.

"I'll stay up here to simplify matters," I volunteered.

"No, Henry," answered the sheriff, "you're going down like the rest of us. The ride'll give you an idea of what it's like in a grave."

Now I was certain the constable knew my true identity, although I was undecided whether he figured it out on his own or with Locke's help. I prayed if they sent me to the gallows that I at least got to change out of the ridiculous clothes I was wearing.

The lawman turned to the mine superintendent. "In fact, Pishon, why don't you let Lo—err, I mean Henry Harris and I go down in the first bucket to make sure it's safe for our esteemed visitor, Oscar Wilde."

"Fine idea, Sheriff. Next, we'll send the mayor down and I'll follow with Mister Wilde."

"Perfect," the lawman answered. "Henry and I can ensure there are no murderers down below, someone that would shoot an upstanding citizen like a lawyer in the back with a shotgun." He pointed to the ore canister. "Go ahead, Henry." He was playing with me like a cat tinkers with an injured mouse before killing him.

I hesitated.

"You scared of the dark?" the sheriff asked. He paused. "Or is it your past?"

I gulped, inching to the loading platform by the ore bucket. I lifted my right leg over the bucket rim, then my left and slid in. My law friend climbed in behind me, and we stood facing each other, me biting my lip as I pondered what to do, and the lawman licking his lips as he figured on arresting me and claiming the reward.

"You both ready?" Pishon asked.

My shadow nodded. "Let 'er rip."

Nodding to the hoist operator, Pishon gave us final safety instructions. "Remember not to lean outside the bucket."

As the equipment groaned, the huge kettle jerked upward, stabilizing as the operator said, "Here we go." Slowly my new friend and I disappeared into the earth, immediately enveloped in the pitch black of the shaft. Light and cool gave way to the earth's darkness and heat. On the descent, I thought I was on a slow preview of hell with my executioner beside me. Best I could figure, the journey took ninety seconds, but it seemed like forever with the lawman beside me.

We reached a bottom landing, dimly lit by flickering candles on spikes driven into the wall. A dozen miners greeted us, helping me from the iron container and welcoming me to their domain. From my wig, they mistook me for Oscar Wilde, praising my speech and offering condolences on the death of my friend Benvenuto Cellini.

"This fellow ain't Wilde," the sheriff announced as he climbed out of the bucket. "He's the imposter Oscar."

The miners groaned.

"I'm the illegitimate son of the Prince of Wales," I proclaimed.

"Then welcome to hell, you fishy bastard," cried one miner as another rang the bell and sent the bucket upward to the shaft house.

Two mineworkers grabbed me by the arms and guided me off the platform onto the rock floor surrounded by rock walls, which seeped water, and a rock ceiling that bled droplets of ooze. Thick timbers supported the ceiling. A handful of rats scurried around the chamber, occasionally squeaking when they fought over a scrap of food.

As I studied the rodents, one miner said, "Don't mind the rats. You'll get used to them."

"There's only one rat that worries me." I pointed to the sheriff.

"Yeah, ol' Vern is a pain in the butt."

It occurred to me I didn't even know the sheriff's name. "What's he called?"

"The miners call him a lot of names, but he goes by Vern Middling."

Shortly, the mayor joined us, and the ore bucket returned to the top to bring down the aesthete and the superintendent. When the cable moved, a human squeal echoed down the shaft. My new miner friend chuckled. "Some folks are scared of the drop. Sounds like we got us a fraidy cat coming down."

"The fraidy cat'll have plenty to eat with all the rodents," I noted.

"We've got a dinner set up for our guest in a crosscut."

I laughed. "If the rats get to it, there won't be any left."

The ore bucket arrived at the landing and the miners turned to greet the honored guest as Lord La-de-dah climbed out of the conveyance. Pishon handed a lit candle to a worker and hauled himself out of the bucket, rolling his eyes. "He's scared of the dark."

Wilde enjoyed the attention of the laborers, shaking hands with each, the final one noting, "You don't work much with your hands, now do you?"

"Toiling with your mind is harder than laboring with your hands," Wilde answered, raising his nose in the air.

"Doubt it pays as well," the man responded.

"I've never known of anyone paying a dollar and a quarter to listen to a hard-rock miner speak in the Tabor Opera House," Wilde retorted.

Pishon interrupted the conversation and guided the genius to the rock wall, holding his candle near the slab and pointing out streaks of ore, some high grade, some low grade, but all valuable enough to make a man rich.

Wilde scratched his cheek. "That's silver? It looks so common and somber, unlike anything a silversmith of Cellini's artistry would touch with his talented fingers."

The superintendent pointed to the miners in an arc around them. "Without their callused hands, silver would be scarce for coin, jewelry or art. Mining and smelting are hard, dirty jobs."

Lord La-de-dah had led such a pampered life it shocked him to learn raw silver in the ground lacked the beauty and artistry of the finished products he had enjoyed while visiting with the crown prince and other prissy London socialites.

Pishon told him more about the mining process, but Wilde remained distracted by the revelation of silver ore's inherent ugliness. Finally, the superintendent turned to his employees. "Okay, fellows, he's all yours."

The miners cheered, clapped Wilde on the back and escorted him through the timbered hole to a large crosscut where they had set up a table with sixteen stools. Atop the table sat covered tins of food, overturned tin plates, tin utensils, and a bottle of whiskey at each place. The hosts pointed Wilde to the head of the table, taking their seats and inviting the mayor, sheriff, and superintendent to join them for a late meal.

I was the odd man out, the seventeenth man for sixteen stools. Nobody cared, except Sheriff Middling, who kept twisting around in his seat to watch me, standing by a timbered brace. Everybody else focused on Wilde as they shared drinks to his success and well-being, taking a sip from the whiskey bottle and passing it to the man on the left. With each toast, the bottles slowly worked their way back to their original places. The diners ate beefsteaks, boiled potatoes and bread between toasts. As they drank, I watched Middling take an occasional sip as he kept his eyes on me. Pishon and the mayor avoided the drinks entirely, holding the bottles to their faces, but never to their lips. The miners showed no restraint, thinking they would drink the prissy poet under the table, but he outlasted them, still standing and speaking in his usual monotone. Each time he offered a toast, the laborers wobbled to their feet and slurred their words. After three hours of toasting, drinking and eating, Wilde announced he had a train to catch to Colorado Springs for the next evening's lecture. Standing straight and tall, he thanked his hosts for their hospitality, then strode out of the crosscut toward the ore bucket. As Pishon chased after him, Middling stood up and motioned for me to accompany him.

"Let's go, Henry Harris," he said.

I joined him, and we walked away together. The lawman had consumed enough liquor that his reflexes were slow and wobbly, but not so much that he couldn't pull out his revolver and plug me anytime between this hole and the jail hole.

Ahead, I saw Pishon ring the bell and moments later the ore bucket lifted off the landing and disappeared up the shaft. The mayor caught up with us as we waited for the conveyance to return.

"You go first, Mayor," Middling offered.

Dougan nodded. "Thank you, Sheriff."

We stood in silence until the bucket returned and Dougan scrambled in. He sounded the bell and the lift left again. When it came back, Middling and I climbed in. Once loaded, he reached for the rope to sound the bell, but missed it and stumbled against the iron sides. The sheriff had either consumed more liquor than I imagined or could not handle what little whiskey he had drunk. I yanked the rope and clanged the bell. Moments later, the bucket began its upward journey.

As soon as darkness enveloped us, the lawman grabbed my shoulder to steady himself, I thought, but instead yanked at my wig, pulling it from my head. As it dropped to the iron floor, he leaned into me.

"It was a wig," he scowled.

I could smell whiskey on his breath. "You scalped me," I cried.

"You're not Henry Harris, you're Henry Harrison Lomax, wanted for the killing of Adam Scheisse five years ago in his Leadville office. I'm placing you under arrest for murder and the hanging you deserve."

He leaned into me so hard, I feared he would push my shoulder or my arm outside the ore bucket. I shoved him away.

Middling staggered backward.

I heard a thump and a groan. I felt the weight of his body fall against my knees, pushing me back. Attempting to brace myself, I yanked my head away from the stone shaft, whirring by my ear as the bucket ascended. After the initial moan, the sheriff lay silent. I didn't know if he was dead or alive. At least this time, I knew what happened, unlike the last occasion I had a body at my feet in Leadville.

Overhead, a pinpoint of light grew larger and cold air caressed my face, a refreshing moment after three hours in the hot humidity of the mine. Moments later, the conveyance cleared the hole into the shaft house.

"Where's the sheriff?" Pishon asked.

I pointed to my feet. "He collapsed."

"What happened?"

"Don't know for certain in the darkness, but I heard a thump and a groan as he crumpled in the ore bucket. He must've hit his head."

"Is he dead?"

Looking down at my patent leather shoes, I shrugged. "If he isn't, he'll have a hell of a headache tonight." In the dim light, I could see the bloodied right side of his face, a mangled ear and a goose egg on the side of his head.

As I clambered out of the ore bucket, Pishon brought a candle over and lowered his arm into the iron cask to inspect the damage. "He's in bad shape. Looks like the hit scalped him."

I looked into the bucket, spotting my wig.

"That's my hair."

"You hit your head, too?"

"It's a wig."

The superintendent glanced at the winch operator. "Fetch some help and a wagon to carry the sheriff to town and a doctor."

The fellow dashed away as Pishon climbed into the iron container, picked up my wig tossed it to me, splotches of blood landing on my rubberized mining gear. Wilde, who had removed his underground attire and replaced it with his green, fur-collared coat, strode over.

"What's wrong with him?"

"The sheriff can't handle his liquor and bumped his head on the way up the shaft."

"He's lucky he didn't get it snapped off," Pishon cried, as he lifted the unconscious lawman. "Give me a hand, you two."

Wilde and I moved over as the superintendent wrestled Middling up enough to drape him over the lip of the ore bucket. The poet and I grabbed an arm as the mine boss pushed at his waist. Slowly, we inched him over the top, Pishon grabbing his legs and easing them out of the iron vessel.

The sheriff moaned.

"At least he's alive," Pishon noted.

Wilde and I pulled him fully from the conveyance and the mine superintendent released his lower limbs, so they dropped on the platform.

Lord La-de-dah and I lowered him to the wooden flooring, then rolled him over, the right side of his face distorted with a huge knot atop his head and his cheek sticky with blood and his mangled ear. Wilde gagged, arose, leaned over the ore bucket, and wretched as the mine boss clambered out.

The poet was still throwing up when the winch operator returned with three other employees. "A wagon's on the way," he announced, "and we brought blankets.

I backed away as Pishon knelt beside the sheriff and placed his fingers beneath Middling's nose. "He's still breathing."

As the men with the blankets spread one on the platform beside Middling, Pishon rolled the sheriff over enough for the other two to slide the blanket partially under him. One miner grabbed his ankles, and the other his wrists. They lifted him to the center of the cloth.

From the mineshaft came the sound of the bell as the miners displayed their impatience to emerge.

"Hold your horses," the winch operator shouted into the hole. "We've had an accident."

One mineworker placed a second cover over the lawman, then he and his partner plus the hoist operator and Pishon each grabbed a corner of the lower blanket, gently lifting the sling and carrying it down the platform.

The shaft house door flung open and a breathless miner bolted in. "The wagon's here." As the liter crew eased outside, I moved to the rack where I'd left my coat and shoved the wig inside its pocket. I started removing my rubberized gear. By then Wilde had quit vomiting, but he staggered off the platform, looking pale and weak. I slipped on my jacket and walked to steady him. I led him to a bench where he sat down, bent over and put his elbows on his thighs and his head in his palms.

Outside, the wagon rattled and jangled as it dashed to the doctor. Moments later, Pishon returned. I pointed at Wilde. "He's sick now."

The mine superintendent stepped over, squatted, and placed his hand under Wilde's chin to lift it. He studied the poet and nodded. "Yeah, he's a little puny. If you can get him to a carriage, head back to town. The mayor's already left." Pishon directed the hoist man to return to the machinery and extract the miners from the hole.

"Let's go, Oscar," I instructed.

Slowly, he raised his head, staring blankly at me with his wide eyes. I couldn't determine it if resulted from his drinking or his sudden encounter with the violence of Middling's injury. As he had come from a life of art and beauty, I decided he was not prepared to face the ugliness of life among men with callused hands. I pulled him to his feet and escorted him out of the shaft house to the wagon and drove him back to the Clarendon Hotel.

When I finally got him up the stairs to his suite, it

was five in the morning. I shoved him onto his mattress and left him in his coat and hat. Next, I retreated to the room I shared with William Traquair, who was slowly getting out of bed. He stretched and yawned, then turned on a gas lamp, surprised to see me as I closed the door.

"I wasn't expecting you."

"Why not?"

"After Vale and Locke returned from the saloon visit, they were laughing about you, saying they'd seen the last of your sorry butt now that the sheriff intended to arrest you. They'd told him who you were and agreed to split the reward money with the lawman."

I grinned. "Things didn't quite work out that way."

"I can see that."

"Did you kill the sheriff?"

"Not so far, but he has a nasty headache. I'm tempted to break into their room and plug Locke and Vale for betraying me."

"Don't complicate your life—or mine—any more by shooting those two. What about the sheriff? Did you slug him?"

"No, sir. When we were being hoisted out of the mineshaft, he leaned out of the bucket, hit the shaft wall and knocked himself out. He was still breathing when I last saw him, but had a knot the size of an apple on his head, a bloodied face, and a mutilated ear. Lord La-de-dah did all right in the mine, out-drinking the miners, but once he saw the sheriff's head he threw up and turned sickly. I put him to bed, clothes and all."

Traquair started dressing. "I've a lot of packing to do if we are to make the train to Colorado Springs for tonight's lecture."

"Is it the same one we rode in on?"

"No, sir. This one follows the Arkansas River valley south and then east to Colorado Springs"

"Good, because I'm taking the train back to Denver and leaving Colorado as fast as I can. I don't care to be around if Sheriff Middling dies. The only thing that'll slow me is getting even with Locke and Vale."

"You sure that won't get you in more trouble?"

I shrugged. "We'll see."

Once Traquair left to pack things for Wilde, I flung off my coat, removed my gun belt and ripped off the frilly clothes I had been wearing. I considered throwing them out the window, but figured I shouldn't draw attention to myself or leave them behind, so I stuffed them in my carpetbag. Next, I dressed in my normal pants, shirt and boots, finally feeling like an American again, rather than the illegitimate son of the Price of Wales or Whales or whoever he was.

I checked my money, confirming I had plenty of cash to take me where I wanted to go, assuming I wasn't robbed by bandits or cardsharps or theater promoters. After I put on my hat, I gathered my saddle-bags, my carpetbag, my carbine and my coat and tossed them all on the bed. I slipped into the hallway, making sure no light seeped from under the door of the promoters' room. Entering Wilde's room, I found Traquair quietly folding the furs, trying not to disturb Wilde, who was splayed on his mattress exactly as I had left him, except that he was snoring.

"Good luck to you, Willie," I said, offering him my hand. "I don't see how you put up with all his fool-ishness."

As we shook hands, he said, "I'm getting an education about the States, though I am a little worried, as Massa Wilde wants to tour the South as well. My kind of folks aren't favored in that part of the nation." We broke our grasp.

"You're favored by me, if that's any consolation." I pointed to the snoring poet. "You're certainly better than royalty or aesthetes or whatever the hell he is. Your description of him as a noodle is the one I like best, that and Lord La-de-dah."

Traquair smiled. "Where are you heading?"

"After running into a sister in Utah, I figure I'll head home to see the folks. I owe it to them."

"Is there any place I can write you and let you know how things worked out here?"

I pondered the question, wondering how I would get mail since I didn't want him sending missives to Cane Hill, Arkansas, where I could be tracked. Once I got back to Denver, I planned to go to Cheyenne, then catch the Union Pacific east to Omaha and from there take a steamboat down the Missouri to Kansas City, where I'd board another train to Arkansas and home. "Try general delivery, Kansas City. It may be a spell, but I'll go there if you promise to send me a letter."

"Agreed," Traquair said, stepping to me and wrapping his arms around me for a vigorous hug. Next, he kissed me on the cheek and broke away laughing. "Now you can say you've been kissed on the cheek by an aesthete *and* a Negro."

With that, I wished him luck, turned and marched out the door.

"Don't kill anybody else," he laughed.

I checked the hallway to make sure Vale and Locke weren't up, then scurried to my room, grabbed my things and rushed down the staircase, intent on leaving Leadville for good this time. I walked to the depot. Even though I was exhausted from a night without sleep, I believed the cold air would keep me awake until I got on the train where I could rest all the way to Denver.

Fortunately, I caught the morning iron horse and did not run into any problems. When I wasn't sleeping, I plotted how to get even with Vale and Locke. By the time the conductor shook my shoulder and woke me up at the Denver station, I realize I had quite a story to tell, one that might interest the newspapers. I gathered my belongings and stepped out of the passenger car into air that was thicker than it had been in Leadville and into air where I could breathe.

Now all I had to do was find the office of the *Denver Tribune*.

CHAPTER TWENTY

Outside the station, I hired a buggy to deliver me and my belongings to the *Denver Tribune* office, a stone building off the main street downtown. I paid my fare, grabbed my things, and marched into the newspaper office.

A fellow with garters on the rolled-up sleeves of his ink-stained shirt greeted me, though it was hard to hear him above the clatter of all the typesetting machines behind him. "You here to buy an advertisement?"

"No, I'm wanting to see the fellow that wrote the piece on Oscar Wilde earlier this week. Where would I find him?"

The printer eyed me, his gaze stopping on the carbine tucked under my arm.

"If you didn't like something he penned, then he's not here."

"I intend to give him a lead on a story, one that'll interest him and his readers. It's about Oscar Wilde, some sordid information about the aesthete himself."

The printer shrugged. "Check upstairs. That's where the news hounds stay, but I should warn you, they all go armed. If you shoot one, they'll fill you with enough lead to print a special edition." He pointed to the stairs at the side of the room.

"What's his name?"

"Let them tell you, because I don't want to be blamed if anyone gets shot."

Offering my thanks, I marched upstairs. At the landing, I stopped at a half door and twisted the knob, but it was locked. I leaned over the counter ledge. "Can someone help me?"

"Depends on what you need," said a fellow behind a typewriter the size of a wagon. He stood up and walked over to study me. "This ain't a shooting gallery."

"I just arrived from Leadville and am only passing through, but I thought this was important enough to delay my journey. I want to visit the man who wrote the Oscar Wilde article this week, the one that interviewed him in his suite at the Windsor Hotel."

"Can't help it if you didn't like the story, but that's no reason to shoot him."

"I don't aim to harm anybody. I've information he may find interesting about Wilde."

"Let me check if he'll meet with you."

"What's your name?"

"He won't know it."

The newspaperman turned and strode to the distant corner of the room beyond a dozen desks where men wrote whatever lies were going into the next edition. I intended to give them a whopper. The messenger stopped at the farthest desk and pointed at me. Another newsman stood up, cocked his head and eyed me, finally nodding. I recognized him from the Windsor interview.

My courier returned and picked up a mallet. "He'll see you now."

"What's his name?"

"Ernest Mackovey is his real name, though he writes as Shorty DeLong."

Before he unlocked the door, he took the wooden hammer and struck a bell by the door. For a moment, I thought he was signaling a winch operator to raise the ore bucket. Instead, he was alerting journalists to be on guard. After he unlatched the door, I stepped inside and observed every newsman at a desk pick up a revolver or a derringer.

"Y'all are sure a friendly bunch."

"You came to us, not the other way around."

As I marched across the newsroom, I knew how General Pickett must have felt at Gettysburg during his famous charge. As I reached Mackovey's desk, he extended his hand. In it he held a sawed-off shotgun. He noted my carbine, saddlebags, and carpetbag. "This ain't a rooming house or a hotel."

"I'm not staying, but I thought you'd be interested in a good story about Oscar Wilde." I dropped my gear to the floor, then leaned my long gun against his desk.

Mackovey lowered his weapon and grinned. "Okay. Weren't you Oscar's bodyguard at the Windsor?"

I nodded. "Remind me of your name."

Not caring to give my actual name, I answered, "Snooter Johnson of Buffalo Gap, Texas."

"Snooter! Now that's an odd name."

"Everything's odder in Texas."

"Buffalo Gap, did you say?"

"Yes, sir, that's home."

Mackovey leaned back in his chair and propped his feet on his desk, the holes in his shoe soles failing to impress me. "Buffalo Gap? Seems like I read something in today's edition about Buffalo Gap." He pointed to a stack of papers on the corner of his desk. "Take the latest paper when you leave and see what it says about your hometown. It must've been important news to make the esteemed pages of the *Denver Tribune*. Now tell me, Snooter, what is it you want to visit about?"

I pointed to the chair across from him. "Mind if I sit down?"

"Suit yourself, but get to the point. I'm a busy man, Snooter."

"It's something that's been bothering me about Oscar Wilde and his promoters Charles Locke and J.S. Vale. They've been using imposters at some of his stops and lectures. Folks aren't getting what they pay for."

Mackovey jerked his feet from his desk, and his chair legs landed on the floor with a pop. "You mean people are paying good money to hear a phony pretender?"

I nodded. "Oscar imposter, I call him."

"Don't know if that's illegal, but it is definitely a fraud."

"Sir, I agree and that kept bothering me. My momma back in Buffalo Gap taught me to lead an honest life and not to associate with folks who lied or took advantage of others."

The newspaperman grabbed a pencil and pocket notebook, scribbling things down. "I heard Wilde speak here. He has such a droll delivery that I could barely sit through it. It was like listening to a gnat flying in your ear. Tell me, Snooter, is this imposter a better lecturer? If so, I might pay to hear him."

"He tries to imitate Lord La-de-dah—"

Mackovey laughed. "I like that, and I'll use it if I do a story."

"—and has a flat delivery as well."

"Now, do you have any proof, Snooter? How do I know you're not lying?"

"Ernest, have I ever lied to you?" I bent down to pick up my carpetbag.

Mackovey instantly grabbed his shotgun, pointing it at me.

Lifting the valise for him to see, I answered. "I'm getting the proof." I unlatched the valise and pulled out the patent leather shoes, tossing them before him. Next, I yanked out the stockings and knee britches, pitching them atop the shoes. I unpacked the frilly shirt and huge bowtie and plopped them on the other clothes. "Does anybody else in Colorado wear or even have clothes like these?"

Mackovey placed his shotgun on his desk and picked up the shirt, shaking it like he was ridding it of fleas. "That's Oscar's attire alright, though it appears a bit worn."

"Do you think he would allow someone else to wear his new, finer clothes? Not, Oscar Wilde."

The newspaperman eyed me. "Let me ask you a question. Did you wear these? Were you the imposter?"

Grimacing and lowering my head, I finally nodded. "I'm ashamed to say I did. Mostly I spoke at train stops between Salt Lake City and Denver. His managers told me they hired an actor to portray him at lectures in

California, though I can't swear to that as I didn't hook up with him until Utah."

Mackovey eyed me. "Did you ever give any of his paid talks in Utah or Colorado?"

I cleared my throat and lowered my gaze. "I'd rather not say, sir, as I don't want to get in trouble with the law. This has all bothered my conscience. That's why I'm heading to Buffalo Gap, so my dear mother and my beloved pastor can show me the way to repentance."

Mackovey offered me the shirt.

"Keep it and the rest of the clothes. They are a stain on my honor, one I can never wash away or forget as long as I keep those silly things with me." I latched onto my carpetbag. "I've taken up enough of your time, Ernest, you being a defender of truth and justice. So, I'll catch the next southbound for home and repentance."

"Before you go, Snooter, will you sign your name to a statement to the effect of what you just said?"

"I fear I'll miss my train."

"Give me fifteen minutes to type up your account. You can read and sign it, then the *Tribune* will cover your ride to the depot."

"Okay," I said, nodding to further affirm our agreement and my commitment to the truth.

At that point, the reporter stood up, grabbed his sawed-off weapon and put it in the top drawer of his desk. "Listen, fellows," he shouted across the newsroom, "you can put up your weapons. This is Snooter Johnson from Texas, and he's told me a story of what a fraud Oscar Wilde is. This'll be in the papers tomorrow before Oscar's second speech here in the evening."

The newspapermen clapped and cheered, though I remained uncertain if it was for me or for Ernest Mackovey, who sat down and started pounding away at the typewriter. It took him twenty minutes to finish. When he did, he handed me three pages to review. I skimmed the text and found it to be as accurate as any false affidavit could ever be. As I read, the correspondent cleared the sissy clothes from my corner of the desk, then placed a pen and inkwell within reach.

When I finished reviewing my account, I nodded. "Don't change a thing and thank you for your commitment to the truth."

"If you would sign each page, I'll arrange for one of our news wagons to be out front to take you to the depot."

I picked up the pen, dipped it in the inkwell and enhanced my name, penning *B.S. SNOOTER JOHNSON* to the three pages. By the time I finished signing and blotting the papers, Mackovey had returned, proud as a new poppa.

He looked at each sheet and nodded his appreciation. "The public will be grateful to you for this gesture of conscience. Thank you, Snooter, for your integrity in exposing this fraud."

As I stood up, he shook my hand. After I gathered my things and turned for the door, the newspaperman grabbed my arm.

"Don't forget today's edition. It'll give you something to read on the train." He picked up the paper, folded it and slid it under my arm, then escorted me to the half door, which he unlocked. Mackovey accompanied me down the stairway and out into the street, where a news wagon awaited. I climbed up front, tucked the newspaper into my carpetbag, and held on as the driver raced through the Denver streets to the depot, where I bought a ticket to Cheyenne. Within two hours, I was moving toward Wyoming, sleeping most of the way. In Cheyenne, I bought a ticket to Omaha. Somewhere between Cheyenne and eastern Nebraska, I remembered the newspaper and pulled it from my carpetbag to pass the time.

On the fourth page, I found an article on the progress of the Texas and Pacific Railroad, which had chosen Abilene over Buffalo Gap for its main depot in Taylor County. Not only that, but the citizens of that west Texas County had called a vote to move the county seat to Abilene and passed the measure by a large margin. Whether right or not, I believed I had cost Buffalo Gap the railroad and the county seat, so I smiled all the way into Omaha, where I took a steamboat south down the Missouri to muddy the trail should any lawmen be following me. After a few unfortunate encounters, I made it home for a bittersweet reunion with my surviving family and LouAnne, my first sweetheart who had waited for me to return, but finally given up and married another, more suitable Washington County beau.

Leaving Cane Hill, I decided I would head north to Kansas City on the off chance that William Traquair had written me a letter. After an uneventful journey, I found the post office and asked the clerk if he had any mail for H.H. Lomax. He went to check and ten minutes later returned with an envelope with a penny postage due. I paid the fee, stepped outside, and sat on the building steps. I ripped open the missive and read the news from Traquair.

He first reported that Sheriff Vern Middling had survived his encounter with the mineshaft, but had a hard time remembering his own name, much less the events of the previous month. Next, he reported that the crowds for Wilde had thinned after a Denver newspaper had accused the aesthete and his promoters of using imposters to represent the poet at various appearances. Traquair said he was still getting paid his weekly earnings, but the story had dogged them ever since leaving Colorado and cut into Wilde's take, which had dropped significantly.

I was as proud of that letter as if it been from my girlfriend or a president—a Republican president, at least. My accomplishments in life had amounted to little until then, but I could now take pride in getting Mandy Mae's teeth fixed, in costing Buffalo Gap both a train stop and the county seat, and in damaging Oscar Wilde's ticket sales for the rest of his stay in the States. In the last feat, I took the most satisfaction, as I had saved many Americans—most with callused hands—money, time, and boredom by steering them away from Lord La-de-dah and all his silliness.

A LOOK AT: PRESTON LEWIS WESTERN COLLECTION, VOLUME 1

SPUR AWARD WINNING AUTHOR PRESTON LEWIS BRINGS YOU FIVE TIMELESS WESTERNS IN ONE!

Get swept away by five western heroes all on a bout of good versus evil. From fighting for freedom in the Texas Revolution to fighting the demons and secrets that have been holding one hero back, Lewis will have you captivated the whole time.

In Choctaw Trail, retired U.S. Marshal Doyle Hardy is called back into service to track down the culprit in a brutal double murder in Indian Territory. The no-nonsense lawman working out of Fort Smith, Arkansas, returns to the trail to track down the murderer, who he doesn't want to admit is his own son...Hardy must confront his own son and tough family truths that he had tried to avoid in all his years as a lawman.

The Preston Lewis Western Collection, Volume 1 includes: Blood of Texas, Lone Survivor, Choctaw Trail, Tarnished Badge and Sante Fe Run.

AVAILABLE NOW

ABOUT THE AUTHOR

Growing up in West Texas and loving history, Spur Award-winning author Preston Lewis naturally gravitated to stories of the Old West and religiously read his father's copies of *True West* and *Frontier Times*. Today he is the author of more than 30 western, juvenile and historical novels as well as numerous articles, short stories and book reviews on the American frontier.

Preston Lewis began his writing career with traditional westerns and expanded it to include historical novels, comic westerns and young adult novels. His publishers have included Bantam, HarperCollins, Pinnacle, Eakin Press and Wolfpack Publishing. *Blood of Texas*, his historical novel on the Texas Revolution, received Western Writers of America's Spur Award for best western. His *True West* article "Bluster's Last Stand" also won a Spur Award. Lewis's other short works have appeared in publications as varied as *Louis L'Amour Western Magazine*, *Old West*, *Persimmon Hill* and *Dallas Morning News*.

He is the author of the well-received *Memoirs of H.H. Lomax*, a comic western series, beginning with *The Demise of Billy the Kid*. The second and third books in the series—*The Redemption of Jesse James* and *Mix-Up at the O.K. Corral*—were Spur Finalists. *Bluster's Last Stand*, the fourth book in the Lomax series, won the 2018 Will Rogers Medallion Award for written western humor. His western caper, *The Fleecing of Fort Griffin*, won his third Elmer Kelton Award from the West Texas Historical Association for best creative work on West Texas.

Preston Lewis began his professional career working for four Texas daily newspapers before moving into higher education communications and marketing at Texas Tech University and later Angelo State University, where he retired in 2014. Lewis holds bachelor's and master's degrees in journalism from Baylor and Ohio State respectively and another master's in American history from Angelo State.

Preston Lewis is a past president of WWA and WTHA, which in 2016 named him a fellow. He has served on the boards of the Ranching Heritage Association and the Book Club of Texas. He and his wife Harriet live in San Angelo, Texas.